Claverack
August 12, 1815

Mr. Daniel Hedges
Buffaloe Creek

Dear Mr. Hedges:

Mr. DeWitt Clinton requested specifically that I write to ask if you would do him the valuable service of attending a meeting at the City Hotel, Broadway, New York City, on December 30 this year. He has secured the support of many influential men, and believes that after the lapse due to war, the canal project can again be undertaken. Your expertise in these matters is valued and needed.

I will be attending as well. I look forward to renewing our acquaintance and have much to discuss with you.

Please make every effort to join us then. Hoping that you will respond at your earliest convenience, I remain,

Your humble svt.,
Eleanora Van Rensselaer

Now, here was a predicament. Daniel sought solitude and independence, and she was offering him employment. He held the letter gingerly above the water. If only he could let it slip away, forgotten. But then her image was before him, her aristocratic bearing, her blue eyes and pale lips, her fair hair, long and fragrant.

The sloop was nearly loaded. He was all packed and ready. He reread the letter, then glanced back at the sloop. Before him, over the water, lay a vast wilderness. Yet from the civilized East a grand lady had summoned him.

Daniel read the letter a third time. He walked to the sloop and accepted half of his fare as a refund. Then, whistling and light of step, he returned to the village to find a barber and a bathtub.

A

LAND BEYOND

THE

RIVER

JACK CASEY

BANTAM BOOKS

TORONTO • NEW YORK • LONDON • SYDNEY • AUCKLAND

A LAND BEYOND THE RIVER
A Bantam Book / February 1988

All rights reserved

ISBN 0-553-26993-3

Published simultaneously in the United States and Canada

Bantam Books are published by Bantam Books, Inc. Its trademark, consisting of the words "Bantam Books" and the por-
trayal of a rooster, is Registered in U.S. Patent and Trademark
Office and in other countries. Marca Registrada. Bantam
Books, Inc., 666 Fifth Avenue, New York, New York 10103.

PRINTED IN THE UNITED STATES OF AMERICA

KR   0 9 8 7 6 5 4 3 2 1

Dedicated to my father
JUSTICE JOHN T. CASEY
who gave me a love of literature,
and showed me the value of public service.

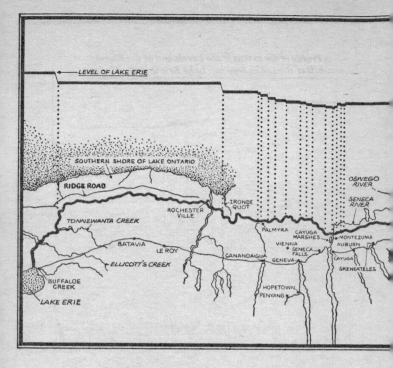

MAP OF THE PROPOSED CANAL ROUTE— LAKE ERIE TO THE HUDSON RIVER

FROM THE ENGINEER'S MAP, 1817

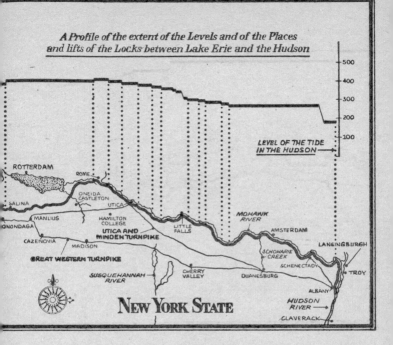

A Profile of the extent of the Levels and of the Places and lifts of the Locks between Lake Erie and the Hudson

LEVEL OF THE TIDE IN THE HUDSON →

500
400
300
200
100

ROTTERDAM

ROME

ONEIDA
CASTLETON

SALINA

UTICA

MANLIUS

HAMILTON
COLLEGE

ONONDAGA

LITTLE
FALLS

MOHAWK
RIVER

AMSTERDAM

LANSINGBURGH

CAZENOVIA

UTICA AND
MINDEN TURNPIKE

MADISON

SCHOHARIE
CREEK

TROY

GREAT WESTERN TURNPIKE

SCHENECTADY

SUSQUEHANNAH
RIVER

CHERRY
VALLEY

DUANESBURG

ALBANY

NEW YORK STATE

HUDSON
RIVER →

CLAVERACK

BOOK I

1

"*Love?*" Lady Eleanora turned and scowled at her maid. "Did you say you were in love?"

Again Kate's idle tongue had betrayed her. Her face flushed and her nimble fingers, braiding her ladyship's hair, darted and wove more quickly. "Yes, mum." Kate thrust up her chin. "I believe I'm in . . . in love."

"And what, poor lamb, would you know of love?" Lady Eleanora's eyes gleamed with mirth. The maid stepped behind the chair, but Eleanora turned fully around and tilted up her chin. "Well?"

Kate pulled the braid, and her ladyship winced. "P'rhaps it weren't that neither."

"But you said you were in love! I heard you!"

Kate's eyes welled with tears. She longed to be away, out in the cool evening river breeze. "Well, to me, mum, it is!" Her breath came short and quick. "And it mayn't be so grand as you knew, neither, but it's the best I can ever hope for!" Now she dared to look into her mistress's eyes, and saw her smile. When Lady Eleanora smiled, it was as if the sun beamed upon a summer's morning, her eyes were such a clear pale blue. Now they held ridicule. Kate concentrated mightily upon her work.

"Who is he?"

Kate threw up her hands and the braid fell, slowly untwining. "You mock me! It's not as though we'll be setting up a household and scrapin' the ground for a few bushels of corn, and raisin' brats and growin' mean and sour to each other! But if he should pr'pose—and mind you, I believe he will—then I must think on it hard, and if I accept, as I'm not saying I won't, then I'll be his wife."

"Kate," Lady Eleanora said softly, "who is he?"

"A groom of the stables here at the general's manor. Joel Kipp's his name. From C'netty-cut. Now turn around, mum, and I'll fetch the wig so's you can descend the stair to the ball. I can hear them fiddles now."

Indeed, the strains of a Viennese waltz lilted up the stair above the low rumble of men's laughter.

"Let them wait, pet." Eleanora turned to face her reflection in the mirror. She wore a low-cut sapphire gown with a lace bodice, and though her blond hair usually hung to her shoulders, tonight it would be tightly pinned under the heavy old-fashioned powdered wig. "Tell me more about him."

"Why, he's ever so nice. He's tall, mum, and lean, and he has such sad gray eyes. He can ride the most spirited of the general's steeds with ease and skill. I bet he could ride your Hecate first time."

"How does this . . . this *love* make you feel?"

Shyly Kate blushed. "It's wonderful, mum! When he speaks my name, I quiver . . . though I'd never compromise my virtue! Never!" Seriously, she shook her head, then her eyes widened. "But I did kiss him once, and it stole away my very breath." Kate pinned up the braid. "A-course it's nothing, mum, like you must've felt with Master Jacob . . ."

The mention of her late husband stung Eleanora.

"Them poems he switched from Latin, why mum, I never knew the meaning of them, so lofty and wondrous even in English, and I despaired of ever feeling such grand emotion. You made the happiest couple!"

Kate brought the powdered wig and placed it like a high crown upon Eleanora's head. Eleanora frowned.

"And poor Master Jacob was so ill so very long, his passing away must have been a relief!"

"Yes," Eleanora said. She inclined her head and listened to the bright violins, the melancholy cello. Tonight would be as always, witty young men after her hand, her lands, making fools of themselves; and aging beaux, whispering they understood a widow's plight. At twenty-four it was over. There would be no new love. She scowled at her reflection, powdered and jeweled and perfumed. The reflection seemed that of a common actor burlesquing the vanities of her class.

Deftly Kate combed the wig. Eleanora watched her in the looking glass and predicted Kate's sad future. The stablehand would have his way, then leave the girl, grieving and bitter, hopefully with no bastard in her arms. Eleanora considered giving advice, then thought better. Each woman must make her own mistakes. Tragic but true. She stood, and the gown rustled elegantly about her.

"Oh, mum, you'll steal every heart!"

"If only, my pet, there were one worth the taking." Then Eleanora brightened and touched Kate's cheek. "But I'll not need you till midnight, so after you finish here, run along. And see you put your time to good use."

Kate curtsied. "Yes, mum." She didn't hide her joy. As she opened the door, music wafted into the room like sweet perfume. Lady Eleanora pulled herself up to regal height, fondly touched Kate's cheek, then glided along the hallway to the stair. The laughter and talk of the men suddenly stopped. The maid dared not look over the banister. She quietly closed the bedroom door, darted to the dressing table, dabbed rouge upon her cheek, a puff of powder, then darkened her eyes with belladonna. She combed her hair, tied it up with a pink bow, and adjusted her gown.

Quickly straightening the clothing and lingerie strewn on the bed and chairs, Kate checked her appearance again in the mirror, flounced her skirts, then scampered down the back stairway to the kitchen, the yard, and the stables beyond.

Descending with queenly grace, Eleanora Van Rensselaer was met by a room of admiring men. She bowed slightly, took the arms of her two escorts, then entered the high, deep ballroom. The cherry paneling glowed in the soft candlelight from ceiling candelabra and wall sconces, and resonated with sweet violin and the laughter of state legislators celebrating the end of the 1810 legislative session.

Eleanora glided to a handsome white-haired man, and thrust out both her gloved hands for him to take.

"You look radiant, my dear," the general said. Stephen Van Rensselaer, her late husband's uncle and her host for the weekend, had tonight assembled the best and brightest of New York society at his elegant manor house.

"I'm so happy I could be here, General."

"Not nearly so happy as we." He bowed. "You remember

Mr. Irving, I'm sure." Gracefully he moved her along so he might greet his next guest.

"Dear Eleanora." The tall man bent to brush her hand with a kiss. "It's been far too long."

"And since we last met you've become our literary lion. I so enjoyed your *Knickerbocker's History!*"

"London and Paris do rave about it so," Washington Irving admitted, then added modestly, "They enjoy ridiculing Americans. Unfortunately, I may have spurred along the image of American buffoons."

"Well, then, you must correct that perception by writing our national epic."

"Actually I returned to undertake something of the sort," the author mused, then his expression grew very sad. "But since my exquisite Matilda passed away, I have no heart to write at all." Gently he touched her hand. "Yet you have had your hardship too. Jacob was my dear friend." The author dropped his eyes, and smiled with effort. "But I must introduce you to Theodosia!"

He led her through the crowd to a striking young woman whose dark eyes were quick and suspicious, and whose prominent nose was poised to smell danger. She wore no outdated powdered wig, no brocade gown, no whalebone stays. She wore a loose-fitting sheath of gold tissue with an Empire waist in the latest Parisian style. Her raven hair hung in luxuriant ringlets, and her lips curled as if she were enjoying a private joke.

"I've heard so much about you," Eleanora said evenly as Irving introduced them. Theodosia's eyes glittered with disdain.

"Yes, there are many stories, so very many stories." Theodosia, seeming weary of it all, shook her head, her ringlets shimmering in the light. "People could spend time far more productively than in spreading gossip."

"I agree completely," Eleanora said with sarcasm, "unless they are generating it."

Theodosia Burr narrowed her eyes like a cat, and her lip curled. "I so enjoy meeting Washington's friends. They're so disarming. Like the characters he creates with his pen."

"Dear me!" said Irving.

"Why, Eleanora!" It was Eleanora's cousin Harriet. "Let me steal you away. Come over and greet Rob! He's been working ever so hard, and only left the boat tonight to talk with some of the legislators."

"It was so nice to see you again, Washington." Eleanora gave him her hand, and she smiled and inclined her head slightly. "And to meet you, Miss Burr."

Theodosia shook her ringlets and turned away.

Harriet, a flighty redhead, rolled her eyes as they moved through the statesmen, soldiers, and aristocrats. "Oh, what they say about her! Her scoundrel father in exile, penniless, and her running from state to state, scraping together shillings and pence to send him." Harriet whispered, "I don't trust her! Never have!"

"Oh, I do," Eleanora said lightly, "her conduct is *always* so impeachable."

"Quite. Quite."

They approached a cluster of men. Harriet's husband, Robert Fulton, and her uncle, Chancellor Robert Livingston, were talking to two men. By their dress, these men were from the West. Instead of breeches, stockings, and sequined waistcoats, they wore trousers and black frock coats. One man had dark features and piercing eyes; the other had curly, sandy hair, bright blue eyes, and against all dictates of fashion, a shaggy moustache.

"Who are they?" Eleanora asked derisively. "Quakers?"

"Oh, no. They're very nice. Really."

"Perhaps we shouldn't interrupt them." Eleanora looked elsewhere for someone to greet.

"Oh, let's do! Expand your circle of friends." Boldly Harriet took her arm and approached the group. "Now there, Rob, this is a ball, not the legislature or your captain's bridge! We're here to celebrate the end to all your political haggling."

"As if it will ever end." Fulton sighed, then bowed to Eleanora. "So good to see you again, my dear."

She inclined her head in greeting to Fulton and to her uncle, the chancellor. Then she looked with unabashed curiosity at the dark-haired westerner. He dropped his eyes respectfully and bowed.

"This is Joseph Ellicott," Fulton said.

Ellicott reached to kiss her hand, and as she yielded it to him, she looked toward the man at his side. He did not bow. He stared directly into her eyes, leaning leisurely backward with a cup of punch resting in his folded arms.

"And this is Daniel Hedges."

Her eyes narrowed at his expression. He was neither impressed nor subservient. A broad smile broke beneath his moustache. "Pleased. Pleased." But his relaxed impertinence completely confounded her when instead of kissing her offered hand, he shook it. This had never happened to her.

"We've been discussing the canal proposal," Fulton explained. "These men are from the frontier, from a hamlet called Buffaloe Creek on Lake Erie. They incorporated their township with the legislature this session, and Mr. Hedges will deliver his survey of the proposed route for the canal to the Canal Commission."

"So, Mr. Hedges." Eleanora turned to him. "Do you think such a major undertaking possible?"

He grinned. "Well, now, I sure hope so." He nodded and looked keenly at her until she looked away. "I'd sure like to get down to these parts more often."

Eleanora narrowed her eye as if to ask, do you know who you're talking to? At that precise moment, as if reading her mind, Daniel Hedges grinned and nodded. It shocked her, though she didn't want him to see. Instead, she joined the conversation about the canal, and found herself striving to demonstrate how informed and involved she was. Hedges didn't seem impressed.

The chancellor's wife was suddenly there. "We must dance, dear. It's the general's waltz."

In desperation, Eleanora looked about for her escorts. She did not want to dance with the frontiersmen, and all the others seemed to be paired.

"Why it's a real shame I don't dance that way." Hedges shrugged. "I'd take you out there myself." Eleanora glared at him. "And yet, you're in luck." He slapped Ellicott on the back. "My friend here is as good a dancer as we have west of Schenectady."

"How comforting." She attempted a smile.

"Madame." Ellicott gave a polished bow. She nodded, took his hand, and glided out upon the dance floor. When the music began, she found Ellicott was indeed accomplished.

"Your friend is impertinent," she observed as they danced.

"That's just Daniel's way. He doesn't let much bother him. He's different, sure, but he's perhaps the most capable man I know."

"What is his...his *occupation*?" She asked this with a distaste for the notion that people had to work.

"A little bit of everything. He owns a brig on Lake Erie.

He plies a trade from Buffaloe Creek and Black Rock to Cleveland and Detroit."

"Oh." She grimaced. "A merchant."

Joseph frowned. The word wasn't sufficient. "Partly. But understand that we don't fit into your conceptions out West. He trades, yes, but he's a ship's captain of considerable skill. He accompanied me to Albany because he is the best surveyor we have. His knowledge of the land west of Oswego is second only to the Iroquois."

"So he is to help on Mr. Clinton's canal survey?"

"When we meet with the commissioners, he will file his preliminary report."

"I see." Her eyes indicated the matter was over, yet she stole a look at the tall ship's captain. He was watching her.

Each time they spun, she looked again, and Hedges's relaxed posture and smile irritated her. They were different from anything she had ever seen at a ball, and when the violins ceased, she thanked Ellicott and crossed the ballroom in the other direction.

Lady Eleanora danced through the evening with many dashing young men. Her grace and skill in the quadrille, the minuet, and the waltz was greatly admired by her partners. Occasionally she peered over to the corner where the impertinent frontiersman stood. He still watched her, and while this unnerved her, it excited her, too, and she found herself dancing more animatedly to impress him. It was with a pang of disappointment, then, when she glanced in his direction after making a difficult pirouette and did not see him. She scanned the room as she continued to dance, but in vain. She told herself he must have left, and resolved to forget him altogether. When the orchestra ceased playing, Eleanora walked out unescorted upon the broad front lawn.

A fat, honey-colored moon floated in the June haze, and under hanging willow, the dark, untroubled river glided by the boat slips. She took a deep breath. The night was warm and close, perfumed with jasmine from the gardens. Here and there on the lawn couples strolled and talked in the soft darkness. The quiet soothed her. Eleanora walked down a graded path to a grove of tall willows. Stretching luxuriantly, she turned to look at the mansion, majestic upon its knoll.

How comforting was the enjoyment of an estate! From a prosperous estate all else flowed—prestige, comfort, the pursuit of elegance and excellence, one's very identity. The general, perhaps the wealthiest man in America, kept a superb house. She had visited before, but had never stayed overnight. The general's capable, fatherly management of his vast lands produced this luxury, this splendor. He was master of Rensselaerwyck as she was mistress of Claverack. And although the general surrounded himself with military men, bankers, land speculators, artists, inventors, governors and judges, the source of his wealth and power were thousands of farmers, blowing to warm their chapped, filthy hands as they waited on wagons each January second to pay their ground rents of wheat and fat hens.

Eleanora loved her estate, too, yet it extracted a heavy price from her. Betrothed at sixteen to the general's nephew, Jacob, and married at nineteen, her dowry and Jacob's patrimony were joined by their families to form their large, comfortable, productive estate, the Clover Reach, in Dutch, Claverack. Yet soon its metes and bounds had closed in upon her, constricting, deadening her spirit. No more did the gracious Claverack mansion host such balls as these. True, Jacob had enjoyed his circle of young literary men who reveled at secluded hunting lodges, but the translations and poetry that had charmed her as a girl did little to satisfy the strong desire that surprised and confused her a year after their wedding.

Eleanora scanned the tall French windows glimmering with candlelight. She watched dancing forms whirl in the faint strains of violins. Like a wondrous abbey she'd read and dreamt about in French romance, Van Rensselaer's seat of wealth, grace, and power seemed tonight how things should always be. She shivered and sighed. Though her marriage had never bloomed, and widowhood proved nagging and lonely, her Claverack was some comfort. For the thousandth time, she told herself to be satisfied with her station and her lands.

Then she smelled the cigar and turned. Not eight feet from her stood the tall ship captain.

"Evening," he said. His voice was deep, resonating, serene.

"I wasn't aware I was being observed."

"Didn't want to interrupt. I was watching the river." He puffed upon the cigar and it lit his features. "Tide's coming in." He turned away.

He was forcing her to decide whether to stay or go. "Mr. Ellicott informs me you are meeting with the Canal Commission Wednesday."

"Yes." He faced her. "I'll help them if I can."

"And beyond your survey, will you be involved?"

"Too early to say. . . . Very ambitious project, though." His voice was inviting.

"Yes." She took a step toward him. "Your friend told me you own a boat on Lake Erie."

"I do." He smiled warmly, the topic pleasing him. "A brig, two-masted, hundred and ten tons. . . . draws five feet of water full-loaded." He puffed from the cigar and gave an easy laugh. "A lively ship she is, and old Lake Erie's mighty rough in a squall. It's then my *Silver Pearl* shows her pluck." He turned fully about. "A sight to see under full sail."

Eleanora took another step forward. "We hear such fabulous tales of your western reaches: Indian scalpings, black bears, wolves, impossible blizzards. It's a wonder anyone chooses to live so far from civilization."

Daniel Hedges laughed and puffed his cigar again. He flicked an ash and looked at her. "Why, it's my home. You should visit and see for yourself instead of relying on stories."

He was ridiculing her notions about the West! Eleanora cleared her throat. "Is this your first visit to Albany?"

"Why, yes it is. The place seems to have its benefits too." He held up the cigar and winked.

He was including her as a "benefit"! She fumed. "Well," she said, "I hope your report is well received by the Canal Commission. Good night." Abruptly she lifted her skirts and glided toward the mansion.

Daniel watched her sweep across the lawn, and he nodded and turned to enjoy the remainder of his cigar.

"She was asking all manner of questions about you," Joseph Ellicott said as they walked into the city after the ball. "I think she was smitten."

"I'll wager that underneath that wig and jewelry and dress she's a handsome woman. Odd notions about the West, though. Got shrewish at one point." Daniel smiled to himself. "Does she have a lover?"

Half a mile before them the roofs of Albany lay in sleepy repose, the cupola of the State Capitol gleaming in soft moonlight.

"It's best to ignore the personal lives of these folks," Ellicott cautioned. "It only leads to trouble. They own everything, they rule everything, and they're all related. Wait until you see how quickly factions form and dissolve in the legislature!"

"But my, she is a handsome woman."

Ellicott scoffed. "Did you tell her you were married?"

"No."

"She'll find out. If she has taken the least notice, she will inquire."

"You always see the sinister side, Joseph."

"Never underestimate these aristocrats," Ellicott advised. "Sure, they prattle on about republicanism and equality, but they rule, and they are very adept at controlling men and events. Eleanora Van Rensselaer is quite a worldly lady, and she's a confidante of Mayor Clinton, the prime sponsor of the canal project. She helped get the needed votes in the legislature last spring to keep the project alive. She'll have you as her lap dog until she tires of you. Then you'll exist no more for her."

"Maybe so," Daniel said. "but my, she's a handsome woman."

"Yes, Kate," Eleanora said pensively as her maid removed the wig, "surprisingly so, I did have a good time. I used to dread the end of session and the long muggy months of inactivity. Albany is a forlorn enough place in summer. But there was a certain excitement about next month's expedition to the West, about the survey and the canal project."

"Anyone of partic'lar interest?"

Eleanora frowned in the mirror. "Why, yes, there was."

"Tell me, mum, what was he like?"

"At first I thought him a Quaker, in that long black coat and trousers. He was...different. He had composure, a self-possession, a...a *relaxed* quality. Not a pretense, but a true serenity. And such impertinence! He used no form of address. He spoke as if to one of his men. And he shook my hand!"

"Wealthy, mum?" Kate clearly believed other things more important than manners.

"He owns a small freehold in the West, but I daresay he's not as wealthy as Cox or Peterson, who hold tenancies of me. He's a merchant too. He captains a ship on Lake Erie, evidently a remarkable feat for those who live there. I suppose from this he derives his air of command."

"And his looks, mum, what are the cuts of him?"

Lady Eleanora smiled warmly. "You might call him hand-some, though in a very rugged way. His face is weathered and brown. His hair is sandy and he wears a moustache. But his eyes, Kate, his eyes... Deep blue, penetrating, wise. You can imagine them scanning the water for shoals and the western horizon for storms."

"It's always in the eyes, mum."

"I suppose so."

With her hair loosened for sleep, Eleanora stood and Kate unlaced the corset. Although slender, Eleanora had her midriff drawn in so tightly by the whalebone corset that she emitted a deep sigh when it was removed. She rubbed her sides, cupped her breasts, and ran her thumbs over her nipples. She turned sideways in the mirror and stood on tiptoe to flex her buttocks. Sighing deeply, Eleanora placed her hands in the small of her back and arched backward, pushing her shoulder blades together until they nearly touched. "Ahh!"

Kate returned the corset to the traveling trunk and pulled out the camisole. "Oh," Eleanora groaned, "I despise Federal-ist fashion. I wish the general would finally notice the French."

As she slipped into the camisole, she remembered Theodosia Burr in her French gown. What disgrace she had lived through; what dark passions she must know. Eleanora nodded to herself. Reputation must be guarded carefully, always and everywhere. Yet she had lived more carelessly before:

"On summer nights such as these, Kate, I would steal out of my father's house and go galloping along the high road, galloping in the moonlight. Oh, if we could only do that tonight! Yet that would not be proper for a respectable widow, would it?"

"No, mum."

Eleanora slipped between the fresh linen of the four-poster bed. A cot had been set up for Kate to share this guest room. Kate stepped out of her dress and into a chemise, then blew out the whale-oil lamps.

"Pleasant dreams, mum," she whispered, wondering how soon her mistress would be asleep and she might escape to her tryst.

"You, too, my pet," Eleanora said tenderly, and stroked Kate's cheek.

She snuggled into the pillows, and the steady gaze of the westerner came into her mind. His mellow intoning of her name had reminded her of someone else, and now she realized it had been like her father's voice. How new and different was his manner. As she drifted off to sleep, hugging her pillow, Eleanora imagined Daniel Hedges piloting his *Silver Pearl* upon the rolling, moonlit breast of Lake Erie so very far away.

2

*S*ince the Revolution, classical columns, pediments, and domes, hallmarks of the New England Yankee, had been rising above the Dutch gables of Albany. A thriving Hudson River port, and capital city of New York State, Albany also served as a threshold to the fertile western valleys. Three gravel turnpikes radiated westward over the gentle hills, and the accommodating Albany merchants sold dry goods and tools to thousands of Connecticut and Massachusetts Yankees who left their rocky hillsides for the loamy bottom lands along the Mohawk, the Susquehanna, the Oswego, and the Genesee.

Bold, enterprising Yankees traded along the waterfront where Robert Fulton's steamboat belched sparks and smoke. To the Yankee, no invention seemed too outlandish, no project too enormous. They knew no word "impossible." A canal three hundred fifty miles through the wilderness? Why not?

On a pleasant Monday morning, two days after the general's ball, Washington Irving encountered a small, dapper young man on State Street's hill. The author had first met Martin Van Buren, Surrogate Judge for Columbia County, while collecting folk tales of the Hudson River Dutch. Van Buren's parents were innkeepers in Kinderhook, and Irving stayed with them. Lacking a formal education, wealth, and family connections, young Martin nevertheless had fared well in law and politics.

"A wonderful, hilarious work." Van Buren praised Irving's recent *Knickerbocker's History*. Although he had only skimmed the satire, Van Buren knew the value of flattery. "It is destined to lift you among the literary immortals."

Irving thanked him, and as they talked, happened to tell Van Buren he was traveling with Miss Burr. When Irving explained that she was visiting her father's old friends, including Joseph Ellicott, to ask for money, Van Buren rubbed his chin thoughtfully. "Interesting, most interesting."

"The poor man is penniless in Paris just now," Irving said. "The Madison Administration adamantly refuses to issue him a passport. Poor Theo despairs of ever seeing her papa again."

"Brilliant man, absolutely brilliant. I idolized him. He should have been president." Van Buren nodded. "Yet he'll never be forgiven for killing Hamilton. The price of a public career."

"Public regard is damnably fickle," Irving agreed, "and not only toward authors."

Van Buren's eyes brightened. "I say, Irving, may I call upon her? I'd certainly make a donation."

"She would be honored, Judge, I'm sure." And Irving gave him the address.

After his noonday meal, Martin Van Buren slipped into a fresh ruffled shirt, buffed his shoes, inscribed a banknote *Miss Theodosia Burr*, and presented his card to the servant at Mrs. Elden's Boarding House for Young Women. Van Buren affected an aristocratic air, and though short of stature, he walked erect and proudly into the waiting parlor to wait for her.

"I'm so very happy to meet you, Judge." At these words Van Buren turned to see a striking young woman with black ringlets offering him her hand. He bestowed a kiss. "It's so kind of you to come."

"Not at all, not at all." They sat. "When I learned you were in Albany, I wanted to call personally. I was an ardent admirer of your father, and I know many others among the Sons of Tammany. Politics has dealt him evil cards." Van Buren neglected to mention that he had worked to defeat Burr in two elections. He reached inside his waistcoat. "I hope this will in some small way ease his situation." He handed her the folded banknote.

Theodosia's eyes brightened; she inclined her head and pressed her lips together. "My father will be most grateful. Above all else, he regrets losing the devotions of the young men who nearly made him president." She touched Van Buren's hand. "If there is anything I can do in return..."

Van Buren flashed his engaging smile, and his pale blue eyes sparkled. "There is, Miss Burr, though it is merely a trifle I ask."

"Name it, sir."

"Mr. Irving informs me you will meet soon with Mr. Ellicott of Batavia."

"This afternoon. Yes."

"I wonder if perhaps you might sound him out upon a delicate matter." Van Buren pressed his fingers together. She nodded. "The canal project greatly intrigues me, and I must know two things about it. First, are the canal commissioners planning a series of locks merely to augment existing streams and lakes, or do they propose an entirely separate ditch three hundred miles long? Secondly, financing. Will they form a private franchise, or do they look to the government for capital?" He smiled pleasantly. "I'm sure you understand the delicacy of this matter..."

"Of course, Judge. I shall notify you directly as I return from the meeting."

"Very good, Miss Burr." Van Buren stood, took her hands and kissed them both. He bowed respectfully, opened the door, and departed with his walking stick and three-cornered hat.

Theodosia dashed up to an oval window on the landing. "A most charming man indeed." She watched his small form pass through the crowded narrow street where pigs and chickens rooted and pecked, and noted that the noise and squalor did not affect him.

When he disappeared around the corner, she unfolded the check. "Twenty-five dollars! A most worthy friend." She smiled, realizing then how important the information must be to him.

Daniel Hedges and Joseph Ellicott shared a suite of rooms at Mrs. Pratt's Boarding House two blocks away.

"Unprecedented!" Ellicott exclaimed. Daniel had just received a note from Mrs. Van Rensselaer. "Suitors and hopeful suitors wait for months to get the smallest glimpse of her, and she invites you to call after one encounter!"

"Strictly business, I'm sure." Daniel held the note in the air. "'Mr. Hedges,'" he read aloud, "'I should be pleased to speak with you regarding some matters of our mutual interest. I hope four o'clock will be convenient for you. Until then, I am respectfully yours, Eleanora Van Rensselaer.' Nice ring to that, 'of our mutual interest.'"

"You take my advice and don't be presuming anything with her," Ellicott warned. "She has some ulterior motive, and it won't be 'mutual interest.'"

"Care to accompany me?" Daniel ribbed him. "Might need some help."

"No, I'll be seeing Miss Burr then."

"Want me to cancel and chaperone?"

"Hardly." Ellicott frowned. "I keep thinking about that scoundrel father of hers. Burr twisted legislative arms for me to get the Holland Land Company charter passed years ago, and that's the reason I agreed to see her."

"No love lost between her and Eleanora Van Rensselaer, if I'm any observer of women."

"Women!" Ellicott threw up his hands. "If they'd only stay out of our affairs!"

"Don't know about that." Daniel held the fragrant note to his nose.

At four o'clock Theodosia Burr paced in the parlor, wringing her handkerchief, waiting for the serving girl's return. Agitation showed in her face. Now and again she checked it in the mantel mirror to assure herself it showed well enough.

When ushered into a spacious third-floor living room, Theodosia turned a woeful look to Mr. Ellicott. He registered no emotion. Theo cleared her throat. "It's very kind of you to see me, sir."

He motioned her to a settee. "I hope I can be of service."

"I'm sure you can." For an awkward minute she sat with a trembling lower lip. Then, "It's my father, sir, my poor papa. I realize you and he are men of the world, and you know how cruel and harsh it can be. Yet it defies my simple understanding of things to see how a man's best and closest friends can turn on him when he is wrongfully disgraced, how people he has helped prey on his property and reputation."

"Your father was a man of great ability."

"He firmly believed in developing our West, and he secured the grant your Dutch investors needed. Everyone involved has benefited from the Holland Land Company, and when the canal is dug, you will all be very wealthy."

"He was a man of great foresight."

"Men's fortunes change so rapidly." She sighed. "Today my poor father sits penniless in Paris, exiled from the America he fought to free, exiled from the British Empire, the whole of the English-speaking world. And I...I have come to you today—" she applied the handkerchief to her eyes—"to implore you, his old friend, whether you might find it in your heart to...to..."

"To extend him a loan?"

"Oh!" She clasped her hands together. "Could you? Would you?" She burst into sobs, covering her face with her handkerchief. "Oh, he'd be so grateful for any consideration whatsoever."

Ellicott glared at her, critiquing her performance. Aaron Burr was now a criminal, an exile, an outcast. Though it had been handy once to know him, helping him now might carry a stigma. Caution was required. And yet, having two daughters home himself, Ellicott sympathized with her plight and admired her courage.

"I can be of service, yes, in some small way, but I must impose one condition."

"Oh, name it, sir!"

"I wish my gift—not a loan, mind you—to remain anonymous."

"You are a true Christian, sir." She bowed her head, humbled by true Christian generosity.

Ellicott arose to write a bank draft. Theo set her lip. How to get Van Buren's information? Flattery usually worked in getting people to talk about themselves.

"Why, it is a grand enterprise you're engaged in, sir," she said casually. He harrumphed from his desk. Theodosia stood, dried her eyes, and walked to the window. "I once rode west with my papa. We had holdings in the lands of the Oneida. Remarkably green and fertile."

"Yes," Ellicott said, sprinkling sand upon the bank draft and setting his quill by the ink pot, "and land farther west becomes even flatter and richer."

"It staggers the imagination, Mr. Ellicott, to consider that these waters of the Hudson"—she waved at the waterfront out the window—"will someday teem with boats sailing all the way from Lake Erie."

"Few undertakings can boast such audacity and magnitude." He stood. Theo tilted her head slightly so her black curls bobbed.

"There already exists a canal company, sir. I saw the small canal once. I know so little about such things. Will your canals also allow boats to avoid the rapids?"

Ellicott held the bank draft between his thumbs and forefingers. "No, young lady. Ours is a far greater plan. We will avoid streams altogether. We'll cut a ditch clear across the wilderness to the lake. No flood or ice jam or spring freshet will hinder the boats. A ribbon of water in all seasons but winter." He held out the draft. She accepted and folded it without looking.

"Your Dutch principals must be very wealthy and bold."

Ellicott frowned. "They are wealthy, but not often bold. Why?"

"By underwriting such a vast—"

"They?" Ellicott said. A smile played, then broke upon his lips. "Oh, now there is a thought." He began to chuckle. "That indeed is a droll notion." After years of listening to the stingy land company's principals complain, the thought that they'd pay for such a canal was hilarious. "Oh, pardon me, Miss." Ellicott laughed out loud. "I do not mock you. It's just the idea is so novel."

"Well, then?" she asked with simplicity, "who is to pay for it?"

"Ah ha! You'd like to know, would you now?"

Theodosia formed an expression of perfect innocence and slowly nodded her head.

"Well, being as you're not involved, I'll share our secret if you promise to keep it." She nodded, and placed the check in her bag. "Everyone!" he exclaimed, waving his arms in the air. "Everyone will pay for it, and everyone will benefit from it!"

Theo looked puzzled.

"The government," Ellicott explained. "This great state of New York, and the United States government, together. That, anyway, is Mr. Clinton's plan." He smiled paternally. "Now be off with you before the banks close for the evening, and remember, this is to be an anonymous gift."

"Oh, thank you! Thank you, sir!" She curtsied. "You're so kind and Christian to remember my poor papa in his adversity. If he...if he can ever help you, just let me know. Only then will I number you by name among his benefactors."

Ellicott held the door for her, then reentered his rooms. He mused how such a scoundrel could sire such a forthright, intelligent, caring daughter. His thoughts turned to his own daughters, and he longed to wrap up his business in the capital so he might return home.

Around the corner Theodosia unfolded the bank draft—ten dollars. She was angry. Her father had bullied and bribed

Ellicott's charter and land grant through the legislature, and his return? Ten dollars! And she had groveled before him—her poor father, most excellent of men, starving and friendless in Paris. Ten dollars was infuriating, and even that begrudged! But at least she had Judge Van Buren's information. Theo cashed the draft, then called on Van Buren.

"You are most kind to return so soon," he said.

"The very least I can do." She relayed what she had found out—the canal would cut through three hundred fifty miles of farmland, swamp, mountain spurs, virgin forest, cliffs and torrents, much of the land still unexplored, and would be publicly funded.

"Excellent." Van Buren smiled radiantly. "Precisely what I needed to know. If I can be of further service, Miss Burr, please do not hesitate to call." He motioned for her to stand.

"Judge Van Buren." She looked at the floor. "There is one thing." She sighed. "I have been rebuffed countless times trying to secure a passport for my dear father. The Madison Administration refuses even to hear my requests. If you might intercede . . . ?"

"I'll most certainly try. I know some people in Washington who hold your father in the greatest esteem. I'd be more than happy to help. Promise me you'll call on your next visit to Albany. I can be reached here at the Mansion House if I'm in town, and if not, they relay my mail. Leave a note."

She smiled and nodded. "I certainly will."

Van Buren took her hands and kissed them, then showed her out the door. He watched approvingly as she swayed descending to the street. Closing the door, he quickly calculated where this new information best fit in his plans.

3

*P*lasterers, painters, carpenters, and masons busily refurbished the gabled brick town house as Daniel Hedges approached. Surprised, he stepped up the stairs and hammered the brass knocker of the open door. Down the dim hall a butler approached with a silver tray.

"Good day, sir. May I help you?"

"Mrs. Van Rensselaer asked me to call."

"Have you a card?" The butler held out the tray.

"No. Just this." Daniel placed Eleanora's note on the tray. The butler scowled, but was back in two minutes, smiling.

"Please step this way." Guiding Daniel through the plaster dust and wood shavings, he opened a high door to a sitting room. It was furnished with a German pianoforte, a wide set of bookcases, a Louis XIV writing desk, four sturdy Dutch chairs, and an elegant chaise longue. As the butler left, Daniel catalogued the haphazard furnishings. The wallpaper was faded, the drapes antique and dusty. A threadbare carpet lay upon the floorboards. Daniel admired four canvases, one an idealized landscape of a Catskill gorge, another a view of the Hudson, and two stiff portraits of a husband and wife. He was inspecting an old Dutch clock when the door opened. Eleanora entered in a loose white gown, her blond hair undone, falling past her shoulders.

"Please forgive the chaos, Mr. Hedges." She was all business. "We haven't opened this house in town for a decade. Now, after a year of mourning, I've decided to sweep away the cobwebs and reenter the life of our capital city. Won't you have a seat?" Eleanora rang a little golden bell. The butler answered. "You may serve the tea now, Edward." He bowed and closed the door.

Daniel sat in one of the sturdy Dutch chairs, hooked a boot heel on a rung to lift up his leg, then leaned his elbow on his knee and regarded her with interest.

"I was intrigued Saturday night by our conversation," she said. "I don't believe I've ever met anyone from the frontier, let alone the captain of a trading vessel so far from civilization. Have you lived your whole life there, Mr. Hedges?"

"As much as I remember."

"Your parents, were they westerners as well?"

"Don't really know." He looked at her quizzically, wondering what interest his past could possibly hold for her. "They were massacred near Cherry Valley during the Revolution. I was among the Iroquois for two years, until Sullivan's army burned the village. After being exchanged for a prisoner of war on the Niagara frontier, I was apprenticed to a ship captain in the lake trade."

"How fascinating."

They stared awkwardly at each other.

"And Mr. Ellicott then secured your services as a surveyor?"

"Yes. Years back, I helped him lay out the tract of the Holland Land Company, and I knew the area well. He wants the canal to come west through his lands, to increase their value. He asked me to help, so I left the brig with my first mate and came east."

"And you're meeting with the Canal Commission Wednesday?"

"Yes." He narrowed his eyes. Her interest in his life did not quite square with her businesslike manner.

"And you'll discuss the survey you have undertaken?"

"As much as they wish to."

Eleanora reclined slightly. "As you know the territory so well, do you believe a canal can be dug?"

Daniel extended his arms candidly. "I'd like to help, ma'am, but won't you first tell me what all the questions are for?"

She was momentarily flustered, and tried to hide it by reclining farther away on the sofa. The butler entered with a silver tea service—teapot, sugar bowl, cream urn, tongs, spoons—and a delicate pair of porcelain cups and saucers. Placing it on the table, he left.

"Shall I pour?" she asked. Daniel shrugged and nodded. He watched how she gracefully poured the two steaming cups of tea. "Milk or lemon?"

"Lemon."

"Sugar?"

"No, no thank you." He accepted the cup, stirred it, and took a sip. He couldn't remember having had tea before, preferring whiskey and ale late in the afternoon. It was pleasantly fragrant, hot and tart.

Eleanora leaned back again and sipped her tea. Daniel watched as her pale lips delicately touched the cup.

"You were about to say whether you believed such a canal could be built."

"Well, sure, sure it can. I don't believe there's a damned thing that men can't do when they put their minds to it."

"But we understand the terrain to Lake Erie is quite rugged."

Daniel nodded. "It is that. Land west of here looks like a great claw gouged it from south to north, leaving long narrow lakes and swamps in the low places, great heaps of boulders and gravel in long, narrow mounds."

"Then it's possible to bridge those low places?"

Again he nodded. "You'll have to lay culverts and bridges over the gullies and valleys, and you'll have to blast through the mountains. It's not something you'd plan if you want an immediate profit. It'll take years, and men will die."

"But you have walked it? What are the most serious obstacles?"

Daniel gave a low, ironic laugh. Although she presented a most pleasant sight, reclining with her teacup in the sun, he was suspicious. "Still haven't told me what this is all about. You're asking more than the commissioners will."

Eleanora pursed her lips. "Let's just say, Mr. Hedges, that I'm extremely interested in this project, and that I want to see it through to completion. I can help both you and the project if you'll cooperate, and things that I am not at liberty to discuss just now will become more apparent as soon as they need to."

Daniel nodded and set down his cup. "Fair enough. Mind you, I haven't looked at the easternmost sections, and I understand there's quite a cascade at Cohoes, but from Utica west there are three major obstacles. First, near Salina there's the Montezuma swamp, hell's own land breathing malaria and plagues. Second, two great valleys must be bridged, the Irondequoit Creek and the Genesee River. They'll require stone breastworks to carry the canal over the water, aqueducts strong enough to withstand the spring ice floes."

"And the third?"

"A great cliff must be scaled by the canal, the same cliff the Niagara cascade plunges over. We'll need to get up and over it to reach the altitude of Lake Erie. Much blasting will be required, and many locks. Men will die."

She nodded, satisfied.

"But those are only the prime obstacles." Daniel regarded her. "There are problems the entire length of the project, trees as old as time, streams to be dammed and forded, boulders and cliffs to be blasted away. Least of all the worries, a smaller network of canals must be built just to keep the main ditch filled. An army of men will be needed, and of course that will bring labor problems."

She nodded. "Are you aware of the essays written by Jesse Hawley?"

"No."

She set down her cup and crossed the room, returning

with an envelope of newspapers. "While serving a jail sentence for debt, Mr. Hawley wrote these fourteen pieces about digging just such a canal. You should read them, as they will help you with the commissioners."

She leaned over him, and as Daniel accepted the envelope, he looked up, openly flirting. She backed away, picked up her teacup and hid her lips behind it.

"I should like to meet with you after you speak with the commissioners, and I hope you will consider me a confidante. I cannot tell you my role just now, but I can answer your questions, and carry your concerns to a level where most difficulties may be overcome."

Daniel stood. "Well, then, if we're to be working so closely, call me Daniel, and I'll call you Eleanora." He put out his hand to shake. "Out west folks don't simper around with mister and missus. Wastes too damned much time."

She stepped back, unsettled by his frankness, surprised by his sudden height. She reached to place her teacup in its saucer, but missed her mark. The cup fell to the floor and shattered. Instead of calling the butler, she yielded to her first nervous instinct, knelt and placed the broken porcelain in her left palm. Daniel retrieved a piece that had flown across the floor, then joined her. Side by side they picked up the smallest particles.

"There," he said. "I think we got it all."

Eleanora turned and looked in his eyes. She paused, her eyes opening wider as Daniel gazed deeply into them. He saw there a loneliness that shocked and surprised him. She had let her guard down, and now inclined her head and opened her lips slightly, looking from his eyes to his lips and back again.

She wanted to be kissed, he knew, but he held back. He looked from her wide clear forehead, down her long blond tresses, then returned to her eyes again. Yet it was as if her eyes had closed, for he could no longer see into them. She sighed, then pressed her lips together. The moment had passed. "Thank you, Mr. Hedges. That was clumsy of me."

"Not at all." He stood and reached down, and as she placed her hand in his palm, he felt it trembling.

"And thank you, also, for sharing your observations with me," she said, a tremor in her voice. She turned away and walked toward the door.

"I'll call Thursday before I leave for home."

The mention of his leaving did not please her. She opened

the door and suddenly the reality of plastering and sawing was upon them.

"Good day, Eleanora."

"Good day, Mr. Hedges." She stood in the doorway watching him pass through the workmen. He turned once and looked back, but did not wave. She raised her hand and gently brushed her lips.

When he had passed from sight, Eleanora turned down the hall and entered a rear sitting room. Gazing into a mirror, she saw a certain rebelliousness in her eyes. She swept up her hair with a black ribbon. then threw on a velvet riding habit. With the hood up, she left by the back door, passed through the empty stables behind her town house, and walked up the alley to a cross street. Entering Gregory's Tavern, she hurried past the open door of the taproom and upstairs to room 307. The door was opened by a handsome, dark-haired man of forty.

Neither spoke as she entered and deposited her riding habit on a sofa. Books, charts, and papers lay strewn about the writing desk and floor. A closed portmanteau rested in the doorway to the bedroom. Just after arriving that morning, DeWitt Clinton had immediately plunged into his work. He was a tall man, as tall as Daniel Hedges, but massive, bulky. A restless energy burned in his intense blue eyes, at variance with the deliberately slow and patrician cadence of his speech.

When she was seated, Clinton stood opposite her. "I sent Carr away. What news do you bring?"

Eleanora gave an account of her interview with Daniel, conveying to Clinton the surveyor's opinion about the project, the three most difficult obstacles, and Daniel's daring sense of enterprise. As he listened, Clinton crossed the room, his penetrating eyes weighing each piece of information.

When Eleanora finished, Clinton spoke conclusively: "All you have said marks this fellow as a valuable asset. Can he be trusted?" Clinton fixed her with an imperious stare.

For a moment Eleanora tried to separate her personal attraction to Daniel Hedges from her assessment of his character. "I believe, DeWitt, he can."

"I defer to your judgment then." Clinton walked to the window and looked out. "Your instincts about people are infallible, and so they are invaluable to me."

Eleanora winced at the high-handedness of the compliment. Clinton's chief flaw was an inability to understand normal human emotions.

"You can work with him, then, and you will be my intermediary until I choose to work with him directly?"

"Yes, DeWitt. It would be a pleasure. He's refreshingly different from the men I have known here in Albany."

The big man wheeled around and scrutinized her. "Is there any personal interest?" His suspicion unsettled Eleanora, and she faltered.

"I find him amiable and talented . . . yet certainly unsophisticated in the ways of public men. He knows much about the western lands—more, probably, than any other white man. But be assured, DeWitt, I am ever mindful of my station and the decorum required of widows." Still he stared at her. She sought refuge in a platitude, "Reason must always govern passion," then laughed half-heartedly. "Not that I could ever feel passion for a son of the forests and lakes."

Clinton nodded abruptly. "Very well, but I trust you will inform me if your feelings change. We all are, unfortunately, susceptible to such emotions. And they can prove very dangerous to our undertaking."

"Of course." Eleanora suppressed her annoyance. "I have asked him to read Jesse Hawley's essays, as you suggested, and he will meet with me after the full commission sits. I will, of course, convey his impressions of the other commissioners to you."

Clinton crossed to her and held out his hand to raise her up from her seat. "I will call for you Thursday, Eleanora. Until then, farewell. Your services, as always, are deeply appreciated." He retrieved her riding habit, held it for her, and smiled affably as he escorted her to the door. "How does work progress on the town house?"

"Very well."

"Spare no expense. We will establish a salon where the necessary votes may be cajoled, bought, or forced next session. It will be the talk of New York and Washington. Send Carr the bills as they come in." He opened the door. "You look well, Eleanora. Returning to the world of politics and society has put some color in your cheek."

She smiled and touched his hand with hers. He began to close the door, then opened it again. "Eleanora?" She turned, adjusting her riding habit. "Did that fellow Hedges happen to mention he's married?"

"Yes," she lied, and she smiled at him. "Why, yes, he did."

Clinton nodded approval, then closed the door. Eleanora turned away, her mind stunned by the news. Married? Hedges was married? The mere thought of his being married infuriated her. Blindly she descended the stairway, passed through the hotel lobby and out into the sunshine. Her quick thinking had just now saved her from humiliation in Clinton's view as the lonely, impressionable widow she believed herself to be. Clinton had deliberately saved that tidbit for her departure to throw her off guard, and she despised him for it. Tears pressed at her eyes. How could he know Hedges was married? But DeWitt always knew everything.

Eleanora dined with Kate in a private room of Foley's Chop House. She deliberately steered the talk away from love. And as she went to bed that night in a makeshift boudoir in the town house filled with the smells of drying plaster and reawakened wood, her mind was in a hot confusion. She tossed and turned, plotting how she might confront Hedges with the news, how she might let him know she was not to be trifled with, how she might accuse him of...of...of what? Of being married? Of raising her expectations? Yet beyond the events of the day one image kept arising out of the tumult of anger, doubts, and desire. She saw a helpless baby ripped from the arms of its mother as she was being raped and scalped behind the burning cabin; then the baby was carried off into the forest in the swarthy arms of its captors.

4

A recent political upheaval had stripped DeWitt Clinton of his robes of office as mayor of New York City. He had adopted the canal project to regain office, to keep busy, and to broaden his political base. With a statewide presence he might succeed his uncle to the governorship and then grasp at national laurels. With sway over the Pennsylvania, Michigan, and Illinois frontiers being contested by territorial leaders and by Britain, the canal held vast national and international strategic possibilities. Although General Stephen Van Rensselaer chaired the Canal Commission, Clinton's foresight and energy guided the group, and so he was allowed to preside over the meetings.

"Motion..." Thomas Eddy, a thin, fiery zealot, stood up. "That the New York State Canal Commission christen the two flatboats upon its upcoming westward exploration as the *Argo* and the *Cosmo*."

"Mr. Eddy's motion is on the floor. Discussion?" Silence. "Very well," Clinton said, "Call the vote. All those in favor of the motion?"

"Aye," said Thomas Eddy alone.

"All those opposed?"

"Nay." Everyone but Eddy.

"Next item: Mr. Morris."

The plump Gouverneur Morris arose: "As General Van Rensselaer and myself will employ his coach and four to propel us westward, I move that we split the sum granted us by the legislature in half." In that room Morris's wealth was second only to Van Rensselaer's.

"Point of order!"

"The chair recognizes Mr. Eddy once more."

"Mr. President. Colonel Porter has not seen fit to grace us with his presence this morning. The fund appropriated by the legislature is for the express purpose of viewing these wild lands, and not to provide fine Madeira for the commissioners." This caused a stir. Eddy's garrulity and temperance were widely known, as was his dislike of Morris. "I suggest therefore that thou divide the fund into six equal parts, disburse it, and let each man be accountable, even as he is to his maker. Thy proposal, Mr. Morris, is avaricious."

"Order. Order." Clinton tried to remain patient. Joseph Ellicott turned and regarded Daniel Hedges. They were sitting in Simeon DeWitt's dusty office. DeWitt held the post of Surveyor to the State of New York, and his office was strewn with maps and charts, quadrants, an astrolabe, sextants and telescopes. Ellicott rolled his eyes at Daniel, and Daniel set his lips impatiently and nodded.

"Many of our expenses will be communal," Clinton tried compromise. "It would be premature to make a disbursement at this juncture. Yet the matter is open for discussion." The discussion lasted twenty minutes and at times became very heated. During it, Clinton seemed very much a god gazing down at the petty squabbling of mortals. Finally he intervened. "The chair recognizes Mr. DeWitt, who will call a vote."

Dutifully his elder cousin called a vote and Morris's motion to split the fund was approved five to one.

"Next item: the Survey. A Mr. Daniel Hedges joins us this morning to inform us about the survey he has conducted in our western lands, and to answer questions as to what we should be looking for upon our expedition. The chair recognizes Mr. Ellicott.

"Gentlemen." Ellicott stood and spoke with utmost formality. "I have known Daniel Hedges for fifteen years. He surveyed the entire tract of the Holland Land grant and has been invaluable to me on many, many occasions. At my behest he left his mercantile pursuit in plying the waters of Lake Erie to lend us his talents on a survey of the hills and ridges, the lakes and streams that now separate the Hudson from the distant western lakes. Mr. Hedges."

Daniel stood and informed the commissioners in his succinct and straightforward manner what land formations and watercourses they could expect to see, what must be cut across, bridged, and blasted through.

"Young man!" harrumphed Mr. Morris. "Do you believe locks will be necessary for this canal?"

Daniel looked to Joseph, and Joseph rolled his eyes. "Haven't seen a better way, sir, to raise or lower a boat. Be a mighty lot of that going on from here to Buffaloe Creek."

Morris laughed derisively. "Does it not strike you, sir, that Lake Erie being six hundred feet above the Hudson at Troy, an easier method might be employed?"

"I have an open mind."

Morris scanned the table with a superior attitude. "We start at Troy"—he held his hand high in the air with the fingers sloped upward—"and we incline the canal half a foot every mile up to the lake." He demonstrated with his hand. "Thus the water of Lake Erie will pour by gravity into the Hudson, making a natural, man-made river, and we may avoid the building of locks."

Daniel looked to the chair for a reaction. Clinton's eyes bored into his. "I must confess, sir, the thought never occurred to me."

"No, young man, I suppose it never did." Testily Morris

folded his arms across his chest and proceeded to look out the window.

Clinton interposed. "Mr. Morris, the surveyor-general has asked Mr. Hedges to join our expedition at Utica. We will have ample time along the route to question him about engineering possibilities." Clinton nodded to Daniel, and Daniel resumed his seat. Again he exchanged a baffled look with Ellicott.

The remainder of the meeting was devoted to discussing what sort of clothes and fowling pieces, boots and sketch pads, wines and cheeses to bring along; how ferocious were the Indians and wild beasts they would encounter; and how they would locate taverns to put up for the night. Ellicott, the western expert on the commission, diplomatically addressed each of these concerns.

General Van Rensselaer then delivered a lofty speech about the trust placed in them by the people of New York State, the high purpose of their expedition, and the tremendous benefits they would bring home both in knowledge and expanded opportunity for the legislature to consider.

On the street afterward, Joseph asked, "What did you think?"

Daniel raised his eyebrows. "Remarkable."

Joseph laughed. "Truly, though what did you think?"

"Good they live along the Hudson. Good they're all wealthy and have servants. If they lived where we come from, they'd starve." Joseph clapped him on the back and Daniel shook his head sadly. "Be a fine afternoon's enjoyment watching them design and build a boat. After a year they might get a raft . . . and then it wouldn't float."

"Van Rensselaer, though, is well-intentioned. North and Eddy are useless. Morris is senile. There's our majority. But then there's Peter Porter from Niagara. Know him?" Daniel nodded. "And there's myself."

"Two shining stars."

"Don't overlook Clinton, Dan. You didn't see him at his best. He couldn't be today, with the others present. He has a first-rate mind, extraordinary political talents and connections, and an uncle who's vice president. He's related to half the aristocracy in New York, including your Lady Van Rensselaer. Arrogant, ruthless, and insatiable when it comes to power—today he was laying back, playing mediator, letting all of them prattle on and feel as though they were making decisions and participating. He can't afford to alienate any of them because they have the influence and the votes he needs. He was observing you too."

"But ain't the pretense silly, Joe?"

"Yes, but it's the way it has to be. We can either cooperate or not. Here in Albany the secret in getting what you want is not antagonizing anyone needlessly. Here's Mrs. Pratt's. Let's start packing."

"You go in and pack. I have a visit to make."

"Eleanora?"

Daniel nodded.

"Be careful what you say. Clinton's secretary, Edward Carr, was asking questions about you just as soon as Fulton's steamboat docked yesterday."

"Questions?"

"Yes. And one of them regarded your marital status."

Daniel grinned widely. "So that's the game? I'm walking into an ambush."

Joseph slapped him on the back. "Yeah, but a fond one, to be sure."

"See you in an hour."

As Daniel walked along, he observed the town houses, carriages, horsemen, women carrying baskets, shopkeepers, and boys with wooden pails from the well. Looking high to the hill, the tower and cupola and statue atop the State Capitol, Daniel took a deep breath. In that building decisions were made that affected every phase of life here in the street. He understood better now. Before, Albany had seemed vague and strange to him. Stealth, gossip, feints, and fakes were how things were done here. It was much like hunting in the forest. The rules were made by men in power. That commission could no more build a canal than it could raise a house or dam a stream or build a wagon, yet it was vested with the authority to keep the canal issue alive. Without them there wouldn't even be curiosity.

The workmen were nearly finished in the hall of Eleanora's town house. The butler showed Daniel into the same parlor as two days before. Drastic changes had been made nearly overnight: a new carpet, graciously upholstered chairs, a settee and new drapes. The walls, the ceiling, and floor needed more work, and the furniture seemed to be on display so Eleanora might approve it.

She entered in a loose green gown, her hair pinned up. She looked pale.

"You've done much work since the other day," Daniel observed. "Yes. I'm returning to Claverack tonight and I wanted to be sure the furniture would be acceptable." She motioned him to a chair, and she reclined upon the settee. "How was the meeting?"

His smile spread his bushy moustache broadly and made her smile in spite of her serious purpose. "Got to get those boys out West, teach them a few things."

She inclined her head quizzically. "Yes?"

"Why, I can draw a line 'cross a map and say this is where a canal will go, but nature, why, she might not be so accommodating." He shook his head. "They're smart enough, those boys, so they'll learn when they actually see the land they're up against."

"What if there are disagreements?"

"Always are. Best you can hope for is to show them everything and let Clinton pull them together into a team."

She gave a small start at the mention of Clinton's name. Daniel noticed. "What did you think of Mr. Clinton?"

"Reserved, very reserved. I'm leaving Albany first thing tomorrow, overland, and I'll meet up with them in Utica. When I can get his ear alone, I'm sure we'll get a few things sorted out. He has a chore getting the rest of them boys to see his way, but he's equal to it. He'll be all right."

Eleanora relaxed. "You must understand Mr. Clinton. Often only he knows why he does certain things. Those around him must trust him. Support and loyalty are the prime qualities he demands."

Daniel nodded. "I look forward to showing him the West. Once he sees it, he'll know."

"Will you attend him during the entire month?"

"No. I can only spare two weeks. Obligations."

"Business?"

"Yes, business and family. My wife is very tolerant, but I don't like to leave her with the little ones for more than a month at a time."

"Oh," she said, feigning surprise, "You have children?"

"Didn't I tell you? A son and a daughter."

"I had no idea."

"Make a difference?"

"No," she said quickly, "of course not. Not at all." Daniel

scrutinized her. She returned his gaze. There was a strong animal attraction between them. Daniel had passed her test, and he saw now the need for her caution: her widowhood and station made her vulnerable.

"Will you want to participate in the building of the canal, or will your business and family absorb your time?"

"Business could run itself for a while." He didn't tell her his current business interest included smuggling pelts, wood, rum, potash, and salt to the British in defiance of Madison's embargo. "Salary attached?"

"Of course, of course." Now she saw danger. She could not very well offer him a position, yet she was supposed to test his willingness to accept one.

"Don't know what I could do. Project intrigues me, though. That fellow Clinton's a bold one, ain't he?"

She panicked. He had seen through her charade. "How so?"

"Why, who else would set sail on such a long voyage with such a crew?"

The image pleased her. She envisioned staid General Van Rensselaer climbing the rigging, portly Gouverneur Morris at the wheel. General North would be in the crow's nest, and garrulous Thomas Eddy spouting "thee's" and "thou's" as bosun.

"Perhaps Mr. Clinton has other plans," she suggested. "And he'll need other sailors on board."

Daniel nodded. She had just confirmed the identity of her patron. Daniel stood. "Well, Eleanora, ma'am, my journey has been most rewarding. I'm thankful Joseph asked me along." He extended his hand and shook hers. She was getting used to this custom of his. "I'm happy we met, and hope I can get east soon again." He started for the door.

Suddenly Eleanora wanted to dash after him, to hold him back, perhaps blurt out something foolish, something girlish. She held back, but the opportunity was being lost even as she hesitated.

Daniel turned, drew himself up to his full height and leaned his head back in an air of detachment. "Won't you see me out?"

Eleanora smiled and pulled herself from the settee. "Of course." She pressed her lips together and narrowed her eyes in anticipation as she approached him. For once in her life she couldn't predict what she would do. Her flesh tingled. Daniel grinned and nodded. He felt it, too, and it was pleasurable. Eleanora walked very close to him, so close he might have encircled her with his arms. She looked up into his eyes, daring him to embrace her. For a long moment he looked from her lips, into her eyes, up to the masses of blond hair upon her head, then down past her eyes, her lips, down her long neck to her breasts. His eyes returned to hers and he acknowledged her desire.

Gently, ever so gently, he reached down, placed his hands upon her hips, bent down and brushed his lips over hers. His moustache tickled her upper lip, and faintly she felt his lips touch hers. She reached up, the room falling away, and circled her arms about his neck. She pressed her open lips to his. Hungrily they kissed, delight and pleasure and discovery drawing them together. Their fingers twined in each other's hair; their arms, strong and fearless now, tightly clinging.

When they parted, it was as if they had just surfaced together from underwater. They breathed deeply, and their eyes smoldered. Again they came together in a kiss, more passionately than before. Her breasts pressed against him, her hips sought his, the abandon of her lips and tongue was cleansing, purifying, delicious. She felt the tremendous power of his shoulders and arms, the firmness of his jaw, the tenderness of his lips and tongue, the strength of his hips. Then she felt his eagerness, and it shocked her. She pulled herself away and caught her breath, felt her lips with her fingertips. A thousand voices within her spoke about what she should not, could not, must not, dare not do, and she knew those scruples were correct even while her breasts and her thighs ached for him.

"Have to go," he said. He suddenly felt thirsty. He saw her discomposure, saw the battle within her, so he leaned over and kissed her gently on the cheek. "I'll miss you. But I'll be back."

This soft intimacy made her shudder. She took his hands and held them up. Large, strong hands, callused and scarred from work, the nails split and jagged. She held them to her lips and gently kissed them. When she looked up at him, the faintest moisture was in her eye. "Good-bye," she whispered, then opened the door so he might leave. Daniel looked longingly into her eyes, then dropped her hand, turned, and was gone.

She didn't watch him walk away. Slowly she closed the

drawing room door, and the sound seemed that of the door to a tomb. She leaned against the door with closed eyes and breathed heavily to calm her heart. She bit her lips. She wanted to explode in rage. She wanted to weep. She wanted to purge herself, to feel clean and whole and pure. "Kate!" she cried, "Kate!" There were footfalls on the steps up from the kitchen, and the small door by the chimney opened.

"Mum?"

"Have Guy ready Hecate. We will ride."

"Hecate, mum, are you sure? She is so black and wild."

Eleanora glared at her.

"Yes, mum. Hecate, mum."

"And not the sidesaddle either."

"No, mum."

The maid left for the livery stable in the next street to deliver the orders. Eleanora stormed into her temporary bedroom and ripped off her clothes. She stood naked in the afternoon sunlight, and the sun felt warm and pleasing. Thankfully, she'd packed the riding trousers she wore at home in the country. She opened the trunk, thrust aside the gowns and lingerie and pulled out a pair of jodphurs and riding boots. Quickly she changed and put her hair up under a three-cornered hat so passing horsemen would not gape at a woman riding as a man.

Soon the horses were at the vacant stable behind the town house. Hecate, the spirited black mare, pawed impatiently at the ground. When they'd gained the top of the hill by the Capitol, Eleanora whipped Hecate into a gallop, and continued to whip and spur, ride and whip the horse toward the distant blue escarpment, the Helderbergs. Her thighs tightly clasped the horse, she bent far forward, tightened up on the reins, and rode hard, as hard as she'd ever ridden. She felt the exhilaration of the wind in her face, the horse's pounding hooves, the churning, heaving rhythm of the horse's back arching then straightening, arching then straightening, and she thrust herself down into the saddle, losing herself in the pounding and furious rhythm of the ride until she was gulping at the wind, panting to catch her breath, dizzy. On and on and on she rode, and the sky suddenly burst with sunlight, and a bird screamed, and slowly as she rushed onward, the trees and the mountains returned.

At last Eleanora reined in the mare. Hecate resisted, rose up pawing the air, but stopped. Eleanora was perspiring. She took a deep breath and shuddered, then turned in the saddle. Far behind her, a mere speck in the road, Kate was striving to keep up. Eleanora threw her head back and laughed at the sky. She was in love! She could admit it! She could call it out in the bright afternoon: I am in love! She felt weightless and free. How extraordinarily simple! And such a man! Such an unusual man. She patted Hecate's long black muscular neck, perspiring now from the gallop. "Come on, girl," Eleanora whispered. "Let's collect Kate."

Eleanora suggested they graze the horses and sit on a knoll overlooking Albany, the Hudson, and the knobby silhouette of Rensselaer County across the river. They tethered the horses to graze on the sweet grass, and sat looking eastward.

"And how is your young man?" Eleanora asked.

"Fine enough, mum. But too polite. 'Tis a bad sign."

"What?"

"I don't know if I like it or don't mum." Kate scowled. "What with all the 'by your leave's' and 'with your permission's.' It's not like him." She regarded her mistress. "And the gentleman from the West?"

"Oh." Eleanora smiled, and a shiver passed through her. "A fine man, a very fine man. Married. Yes, but a fine man nonetheless." She slapped the riding crop twice upon her thigh.

"Married?" Kate cried in horror. "Oh, mum, I'm so sorry!"

"That's his affair, not mine," Eleanora said, more to herself than to Kate. She pointed to a farmhouse, then swept the riding crop in a semicircle in the air. "See these lands, my pet? Do you know how they're held, how they're owned and transferred?" Kate scowled again, not understanding. "They're owned by the general, and they descend eldest son to eldest son, forever... forever. The farmers never own the land they work. They only have the right plant and harvest so long as they pay rent. And so it is at Claverack. Who made it that way? Someone long ago and far away. Someone we've never met. Yet someone, even though he's dead, controls all their lives with his dead hand, general and farmer alike. The dead hand, Kate, is what they call it, the dead hand's shadow falls over me and you today even as we sit in the sun. Our dead ancestors steer the course of our lives, allowing us property or freedom as they saw fit long ago, or else taking it away. They don't know us today, they can't know what we feel, yet they run our lives."

Kate nodded, but did not understand. She watched the clouds pass and their shadows sweep over the fields, the river, and the forests.

"But it must not be that way, pet. It must not!" Again Eleanora slapped her thigh with the riding crop. "We must summon all our courage and it will not be so. The dead hand must not control us, and it *shall* not! This day, this sun, this sky, this world belong only to the living, Kate, only to us who breathe and walk and see and...and love. Come, my girl, let us return."

"Can't keep up with yourself and that mare, mum."

Eleanora smiled fondly and patted Kate's head. "Then we shall proceed more slowly, and we'll stop and pick some flowers along the way. And tonight, why tonight we'll remain in the house again, and we'll have a hearty meal sent from Hawley's Pilot House."

"I'd like that, mum." Oysters and ale were Kate's favorite fare. Eleanora helped Kate into her saddle, then vaulted into her own, and they rode leisurely back toward Albany as the sun set behind the escarpment of deepening blue.

5

A black coach clattered through Albany's rutted streets the next morning. Drawn by four plumed white horses, the coach bore a monogram SVR, and led a procession of two open carriages, a large baggage dray, and two men on horseback through the morning fog.

The party paused at the toll keeper's gate. As a hand in a frilled cuff reached from the coach window with money, the gatekeeper turned his pike to allow entrance to the gravel highway. The four plumed horses jerked the coach into motion, and soon were galloping west.

The two horsemen, Ellicott and Hedges, trotted briskly behind, discussing how soon the commissioners' pride would be dampened by corduroy roads, waterfalls, slippery portages, mosquitoes, the rain and mud and humid sun; by drunken

Yankee frontiersmen, surly boatmen, flea-infested inns, rancid meat and butter.

"They'll come to love the West," Hedges observed sardonically.

The procession reached Schenectady by noon and split in three. Ellicott and Hedges rode directly out of town on the Utica turnpike. Later, General Van Rensselaer and Gouverneur Morris, the gentlemen of the coach, selected a case of Madeira to ride with them inside. Uncorking a bottle, the general knocked upon the ceiling trapdoor: "Onward, Joel!" And the coach lurched forward.

"Fine vintage, General."

"Imported, Morris, imported. Just the thing to cut the dust." The general held up his glass, smacked his lips, and the four horses stepped high on the gravel turnpike as the coach attained the breakneck speed of nine miles an hour.

DeWitt Clinton, leader of the third group, found he could not leave Schenectady that day. The boats were still being caulked and painted because Thomas Eddy had commissioned their preparation only the day before. To keep up spirits, Clinton suggested they elect Eddy "Commodore" of the expedition, and that they name the baggage boat after him. Yet Clinton was not amused. He instructed the workmen to erect an awning and curtains to shield out the sun, something Eddy had overlooked, and he delivered two flags for the passenger boat: an American flag with fifteen stars and fifteen red and white stripes, and a flag with the seal of New York State upon a royal blue background.

They awoke to Independence Day fireworks. Realizing they had a dignitary among them, the citizens of Schenectady asked Clinton to address an assembly in the old stockade. Clinton discussed the need for internal improvements for the nation and for the state, and he urged that the people avoid war with Britain at all costs. Immediately afterward he visited the boatyard, and the two boats were ready by three o'clock.

The entire village followed the expedition party to the river. Baggage filled *The Eddy*, and the men took their seats in *The Morris*. An eight-piece band played, and the crowd cheered as the boatmen cast off, planted their long poles in the river bottom, and propelled the long, flat boats into the current.

Progress upstream was slow. A sail did not help, since the boats had little ballast and no keel. Their undersides were smooth and shallow so they might be dragged over rapids. In his leather slouch hat Clinton stood hour after hour for three days, smoking cigars, gazing moodily into the wind. The others seemed festive, but Clinton was restless. This was no Sunday outing. At each bend or shoal or creek that spilled into the river, he referred to Wright's map, checking its accuracy. He questioned the boatmen incessantly about the river's depth and currents, what goods were shipped each way, the prices and quantities, the length of the shipping season and the number of boats in active trade. Great leaders he emulated had opened new trade routes—Henry the Navigator of Portugal, Ferdinand and Isabella of Spain, Peter the Great of Russia—and wealth poured into their treasuries. New York State might open an inland route to connect the virgin territories of the Great Lakes and beyond with the maritime cities and with Europe. Then through New York State such goods and wealth would pass, diverted from the Louisiana French in the Mississippi Valley and the British down the St. Lawrence.

In five days they ascended the Mohawk to its source at Rome, and their boats passed into a channel that a private canal company had constructed. The wooden locks that lifted boats over the hill and into Wood Creek were rotting. Bridges were so low, the awnings and flagpoles had to be removed. As the boatmen poled the boats into the first lock, Clinton jumped ashore to survey the western slope and Wood Creek. He scanned the horizon with the eye of a general. The Mohawk, downstream broad and placid, had recently become swift and narrow near its source. On the other side of the hill Wood Creek meandered westward through the willows into salt marshes, swamps, and shallow lakes—a foreboding land.

As he sat beneath a tree with his journal and pencil, Clinton heard a harness jingle, and into view rolled Van Rensselaer's coach.

"Hey-ho!" Morris deposited his bulk on the roadway and the general stepped out behind. "You made it, Clinton!" Morris called in high spirits. Clinton slapped his journal shut; they had been drinking all morning.

"We heard from a chap who saw you at Engster's Tavern last night," Van Rensselaer called. "We took the liberty of preparing breakfast. Come!" The general led them down an embankment to a cool brook where a table was set beneath tall pines. They ate a breakfast of fried pork, ham, boiled pork, bologna sausages, Oswego bread, biscuits, coffee and tea, old and new cheese, partridge, duck, boiled eggs, perch, salmon, and bass. A keg of strong ale was tapped, and in the shade they regaled each other with humorous anecdotes of their discomforts. The boats would be another hour in passing through the locks. Growing impatient again, Clinton walked to inspect the primitive locks.

The Inland Navigation Company that had built them was bankrupt, only kept solvent with state funds. Poor design, lax management, and far too little trade taught harsh lessons, Clinton reflected as he measured and considered the locks.

"Had an eventful week?" he heard at his elbow, and it was the surveyor, Daniel Hedges.

"We've seen much." He squinted at the horizon.

"I was through here in April when all the streams were swollen with rain," Daniel observed. "This is the tamest segment from the Hudson to Buffaloe. I'd begin construction here and continue westward." Clinton searched Hedges's eye. Often his penetrating gaze intimidated men and women, yet Hedges simply smiled good-naturedly and nodded. "That's what I'd do."

"Why?" the great man asked.

Daniel looked to the west. "Two reasons. First, it will be the easiest leg to construct—only a dozen locks in ninety miles. With rapid progress, the public will see success quickly and will support the canal. Second, if the project is stalled or abandoned afterward, this portion will still benefit the people hereabouts by linking them directly with the Mohawk. The effort won't be wasted."

Clinton nodded. These were the first sensible observations he had heard all week. "What is your impression of the locks operated by this company?" he asked.

"Dismal. Their use and demand greatly exceed their engineering. Certainly they ease the loading and unloading of goods, but they are too wide, and so require too much time and water to fill." Hedges pointed to the rotting beams. "Also, they're made of wood and will need to be replaced in three years. The greatest cost of a canal lock is labor, not materials."

"What would you use?"

Hedges pointed south. "There's an outcropping of granite not half a mile from here. The land supplies the materials if you know what to look for. With proper maintenance, a stone lock will last forever."

The boatman's cry interrupted them. Flags fluttering and

awnings re-erected, the two boats had passed from the eastern waters of the Mohawk into the western waters of Wood Creek, and were ready for boarding.

"You are accompanying us now, Mr. Hedges?"

"I'd planned on it, sir."

"Sit with me, then." Clinton led him to the waiting boats.

The boatman poled with the current down the winding course of Wood Creek, and the stifling, mosquito-ridden air closed in upon them. Yet Clinton was refreshed, for he found Hedges not only knowledgeable about the lay of the land, the beasts and fish and trees and plants, but also about inland trade routes, products shipped, and prices per hundredweight. Hedges knew distances between towns both by horse path and by water, and he related all he knew with the practical good sense of a backwoodsman.

True to Hedges's account, the land westward was flat, and the creeks wound around and back upon themselves so a distance by water route was often twice or thrice that by land. Shallow lakes filled with bass and pike stretched into marshes choked with sea grass, cattails, cranberry, and scrub pine.

They paused for the night at Cicero near the mouth of Oneida Lake. As the sun set and darkness sifted in, Hedges and Clinton walked the ruined battlements of Fort Brewster which brooded over the lake.

"You have an admirable knowledge of this land," Clinton said.

"I've lived here all my life."

"Yes, but so have so many others." Clinton squinted ahead to see men paddling bark canoes upon the placid breast of the lake. Sparks from flint and iron lit flames in the canoes in fixtures high above the water. "What are they doing?"

"Fishing. They're Onondagas. They set braziers up in their canoes and light fires of pine knots. The light draws the salmon up to the surface of the water for spearing."

Both men watched the canoes glide to and fro, flames reflecting eerily in the water. The soft, mournful complaint of the loon edged the evening with melancholy.

"It's pagan sorcery," Clinton whispered. "Quite pleasing to watch how they fish." The loon persisted, and bats flitted over the water. "We who live in the cities consider this land wild, yet it possesses a quiet and a mystery we lack." He produced two cigars and handed one to Daniel. They lit them, then leaned against the abandoned ramparts and watched the canoes and the reflected firelight pass back and forth peacefully.

They poled down from the lake the next morning, reaching the Oswego River. Then, after twelve miles of slippery portages and waterfalls, they drifted into Lake Ontario. The village of Oswego was a cluster of fourteen houses and six log cabins.

"You would think you were on the shores of the Atlantic," Clinton observed in the stiff breeze that raised surf.

"Ontario never freezes," Daniel remarked. "Erie does. Erie is not nearly as deep."

"It has been proposed, Mr. Hedges, to end the canal here." Clinton was testing him.

"No, it must flow from Erie," Daniel said conclusively. "From here it's just as easy for goods to continue down the St. Lawrence. No reason to unload and go to Albany and New York harbor. Oswego can continue as a lake port, certainly, but the canal should pass through Salina. Salina's salt mines produce great quantities of salt that need to be shipped. Other minerals as well may be discovered there. Besides, the land is flat and the digging will be fairly simple. The canal should steer away from Oswego."

"I should like next to visit the salt mines at Salina."

For two days they toiled back upstream to Onondaga Lake. They visited the Galen Salt Works at Salina, where thousands of gallons of brine were pumped from the earth, boiled night and day over cordwood fires in rows of great black caldrons, then the salt packed in oak casks. The endless boiling muted all sound, so Hedges waited until they were returning to the boats. He showed on his survey map how the canal could be routed directly by the salt refineries to ship tens of thousands of barrels annually both east and west. "It will foster the industry of these men," he reasoned, "and provide money in tolls."

After detouring from the proposed canal route for three days to view the Finger Lakes, they planned to meet Van Rensselaer and Morris at the comfortable Powell Hotel in Geneva. A note awaited them there:

July 22, 1810

My dear Clinton:
    The General and myself, finding our port and Madei-

ra supply dangerously low, have repaired to Batavia where, we're told, Mr. Ellicott keeps an admirable cellar. We shall meet you at the Niagara cataract August 2nd, instant.

Your most obt. svt.
G. Morris

"I pity Ellicott," Clinton remarked.

"Not at all," Daniel said. "He'll enlist Morris and the general to support some bill or other for his Dutch principals. And if the digging begins next summer, as we all hope, his reputation will be enhanced."

The expedition dined that evening on venison steaks, trout, bass, salmon, wheat and corn bread, squash and tomatoes from the hotel's garden, and plums, peaches, and apples from its orchards. All agreed it was a very fine stopping place. They relaxed this night, for having completed all but ninety miles of the route, they would continue the next day by land.

"Many canal supporters propose the canal follow the Genesee River into Lake Ontario," Clinton mused as they lingered over brandy, coffee, and cigars in the candlelight of the grape arbor. "They say the remaining mileage to Lake Erie is a needless expense." Clinton looked to Hedges for the response he'd heard days before. Clinton wanted the other commissioners and scientists to hear Hedges bear out what he himself had told them.

"That would be a mistake, a great mistake," Daniel said. "It must begin at Lake Erie, and I speak not merely as a landowner of Buffaloe Creek, but as a merchant. The greatest expense in shipping goods east from Huron, Superior, Michigan, and Erie is to get them around Niagara Falls. Once on Lake Ontario, they can easily sail down the St. Lawrence, and the trade will enrich Montreal, Three Rivers, and Quebec."

The others nodded in the candlelight.

"Western farmers and traders don't really care whether their goods to go Canada or to Albany and New York City. They will ship to the readiest market. To benefit New York State, the canal must bypass the treacherous portage at Niagara Falls, and only then will the canal become the prime transportation link with the Great Lakes. We must go all the way to Lake Erie or not bother at all."

"How difficult will the dig be from the Genesee to Buffaloe?" Eddy asked.

Daniel unrolled a map and traced a line roughly parallel to the south shore of Lake Ontario. "West of the Genesee there is a level ridge over seventy miles long. It rises fifty-five feet above the lower land, and if we can route the canal along it, we won't need a lock for seventy-five miles."

"Preposterous!" Eddy sputtered. "After we have struggled up and down rapids and falls, climbed tortuous portages, dost thou mean the rest of the course is level?"

"Exactly," Daniel said. The others at the table were amused, for Eddy had become something of a blustering mascot of the expedition. "This was originally the shore of the lake when it was higher than now. I have taken the level, and the ridge is four hundred eighty feet above the level of the sea—only eighty feet below the level of Lake Erie. If we use this ridge, gentlemen, we need only scale one cliff afterward with locks, and the canal will be a straight dig to Buffaloe Creek."

Clinton nodded. "So all of the canal is divided into three parts. Simple. From Schenectady to Rome, a river valley; after Rome, swamps and lakes; from the Genesee westward, a level ridge. So, too, should construction be divided into three parts, requiring different engineering skills."

"I don't see why," Daniel said facetiously. The entire table looked to him, now the acknowledged expert, to see why he was challenging Clinton. "What skill do we need to build an inclined plane?"

It took a moment for this joke to register, then as they all considered the ruggedness and variety of the land they had explored, they laughed at Morris's original plan for a man-made river.

"Mr. Morris, no doubt, is enjoying Ellicott's wine and designing new engineering feats," Clinton said. "We shall hear them presently."

They set off at daybreak upon a turnpike graded by the Holland Land Company for its settlers. The horses galloped along as if on a racetrack, and though the party could not see the lake ten miles north, they could smell the clean wind blowing as if from the sea. Clinton ordered the driver to stop after five miles, and bareheaded he emerged from the coach to climb and observe the height, width, and surface of the ridge. Fifty-five feet above the Ridge Road it roughly paralleled the road, and ran as level as the road itself.

"It most certainly was the lake's shore in some ancient

time, just as the road is a more recent shoreline." Clinton bent down and felt the sand. "Imagine, Hedges, the upheaval when this lake burst its natural dam and the waters ran down the St. Lawrence Valley to the sea! These ridges show that it happened twice. Ah, this mocks our human vanity in digging a canal. These shorelines have lain here for thousands of years, evidence of untold violence and upheaval, and we look upon them as if they were formed for our convenience. Yet enough of that." He smiled up to Daniel. "A brief glimpse at the eternal is enough for practical men, eh? The convenience this ridge affords can hardly be believed after so much rugged country. Come, I have much to discuss with the commissioners."

Below Niagara Falls the port of Lewiston bustled with traders, teamsters, and stevedores. Barrels of salt and potash were loaded and hauled on sleds by snorting teams of oxen up the Niagara gorge to the level of Lake Erie. A team could haul a mere twelve barrels a day. The slow plodding of the beasts was matched for inconvenience only by the danger of the trail.

The party visited Fort Niagara the afternoon they arrived. The red-faced, sputtering American captain discussed Canadian politics.

"The Brits use Canada as they did our states before the Revolution. They milk the province of men and materials. Compare our fair state with the land just across the river. Same land, only different governments. Here we have farms and orchards. There it's nearly barren. Last year eighteen thousand barrels of salt were lifted up the American side of the falls, and only four thousand on the Canadian. The Canucks are fed up. They promise secretly that if America declares war, they will side with us and run the Brits out."

"Interesting perception," Clinton observed. Later, as he and Daniel Hedges walked the battlements high above the river, Clinton asked if this were true, if the Canadians were so dissatisfied.

"He's half right," Daniel said. "The Canadians are upset with the British; yet I doubt they'd join us. Too much to lose. A war would be disastrous for both sides."

"It always is." Clinton scowled. "Always and everywhere."

Morris and Van Rensselaer arrived August second. Three of their original four horses had been traded at tavern yards along the route, and the remaining one had lost its plume. Stiffly the two gentlemen stepped down from the coach. After a rousing evening in Batavia, they needed sleep, yet Clinton insisted they view Niagara Falls together that day.

Daniel Hedges was an able guide. Pointing out abandoned cranes and sleds used by the French fifty years before to haul goods up the escarpment, he compared it with the teams and oxen for safety and convenience. He shared with them anecdotes of pets and cattle who'd plummeted over the falls and survived.

"An interesting legend is told about going over the falls," Daniel said when the band collected to hike along the brink. "An Indian chief moored his canoe at the shore near Chippewa and fell asleep. A British soldier loosened the rope, and the current carried the canoe away. Drifting along, the chief awoke to the roar of the rapids, and he tried to paddle first to one bank and then to the other. But the current had him in its grip. At last he wrapped himself in his blanket and met his death, singing his death song in defiance."

Clinton brooded as Daniel told this legend, and he gazed upon the white water thoughtfully. "I say, Hedges, that tale would make an admirable topic for one of our poets if properly rendered."

"How so, Clinton, how so?" asked General Van Rensselaer.

"Think on it, General, the pagan stoic meeting death. No folderol about heaven or funerals or wills. A man and this cataract. Ah," He breathed deeply, "the fatality. This land is inspiring. I shall recommend the story to our own Mr. Irving when I return to New York. He should shun those European capitals, and visit this land for his subject matter. It's got a far bigger heart."

As they approached the thundering cataract, froth from the rapids pitched over the edges, and beyond, a great billowing cloud of spray rose into a glorious rainbow. No one spoke. Beneath them the earth rumbled. They picked their way along in single file until suddenly, one by one, they emerged from the dim forest to view the spectacle. Before them a full mile of water spilled over the lip of the falls in a luminous green until whipped into foam by the air, falling, falling, then dashing itself upon the dislodged rubble, spray ascending into the air, into the sun, blushing with colors of the rainbow.

Silently the commissioners gazed for a quarter of an hour. The vastness of the sight defied words: The wide semicircle of rock; the free-fall height from the sharp brink to the enormous stone blocks torn and plunged and mercilessly pounded below; yet above all, the immense volume of water that poured over second by second, day and night, year by year, century after century.

"Makes our concerns seem rather small, don't it?" Hedges asked Clinton.

"It is magnificent." Clinton's eyes burned intensely. "The land this river drains must rival the size of all Europe. And our canal will join those lands, those lakes and river valleys, with the sea." He placed his hand upon Hedges's shoulder. "If only we could stand every legislator and congressman here, we'd never want for funds."

Yet the legislators couldn't share Clinton's lofty vantage point. Other business now kept them in the lowlands, and sluggishness would always keep them there. Martin Van Buren saw this. Clinton was so far out front that the Democratic-Republican Party could hardly keep track of his whereabouts, much less keep pace. Van Buren saw his chance to lead, and he moved to the forefront by opposing the canal in the party's ranks. He believed the canal a physical impossibility and therefore politically suicidal. Posturing himself as a voice of reason and caution, he met in Albany with Tammany Hall legislators from New York City while Clinton was scouting in the hinterlands.

The Tammany sachems loathed Clinton, frowned upon spending tax money upstate, and feared any progress that threatened workingmen's jobs. They agreed that a three hundred fifty mile ditch was foolhardy, wasteful, and impossible; yet they didn't quite trust Van Buren. Why was a judge meddling in legislative and executive matters? Recognizing that he had valuable information and a quick and persuasive manner, they urged him to meet with the great chief of Tammany Hall, Brody O'Hanlon. "Talk with him," they advised, "he'll know what he wants, and he's never shy about telling us how to vote."

Van Buren was encouraged. He had tapped into a large and powerful political organization and was immediately directed to its leader. If he persuaded O'Hanlon, the Tammany boys in Albany would begin to look to him for guidance. Van Buren planned to run for Senate from Columbia County when the seat was vacant in 1812, and he believed he could organize canal resistance upstate, marry it to Tammany Hall, and thus lay a foundation wide and deep enough for his own ambitious political future. He'd force Clinton to deal with him, and thus rise in people's esteem to a stature equal to the great man. Let Clinton explore the state's wilderness and appeal to men's hopes and dreams of the future. Van Buren knew where fear lurked in men's hearts, which caused them to huddle together in political organizations, and he knew how to harness it. The more ambitious the canal seemed, the greater the skepticism he might arouse. Van Buren's only regret, as he girded his loins for the David and Goliath contest, was that his brilliant strategy must be kept secret. Sharing it would ruin it, and bearing such a burden alone would be lonely and tiring work until the time when it began to succeed.

DeWitt Clinton had discussed the appointment of a surveyor to the canal project individually with each of the commissioners to make each man believe the appointment had been his idea. When they met the next day at the small Canadian village of Chippawa, Clinton diplomatically allowed General Van Rensselaer to chair the meeting.

"We have, in the past four weeks, traversed the entire course of the proposed canal," the general began grandiosely. "We know now firsthand what difficulties lie in our path. Inland navigation today is rough and primitive, so rough and primitive"—he held up his tankard of ale—"that Mr. Morris and I chose the turnpikes and corduroy roads rather than the portages and Durham boats that you suffered along in." This brought cheers and applause. He stopped them and looked about the tavern.

"Not too far in the future we will build the longest, smoothest, most efficient waterway the world has ever seen." The commissioners applauded and cheered. "I have spoken with Mr. DeWitt, and his duties as surveyor-general will keep him busy as our great state of New York continues laying out townships, and as he lays out the streets for a city of the future on Manhattan Isle. Today we have the task, and the privilege, of naming someone to survey the actual course the canal will take, a thorough survey that will allow our august legislature to make an informed decision about appropriating funds. Therefore, it greatly pleases me to nominate Mr. Daniel

Hedges of Buffaloe Creek as Chief Surveyor for the Grand Canal."

This took Daniel completely by surprise. Joseph Ellicott, his usual informant, had not attended. Daniel looked about the tavern at the pleased, congratulating faces, and he nodded. Duly seconded by Clinton, Eddy called the vote.

"Aye!" rang out from all.

"It's unanimous, then. Mr. Hedges is our chief surveyor. Congratulations, Mr. Hedges. I see no reason to be stingy, so let us affix a salary of five hundred dollars, and we shall secure this appropriation from the legislature when it convenes. Edna, my good lass," he called to the buxom barmaid, "more ale."

Applause and laughter filled the room, and the barmaid brought each man a full tankard. Daniel stood to accept a list of places the commissioners wanted surveyed in greater detail. He stood easily and spoke slowly, "Gentlemen, I'm mighty thankful for the honor you give me today, and I will work as hard and as well as I can to get the canal under way. Now, Mr. Clinton and I have been together for three weeks discussing any number of things—plants, birds, beasts, rock formations, clouds, even some ancient Indian mounds I never explored before. His questions have been constant and not always easy to answer, but I've tried my damnedest. Now, I'd like to put one to him here and now, just one. You see"—he slouched a bit and grinned—"I ain't a political man by nature, and I don't understand much of what goes on in Albany. But as we've traveled three hundred miles to view the wildest reaches of this state, I'd like to know, Mr. Clinton, just what in hell does all this mean to an ex-mayor of New York City?"

The taproom erupted in laughter, men crying, "Clinton for governor! Clinton for president!"

Then DeWitt Clinton himself stood with a benign smile, calming the applause. "Gentlemen, gentlemen...as Mr. Hedges asks, I must respond. Don't ever believe anyone who tells you I'm not just another concerned citizen." Again, resounding applause.

"Seriously, though, we have walked this land together, you and I, and we have just appointed a most capable surveyor. The only obstacle to construction now is money. If I may, I'd like to leave today with something you can give me." Attentively they listened. "I move, as a member of this commission that we petition the United States Congress for funds to help the people of New York undertake this great endeavor. With a favorable vote on my motion, I will personally travel to Washington and lobby strenuously for federal dollars. We believe this canal will serve not only our national goals, but even as we sit today in Chippawa, in British territory, it will serve our international interests as well."

Gouverneur Morris had been flirting with the barmaid. Anxious to participate in the meeting, he clumsily stood and wiped a moustache of foam from his lip. "Not only do I second the motion," the old Federalist blustered, "but I will accompany you to Washington, Clinton, and I'll twist a few arms of my Revolutionary comrades who are now sitting in Congress. Jemmy Madison won't keep all the federal money for Virginia."

"The motion is on the floor," Van Rensselaer called. "All those in favor?"

"Aye!"

"Opposed?"

Silence.

"Mr. Clinton's motion carries. Let us adjourn this meeting" —the General held up his tankard—"with a toast. I raise my glass to the people of the State of New York and the great destiny that awaits them."

6

As the packet from Chippawa ran before the wind, Daniel Hedges scanned the shoreline past Black Rock for the sandbar and mouth of Buffaloe Creek. Holding a hawser of the packet boat, he longed again to pace the deck of his *Silver Pearl* and feel her sails swell in the wind, her sleek prow cut the waves.

The packet entered the mouth of Buffaloe Creek, and Daniel looked fondly and critically at his brig. Her lines were true and sure, and riding at anchor, she seemed anxious to be out on the lake. Yet he had other obligations. A rowboat brought him to shore, and walking along the dock, then up a rise into town, he paused. Although he was glad after eight weeks to be home, to see Carrie and the children, he scanned the forty-odd buildings clustered together on the shore of the lake: the new stone courthouse and jail, the one-story customs house, Cook's Tavern, Buffaloe Creek's gathering place. After Albany the village seemed dismally small, primitive, and quiet. The town fathers had shown themselves distinctly petty the year before when, insisting upon straightening a road, they bisected Joseph Ellicott's property, the land where he had planned to build a stately mansion. Bitterly, Ellicott canceled his plan, sold the stone to the Holland Land Company—to be used for the courthouse and jail—and returned to Batavia, abandoning his plans to move. What would these same town fathers think of the ambitious canal project?

Smoke trailed up through the shade of virgin pine where log cabins nestled, their frontier slumber unbroken. Daniel and Carrie lived in such a cabin, but earlier that year Daniel had dug a cellar and laid a foundation at his large lot on Washington Street, secured lumber, and window glass, and roofing shakes. He had planned a large frame house for his family, but Ellicott and the canal had intervened. Daniel passed the site and inspected the sail canvas protecting the lumber from rain and sun. The foundation lay ready for flooring beams and walls. The commissioners wanted their surveying done by October, and he wanted the house ready for the first snow. Many plans needed to be made.

He passed along the path south and east, his seabag over his shoulder. As he turned a corner, he saw Carrie and stopped to watch her scold Eli, who'd been teasing his sister. The scene was so domestic and familiar, yet so new. Clothes hung on a line between two trees, and the cabin seemed so very small, yet far more comforting than he remembered.

"Carrie!" he called. She turned, squinted into the shade, then her mouth opened and her eyes widened. "Danny!" Her arms extended as she ran to embrace him.

"Papa's home!" squealed Rachel, and she bolted up. Eli dropped his toy rifle and dashed after her.

"Oh, Danny, you're home!" Carrie cried, and she hugged him and kissed him on the neck and the lips. "It's been so long!" She pulled back to look at him, and he smiled down at her.

"You look wonderful, girl," he said, then lifted her up and spun her about. By now the children had reached him and were hugging his legs.

"Wait, wait, I have presents for you." Daniel pulled away from Carrie, opened his seabag, and produced a doll with a ceramic head and a wood ship resembling the *Silver Pearl*. The children fell quiet with the gifts.

"Ah, Carrie." He patted her backside and led her toward the house. "It is a grand enterprise Ellicott's involved me with, but I so hate being away from you."

She reached up to kiss him, and rested her head upon his shoulder as they walked together. "Things have been well here. Lester has completed eight voyages—four to Presque Isle and the Pittsburgh Road, two to Cleveland, and one each to Detroit and Port Colborne. We have wanted for nothing, and I have kept the account books."

"I'll see Lester in the morning." He hugged her again and viewed the cabin as if seeing it for the first time. "Must get reacquainted with you and home first."

They sat together on a bench, and through a clearing in the trees, they could see the buildings of town, the creek, and the lake beyond the sandbar.

"So the trip overland was good?"

"Yes. Mr. Clinton is a capital fellow, and it was with him that I returned. But politics! I don't know how he stomachs it. The canal that people talk about has become his personal ambition, and he wants to build New York State into the foremost state of the nation. He is a wise man, and his questions and comments brought the land alive in ways I'd never seen." He paused and slipped his arm around her neck. "I'll be working with them again. That's the news. They have appointed me the chief surveyor."

"Oh, that's wonderful, Daniel! What an honor." Then her expression clouded. "Will it require you to be away from home often?"

"Can't tell yet. I have another survey to do before winter, but that should take only three weeks."

She nodded somberly. "I see." Then she brightened. "But you're home now, and that's what's important."

They talked together for an hour, then Carrie prepared a dinner of venison steak, cornbread, baked beans, and bass fried with onions and potatoes. Daniel brought a pail of beer from Cook's Tavern, and they dined under the pines as the sunset burnished the lake. Daniel held the children. They had grown surprisingly since he left, and he admired their clear, innocent beauty. He coddled and teased them until their bedtime, then tucked them in with a story about the great man who would dig a canal from the state capital through the forest to their own town, and how this someday soon would allow them to travel in boats and see great cities.

"It's wonderful to be home," he said, returning to Carrie sitting by the hearth. He place his hand upon hers and sat beside her. "Often as we lay down for the night upon the expedition, I'd think of you and the children, and you'd seem so very far away. I'd ache to be here with you, and I'd gaze up into the stars as I do when navigating at night, and wonder how long it would be."

"I know, I know."

"It's difficult when I'm away...."

"I wish you could always be here, but..."

"Someday." He patted her hand and nodded. "Someday, and the work I do will make all our lives so very much better."

She agreed, and Daniel suggested they lay on the bearskin rug. Together they looked into the fire and played a game they had played while courting—predicting the future. After that Daniel told her about the aristocrats he had met at the General's Ball and the wonders of the expedition. He neglected mentioning Eleanora Van Rensselaer, though. As the embers burned low, they made love slowly, tenderly. A soft wind played through the pines outside, crickets chirped, and the moon cast its light in through the doorway.

After each had pleasure, Carrie nestled in Daniel's arms and drifted into a deep slumber. He held her, soothed and comforted to feel her breathing once again in his arms as he watched the embers burn like rubies and the cool moonlight spilling into the room.

"Hey-ho, Lester!" Daniel called next morning as his row-boat pulled alongside the anchored brig.

Lester Frye, a burly, whiskered, sunburnt fellow in his mid-forties, peered over the rail. "Danny!" He ran to the stern and heaved over a rope ladder. "Come aboard."

Daniel clambered up the ladder and vaulted the rail. He scrutinized the masts, the furled sails, the rigging, and the deck. "Everything appears shipshape," he said, and thrust out his hand for his first mate to shake.

"You didn't doubt it would?" Lester asked suspiciously. "I'm sure your beautiful bride informed you of the good news? The runs we've made in your absence?" Daniel nodded. "Well, then, how was your trip?"

"Long. I leave again the tenth of September."

"So soon? But they must value your services, eh?"

"Yes. And we have our work cut out until then. It's time to make some quick money, Lester. What's in the wind?"

Lester looked comically shocked. "Oh-ho! Danny! Not me, says you, never again will I turn to smuggling, says you. Once the embargo is lifted, it's by the book, says you. Ho, ho, ho."

"We all need to make sacrifices." Daniel shrugged. "For a worthy cause, mind you. I must hire some men to help raise the house in town and finish it while I'm away. Otherwise Carrie will make good her threat and move onto the Seneca reservation. The two little ones in that cabin, we can't be snowed in there again this winter."

"Well," Lester licked his lips, "I hear tell there's six hunnerd barrels of corn liquor from Ohio arriving at Presque Isle in a fortnight, and that the man's seeking transportation, name of Sims. He wants to walk away clean."

"Buy-and-sell arrangement?" Daniel scowled.

Lester nodded.

"But why? They never do that. What's the price?"

"Ten-fifty a barrel."

"Is it quality at that price?"

Lester nodded. "Only hitch is, whoever takes it must take all."

"That's sixty-three hundred, twice the value of the *Pearl*."

"Yes," said Lester, "but worth ten thousand in the right hands."

"Does this Sims have a customer?"

"A merchant in Port Colborne, name of McFarland. He'll pay ten thousand, maybe an additional five hunnerd for timely delivery."

"But why?" Daniel asked. "It's only a thirty-hour sail."

"Customs. You weren't here when the embargo lifted. This new agent Wiley takes it as his personal mission to collect every shillin' in duty."

"Well, then," Daniel peered over toward the customs house, "we'll have a little fun at Wiley's expense. Tell Sims we'll be there." He went below to inspect the condition of the ship. It was as orderly and as clean as he kept it, and he returned to the deck satisfied. "Did you have any plans today?"

"No, sir, cap'n."

"Well, let's hang some sail and take her out. Those Durham boats I've been on lately are damned plodding craft. Call the lads!"

The first mate called two boys who were splicing cable at the bow. They sprang to the masts and unfurled the topsails. Lester cast off from the mooring, and Daniel carefully steered the *Silver Pearl* over the sandbar and onto the lake. The boys then unfurled the top gallants and the mainsails.

Pregnant with wind, the sleek ship responded, and soon the prow was slicing through the pale blue waves. With the wind in his hair, his blue eyes keen and happy, Daniel Hedges steered away from land. The day was bright and sunny, great cumulus clouds piled in the sky. Gulls screamed and dipped behind the ship. Away from land and its concerns, upon the sunny breast of the lake, Daniel at last had the freedom to think.

He tacked back and forth, examining things from both sides. What had Ellicott enmeshed him in? He considered the maneuvers and strategies of Albany. The contortions those people went through! Like the dancers at the General's Ball moving in patterns of the quadrille and minuet, they all knew the steps, and they enjoyed the ritual. He did not belong to that world, among those people, and yet the grand enterprise of the canal lured him. It was grander than anything he had ever done, ever attempted.

Then he remembered Eleanora. She had somehow worked things out with Clinton, and might even have known about his appointment before he left Albany. Had she used him? Perhaps. Yet the hunger in her eye, the nervous tension in her smile and coiled in her limbs even as she reclined—her passion awakened a need in him stronger than he knew he possessed. He contrasted Eleanora and Carrie.

Carrie's bright, candid green eyes and impish smile summoned him to a haven where life was sedate, happy, and complete. Her tenderness, her sensuality, satisfied him, made him feel whole and domestic and fulfilled. Her black curls, luxuriant as the flowering vines about their cabin, her sweet laugh, the grace of her step, and her calm acceptance embodied innocence, health, and well-being. Her maternal instincts, the patience in nurturing the children she had borne, awakened him to the voice of the future, of a new generation that must be guided and provided for. An orphan himself, Daniel took fatherhood most seriously.

He thought back to their wedding day six years before: that sunny afternoon Carrie had stepped out of the shadows in a dress of white buckskin a Seneca woman had sewn. The ceremony by the local justice was held in a glade, and with white moccasins and her hair braided with white flowers, Carrie seemed like a nymph of the wood. After the vows, her lively nature spurred others to dance to the fiddles, to eat heartily from the tables of game, vegetables, and fruit, to drink from jugs of cider and corn liquor. Last night Carrie had again lavished on him such joy and peace. He didn't want to leave again. Then he remembered Eleanora.

How different was Lady Van Rensselaer! Some deep sadness, deeper than a widow's grief for her husband, burned with a subdued flame, a flame of outrage deep within. Insulated by her position and her wealth, she dared not express that rage, but though she held it in, it burned and rebelled and demanded to be heard. That woman knew a loneliness Daniel hadn't felt since childhood. Amid the social whirl, political intrigues, and escapades of aristocrats, she knew how horribly alone each man and woman was, and this knowledge tormented her. Why her interest in the canal? He saw and he knew. She longed for a grand passion to sweep her up, to engage her energies and talents in an intense communion with something that would convince her—even if just for a day—that she was wrong about life, wrong about desire, wrong, above all, about love.

Daniel hated to see suffering, yet he wondered what he could do. Ellicott didn't understand. Eleanora wasn't using him. She was simply curious as to whether he saw into the source of her sadness, her despair; and if he saw, what he would do about it. He couldn't do much. His life was settled here on the frontier, here with his wife and his two beautiful babies, in his village, with his beloved ship. And while the thought of gazing for hours into her eyes, of feeling the slim lines of her body, the passion pent up, caged within her breasts and thighs—

"Danny! Say, Danny!" Lester cried. Daniel shook himself awake. "Ye've been too long upon the land, lad. We're luffing!" Startled, Daniel looked up at the sails luffing idly in the wind.

"Decide which side you want the wind on, lad, and keep to your course."

"Sure, old man!" Daniel yelled to cover his embarrassment. "My ship's been too long in your care and forgot its master's hand."

Daniel vowed then and there to forget the grand lady and to concentrate solely upon his role as surveyor.

7

*E*leanora returned to her Claverack estate. The crops were planted, foals and lambs and calves grazed in the pastures, the mills ground winter wheat and sawed her lumber, but she felt strangely unsettled being home. The outward appearance of everything, the order was the same, but the essence of it all had changed. She wandered through the mansion at all times of day and night. She gazed out the window when her foremen discussed business matters. She sat before portraits of her ancestors and Jacob's ancestors, wishing she might ask them questions. Most disturbing, though, she awoke from dark dreams, tangled in the sheets, dreams that she'd been disgraced, dispossessed, turned away from her home.

Daniel Hedges occupied more of her thoughts and dreams than she cared to admit. She told herself not to think of him, and she felt foolish when she did. What was he, a merchant? A surveyor? There were yeomen and tradesmen all about her more accomplished in their callings. He had callused hands with cracked nails. He ignored the most fundamental of the social graces. Yet in moments when she least expected, his smile and his mellow voice were with her. Worst of all, she allowed herself to remember his kiss. Other than her husband, he was the only man she had allowed to kiss her so. But the difference!

By late August the workmen had finished and the town house in Albany was ready. Eleanora left her Claverack mansion to wait in Albany for Clinton. She admired what the decorator had done, and she walked from room to handsomely appointed room: a dining room where eight could dine in intimacy, discussing delicate matters of state; the drawing room where brandy and cigars might be enjoyed, where she would play the newest Parisian and Viennese compositions on the pianoforte; the library stocked with the classics and with Locke and Rosseau, Hume and Hobbes; the comfortable parlor with a Chippendale sofa, love seat and parlor chairs, and Vanderlyn canvases of the pastoral Hudson Valley upon the walls.

Upstairs were three bedrooms: hers, the master bedroom with a four-poster bed, full-length mirror, vanity table, and spacious closet; and two guest rooms, simply but tastefully furnished. Servants quarters were in the attic, a kitchen and wine cellar in the basement. The stable likewise was complete, and a flower garden planted in the back. After a week Eleanora felt strangely more at home here than in Claverack, for it represented the new life she was beginning.

Clinton called upon his return from the West and he viewed the furniture and paintings, the arrangement of the first floor rooms with approval. "They've done a remarkable job."

"I'll show you upstairs."

"No need, no need."

"Please sit." She motioned him to one of the chairs. "How was your expedition?"

Clinton was excited, and he ignored the chair. "Inspiring, inspiring. We saw lands I never dreamed existed. You have seen the coastal cities, Boston, New York, Philadelphia, as I had. But our nation now only hugs the edge of this continent. There is so very much land. These cities along the coast are mere shadows of what will spring up when the west is developed."

He paced to the window, then back again. "After so much forest, so many rapids and mountain lakes, we traveled along a ridge nearly eighty miles long and perfectly flat. A marvel. And just when we considered we'd beheld all the wonders of the country, we were shown the Niagara cataract. Why, Eleanora, I felt as Moses must have on Mount Nebo, when Jehovah allowed him to view but not enter the Promised Land."

She smiled at the allusion.

"Vast empires lie to the west, waiting to be developed. If my reappointment as mayor weren't imminent, I would undertake a journey such as Lewis and Clark did for Jefferson. The West, Eleanora, holds our future, but so few of us back here know it."

"Then we should begin work to secure funds?"

"Absolutely. It is imperative now to connect those lands with our seaboard."

Edward the butler brought tea, and Eleanora poured and handed Clinton a cup. "How were the rigors of camp life?"

He smiled, then sat down. "We stayed in some true hellholes: mosquitoes, drunken lumberjacks, bedbugs, moths, even a snake in one elegant hostelry. The land is very primitive, mere clusters of sheds they call towns. But there is ample wood and stone for building. I spent most of the time with that Daniel Hedges. A capital fellow."

Eleanora shifted her position. "Oh?"

"Yes. The others looked at everything. Hedges helped me look *through* much of it. We discussed elevations, rock formations, methods to circumvent the rougher land with locks. He was a salvation to me, trapped as I was in the company of Eddy, DeWitt, and North. We elected him chief surveyor of the canal project. Simeon DeWitt grows old and I've commissioned him to survey and lay out the streets of Manhattan above Canal next year. Hedges will be taking a second look at some places we viewed."

"He'll be reporting to the commission?" She tried to hide the hope in her voice, but Clinton heard it.

He raised an eyebrow. "We expect him to deliver a report early in October." He watched. She nodded, stared into the tea leaves in her cup and said nothing.

"So, Eleanora, I have come today to enlist your help."

She peered up, smiled. "You know I'll do anything I can."

"Yes. And this might even be a bit of fun. I'd like you to accompany me and Mr. Morris to Washington. We'll ask Congress for funds to help us start. Now is a good time to force the issue since a bill for a mountain road in Cumberland, Virginia, is before the lawmakers. But beyond the finances, federal money will give our project a boost in the public eye."

"When do we leave?"

"As soon as Hedges delivers his report. Sometime in October, I should think. If I cannot make it here, then you should bring his report to New York. We'll set out together from there."

"I look forward to it."

Clinton nodded and stood. "I must return this afternoon to New York. I expect my reappointment as mayor any day, and I must immerse myself in city council matters."

"Have a safe trip in Fulton's boat. Frankly, I prefer coaches. The sparks and noise frighten me."

"Progress, Eleanora, progress."

Clinton stood that night at the railing aboard Fulton's steamboat *North River*, enjoying a cigar and the moonlight on the waves. He thought of the expedition, and he thought in particular about ancient mounds Hedges had showed him south of the level ridge. They were forts built along the ancient shoreline, surely before Rome was sacked, perhaps before the Greeks sailed to wage war on Troy. The civilization that built them was now extinct. Clinton had wondered, gazing at the surrounding countryside, who the mound builders were and where they went. How did they live? By hunting or planting? What gods did they worship? What were their boats like? Did fierce invaders, ancestors of the Iroquois, perhaps, conquer and disperse them?

Clinton saw in the mounds exactly what he now was pressing with New Yorkers. Those mounds were public works, ancient public works, now mute and ruined. Directed by chiefs and priests, the thousands of laborers had built them basket by basket of earth. Clinton had considered himself such a leader of multitudes. "Nothing makes a leader so admired as the undertaking of great enterprises." Machiavelli, but so be it. He would construct this vast canal for the common good. He'd persuade, cajole, intimidate, and force New Yorkers to see its value, vote for its funds, engineer and dig it. Its completion could very well lift him into the presidency.

Clinton was suddenly aware of someone nearby. A small man with blond hair, a man he knew but couldn't immediately place.

"You seemed so absorbed in thought, I didn't want to interrupt," the man said. He was a lawyer, no, a judge…a judge in an upstate county. He had a Dutch name.

"It is a fine evening," Clinton stalled.

"Have you been long in the West, Mr. Clinton?"

"Yes." Van Buren, Matthew? No, Martin, and they called him Matty. Martin Van Buren, surrogate judge of Columbia

County, Eleanora's county. "Why, yes, Judge Van Buren, I have."

The small man preened at the recognition of his name. "And how fares our canal project?"

"Well, sir, well."

Van Buren nodded. Clinton said no more. Yet Van Buren was not put off by the pause.

"I have business in the city," he announced with a certain self-importance.

"Business is an honorable pursuit," Clinton patronized him.

"No, no, no," Van Buren grinned. "Political business."

"There surely is much of that to be done."

"I am upset our noble party is being torn in two by a war faction and a peace faction—"

"And to which do you belong?" Clinton interrupted.

Van Buren smiled quickly. "I do not think factions accomplish much, Mr. Clinton. I believe we all stand or fall together."

Clinton agreed with him. "And your errand?"

"Hardly an errand, sir. More of a mission." Van Buren knit his fingers together. "I am hoping to help bind the two viewpoints together."

"Well, then, sir, I hope your efforts have success." The sarcasm was slight.

"Perhaps we might meet in New York and discuss where you stand on the war question..."

Clinton viewed this young upstart with disdain. "Contact my man Carr for an appointment."

"Very good." Van Buren nodded.

"I am sorry, sir, I hope you will forgive me. I simply must repair to my cabin and rest."

Van Buren bowed. "Good night, Mr. Clinton."

Clinton returned the bow and departed for his berth.

"Yes," Van Buren muttered, "I'll forgive you. Sleep well." And he grinned, pleased with the informal encounter. Men were approachable when met unexpectedly, and though Clinton had brushed him off, that mistake would soon be corrected and punished. "Ah, my fine aristocrat, you'll soon have to reckon with me." Van Buren stretched and gazed at the moonlight on the water. It was indeed a fine night to be on the river.

The steamboat docked at sunrise among a tangle of masts and riggings. Impeccably dressed and groomed, Van Buren marched along the wharf and into the streets of the metropolis. He knew New York City well. As a penniless law clerk seven years before, he had heeled votes in the rougher wards, his boyish physique jostled by the thick, rough hands of blacklegs and thugs. Thanks to the canal proposal, he now had an appointment with the Tammany chief. Better than venting the resentment and envy he felt for the education, wealth, and connections Clinton had enjoyed—indeed, Clinton had been serving as United States Senator from New York in 1803 when Van Buren struggled to find voters and clients— Van Buren now had sipped and savored the sweetest wine of all: power. If he might ally the interest of Clinton opponents upstate with Tammany Hall and get himself elected to the State Senate, he could single-handedly bring Clinton down and build his own political temple upon the ruins.

Brody O'Hanlon, boss of Tammany Hall, ran a foundry on the East River, and his "office" was a small cluttered room whose cold hearth served as a spitoon.

"What can I do for ye, sir?" O'Hanlon had a thick brogue.

"It's more what I can do for you." Van Buren flashed a ready smile, rubbed his hands together. "I've been discussing sensitive matters regarding Clinton's canal project with your legislators in Albany. They suggested I share this information directly with you."

O'Hanlon nodded his white bushy head.

"I know there's no love lost between the Loyal Sons of Tammany and Mayor Clinton—"

"Silk-stockinged bastard!" O'Hanlon spat.

"And yet the Council of Appointment is about to reinstate him as your mayor?"

"Aye, the boys go back on their word. They'll be punished, sure enough."

"Clinton is posturing himself to run either for governor or for president. He believes the canal project will lend him the notoriety he needs. Clinton is very shrewd, as you no doubt know, but he has a glaring flaw—arrogance—and in our business of politics, we work toward men's flaws." Van Buren raised his eyebrows, and O'Hanlon nodded for him to continue. "With his education and his connections, he truly believes office should be conferred upon him rather than earned. He despises the political process."

"Aye, until the bleedin' Federalists acknowledge him, then

he jumps into bed with 'em." O'Hanlon grew testy. "What is it, Van Buren? What have ye come for?" He spat a line of tobacco juice into the fireplace.

Seeing that delicacy was futile, Van Buren grew more direct. "I'm running for State Senate next election, and I want to offer my services to the Sons of Tammany."

"What district?"

"Columbia County."

"Why, we own half the legislature now, and we can't get out the vote away up there." O'Hanlon squinted. "What can you offer us?"

"Clinton." Van Buren let the one word register.

"Well, that would be grand, sir, but better men than you and me have tried to bring him down."

"Don't misunderstand me. I don't want to topple him. At least not yet. Good enemies are scarce, and therefore valuable. I suggest we use him as our adversary to strengthen the party. We minimize his accomplishments by taking credit for them ourselves, and we blame all our misfortunes on him."

"Aye, we've been trying to do that, but ain't as easy as it sounds. He always seems to rise above the fray. What will you win for yourself, sir?"

"Your undying friendship." This made the Irishman smile. Van Buren continued: "As a preliminary matter, I've made some inquiries about Clinton and the canal project."

"Have you now?"

"Yes, and I offer them not for general circulation, but to indicate how we may work together, what sort of information I may provide in the future."

"Let's hear." Again O'Hanlon spat a line of brown juice at the fireplace.

"First of all, it is not merely an improvement of existing watercourses he's proposing. It's digging a ditch from Albany clear across the wilderness to Lake Erie. In and of itself, that ignores all reason. You should know he'll need immigrant labor to do it, and the foreigners will need work when the project falls through, flooding the labor market and driving Tammany members from jobs." Gravely the Tammany leader nodded. "Secondly, and more importantly, Clinton is trying to finance the thing publicly."

O'Hanlon scowled. "The whole thing?" Van Buren nodded. "But who's to own it and run it?"

"The state."

"The state?" O'Hanlon nearly choked on his tobacco wad, and he hawked it into the fireplace, coughed and regained his breath. "Since when does a government go into business building canals?"

"Never, if we're successful. The whole scheme is preposterous. And Clinton's arrogance will undo him. Why, if his plan were widely known, and cast in the proper editorial light"—he winked—"you do have friends who are editors?"

"We own two newspapers, man. Don't you know that?"

Van Buren dodged the question. "Well, when this becomes public, the outpouring of scorn will make it impossible for Clinton to hold his head up. Think of it! A four hundred mile ditch."

"Aye, and it baffles me what our dandy mayor wants with farmers and trappers and woodsmen."

Van Buren leaned across the table. "I have just learned that Mr. Clinton is planning to go to Washington to seek federal money for the project. He will tout his recent expedition westward as a personal quest in the interests of a nation."

"And so, what do you recommend?"

"If you have any access to Madison or his cabinet, work to forestall the federal funds. Clinton wants to run for president, and the suggestion that he'll be Madison's opponent in 1812 should sabotage any federal help. The public, I think, may enjoy learning of Clinton's Washington trip too. They may like to know when their mayor is out of town. Perhaps the notion of a publicly-owned ditch through the forest might stimulate some interest here in the metropolis." Van Buren opened his arms in candor. "I will leave all of this in your hands."

"Aye." O'Hanlon's expression grew sly. "Have you talked with any of the lawmakers about the canal specifically?"

"Only the Loyal Sons and three of my closest allies. If I may count on Tammany's opposition, I shall begin working with other legislators. Your say-so must come first, of course."

O'Hanlon tapped his temple and winked. "Wise, Van Buren, very wise."

"Of course, my name in no way must be connected with—"

"Never, sir, never. We have never met."

Van Buren stood and extended his hand. "The accounts I have heard of the Loyal Sons were not exaggerations."

"We do our best." O'Hanlon shook Van Buren's hand and

dismissed him from the office, and the judge strutted through the grimy, clanging foundry wearing a broad smile.

8

Under the nose of Wiley, the new customs agent, Daniel Hedges and Lester Frye carried on business as usual until, late one September night, they quietly cast off and were away. The *Silver Pearl* could reach fourteen knots in a good wind.

Presque Isle rose into sight on the evening of the second day out. Two miles to the west of the Pittsburgh Road, smugglers had built a port during President Jefferson's embargo. It was reached through a narrow channel which the proprietors camouflaged with evergreen trees so the shore appeared unbroken. In the lagoon stood six log warehouses and eight docks.

While his crew moored the ship, Daniel went to negotiate with Emmanuel Krabb. Daniel had borrowed two thousand dollars. Lester had put up two hundred, and Daniel had staked forty-three hundred of his own money—every penny he possessed—on this venture. The fat, bearded dealer sat behind a counting table, a jug of whiskey and a glass in reach.

"Sims sent me." Daniel threw down the leather satchel. "There's the price, six thousand dollars. We can be gone by morning."

"Price is seven thousand." Krabb did not look up.

"Too bad." Daniel picked up the satchel. "I won't waste your time." He walked out of the office and back to the ship.

"All set to load?" Lester asked.

"No. Cast off."

"Cast off? But our investment!"

Daniel glared at him until Lester hurried about his business Just as they had loosened the lines and were beginning to leave the lagoon, the fat man appeared in the doorway.

"Hey, horse trader! Want to sample my wares?" He held up a jug.

"Tie up," Daniel said.

In exasperation Lester shouted orders to the two lads. "What gives?"

"That little antic just cost the son of a whore five hundred." Daniel took a wad of greenbacks from his pocket, his bargaining money, and handed it to Lester. "Hold this."

He hopped to the dock, walked up the path, and again entered the counting room. He sat and accepted a glass of whiskey from Krabb, and though it was smooth and well-blended, he spat it on the floor. "That's the best you can peddle? The farmers should keep it as corn."

The fat man tried not to seem disturbed. He extended his hands. "I'm going to do you a favor. Sixty-eight hundred, take it all."

"Do me a real favor," Daniel spat the taste out of his mouth. "Don't waste my time. Sims said six thousand and that's what I brought, no more, no less. That's ten dollars a barrel, and I take all the risks."

"That liquor would fetch twenty-two at Montreal."

"Good. You get it there. You want the six or you want the liquor? I don't exactly see the sloops lining up." Again he tossed the satchel on the rough plank table. The fat man licked his lips, poured another drink and swallowed it.

"Six thousand it is." He slapped his fat palm on the table. "But you leave me fifty barrels."

"I leave you ten." Daniel stood and walked through the door. He turned outside. "Count the money. We'll be loaded and gone before sunrise."

Back at the ship Daniel ordered the lads and Lester to begin loading. Oil lamps were lit, hatches opened, and all night long they sweated, stacking the barrels in the hold. "Smell each one," Daniel cautioned. "We're not buying a load of Cuyahoga water."

By sunrise they had loaded five hundred ninety barrels. The six hundred barrel cargo had been two barrels short. Krabb had appropriated two for himself. He was now sleeping on a heap of gunnysacks in the corner of his countinghouse, so Daniel did not disturb him. Because the farmers who preferred to ship a few barrels of liquor rather than wagonloads of corn had avoided paying the whiskey tax, no bill of lading was supplied to Daniel. As the sun rose above the treetops, he cast off and slowly made his way through the narrow channel to the lake.

"Will we run straight across?" Lester asked.

"Not today. The lads are tired from loading, and I'd prefer to set out at dark. I know a cove to the east. We'll anchor there, rest, and take on some drinking water." They sailed around an island to a hidden cove with a sandy beach, a clear brook, and ferns beneath the tall pine. A boulder at the waterline offered them mooring, and Daniel, Lester, and the lads stripped off their clothes and plunged into the water to wash away the night's sweat. One of the lads cooked salt pork and beans, and with a dram of whiskey and some biscuit, they had breakfast. The youngest lad, Jim, who'd worked the least, was sent aloft for the first watch, and the rest strung their hammocks between the masts and the railing. Soon Lester was snoring.

Daniel folded his hands on his chest and gazed up in the rigging. The boat rocked gently, like a cradle. He thought of Eleanora. He had tried to forget her many times, but her image came to him again and again. Perhaps when he was in Albany next he'd visit her. He tried to imagine her upon the ship, her hair in the wind, but he couldn't. Their worlds were far too different. Yet thinking of her was quite pleasant.

He was awakened by the lad Jim. "A cruiser, sir."

Daniel sprang up the rigging with his telescope. Half a mile off shore he spied a two-masted schooner tacking back and forth aimlessly. He looked for her colors, but the schooner was flying none. Very odd. "This is more than a coincidence," he muttered, and he told Jim to get some sleep. Daniel took the watch, and high in the crow's nest he watched the ship pass. He felt safer at sunset when it stopped patrolling and sailed northward.

A gentle September night came on. The moon wouldn't rise until daybreak. They blew out all lamps, cast off, then out on the lake they hung every square inch of sail. With a stiff westerly wind they began the wide tacking that would take them to Canada. All night and all the next day Daniel manned the wheel and the lad in the crow's nest warily scanned the horizon for any sign of sail. None appeared. Near evening the lad in the lookout shouted, "Land off the starboard bow."

Daniel sighed with relief; his fortune was secure. Yet the relief was short-lived, for soon the boy announced, "Ship off the port bow, approaching fast."

"What are her colors?"

The lad squinted through the glass and said nothing. "A two-masted schooner?" Daniel called up.

"Aye, sir, but I can't see any colors."

Daniel ripped out his own telescope and looked across the waves. "It's the schooner I saw yesterday."

This set them all buzzing.

"Will we outrun her, Danny?" Lester asked anxiously.

"We'll try, as loaded down as we are." He fired off orders to his crew.

"Approaching quickly on the starboard side!" called the boy.

Daniel looked anxiously for land through his glass. It was too far to run. He looked to the west to see if a heaven-sent bank of fog would roll in. The night was clear.

"They have no right to stop us!" Lester cried.

"And we have no right to be smuggling liquor," Daniel said quietly.

"They can't catch us!"

Daniel looked grimly ahead.

Soon the schooner was within shouting distance. "Ahoy, there!" a large bearded man called through a megaphone. "Slack your sail. I'm coming aboard."

"Who are you?" Daniel demanded.

"British customs officer."

He swallowed hard. This was the end for him, and it all flashed before him: arrested, tried, imprisoned, his family destitute. Yet he could do nothing but obey. He gave orders to slacken sail.

"I've got two hunnerd dollars invested!" Lester cried. "Do something, Danny!"

"Let's hear him out. Throw down a ladder and a line."

The schooner pulled alongside, and the waves rocked the two boats together, then away, together, then away. The Canadian fastened the line and clambered up the ladder.

"Customs," he announced. "I need your bills of lading, a view of your cargo and your log."

"We're hauling potash. We've come from Erie and are bound for Port Colborne."

"I need to see the bills, the log, and the cargo."

Daniel whistled, and one of the lads swung down from the rigging. "Take this man to the hold. I'll get the paperwork."

The lad escorted the man, and Daniel looked to the

schooner and saw three raffish, barefoot sailors on deck. That was unusual for an official British customs ship.

"What do we do?" Lester groaned.

"See what happens. They look more like pirates than customs agents to me."

"But my two hunnerd dollars!"

"Quiet. Here he comes."

"Sir—" the Canadian said, but the boy aloft interrupted him with a cry of "Sail off the port bow, closing quickly." All faces turned eastward.

"Her colors?"

"United States."

"Yes," the Canadian turned, "but we were here first. Sir, you are transporting liquor into Canada, and I demand to see your bill of lading and a receipt. Otherwise I must immediately impound the ship and its contents."

"Sure," Daniel nodded, "but I need to see your commission first."

The man's face flushed and twitched. "Those documents will be in my hands inside of two minutes or you'll be in the brig aboard my ship."

"All right. Lester, help me."

They went down into Daniel's cabin, and Lester was wailing, "My two hunnerd dollars."

"Quiet!" Daniel whispered. "The American ship is probably Wiley, looking for us. We have to stall until the American ship arrives."

"But if the Canuck feller don't impound us, Wiley will."

"Stall him," Daniel ordered. He thrust a pistol into Lester's hand. "Hide this in the companionway."

"Ahoy, there!" was called from the American ship, "Name yourself!"

"The *Silver Pearl* of Buffaloe Creek," Jim from the crow's nest called. Daniel rummaged about his desk and collected all the papers he could find. Arming himself with the other pistol, he put on his coat to hide it, then carried the papers up to the deck.

"Ah." The Canadian reached for the papers, but just as he touched them, Daniel dropped them to the deck and they scattered in the wind. The Canadian looked alarmed, then raised his eyes to behold Daniel's pistol pointed at his heart. "You're not a customs officer, friend. You and the boys look like pirates to me. So we'll just wait a few minutes together."

"Amos!" the Canadian called to his own crew, and there was the sound of men clambering up the rope ladder.

"Lester!" Daniel cried, but the first mate already had a belaying pin at the top of the rope ladder. A shot was fired from the schooner's deck, and the boy in the crow's nest cried and fell forty-five feet to the deck. The Canadian grappled with Daniel, trying to wrest away the pistol. The pistol fired into the sails, then Daniel kneed the man in the groin and punched him squarely in the face, sending him reeling backward. With his one pistol shot spent, Daniel jumped for a belaying pin as the man hit the mast, shook his head, then lumbered forward.

"We're coming aboard!" the American officer cried.

Lester was busy keeping the Canadian pirates from climbing over the railing. The other lad threw a ladder over the port side as Daniel wrestled again with the big Canadian. A third gunshot sounded, and all eyes turned toward a man in uniform—Wiley, standing at the rail. This distracted the Canadian, and Daniel dealt him a blow to the side of the head which sent him sprawling on the deck.

"In the name of the United States government, cease and desist!"

"Yes, sir," Daniel said.

Lester had sent one of the sailors into the lake and two others back to the ship. "They're casting off," he cried. Wiley approached.

"We heard shots, Captain Hedges, as we came to inspect your ship. What is going on here?"

"They're getting away!" Lester cried, pointing.

Daniel paused, then nodded. "This fellow here says he's a British customs officer, but I believe he is a pirate, trying to steal the potash we're hauling. His ship is now escaping, leaving him behind."

"Can I trust you to put him in irons and produce him at Buffaloe Creek?"

"Yes, sir."

Wiley turned, vaulted the railing, and ordered his craft to chase the escaping pirate ship. Bleeding and sore, Daniel went to the boy who lay lifeless on the deck.

"My God!" the other lad cried, cradling the lifeless head. "Jimmy! Jimmy!" Hedges looked down, and by the angle of the boy's neck he knew that if the shot hadn't killed him, the fall had. He turned and walked to Lester.

"What the hell just happened?" Lester asked with terrified eyes.

"Don't know, mate. Help me haul that blackguard below."

Together they dragged the moaning Canadian down the companionway and tied him to the mainmast between decks.

"What now?" Lester asked.

"Your two hundred dollars."

"Don't joke, Danny. What now?"

"We'll look to the boy, then deliver our cargo."

The boy was dead. They brought him to Daniel's cabin and lay him in the bunk, then Daniel took a reading to see how far off course they had drifted. He consulted his charts, and set a new course to Port Colborne.

They delivered the corn liquor to the McFarland warehouse in Port Colborne late that night, and received sixteen dollars a barrel. A stiff westerly wind allowed the *Silver Pearl* to clear the sandbar at Buffaloe Creek two days after the lad had died. His body was beginning to putrefy, so Daniel and Lester and the other lad immediately delivered it to his mother. As she was a widow and her son was her sole support, Daniel gave her five hundred dollars of his profit. Returning to the brig, they untied the Canadian pirate, who staunchly refused to identify himself, and delivered him to the sheriff.

Daniel reserved a thousand dollars for his backers to give them the promised fifty percent return, and he computed Lester's share to be eighty-three dollars, plus his original two hundred. Because of his heroics, though, Daniel gave Lester an extra hundred, and he gave the other lad a hundred. Daniel earned sixteen hundred fifty-seven dollars clear profit on the venture, and he considered himself damned lucky not to be serving a long prison sentence in shackles.

The story unfolded in Cook's Tavern four days later. Daniel and Lester had not told a soul, yet when the customs pilot boat returned, they were celebrated heroes. The schooner belonged not to British customs, but to the pirate Jack Layland. During the embargo Layland preyed on American smugglers who, if they survived Layland's men, would not be likely to report the theft. Layland hadn't ventured out since the embargo ended in July, yet when he had late in August, Daniel Hedges and Lester Frye had captured him. Happening upon the scene, the American customs packet gave chase. A gun battle ensued and Customs Agent Wiley was slain. The three surviving inspectors subdued the pirate crew and brought them before the federal circuit judge in Buffaloe Creek to be tried with Layland on charges of piracy and murdering a customs officer. In all the excitement, no one thought to ask what the *Silver Pearl* had been shipping.

Characteristically, Daniel shied from notoriety. He credited his ship's hand who perished, James Dougal, as the true hero of the incident. Lester, though, reveled in his newfound importance, and the tale improved each time he told it in the taproom of Cook's.

"Danny, Danny, I can't buy a dram no more," Lester bragged when Daniel met him a week later. "The folks love me."

"Ain't good to get your head up too high, mate. That's when it gets shot off."

"Ah, loosen up, Daniel. We're heroes."

"Yeah, Lester, sure we are. We could have been true heroes resting in jail. Those barrels weren't stamped."

"What's happened to you, Danny? You ain't been the same since you went to Albany with Ellicott. You take things too seriously. What's the difference? It come out our way. You never cared before. Remember the good old days of the embargo? This was nothing compared."

"You're right, Lester. Let's have a drink. You can buy for me today."

"Sure, Daniel, sure."

9

Daniel left late in September, the day after the pirates were hanged. He was not happy about leaving. His new house was framed and roofed, and he wanted to work on it, to finish it. True, it would be good to complete the survey, fulfill his duty to the commission and get paid, but a certain dread attended the leaving. The last nights with Carrie had been exceedingly lovely and tender, and he did not want to leave her. The children, so bright and lively running in the sun, needed to be protected, he felt, from some vague threat.

And yet as he set about surveying and mapping, camping alone in the evening, he had much time to think, and he enjoyed the solitude. The survey took him three weeks, and he reached Albany as the leaves were turning. In those long nights alone, he had vowed to keep away from Eleanora, not for anything she had done, but because he wanted his life to remain simple.

He reviewed his findings with the commissioners, then Simeon DeWitt made a surprising request: "Mr. Clinton is unable to be here, so he asked that you deliver your maps and observations to a Mrs. Eleanora Van Rensselaer."

The old surveyor fumbled among his papers to find her address, and Daniel allowed him to search. He took the address offered him as an instrument of fate, and dispatched a young boy with a note to Eleanora's town house announcing he would call that afternoon. He vowed to leave Albany the next day, return to his family as quickly as possible, and leave temptation behind.

Before he went to see her, though, he bathed and clipped his moustache, shaved his cheeks and chin, combed his hair, put on clean linen, and had the boy brush his suit and blacken his boots. He regarded himself with approval in the mirror, and he gazed into his eyes for a long moment, trying to read something there.

Meanwhile, Eleanora was running Kate in circles as she tried various gowns and hairstyles to achieve some undefined effect. She wanted to be casual, yet she wanted to impress. "The yellow gown, Kate. Bring it back. And the green sash. Yes, it has a certain rustic look. The white slippers? Yes, I think they will do. Now, shall we weave flowers in my hair? No, I agree. A ribbon, yes, but green or white? Green to match the bow. Jewelry. The emerald necklace. No, too gaudy. The stickpin, though, yes."

At the appointed hour, Daniel knocked and was shown into the drawing room. He watched the pendulum of the Dutch clock swing back and forth, back and forth.

After ten long minutes the door opened and slowly he turned. Eleanora stood in the doorway in a loose yellow gown with a bright green sash, and a bright green ribbon in her hair. Yet it was her smile, the gleam in her eye that pleased him. She radiated health and joy.

"So nice to see you again." She swept into the room.

Daniel looked down to the roll of maps and papers in his

hand. "Mr. Dewitt asked if I'd deliver these to you for Mr. Clinton."

"Have you a moment, or must you rush off?"

"I'm leaving tomorrow."

"Well, then." She motioned him to an upholstered chair, and she reclined in the love seat. "Mr. Clinton told me of your expedition and the unanimous choice of the commissioners to name you chief surveyor."

"It's an honor to work with them." He held up the papers. "I hope these will be helpful." He stared at her until she looked at the floor. "Why was I asked to bring them to you?"

"Oh." She blushed and looked away, "I'm to accompany Mr. Clinton and Mr. Morris to Washington. We're trying to get federal money for the project."

Daniel nodded. "I see. Tell me, just how does one proceed to get money in Washington?"

"You need only understand greed." She was being flippant, coy. It annoyed him. "Certain things in Washington are taken for granted—greed and power are the only motives for going there and the only drives that get things done. So that's where you begin, by understanding greed and power."

"And do you?"

Eleanora raised her eyebrows, smiled, but did not answer directly. "You show each legislator what he stands to gain from giving you what you want. You do all the groundwork before the matter comes to a vote on the floor. Then, if you get a favorable vote, you go the president and try to show him how he will benefit."

"He and Mr. Clinton are in the same party."

"That means nothing. Madison sees DeWitt as a threat in 1812, so convincing him to help will be no small feat. But politics grows tiresome, Daniel. How are things in Buffaloe Creek?"

Daniel described the town, his brig, his cabin, and his new house, and he related a few anecdotes about the townspeople.

"Sometimes I envy you and the people out west. Everything seems so straightforward and simple."

"Envy?" Daniel scowled. "People in the West are simply working to get what you already have."

"Yes, I know." A weariness was in her voice. "But they don't see what I see. They don't see what wealth does, how it comes to own the person who has it."

Daniel shifted uncomfortably in his chair and scowled, wondering why she was telling him this.

"Of course, I didn't always feel so." Eleanora lay back and looked at the ceiling. She seemed in a mood for candor. "When I was a girl, I discovered the poet Rabelais. Do you know of him?" Daniel shook his head. She grew excited that she might tell him about Rabelais. "Oh, he was a revelation to me at sixteen! His elegance, his crudeness, his flights of fancy, his genteel amusement with the world. He wrote of the Abbey of Thélème, founded for men and women of elegant taste, apart from the world where the poetic and the sensual might bloom, where greed and power and other vulgar clamorings were unknown.

"For a time I dreamed the abbey existed somewhere, and fine ladies danced and made love with elegant men. In tapes-tried halls they'd walk, music always playing, and with good taste and humor they'd follow the abbey's one command-ment: 'Do what you wish.' No gluttony, no lechery, no greed or lust for power."

She smiled, amused by her naiveté. "And so, even with my wealth I hated my life. I despised the provincial world about me for it never reached the poet's ideal. Our income came not from some heavenly unnamed source, but from crude men and women, tenant farmers who sowed the fields and bred cattle. Where were the fine people? Our houses were drafty, our carriages squeaked, and we entertained ourselves with churlish songs and doggerel."

Daniel frowned and shifted uncomfortably in his chair.

"I married," she said as if admitting a frailty. "I married a man who saw more than the crude people, whose devotion to poetry elevated him into a sublime realm. Ours was to be a communion of souls, Daniel, and together we were to have what no man and woman dared to have on this continent, a platonic love."

"What's that?"

Eleanora smiled. "I'm sorry." Her tone was only slightly patronizing. "It is a love without physical passion."

"And he was your husband?" Daniel asked in disbelief.

"Silly, wasn't it? Yet he lived up to our pledge. He preferred his circle of young poets who drank together and visited hunting lodges together, recited poetry and dedicated their lives to art. And I"—she looked wistfully down—"I needed more. Oh, men came to me," she nodded, "they whispered in my ear, passed me notes, but I despised how their eyes shifted, how their breath came more quickly, how they licked their lips as if I were some barnyard bitch in heat." She sighed. "Perhaps that is the impression I gave; or perhaps they lusted after my lands. My lands"—she gave a short laugh—"but of course they are mine."

"And no doubt very valuable."

She nodded. "Yes, and undoubtedly worth the price I pay every single hour of every single day." Daniel knit his brow at her sarcasm. He didn't understand much of what she was trying to say. "But then I met DeWitt." She smiled. "No, there was no physical attraction, ever. His lovely wife Maria and I are very close, and he has four beautiful children. But DeWitt replaced all that nonsense about abbeys and genteel folk with practical concerns. Instead of pining for what could not be, I looked instead to see what I could do to improve what was. And I found, much to my surprise, that I was good at it, at politics, able to find values behind the rhetoric, willing to work for something I believed in."

Eleanora stared at him for a long moment. The purpose of the revelation was unclear, and Daniel was noticeably uneasy.

"I have worked with DeWitt on establishing free schools in New York City, on advancing history and literature in New York, on getting Mr. Fulton a monopoly for steam navigation, on chartering turnpike companies to build roads. And now the canal. DeWitt is a natural leader of men. He uses his position and his wealth to better the lot of all. I sincerely believe he will be president someday. Since working with him, I've found new meaning in my life"—her voice dropped—"and widowhood bothers me far less."

Daniel winced and shifted in his seat. "But canals and turnpikes? They hardly seem worthy of your attention."

Eleanora nodded, thought, then answered. "It does seem odd. It certainly seems odd to the women friends I have, or used to have. They fill up their days with floral arrangements and dinner invitations. Yet I see so much happening just now. You should hear DeWitt speak on this point. A new order is struggling to be born, Daniel. Commerce, manufacturing, these right now are redefining all our notions of wealth and power. Observe how Fulton's steamboat has altered travel between here and New York—nineteen hours! Read Adam Smith. Soon trade will supplant land as the basis of wealth. DeWitt sees this occurring, and believes that by helping commerce he will help build and strengthen our state and our nation." She shrugged and waved at the maps in his hand. "And so now I go to Washington."

Daniel scowled. Her talk was inconsistent. "You say a new age is being born, yet you hold an estate as old fashioned, as absolute as an English manor."

She shrugged again. "It is a dilemma, but how else shall I live? I have no husband. I have no other way to gain the means to live. I need what I have. That cannot be escaped. I am reaching out for the new, yes, but I must cling to the old. Helping DeWitt gives my life a purpose. He is so remarkable. You should be happy he has seen fit to favor you."

Daniel bristled indignantly. "Any appreciation that is given should be mutual."

Eleanora laughed. "Yes, Daniel, yes, of course you're right. Absolutely. Sometimes I get carried away in my admiration of him. He is pleased with your work, your commitment. Very pleased."

"And so, what now?" Daniel was visibly annoyed.

"We see how we fare in Washington. That will determine the next move."

"So I should wait to be summoned?"

"I'm afraid so." Eleanora showed regret.

"Well, then." Daniel handed the papers to her. "I will wait at home."

"Daniel?" she asked softly. "Would you care to stay for dinner?"

He searched her expression for some ulterior motive. "No, no thank you. I've made other plans."

She seemed shocked, but she quickly retreated behind arid formality. "Well, thank you for delivering your report. I am sure it'll be most helpful in Washington."

"That's what matters," he said with sarcasm. He walked to the door, opened it, then turned to look at her for a last time. "Good-bye."

Eleanora attempted a smile and held up her hand in a wave. He closed the door behind him. She tapped her fingers on the table beside the love seat. She looked down at the yellow gown, as open and fragile as the petals of a yellow flower. She heard the front door close. She had fussed over details with the cook. She'd had flowers picked for the table, and he had walked out. Viciously she hurled the maps and papers to the floor, and chewed her knuckles. Her eyes lurched about the room as if looking for an escape. There was none.

"Has Mr. Hedges left?" Kate asked as Eleanora stormed along the hallway. The look she received in answer quieted her. "Oh, mum, I'm so sorry for you."

"I don't need your pity! Take this ridiculous gown off of me."

"Yes, mum." Obediently Kate followed upstairs, removed the dress, and hung it in the closet.

"Tell Rufus to make the coach ready. We'll return to Claverack tonight."

"Yes, mum."

Eleanora brusquely grabbed her camisole off the hook in the closet, picked up a novel, and reclined upon the bed to spend the afternoon vicariously enjoying the passions of fictional people. It was Walter Scott, and it was about ladies and knights, and it didn't work.

Kate returned in a few minutes with a hangdog expression. "Sorry, mum, to trouble you. P'rhaps I should go 'round to the livery stable?"

"Whatever are you babbling about?"

"The coach, mum. Rufus is repairing the axle that was bent and 'twon't be ready till mornin'."

"And your groom, where is he?" Eleanora asked suspiciously.

"He's tending to his chores at the general's, I'd be thinking."

"And there's not the slightest possibility you have planned a tryst for tonight?"

Kate's eyes opened in shock. "Oh, mum, you don't suspeck me of lyin', do ye?"

"I wouldn't be surprised by anything today!"

"Oh, mum!" Kate cried, holding her apron up to her eyes, "How can you say such horrible things?"

"Be gone! Take yourself away! Go meet your groom! Do whatever it is you do with him. Just leave me alone!"

Kate set her jaw in defiance. "I'd be thinking that's not the way I'd speak to my poor girl even if a gentleman upset me badly. And, mum, you may do with me what you wish, for that is your right, but servants ain't dogs to kick, neither. That's what I'd be thinking." And Kate spun about, slammed the door, and clomped down the back stairs.

Eleanora gritted her teeth and tried to focus on the words of the novel. She read the same sentence four times. The words danced about the page. Tears of anger filled her eyes. She shook the book as if commanding the words to be still, yet merrily they leapt about. Angrily she slammed the book shut, stood and paced. She looked out the window. The flower beds were in an autumn bloom, and the fragrance of roses wafted up. Savagely she slammed the window shut, thrust her fist into her mouth and gnawed on it so she wouldn't weep. She loved him, she loved him desperately and without reason. She had told him things she never told anyone else, and because of one slip of the tongue, he had left. He had left! How could he leave?

Now the tears came hot and cleansing. Eleanora leaned against the windowpane and sobbed uncontrollably. Her grief, her loneliness, her despair that she would never again love or be loved poured out in violent sobs. She saw her vanity and it disgusted her. Oh, how she loved him! But why should she expect anything else? The sight of him, his tales of the West—her breasts and thighs had tingled this afternoon as she listened to his deep mellow voice, as she looked into his eyes and considered asking him to be her lover. Yet she was afraid of him, and of herself. Afraid. His face would not leave her mind. She beat her fist upon the windowsill. "What a mess, what a perfect mess."

She stumbled to the bed and threw herself across it, embraced her pillow, curled her knees up with the pillow in the pit of her stomach. There was no end to it. There was no comfort. She conducted herself exactly as everyone expected, with perfect virtue. Her virtue and her wealth were wonderful consolations for this emptiness! Why couldn't she be selfish just once, just once do something forbidden, shocking, wicked? But that would lose her this gilded cage. Eleanora rolled onto her back and looked up through her tears at the frilled canopy, buoyant with afternoon sunlight. She stared at it for a very long time.

As he left, Daniel burned with anger. The nine blocks to his rooming house flew past. Ellicott, damn him, had been right. Eleanora was playing games with him. Not only must he carry out Clinton's orders, he must feel privileged to do so. Yes, he had made other plans. He had planned, he admitted it now, to share her bed. He had not planned to listen to her extol Clinton's virtues, or to sit across the dinner table wondering which spoon to use.

Though he had paid Mrs. Pratt, he decided as he hastened

along the street to leave Albany immediately. A cool ride through the pine bush country west of Albany, perhaps a bed at a Schenectady inn would be welcome. Yet at Mrs. Pratt's a note awaited him that Simeon DeWitt wanted him to call in the morning. Daniel nodded and set his lip disgustedly. "Now I'm completely at their beck and call," he muttered.

He dined at Mulligan's Oyster House—oysters, steak, and lager—and he read the newspapers the house offered, and tried not to think.

After dinner Daniel walked along the river. He studied the lines of Fulton's steamboat. With its smokestacks and paddlewheel, it was a grotesque craft compared to his *Silver Pearl*, but no doubt there'd be one on Lake Erie soon. Progress.

He passed by riverfront bars, boisterous this Saturday night, but had no desire to drink. He threw his cigar in the river and walked back up to his rooming house. "A young woman is waiting for ye," the serving girl told him.

"A lady?"

"No lady, sir, neither by her dress nor by her conduct. You're aware of the house rules about visitors?"

"Yes, thank you."

"Said she'd wait no matter how late you were." The girl raised her eye.

"Yes, thank you."

"She was crying!" the girl said accusingly. "Must be someone has wronged her."

"Thank you!"

Daniel climbed the stairs and opened his door. A plain young woman sat sobbing in his chair. "Miss, can I help you?"

"If you can't, then maybe there's no one what can. You are Mr. Hedges. I'm Kate McCarthy, Miz Van Rensselaer's girl."

"Eleanora?"

Kate nodded and started to sob.

"Has something happened to her?"

"She's . . . she's not well," Kate said. "She . . . she . . . she yelled at me today and accused me of the most horrible crimes. She has never, ever yelled so at me, sir. But today she lit into me." Kate turned away to sob. "To see the change in her from the time she was dressing to meet yourself till she came storming upstairs, 'twas a different woman altogether."

Daniel scowled. "Has she sent you here?"

"Oh, no, sir, no, no, no. If she knew I came, why, that'd be the end of me, sir." Kate gulped. "While I was picking up the papers she strewed through the drawing room, why, I come acrost a note with this address, and I think to myself, I think, p'rhaps I should ask the gentleman's advice on what to do."

"I don't see how I can help."

"It's you, sir, it's you she pines for. Oh, to see how excited she was before you came! Like a lass waiting for Kris Kringle. Then, like day and night! Oh, sir, if you'd come 'round to see her, I know 'twould have the most pleasing effect."

Daniel scowled again. "You say I should call uninvited? At this time of night?"

"Oh, yes, sir, and unannounced. Otherwise she'd thrust you from her out of pride. Just go to her and hold her. I heard such terrible sounds from her room just before I departed."

"And she knows nothing of this!"

"Cross my heart and hope to die she don't, sir." Kate crossed her heart and held her hand up.

"I make no promises," he warned. "Your mistress is a very important, very powerful lady."

"Yes, sir," Kate said, looking up imploringly, "but above all else she's a woman."

Daniel opened the door and led Kate down the stairs and out into the street. They walked the nine blocks in silence, Daniel's nerves racing with anticipation. Beneath the oil lamp outside the town house, Kate took Daniel by the sleeve. "Her room is up the stairs and to the end of the hall, overlooking the garden, sir. I am not my mistress's bawd, but I know her, and if any impropriety is suggested, she will flee from it. Knock at her door, sir, announce yourself. Tell her I'm away from the house and that you were concerned about her. Go, sir, go to her."

Daniel clenched his teeth, ascended the steps. turned once to look at Kate, and she urged him on with a flick of her hand. He lifted the latch.

A single candle burned in a hallway wall sconce. Daniel took it and ascended. The quiet of the house and the shadow cast by the candle cause him to squint and further clench his teeth. Down the hall, at the last door, he paused and listened. He heard nothing. Gently he knocked. No answer. The candle trembled in his hand. He pinched it out. He knocked again, louder.

"Yes?" The voice was weary, despondent. Daniel swallowed, but said nothing. He lifted the latch and opened the door. The room was dark and fragrant, and cool with autumn. Dimly the white canopy of the bed materialized out of the gloom in a faint moonlight. "What is it, Kate?" Again, weary, despondent.

"Eleanora?" His voice was deep and raspy. She whirled in the bed and her white camisole seemed luminescent in the pale light. She started to climb from the bed, but stopped.

"You've come!" she whispered, surprised. "You've come!" Slowly, like an apparition, she rose from the bed. She stood on tiptoes, wrapped her arms about his back and neck, and drew him down to her in a kiss. Gently, ever so gently, she kissed him, just brushing his lips with hers. then parting her lips, she kissed him gently with her tongue. Up she thrust her hips, and she pressed her breasts against him and moaned.

"I was concerned—" he began. She put her finger to his lips as if words would break the spell. She helped him remove his coat, then led him to the bed. She lay down, her blond hair spilling upon the pillow in the moonlight, and she beckoned him with outstretched arms.

Daniel lay down beside her and drew in her fragrance. He buried his face in her hair and nibbled her ear. She shuddered and rolled upon him, draped her hair over him, pressed her breasts against his face, pressed her hips against him, then smothered his face with kisses, lingering upon his lips with her tongue.

"Ohhh!" she sighed in his ear. "I cannot believe you are here. It's like a dream."

Daniel massaged tension knots in her back, her neck, her buttocks, and she rose to his touch, arching her back. Over they rolled together, and Daniel unbuttoned his shirt, kicked off his boots, and removed his trousers. He kissed her, first on the face, then on her breasts, then upon her belly and thighs.

"Ohhh!" she moaned, and she thrust her hips up at him. He answered with a surprising thirst. For long minutes they continued this play, Eleanora thrashing and moaning, chewing the corner of the pillow slip, until finally she cried out, arched her back, emitted the slightest moan, then pulled him upward and guided him. The size and strength of him astonished her, yet she did not simply surrender. She bit his shoulder and clawed his back, clasped his waist with her thighs, kicked his buttocks with her heels, demanding more and more. Daniel responded, thrusting deeply, his nostrils filled with her, squeezing the very breath from her with his arms, until his fury intensified. Eleanora moved as if possessed, and he drove himself into her again and again and again; he gulped and held his breath, and it felt as though at that one split second he would die; and hot fires burned, then explosions and involuntary spasms shook him as if the earth itself were erupting...

...and she, reaching new plateaus of pleasure, her breath crushed from her by the strength of his arms, the fury of his thighs and buttocks and loins making her squirm with pleasure...and she arched her back so she might feel the thrusts just there, just there, and she kicked up her heels, spread her thighs as wide as she could, drove her long fingernails into his buttocks and drank him in with her hips, demanding more and more and more until the pressure built and built, impossibly strong, like dark water pressing against a dam, building, dark and turbulent and deep, and she kicked and sank her teeth into his shoulder, squeezed his sweating body with her thighs, drinking, drinking, as if dark, turbulent water were pressing deeply, surging and pressing; then it raged hot and white and out of control, as if the dam had burst, and she was swept away with it, oblivious to who she was and where, and her head whipped her long hair from side to side on the pillow; then suddenly she went limp in his arms.

"Oh!" she moaned, and strove to catch her breath. Though beads of perspiration appeared above her upper lip, her lips were dry, and she licked them, brushed her damp brow, then turned and gazed into his eyes.

They lay together for long moments, petting and kissing. Neither spoke, but in the moonlight their eyes gleamed. As he twined her hair in his fingers, Daniel longed to tell her of a time while hunting, hearing a panther scream in her mating, and the scream echoed through a mountain defile—how that wild, echoing cry had stirred him. And as she stroked his perspiring back and thighs, she wanted to tell him how his tenderness, his strength, his self-possession made him stand like a colossus of the West, larger than life, unspoiled, good and kind, immensely virile. Yet they communicated only with their eyes and kisses, and their joy flowed with the purity of a forest spring.

Daniel and Eleanora made love twice more that night. As the sun was rising, the awakening it brought to the two lovers brought also the realization that the entire winter and much of the spring must pass before they met again.

"Oh, Daniel, I shall think of you often aboard your *Silver Pearl* in the winds and storms of that vast lake, and I will believe that sometime as you look into the mists and sun, you'll think of me."

He held her and whispered into her ear: "When the lake runs wild and free I'll think of you"—he lifted her chin and peered into her eye—"and I'll look upon resuming my duties for Clinton as a chance to be near you."

Her face showed momentary alarm, then she smiled. "We must, though, we must keep our...our...*this* a secret. You are married, and I have other reasons, good reasons, unfortunately, reasons that are all too good."

"Yes."

"And you must not be surprised if I don't acknowledge *this* sometimes, even when we're alone."

"I understand."

They kissed and made love again with a hint of desperation. As Daniel rose to dress, she lay back on the pillow in a most attractive languor.

"It is customary for a lover leaving his lady at dawn to sing her a song, an aubade."

Daniel smiled again. "My singing would not please you." He sat on the edge of the bed and held both of her hands in his. "But dear Eleanora, know that I will never forget this night, and that you will be in my thoughts until we meet again."

"Oh, Daniel!" She kissed him.

"I must go."

"Yes, before Kate is stirring. She must know nothing of this."

"Kate?"

"My maid."

Daniel nodded, kissed her again, then tiptoed from the room. He turned for a last look at her reclining naked upon the sheets, then closed the door and descended the back stair. The sun was fully up as he passed through the garden, turned up the alley, and proceeded down the street. He felt clean and whole and exceedingly happy.

Eleanora lay back upon her pillow and savored the warm delicious glow that infused her. "What a distinctive man," she murmured. "An absolutely wonderful man!"

BOOK II

10

Although on paper a magnificent city whose streets formed the spokes of a wheel, Washington, D.C., was little more than wilderness. Few streets were wider than paths, some not yet located through the brush and woods. Besides a few public buildings of white sandstone, and the twelve homes cabinet members and other Virginians had built, boardinghouses dominated the landscape. Clinton, Eleanora, and Morris took rooms at Quinn's.

Immediately they set to work lobbying. The Capitol dome existed only in an architect's drawing, and the Senate and House were connected by a wooden walkway, dark and narrow as a covered bridge. Back and forth the three passed day by day, showing warhawks how strategic the canal was for defense against the British, and doves how useful in developing commerce and manufacturing.

Each evening they dined together and tallied up the favorable, the wavering, and the unfavorable votes. If a legislator was fence-sitting and Clinton considered him ready to fall their way, he dispatched Eleanora to charm him. Her Livingston maiden name stood her well with Democratic-Republicans, and her Van Rensselaer married name appealed to Federalists. Her beauty, her wit and logic, her feminine appeal to their "better sense," won many votes, especially from chivalric southerners who saw no better reason to divert federal money to the north than having a beautiful woman ask for it. Yet Eleanora chafed at this ploy.

"What difference should it make whether it's me or you or Mr. Morris asking? The soundness of argument, the reasons and the benefits in each case are the same."

"Ah," Clinton replied, "but the results are not."

In three weeks they'd secured the necessary votes, and while drafting the congressional intent, they were invited to the President's house for a gathering of the New York congressional delegation and other New Yorkers who were in town. This encouraged them, for President Madison at least would discuss the project.

The Executive Mansion had been extensively changed since George Clinton's swearing in as vice president six years before. Dolly Madison had transformed the great barnlike rooms. Staircases were completed and mantels set over open chimneys; draperies and furniture and carpets, china, silver and crystal, chandeliers and candelabra, had been bought in Baltimore, New York, and Philadelphia and tastefully arrayed. The President's house now had the aspect of a home after Jefferson's eight dour years.

The first lady received them in the Oval Room. She sat on a settee in a gown of yellow satin, and a white Parisian turban with colorful plumage.

"Delightful of you to come." She nodded to Clinton. "So nice to meet you, my dear," she said to Eleanora. For Morris she had a fond handshake—Morris and Madison had become intimate friends while drafting the Constitution. A warm fire burned in the grate, and punch and pastries were set out on tables. Clinton led Morris and Eleanora among the assembled and conducted the introductions to New York's congressmen and to the merchants and manufacturers in Washington to push trade and tariff bills.

Eleanora wore a flimsy sheath of silver batiste with an Empire waist. With only loose underclothing, her figure was flatteringly revealed as she walked. Instead of cropped hair *à la guillotine* as was high style this season, she had collected her tresses in a jeweled headband with peacock feathers.

"Eleanora? You look absolutely ravishing!" She was startled with a hand on her elbow. It was Washington Irving.

"Why, our literary lion! What a pleasant surprise. What brings you to the capital? Have you turned to satire?"

Irving smiled broadly. "Alas, I'm lured here, moth to candle flame, by self-interest." He scanned the room. "The same animating emotion that draws every other soul, except yourself of course." He bowed. "I'm seeking an appointment."

"How wonderful! A cabinet post? Tell me! You're to become Secretary of Literature!"

"Oh, no, no, my dear, nothing that would anchor me *here* in this wilderness. A foreign ministry, an exotic port of call—Paris, Lisbon, Barcelona, London."

"Who could better represent America than its foremost man of letters?" Her eyes gleamed with mirth. The recent success with Congress had raised her spirits, and she enjoyed ribbing the rather sad and serious author.

"I agree, but literary fame and politics are strange bedfellows."

"Optimism, Mr. Irving, optimism. And our good friend Miss Burr? How is she faring?"

"Married now, to a good family in the Carolinas. I see little of her, but her letters are filled with pining for her father, poor heart." Irving pointed across the room, and Eleanora turned to see a smart little man with strawberry-blond hair and bright blue eyes. He was dressed in the height of Republican fashion, amiably addressing a circle of ladies. "Have you met Judge Van Buren?"

"I don't think I've had the pleasure, though I believe he's some county functionary where my beloved Claverack lies."

"He and I have taken lodging together in Lynch's. Among other matters, he seeks a passport for Theo's poor papa. He expects to have better luck when Mr. Monroe becomes Secretary of State, as is rumored."

"This certainly is a place where rumor thrives."

"And what ones may I convey about you? Why are you here?"

"Our canal project. DeWitt, Mr. Morris and I have been lobbying for federal money. We now have the necessary votes in Congress, and we hope the president will be persuaded."

Irving nodded to the far side of the Oval Room, where Clinton had Madison backed against the wall. Towering over the little Virginian, Clinton energetically explained the need and correctness of spending federal money on internal improvements.

"Ah, Mr. Clinton and the lure of the wilderness. He sought me out in New York to write an epic about some Indian chief swept over the Niagara Falls." Irving shook his head.

"When may we expect it?"

Irving rolled his eyes. "I prefer more...shall we say,

civilized subjects. Who wants to read about Indians and trappers? For his surpassing intellect, Clinton certainly displays peculiar tastes."

"He has vision, Washington. Soon the canal will open up that frontier and alter the way we think about the West. Who knows? Indians and frontiersmen may then become popular subjects of romance."

Irving laughed. "I should like to speak with Sir Walter Scott on that score! But as to the canal, Clinton must get past Madison, and Madison is spoiling for war. That's where he wants to spend federal money. Sad comment that Jefferson the titan avoided war, but poor little Jemmy will be the one to fight."

"Excuse me, Mr. Irving. DeWitt summons me." She bowed and smiled. "Best of luck on the appointment."

"Lovely to see you again."

As she glided across the room, Eleanora turned many heads.

"Mr. President, Eleanora Livingston Van Rensselaer. Eleanora, President Madison."

She curtsied. The small, scholarly man had a pale complexion and nervous, shifting eyes. He wore a simple Democrat ponytail tied with a black ribbon, and he seemed quite ill at ease in his own drawing room.

"I was just informing the president of the immense national benefits to be gained with a federal subsidy, and that the necessary votes will soon land the proposal on his desk."

"I'm sure the president would prefer discussing less weighty matters at a social gathering." Eleanora smiled.

Indeed, Madison seemed uneasy. Clinton's massive form, forceful logic, and now his beautiful, intelligent associate intimidated the little man. Madison nodded appreciatively at her comment. "The plan has merit," he said noncommittally. "If nothing else, it has the advantage of being wildly ambitious."

Clinton nodded confidently. "With congressional approval, I hope we can rely on the president's gracious support."

Eleanora looked directly at Madison. "I have every confidence the president will act in the best interests of the nation."

Madison approved of her tact and diplomacy, bowed, and muttered, "I thank you for saying so." With that he fled across the room, held a hurried whispered conference with his Secretary of War, then escaped.

Like a mother hen, Dolly Madison circulated through the

crowd, urging everyone to eat and drink. "You'd never guess she was a Quaker," Clinton said. "Often times I think she is the president and he her advisor. Let's find Morris. There's no advantage in staying now that Jemmy's left."

Over dinner the New Yorkers discussed their campaign and agreed that other than monitor the vote, they had done all they could for now.

"After Thursday's vote in the House, it'll be completely up to Madison. We'll know in two weeks."

"He didn't seem overly receptive," Eleanora observed. "He's got as much charisma as a coat of whitewash."

"Ah, but he's a shrewd one." Morris raised his index finger instructively. "He reads men as critically as he reads books. Though he looks careworn and ill at ease, he's ruthless and tyrannical when crossed. That Tammany crowd has no doubt informed him of your ultimate ambition, DeWitt."

"Yes." Clinton scowled. "I saw that Van Buren fellow today. Odd that an upstate judge would be at the Executive Mansion. Perhaps he has some connection with Tammany, though I can't imagine why."

"With Congress on our side," Eleanora said, "I don't see how Madison can simply ignore us."

"I agree," Clinton nodded. "I don't believe Madison has the backbone to veto this. On our side we have both houses of Congress, with a hearty majority in the House, where it counts; we have Uncle George, the people of New York, and a precedent. Madison just signed a bill giving funds to build the Cumberland Road. He must sign our bill."

"Well," Eleanora said, "all we can do is wait and see." She raised her glass and they toasted their success.

With much rhetoric and fanfare, a half-million dollar canal appropriation for fiscal 1811–12 passed Congress and went to Madison for his signature. Clinton, Morris, and Eleanora were ecstatic. Only Madison stood in their way now, and to defeat them at this juncture, he must veto a popular bill, supported by both war and peace factions. Clinton calculated that a veto wasn't very likely.

On the strength of his Tammany connection, Judge Martin Van Buren met with Madison. The President anxiously put questions to Van Buren about the project within New York State.

"Not more than a third of the population supports the

ditch," Van Buren told him with a ready smile. The President seemed troubled, and Van Buren enjoyed allaying his distress. "One-third actively opposes it, the Sons of Tammany in the forefront of these. You may rely on Tammany's support, of course, if you veto this bill, and those votes will more than compensate for what you lose upstate."

Van Buren described moves Clinton had made to position himself as a candidate for the presidency. "On the other hand, sir, approval of this bill will fuel Clinton's ambitions to oppose you next year. And as much as New York would like to be rid of him, we realize we need you, Mr. President, to lead us to victory over Great Britain."

Madison nodded and stood to end the interview. "Thank you, Judge, and I'll inquire about the passport for Mr. Burr. He has known enough disgrace, I should think, and both the nation and the times have changed so his kind of political machinations will no longer be tolerated."

Van Buren left the Executive Mansion pleased. He had taken three decisive steps to further his own ambition: he'd given Madison good cause to veto Clinton's bill; he'd strengthened his position as a political force in New York, as an ambassador for Tammany Hall; and he had seen firsthand how a President acted in office and under pressure. He knew he could do a better job. Van Buren left Washington the next day, before Madison took official action, with two strategies for the future: he must at all costs get himself elected to the State Senate from Columbia County so he could begin organizing there; and he must stay out of the war. Let others fight battles with muskets, cannon, and sword. He would work behind the scenes to consolidate power so that when the war ended, the returning leaders would have to deal with him in reestablishing peacetime order.

During the week, as they waited for Madison's action, a shred of news from Washington gossip mills diverted Eleanora's attention from the canal. The President was moving the customs house for Lake Erie from Buffaloe Creek to the more easily fortified Black Rock because the previous summer a customs officer had been murdered. She heard also that a heroic ship captain named Hedges had brought the criminals to justice and they were hanged for piracy. Daniel hadn't even mentioned it when they last met. Among the prattling, gossiping politicians, Eleanora thrilled to such an account of a man of action, and she daydreamed about him at the helm of his *Silver Pearl*.

The three New Yorkers busied themselves with reading, correspondence, returning visits each day and with long dinners each evening. It surprised Eleanora when she entered the parlor of Quinn's after an energetic ramble through town to find Clinton sitting, staring into the fire. He offered a wan smile. She reclined on the armrest of the sofa.

"What is it, DeWitt?"

"Madison vetoed our bill."

"No! How could he?"

Clinton shrugged. "Said he had 'constitutional scruples' about signing it, confusing federal and state obligations. Tenth Amendment or some such drivel."

"Oh, I'm so sorry."

Clinton set his lip stoically. "Everything is clear now. We're destined for war."

She winced. "How soon?"

"Six months. Perhaps a year. Instead of financing improvements to strengthen our nation, Madison believes he can chastise Britain. This could very well plunge our continent into the dark ages. Our little scholar believes the world is his personal chessboard. His vainglory will reduce us to a smoking ruin." Clinton shook his head sadly. "If only men would think! Jefferson's embargo paralyzed us for over a year, but that will seem like a bankers' holiday to this."

"So, what are we to do?"

Clinton fixed her with a stare. Sadness and regret showed in his face. "Two things for the present. First, if the national government won't underwrite the canal, we must turn to the people of New York. We'll need to plead our case well. If New York builds and owns the canal exclusively, then New York alone will reap the benefits. Secondly, I will immediately put my name before our committee as a presidential contender. I'll offer the voters a clear choice: peace instead of war." He opened his hands and raised his eyebrows. "In both cases, let the people decide."

11

"The first Christmas in Daniel's new home was a time of rejoicing. Daniel had brought presents from the East. He and Lester Frye cut a tall fir tree, and the children and Carrie decorated it as the merciless wind blew off Lake Erie. They sang carols, played games, and feasted on a suckling pig. Daniel immensely enjoyed the day with his children.

Each Sunday that spring, instead of attending the new church with the other villagers, Daniel took Carrie, Eli, and Rachel on outings: rowing on the lake, into the forest, visiting friends on the Seneca Reservation. One night as they lay in bed, Carrie remarked about a change in him, how quiet, how pensive, how joyful he had become.

"You take such pleasure in being home."

"Ah, girl, I'm just waking up to it, is all."

"You must tell me what Albany is like. Each time you go there, you come back changed. Happier, more thoughtful."

"It's a fine enough place, far different from here. Yet I see everything through new eyes when I return. I appreciate everything more, don't take so much for granted."

"It's a good change, Danny."

"Aye, but Cook's not pleased. He's complaining I don't spend my money in his tavern. Can't please them all."

This new happiness, though, lasted less than a year. As Daniel rowed out to the brig one bright September morning, Lester met him at the ladder. He was shaken and had been drinking already.

"They been here, Danny. They was asking all manner of questions about the *Pearl*." He licked his whiskered lip. "Then they went away. They just went away." His eyes lurched about. "Just like that. They just... went away."

"Who?"

"Federal marshals." Lester shook his head with regret.

"Do they want to talk with us?"

"Don't know. You seen them boys operate before. Tight lips they got till the evidence is collected."

"I told you not to go bragging about, to keep your head down, Lester. Did they ask at all about Sims or Kraab or the liquor?"

"No."

"Good. Best think to do now is to go meet them."

"Us?"

"Sure. Ask them what's on their mind. Worst thing to do is show fear. Come on." He and Lester rowed to shore, walked to the customs house in the post office and knocked. Shown into a room cluttered with maps and papers, Daniel introduced himself. "My first mate says you fellows were at the *Silver Pearl* this morning. Something I can help you with?"

One of the marshals looked to the other. "Perhaps there is." They motioned Daniel and Lester to the chairs. "We're handling a matter that requires the utmost secrecy." Daniel nodded that he understood. "You captured Jack Layland last summer?" Daniel nodded, but Lester began to fidget. "We understand you know much about smuggling hereabouts, the various coves and trade routes."

"As much as anyone," Daniel said noncommittally. Lester wiped his brow, nervously chewed his lip.

"Perhaps it's no secret on the frontier, but by this time next year we will be at war with Britain. We have come to begin preparations, and we need your help."

"We looked over your ship this morning," the other said, "and we understand you built her." Daniel nodded. "We've just bought four schooners from Mr. Ellicott, and we wish to reinforce their hulls and arm them as gunboats to patrol the lake. We have leased land for a shipyard near Black Rock, and a hundred carpenters will soon arrive overland from Brooklyn. In order to avoid suspicion, it would be better if a civilian were supervising the work."

Daniel smiled broadly at Lester. "We could use employment for the winter, eh, mate?"

"Yes. Why, yes."

After they discussed salary and other details, they shook hands and Daniel and Lester adjourned to Cook's Tavern for a tankard of ale to calm Lester's nerves.

Daniel soon got his first taste of working for the federal government. By his sale of the boats, Ellicott had pocketed a tidy profit, but the sloops were castoffs, hardly salvageable, and needed to be rebuilt before they could be reinforced. The promised carpenters didn't arrive until November, and they spent three weeks building ramshackle sheds to live in, using all the lumber Daniel had collected. The fierce December and January snows prevented any work beyond stripping the hulls. Over the men's complaints, Daniel had them cut, haul, and kiln—dry lumber for spring construction. Other needed supplies were not available—canvas for sails, cordage for rigging, tar, cannon, powder, and shot, as well as food for the men. Though Daniel complained and fumed and threatened, supplies only trickled in. And not the least of his worries, his promised salary was never paid.

By June the hulls had been strengthened and fitted with bulwarks to repel enemy cannonballs, but the masts lay on the ground nearby for want of rigging. Now came a new threat. Congress officially declared war on June 12, 1812. The gun ports of Fort Erie opened directly across the Niagara River, and the muzzles of cannon thrust out to shell the shipyard. Unpredictably, the guns would roar, docks would splinter and sink, and sheds would be blown to matchsticks. The ships were just beyond cannon range, and Daniel had the men move the workers' camp to safety. During periods of calm he kept work progressing, yet the men howled and ran for cover during the bombardment. In early July, when a young lad was killed as he sat in an outhouse, the carpenters deserted and together began the long trek back to Brooklyn.

The two marshals returned to inspect Hedges's progress, and he responded to their criticisms with a volley of oaths. They assured him the command would soon be assumed by a military man, that he would be paid and relieved of responsibility. Yet when naval lieutenant Jesse Elliott reached Buffaloe Creek in late July, he asked that Daniel remain at work commanding the locals in building the fleet.

"We cannot continue at this site," Daniel told Elliott. "The shelling makes work impossible."

"But it is the only harbor where British cruisers can't destroy our work before it reaches the lake." Indeed, the small customs boat was the only American vessel on the lake, while the British had three cruisers under sail and three more under construction.

"I know a sheltered port near the Pittsburgh Road," Hedges said.

"I am not authorized—"

"Who is?"

"You'll have to speak with the Secretary of the Navy."

"Can he speed up payment of my salary?"

"If he can't, no one can."

"Very well."

During the dog days of August when malaria and lake fever prostrated many of his workers, Daniel and Lester sailed to Presque Isle, and on rented horses they rode toward Washington, D.C. On the dusty roads of Pennsylvania they seemed more like two backwoods peddlers than architects of the American navy.

Daniel had never seen the Atlantic. Though he captained a proud vessel on the fresh-water sea of Lake Erie, he never had seen the low sandy coastal lands, and he made a quick study of the river deltas, the estuaries, the dunes and outcroppings of rock as he journeyed along the coast from Philadelphia. The nation's capital was a wretched enough place—clusters of rooming houses and public buildings at odd intervals among the swamps and meadows of the Potomac. Its dismal prospect was heightened by a swollen, oppressive sky, unbearable humidity, and swamp fever. Though government officials usually retreated to the cooler Virginia hills in August, this year the war kept them in town.

With no letter of introduction, no commission, and no recognizable name, Daniel Hedges was rebuffed by the offices of the secretaries of War and the Navy. The town was crawling with ambitious soldiers and sailors anxious for commissions, and with merchants and manufacturers greedy for lucrative war contracts. Daniel was just one more voice in the general clamor.

He sought an appointment in vain. About to leave in disgust, he fell into conversation with a fellow New Yorker in the sitting room of his boardinghouse. The gentlemen, Washington Irving, had just been named aide de camp to New York Governor Tompkins. Daniel was pleased to learn from Irving that DeWitt Clinton was also in town, and dressed in his buckskins, he went the next morning to Clinton's boardinghouse. The serving girl told him to wait in the parlor. As he entered the room, to his immense surprise he saw Eleanora Van Rensselaer reading a book. She peered up at him, nodded, then returned to her reading. Daniel stared at her white morning gown, the bright blue sash, and the blue scarf tying up her hair.

"Eleanora?"

She looked up in surprise. "Daniel?" She put aside the book, stood and walked to him. "Look at you!" He took her outstretched hands. "You look like a Kentuckian! What are you doing here?"

"Trying to win the war."

She laughed, and her laughter pleased him. "I heard about your capture of the pirates. You're quite a hero."

He nodded. "We would all benefit from fewer professional soldiers. They seem to enjoy their rank and their uniforms, and have little stomach for fighting."

"DeWitt and I are here asking for money again—this time to fortify New York City. We expect the British will attack our harbor first."

She dropped her eyes, then looked up uncertainly. "The canal is forgotten in the general din. This war is so ill-advised. It will accomplish nothing, and may do very great harm."

Daniel nodded. "How does Clinton's presidential campaign go?"

Eleanora sighed. "As well as can be expected for the peace candidate in these times. Unfortunately, everyone's in a war frenzy. DeWitt and I and a handful of energetic people have been forming political coalitions to wrest the government away from these Virginians. Half of New England wants to secede. It's weary, frustrating work. How are things with you?"

Daniel frowned. "The war hits us very hard in Buffaloe Creek. We're the first line of defense. Joseph Ellicott's warehouse is just beyond the range of British cannon. They have already destroyed his docks. I'm helping build and arm ships to win control of the lake."

"All this effort..." She sighed.

The door opened and DeWitt Clinton entered. "Mr. Hedges! How kind of you to call!" His familiarity was excessive; Daniel ignored it. Clinton looked from Daniel to Eleanora, then back again. "I trust all is well with you."

"I've come to ask for your help," Daniel said directly. Clinton's expression changed to one of concern. "I need to talk with the Navy secretary about a very important matter, and he has refused to see me."

Daniel outlined his plan to move the shipyard to Presque Isle to build larger, stronger warships. Clinton showed interest.

"It has merit," the mayor said. "I am meeting with Secretary Jones this afternoon to discuss the British blockade of New York harbor. You are welcome to attend if..." He looked down at Daniel's buckskins.

"Of course."

"Very well, then, meet me here at two o'clock. I have pressing business that calls me away just now."

"Will you be needing me?" Eleanora asked.

Clinton looked from her to Daniel, then back to her. "No, not for the present."

"Very well. I will show our surveyor what there is to see in this forlorn place."

The slightest annoyance passed over Clinton's features, and he bowed and bustled from the room. Eleanora's eyes positively burned with excitement. "Come, Daniel," she whispered conspiratorially, "we'll make you presentable."

Their joy at the unexpected encounter was sublime. They walked arm in arm in the close muggy air along the muddy streets, talking animatedly, buying the necessary clothes, enjoying the morning despite somber discussions of war in the shops. They returned with the clothes to Daniel's lodging house. Eleanora waited in the parlor while Daniel bathed, shaved, and changed, and he emerged looking clean and civilized. Eleanora sat quietly, her finger to her lip, approval in her eye.

They ordered lunch at a tavern, yet they hardly tasted the food. Eleanora complained about the stalled canal effort, the hysteria of New York City under the threat of invasion; they discussed Washington Irving's appointment, his attraction to Theodosia Burr, war along the Niagara frontier. Yet it was not the topics or the words, but the tone of their voices, and their eyes, that truly communicated. With a shock, Eleanora realized that two o'clock had arrived and Clinton would be waiting.

She insisted upon billing the meal to Clinton's account. They hustled along the street to the boardinghouse. Clinton was just emerging as they reached the front door. Not looking at Eleanora, he said simply "Come along," to Daniel, and Daniel fell in step with him without bidding farewell to Eleanora. All the way to the naval secretary's office Daniel felt Clinton talked too energetically about New York's fortifications in order to avoid discussing something else.

The meeting was half success, half disappointment. Daniel, whose strategic plan required no outlay of government funds, was given approval and assured the order would reach Lieutenant Elliott authorizing the shipyard move. Clinton, who was challenging this administration at the polls and whose plan required three hundred thousand dollars, was told the citizens of New York must fortify their city as best they could. At a street corner where their ways parted, Daniel paused to thank the mayor. Brusquely Clinton said, "Happy I could be of service," and hurried off. Daniel stood on the corner, watching him walk away, and had an unsettling feeling that Clinton was jealous of him, jealous because of Eleanora!

Yet that was not the only unsettling thought. William Jones, Secretary of the Navy, had asked him if he knew Emmanuel Krabb. Daniel said he knew of him, knew he'd conducted a great deal of smuggling on the lake during Jefferson's embargo. No further questions were asked, but Daniel felt the whole affair with the pirate and his liquor smuggling might be opened up.

A note arrived early the next morning from Eleanora. "The campaign summons us to Philadelphia, and so I must bid adieu this way." Daniel suspected Clinton had intentionally removed her to prevent their seeing each other. He left the purchased clothes on the bed, pulled on his comfortable buckskins, and set out with Lester for home.

12

*E*leanora returned to her estate in September. The war was a distant rumble along the Canadian frontier two hundred miles away. Harvest season was nearing and the weather had mellowed. On an afternoon during Indian summer, she gazed out the window, admiring her lands, her buildings, her livestock. She listened to the groom sing as he combed Hecate, the black mare. Idly she paged through a romance Washington Irving had sent her two years before from Scotland, but her thoughts were on Daniel, pleasant thoughts as she remembered civilizing the backwoodsman in Washington.

"Oh, my lady!" Kate dashed up the stairs and burst into Eleanora's room. "He's done it! He's done it, and there's no undoing it!" She threw herself upon the bed, weeping uncontrollably.

Lady Eleanora marked her place in *The Lady of the Lake* and went to her. "Who did what, my pet?"

"Joel!" she groaned. "He enlisted!" Her despair could not have been greater if he were dead. "Some of them were talking 'bout the war, mum, and Master Solomon and the general are conscriptin' reggy-mints out of the tenants, and they work up one another's pride till they're all struttin' and puffin' like cocks in the henyard, and so it gets to workin' 'round in Joel's head that he'll be left behind. So he visits Master Solomon's office and makes his mark on the paper, and that's it. I'm undone!" She wailed and kicked the bed.

"When do they leave?"

"Two weeks. *Two weeks!*"

"Well, my pet, you can be excused from your duties till then. Spend time with him. I'll get by with Allie and Lynn."

"That's the worstest part!" she cried. "He pr'posed!" Kate buried her face in the pillow.

"Why, that's wonderful! You're very lucky."

"Oh, mum, it ain't s'posed to be this way. It ain't s'posed to be this way a-tall. Two weeks is all we have, then he'll be gone for heaven knows how long and I'll be a widder, truth to tell, and what could be worse than that?" She looked up at her mistress, then her mouth dropped and her eyes widened as she realized what she had said. "Oh, I'm sorry, mum, I'm so sorry."

"Yes, Kate," Eleanora said quietly, "but at least you will have those two weeks. And Joel will come back, I'm sure he will."

"Then you believe I ought to say yes?"

"Absolutely. We'll make arrangements. We'll get you a house—the Preston place is vacant now, and it's ever so nice there with gardens and walks. You and Joel may live their until the regiments march."

"Oh, mum, you're so kind!" She smiled through her tears. "May I tell him?"

"Of course. Tell him today, right now. We'll have the wedding Saturday, and you'll have ten wonderful days together, all your own."

Kate began to sob, and fell into her mistress's arms. "Oh, thank you, mum!"

"Now, my pet, stop that. Up with you now and face this. Dry your eyes, freshen up, find Joel. Where is he working now?"

"Master Solomon's forge, across the river at Mount Hope."

"Send word. Don't fret about the preparation. I'll make all the arrangements. We'll have the service downstairs in my drawing room."

Kate sobbed again. "It's happening too fast! It ain't s'posed to happen like this."

Eleanora helped her up from the bed. "My pet, it happens as it happens. Accept it."

In two days the staff had prepared roasts, pastries, a tall elegant wedding cake, vegetables, garnishes, and great arrangements of apples, pears, plums, grapes, and peaches. Eleanora's seamstress fashioned a white wedding dress with a long train. From the cellars they had hard cider, wine, and a cask of ale. The minister of the Dutch Reformed Church arrived in his buggy, and the tenant farmers and their wives clustered about the yard and talked in hushed whispers in the great rooms of the mansion.

"You're so very beautiful today, Kate." Eleanora handed her a small box.

"Oh, mum, I'm so fearful something will go wrong!" She opened the box and drew out a modest diamond pendant on a silver chain. "Oh, it's beautiful!" She looked up and tears welled in her eyes. "Oh, thank you, mum, thank you for everything." She kissed her mistress's hand.

Later Kate glided down the graceful staircase to music from a violin, bass, and cello. In ill-fitting clothes the ruddy tenant farmers and their plump wives stood uneasily in the grand rooms. Abel, the gardener, had offered to give Kate away, and he took her hand as she reached the bottom of the stair. Into the drawing room he led her, where Joel stood tall, dignified, and serious in breeches and cotton stockings, his ruffled shirt tied with a black ribbon.

Eleanora watched inconspicuously from the back of the room, remembering her own wedding with mixed emotions. It had been a lavish affair at the Livingston's Clermont estate, the joining of two families, the creation of a new estate, the Van Rensselaer Claverack property nearly doubled by her dowry. Hundreds of relatives and friends had attended. Jacob had been nervous, and his hand trembled as he tried to slip on the wedding band. She had been so young and foolish and happy. A tear slipped from her eye and rolled down her cheek. Kate and Joel seemed so young, so poor and frightened, yet so very happy. They wanted little from life, yet they had so much together. Even in the face of Joel's going off to war, their blind love and innocence blessed them.

Two young farmer's daughters stood in front of Eleanora, whispering comments about the wedding.

"She's so pretty."

"And he, so tall and handsome. Jane used to walk with him, till Kate spied him and flounced herself around."

"I'll be the one to catch the bouquet, Mary, and next year 'twill be Billy and me."

"No, you won't. I'll catch it."

"But you don't have a beau."

"Never you mind."

"You don't, you have no one. You'll be a dried-up old maid!" She laughed, and as she did, she turned and saw Lady Eleanora. She gasped, and the other turned and gasped too. There was no question as to their thoughts.

Eleanora gently lifted her skirts, turned, and hurried from the room just as the vows were being exchanged. Her face burned with anger, and she needed to be alone. She climbed the stairs and noticed the narrow staircase that led to the cupola on top of the mansion. With a sudden impulse to go up there, she climbed to the glassed tower. She closed the trapdoor, sat upon the bench and looked all about her. It was quiet, and she was alone. She scanned her fertile fields rolling toward the horizon in all directions, her forests and creeks, and the cattle lowing in the pastures. Pridefully she held her head. She must not listen to such young girls' prattle. These lands prospered under her hand. Claverack gave her her identity, and she caused Claverack to flourish. So her farmers' daughters thought of her as an old maid. These lands she now viewed were some comfort, some comfort indeed. Then, as the music rose faintly from far below in the house, Eleanora considered that she could not even call Kate to comfort her. She folded her hands in her lap and listened to the bridal song. She must not think of the westerner, and she must not think of romances. She must think only of her land. Claverack would be her comfort, no matter what else happened, Claverack would always be hers.

13

Panic swept through Buffaloe Creek in October. Two British warships, the *Caledonia* and the *Detroit*, anchored below the escarpment of Fort Erie, ready to sink any craft issuing from the Black Rock shipyard.

The citizens of Buffaloe Creek and Black Rock constantly glanced northward, fearing an attack. In his leather apron Daniel went about encouraging his workers day by day, until a daring idea struck him. He sought out Lieutenant Elliott.

"Capture them?" Elliott rose and looked at the warships through his telescope. "Could we?"

"Only way I see to equalize things." Daniel took the telescope and looked out over the lake. "Sure would be welcome additions to our navy."

"They'd never believe we have the cheek to do it," Elliott said. His face brightened. "Let's do it while the benefit of surprise is ours."

Before setting out, Elliott needed permission from General Smyth. The gruff old general balked. "Soldiers and carpenters will be helpless if not dangerous out on the water."

"But, sir, scouts tell us there are only thirty-six sailors aboard the *Detroit*, holding thirty Americans prisoners, and a mere twelve man the *Caledonia*, with ten American prisoners."

Still the general hesitated. Yet the next afternoon a messenger announced that a hundred sailors sent up from New York by the War Department were only a day's march away. Smyth called Elliott to his office.

"Give me those sailors," Elliott promised, "and I will add two ships to our navy."

Smyth agreed. The sailors arrived next morning, ragged and dog tired from their five hundred mile forced march. Elliott ordered them to assemble immediately, and while Daniel and Lester collected every weapon they could find in the villages, Elliott planned his surprise attack. The *Caledonia* carried eight six-pound guns, and Elliott assigned fifty seamen under Daniel Hedges to attempt its capture. He reserved as his own prize the bigger ship, the *Detroit*, with its fourteen guns. Hedges and Lester returned after sunset with twenty pistols and an assortment of axes, cutlasses, knives, and bayonets. As Elliott instructed, the men muffled the oarlocks of the two large scows, and after eating supper and resting a few hours, they boarded the boats just after midnight and rowed silently on the placid lake.

For two hours the men strained at the oars, Elliott piloting one scow, Hedges the other. Slowly the ships loomed larger, until the scows were illuminated by their stern lamps and drunken laughter drifted from open portholes. Into the shadows they rowed, then stealthily the men sprang to their tasks. Five men in each party cut the anchor cables and forty readied to board. Daniel secured a rope ladder for his men, and he was first on deck. He spied two sailors of the watch playing cards on a barrelhead by the light of a lantern. Crouching in the shadows, he led a file of men toward the card game, and they watched and waited for Daniel's signal. Suddenly a shout sounded from across the water aboard the *Detroit* and shots were exchanged—Elliott had encountered trouble. The watchmen sprang to the railing. "Now!" Daniel whispered. His men rushed forward and wrestled the two sailors, clamping hands upon their mouths to prevent screams. Then others went forward and secured the forecastle hatch so none of the sleeping sailors could come up on deck.

Daniel seized one of the captured sailors by the hair and touched his keen blade to the man's neck. "Where's your captain?"

"Ashore."

Daniel pressed the knife deeper into his flesh, and a slim trickle of blood appeared. "Where does he sleep?"

"Amidships, sir."

"And the first mate?"

"The same—across the companionway."

Daniel hurled the sailor toward the others, motioned to Lester, and the two descended through the hatchway. A lone whale-oil lamp burned in the greasy smell of fried pork. A small brass plaque marked one room CAPTAIN and the other FIRST MATE. Daniel signaled to Lester, and they kicked in the doors. Indeed the captain was not ashore, but lay in his narrow berth with a young woman. Hedges placed his pistol to the captain's temple and said, "In the name of the United States of America, I take possession of the *Caledonia*. Get up."

The woman shrieked and bolted up. Hedges threw her a

shirt to cover herself, and he manhandled the naked captain to his feet. The woman cowered with terrified eyes, yet she seemed to recognize Daniel. "Get dressed," he told her, shoved a nightshirt into the captain's hand and led him into the companionway. Just then Lester emerged, roughly pushing the first mate. "Take these two up on deck," Daniel instructed. "I'll be up presently."

Lester bustled them along the narrow passage then up the steps and through the hatch. Shots rang out aboard the *Detroit*, but Hedges's capture of the *Caledonia* was clean. Again Daniel opened the captain's door. The woman had quickly pulled on her dress and was sitting on the edge of the berth, her hair disheveled, panic in her eyes.

"Who are you?"

She looked up at him defiantly. He remembered then. She was the wench who had served ale at the Chippawa tavern to the canal commissioners. Her name was Edna.

"You are our prisoner," he said.

Her lip trembled, and she hid her face and began to sob.

"Now, young lady, this is a war, and it's no business for civilians. You can be taken prisoner or not, as you choose. But I don't believe in involving innocent parties, so if you follow my instructions, I'll see you are returned to Canada."

"Oh, please, sir!"

"Remain here below. The blood of my men is hot, and I'll not answer for what happens if you come on deck. Place the captain's sea chest in front of the door, and don't open it for anyone but me. When I identify myself, open the door and step smartly. You mustn't be seen by anyone. Now do not move from the cabin as we're in for some violent times. Stay below no matter what you hear."

She nodded. Daniel turned and left, closing the door behind him. On deck his sailors had sprung to the rigging and were unfurling sails. Yet there was no wind. Suddenly a roar was heard to the right and fire leapt from a gun port of Fort Erie. The cannonball passed over the bowsprit and threw up a great splash of water.

"Return fire!" Hedges commanded. Four of the carronades pointed out the starboard side, and his sailors sprang to them, loaded them, and touched them off with a flame from the lantern. At intervals the four carronades spoke and their shots slammed into the wooden palisade of the fort, splintering the logs. Yet the stillness of the air damned them. The sails hung limp. With the anchor cables cut, the current entering the mouth of the Niagara River drew both ships downstream, closer beneath the fort.

"Man the oars!" Hedges called, and those men not firing cannon or guarding the crew in the forecastle climbed down into the scow. Lester threw them a line, and the men began rowing, towing the ship away. Again the guns of the fort flared, and this time one of the shots squarely hit the *Detroit*. That ship reeled, and the current, pulling more strongly as it entered the river, drew it just beneath the fort.

"They'll run aground!" Lester cried from the rail.

"There's nothing we can do to help her," Daniel said coolly. He paced up and down his battery of guns, urging the sweating men on. Two guns fired in unison, and the balls hit the top of the battlements, severing the tips of pointed logs. Three flames sprang from the gun ports, then three clouds of smoke rolled out and the mainmast of the *Detroit* groaned, twisted, and fell in a tangle of rigging.

"Again! Fire again!" Daniel ordered, hoping they might draw the fort's guns away from the foundering ship.

"The crew is busting through!" a sailor screamed, pulling on Daniel's sleeve. Daniel walked along the deck to the forecastle hatchway, where the trapdoor groaned and buckled each time a heavy object rammed it. Daniel aimed his pistol at the door and fired. A scream issued from inside and the battering stopped. Suddenly he remembered the American prisoners below.

"Go down into the hold and free the Americans!" he hollered to Lester. With the cannon blazing above his head, Lester crept down through the ship with an oil lamp, then descended into the rank, fetid hold. He heard the rattle of chains, and thrusting the light into the pit that smelled of mold and excrement, he saw a pitiful sight—ten emaciated men, nearly naked, their hair and beards matted, their glazed eyes staring blankly up at him.

"The key!" he cried. "Where's the key"

One of the men pointed to a far corner. Lester shone the light and saw a long iron key on a ring hanging near the ceiling. He stepped down into the bilge and nearly threw up. Wading across the hold shin deep, he took the key and unlocked the padlock on the chain that ran through the rings in their leg irons. He shouted for them to pull and free themselves. Despondently they did and he hauled them one by one to their feet and led them to the deck.

The eastern sky blushed with morning, and the reds and golds of fall foliage greeted Lester as he gulped for clean air. The men in the scow strained every muscle, pulling the *Caldeonia* to safety as all the fort's guns were trained on the *Detroit*. Barely a hundred yards from the fort Elliott had dropped the remaining anchor to prevent the ship from drifting any closer, and the ship took a terrible battering.

"They'll be taken prisoner," Lester cried, affected by his vision of the hold.

"There's nothing we can do for them," Daniel said. "He never used his boat to tow."

They watched as a British officer in a blue coat ascended the ramparts of the fort, cupped his hands and called: "Surrender or we'll sink you where you sit!"

Elliott mounted the rail, but they couldn't hear what he replied. Suddenly four rounds were fired upon them from the fort's battery, and the hull reeled under the impact. A sailor cut the remaining anchor's cable, and again the *Detroit* drifted toward the river.

"They're gone!" Lester groaned.

"Yes, but we're not. Not yet. We're out of range, we have no more ammunition to fight, so take these men, Lester, and relieve those at the oars." Daniel watched as the *Detroit* foundered helplessly closer to shore. Yet soon Elliott found a crosscurrent and the *Detroit* entered shallow rapids, gained speed, then grounded on Squaw Island, tipping precariously over. As the sun rose and the oarsmen towed the *Caledonia* past the point of Black Rock, Elliott lowered his boats, abandoning the battered hulk, ferrying his British prisoners, the thirty freed Americans, and his own men to safety.

"They attacked us as soon as we boarded," Elliott explained as he and Daniel stood together on the dock. "We were fighting, and no one watched where we drifted. The ship's done, but there's plenty of guns, fittings, shot, and powder to salvage."

Elliott ordered the sailors to get some sleep. He, Hedges, Lester Frye, and a contingent of soldiers rowed out to the hulk. Harassed by British fire, they salvaged what they could, then spread pitch over the *Detroit* and set it afire.

Back at Black Rock Daniel boarded the *Caledonia*. It contained a cargo of furs worth well over a hundred fifty thousand dollars. Daniel had no claim to the plunder because he was not a registered privateer. He notified the customs official of the fur cargo, then boarded the ship and went to the captain's cabin. When he announced himself, the woman opened the door. Before she could be discovered, numbered among the British prisoners, and sent to a prisoner-of-war camp, Daniel transferred her to his *Silver Pearl*. In Buffaloe Creek he made arrangements for her return to Chippawa.

"I thank you, sir. May God bless you for the risk you took. If ever I may return the favor..." They stood together on the dock.

"Just keep it quiet." Daniel held her hand, then turned toward the village.

As he opened the door to his home, Eli and Rachel cried, "Daddy!" and ran to hug him. Laughing, he lifted them high, hugged and kissed them. "Where's your mother?"

"Upstairs," Rachel said with a frown.

"Now, what's the matter with you two?" He jostled them, and they both tried to laugh, but Rachel asked to be put down. "Rachel, what is wrong?"

"We saw Mama crying."

"Oh," he said with a nod. "Well, we can't have Mama crying, can we? And if she's sad, why we'll just have to go cheer her up. You two wait here, and if I need your help, I'll call. Then come running upstairs just as fast as you can."

He deposited them on the floor and ascended the stairs. She was in bed staring despondently at the ceiling. His first thought was that she had found out about Eleanora.

"Carrie, is something wrong?"

"No."

"Tell me. The children are upset. They said you were crying."

"Why didn't you tell me?" she blurted. Then she rolled away from him, hugged the pillow and sobbed. "Why did I have to find out through others?"

Daniel said nothing.

"I don't care, I don't care if you go to Albany for the entire summer. I don't care if you sail from here to Sandusky every week. I don't care if you survey for a canal or get into politics or hobnob with the fine rich folks, only you didn't tell me!"

His face burned with shame. *She knows about Eleanora,* he thought. *It was inevitable she'd find out.* "I'm sorry." The words sounded so weak and hollow.

"I was so worried."

"I'll always be here with you," he said. "Why would you worry? I love you, Carrie. I have always loved you! I always *will* love you."

"I never doubted that." She lifted her head. "It's just that you should have told me you were going."

"Going?" He was perplexed.

"Yes, on that foolish mission to capture British ships. I was so worried."

Daniel smiled broadly and breathed with relief. "It wasn't foolish! We captured a ship, destroyed another, and took forty prisoners and a rich cargo of furs."

"But you might have been killed!"

"I'm too smart for that," Daniel said with bravado.

"Or taken prisoner to some camp in the forest, and we wouldn't see you for ten years."

"But it didn't happen, Carrie."

She looked up at him, her eyes brimming with tears. Her eyes this morning were large and dark and imploring. Daniel could not remember seeing them more beautiful. The fear and the sadness in them filled him with regret. He sat on the bed and held her.

"Oh, Danny! Oh, Danny!" she whispered in his ear. "I was so worried! When they told me where you'd gone, I was frantic. I can't imagine life without you. Please, please don't do that again."

He pulled away. "But I must help, Carrie."

"Why?" She was indignant. "What have they ever done for you? For us? You used to smuggle under their very noses. You traded with the same British you're now fighting, and you never cared before. The government doesn't understand how we live here, what we face all the time. They'll use you as far as they can, then discard you. You yourself used to say that."

"I did." He looked away, considering. "But now, Carrie, things are different; times are different. Our future, the future for me, you, Rachel, and Eli depends on winning this war. If we lose, we lose our home, everything."

"But there are soldiers and sailors to fight!"

"Yes, but they don't know the land and the lake as I do. They're strangers, and they'll retreat when it suits them. This is our home. If I can help defend it, I must. Governments don't really care what their decisions bring to the lives of people. It's not the nation I want to protect, it's you and the children. I just can't pretend things aren't the way they are. We must vanquish the British or the British will vanquish us, and if they do, we'll have nothing. We'll be just like the Seneca, cleared from our land."

"But if the British win, you'll be punished."

"They'll never catch me, girl. You, you're the only one who ever caught me." He embraced and comforted her. "You're all I have in this world, and..." he tilted up her chin and looked deeply into her eyes, "and all I truly need."

"Oh, Danny," she said, hugging him tightly. "I'm so glad you're home and safe."

"Watch this!" he said mysteriously, and he tiptoed to the door, opened it and called, "Eli, Rachel, come help!" Footfalls sounded on the stairs and the two children burst into the room, looking alarmed. They paused, looking back and forth. "Come on!" Daniel called playfully. With a squeal of delight they dashed across the room and bounced into the bed, burying their faces in the bedclothes.

After supper and after the children's bedtime, Daniel and Carrie made love slowly in the October chill. He was aroused by the thrill of capturing the British ship, by the afterglow of his raw panic, and Carrie was aroused by her fear that Daniel wouldn't return, and also by the joy that he had. They lay afterward in each other's arms.

"Oh, Danny, I want to have another baby!"

"So do I, girl, so do I. And it will be a grand life we'll show him."

"Or her."

"Or her. A grand life," he repeated, then kissed her tenderly, and they settled back to sleep.

For a second time Daniel was known as a hero to the people of Buffaloe Creek, and for the second time he shunned the attention. But along the frontier the American flush of pride over the capture of the ships was short-lived.

Commander of all New York frontier militia, Major-General Stephen Van Rensselaer, saw a surge of recruits swell his ranks to six thousand strong. He believed a surprise attack would gain America a needed foothold in Canada. Stationed below Niagara Falls, he planned to cross the Niagara River and attack the British emplacement on Queenstown Heights. The morning of the attack, October thirteenth, his cousin, Colonel Solomon Van Rensselaer, ordered three hundred men to cross the river and scale the escarpment. In hand-to-hand combat, they drove the British flank back into the fort. General Van Rensselaer then ordered all his troops across the river. Seven hundred followed in the first wave, but the remaining troops refused.

"Damn it!" he fumed. "What is the matter with them?"

The adjutant gave the order again. Again no response.

"Sir," a captain cried, running up to the general, "the men say that being state militia, they can't invade a foreign country. They'll only defend their own state."

Van Rensselaer gave the order again, but in vain. Seeing such hesitation, the British opened their fort, charged down upon the stranded American troops and captured one thousand men. In disgust General Van Rensselaer resigned his commission and left the frontier, to return to his estate along the same route he and Morris had traveled in happier days. The British bustled the prisoners off to a camp in the Canadian wilds to winter in bark huts, waiting to be ransomed. Among the men that the British marched into the snowbound forests was Van Rensselaer's coachman, Kate's husband, Joel Kipp.

Granted a passport soon after Van Buren met with President Madison, Aaron Burr left Paris for America. But his ship was captured by the British and he was detained nine months for questioning about the American forces and about politics. Burr reached Boston in May 1812, and disembarked wearing a disguise. In a hired coach he traveled the post road to New York City and immediately wrote to Theodosia.

Madison declared war the following month, and New York City was in a fury of preparation. Although Theo rejoiced that her father was again on American soil, a fever prevented her departure for New York. When the autumn months brought cooler days, she recuperated and she was able to embark December twelfth in *The Patriot* out of Charleston harbor. The ship never reached New York. In vain Aaron Burr, Washington Irving, and a dozen friends scanned the gray waters from the Battery, awaiting news of her arrival. Christmas came and went that year, the bright decorations in the City Hotel mocking Aaron Burr's worry that his daughter was lost. Burr's old Tammany crowd threw a New Year's party to acquaint his friends with his return and help stimulate his law business. Burr hid his distress under excessive charm. He grieved at night that fate, which had punished him so severely for the duel with Colonel Hamilton, was now taking away the only person he cherished in the world. He read and reread a letter he had carried next to his breast since receiving it one foul autumn day in Paris. It read in part:

> You appear to me so superior, so elevated above other men; I contemplate you with such a strange mixture of humility, admiration, reverence, love and pride, that very little superstition would be necessary to make me worship you as a god, and I had not rather live than not be the daughter of such a man.

Did she still live? his fatherly worry demanded in those dark midnight hours. Would he ever see her again, she who single-handedly kept him alive in his exile? By mid-January the New York owners of *The Patriot* petitioned their underwriters for recovery. The ship was considered lost at sea. Rumor abounded: It had been captured and scuttled by the British; it had been seized by pirates, its passengers forced to walk the plank; it had foundered and beached on the Carolina coast, then was plundered by looters who murdered all survivors. Aaron Burr went about his daily litigating, walking the streets of Manhattan, sardonically reflecting that this land was as lonely and unfamiliar as any capital of Europe.

In the months that passed, Burr cast about for a protégé, a young man or woman whom he might guide and who would help him forget his dear Theodosia. Speaking with Washington Irving, Burr was reminded that a young judge from upstate exactly Theo's age had met with her and given her a donation for his living expenses in Paris. Burr made inquiries among Tammany people and discovered that Judge Van Buren had risen from obscurity as the son of Kinderhook innkeepers. He now manifested surprising organizational and political skills, and had helped in securing Burr's passport from the Madison Administration. "I should like to meet this young man," Burr told O'Hanlon. "If I can no longer lead our efforts, perhaps I may guide those who help you."

Burr didn't tell O'Hanlon or Irving, but he dimly remembered an inn in Kinderhook, where he usually stopped when riding with the circuit court. There had been numerous indiscretions with tavern wenches, and though he refrained from dishonoring married women, and didn't remember any specific liaison in Kinderhook, was there a chance this upstart genius could be the result of a casual tryst? Had the innkeeper's wife come to him? The lad showed a brilliance that far outstripped the abilities of his Dutch yeoman parents. Perhaps there would be physical similarities....

14

Because of his journey to Washington and capture of the *Caledonia,* Daniel Hedges was offered the commission of "sailing master," a civilian commission in the Navy. He accepted and left immediately for Presque Isle to build two warships. Since the lake trade had halted, Daniel volunteered his *Silver Pearl* as a neutral cartel ship carrying wounded soldiers and traded prisoners between the belligerent forces, from Mackinaw and Fort Malden to Sandusky and Cleveland. In this way he received valuable information from the men transported.

The hills and forests around Presque Isle bristled with rumors of British scouting parties. Residents expected a squadron of redcoats to fall upon the shipyard any day or night. Two one hundred foot keels were laid, and the ribwork was rising. Yet the peril Daniel feared most was arson by a British spy. He insisted on personally screening each of the men who came to work, and he slept in a cabin between the two ship keels.

After a few sabotage episodes—stolen materials, three suspicious fires, and the disappearance of two lumberjacks as they searched for trees suitable for masts—Daniel summoned the federal marshal. Lester learned from a Cleveland merchant that a British agent was operating near Presque Isle. Daniel told the marshal, "His name is Emmanuel Krabb."

"We've been searching for him for two years," the marshal said. "One of Layland's crew confessed that Krabb was conspiring with them."

As Daniel told Lester this, he added, "Nice people you to do business with."

Daniel showed the agent how to enter Krabb's cove, and they hauled the fat man down to face the circuit court in Pittsburgh on an espionage charge. Krabb's arrest and execution ended the sabotage.

Daniel alone commanded the operation until a young naval officer arrived in March. Oliver Hazard Perry had requested active duty on the western frontier, and was assigned to supersede Lieutenant Elliott with the title of Commander.

Daniel's leather apron was covered with sawdust and he was holding a hammer when Perry met him. "How do you like our navy?"

"You have worked with dispatch," Perry said. He was meticulous, demanding. "Yet we'll need much more than lumber and muscle." He scanned the sandbar blocking the harbor's entrance to the lake. "There has been much concern that once built, these vessels can't enter the lake. There's only five feet clearance, and of course no tide."

Daniel nodded with confidence. "The bar only keeps the British out, sir. It allows us to work in peace, something we didn't enjoy with the shelling at Black Rock. As for getting the ships out, they're shallow drafted. We'll buoy them up unloaded, then rig and load them in the bay." Daniel winked. "When men say something can't be done, they're only saying they can't do it."

"Quite so," Perry said perfunctorily. He looked up into the sky as if he could see masts, rigging, sails, and ensign flags fluttering above the pitch and lumber. "We'll need those vessels from Black Rock as well, and all the cannon we can find, powder, shot, cordage, canvas, galley stoves." He stared directly into Daniel's eye. "Above all, we need men."

"The Navy Department has ignored most of my requests."

"The Navy Department is not fighting this battle. I am," Perry snapped. He inspected the hulls, and Daniel followed him. "I see no iron bolts. Why?"

Daniel shrugged. "No iron to spare, sir. As I tell the men, slipshod work will not do, yet we want to spend no extra care for the sake of time. These ships will be needed for one battle only. If we win, they've performed their service; if not, they're good enough to be scuttled or captured."

Perry squinted incisively. "I see you are a practical man." Daniel frowned as the small man walked away, unable to fathom whether it was a compliment or a criticism.

The work proceeded rapidly. While Daniel supervised the men in the shipyard, Perry worked tirelessly to secure equipment that would transform the empty hulks into battleships. Perry traveled to Pittsburgh to hurry the workmen along the road and to speed the shipment of canvas, cables, anchors, swords, muskets, pistols, and powder. He met with an Army officer and arranged for carronades and shot to be cast. A call went out through the countryside, and every frontier village collected scrap iron—nails, harnesses, kettles, horseshoes, farming implements. Hedges shipped a team of oxen to Buffaloe Creek, and despite spring freshets that washed away bridges, he hauled two twelve-pound cannon overland to the shipyard.

The ruins of an ancient French fort and three English blockhouses were refurbished above the bay, and Perry mounted the cannon there to protect the building and launching of his fleet. When the major construction of the hulls was completed, and only the planking, the masts, spars, and weaponry remained to be mounted, Daniel returned to Buffaloe Creek for more cannon. Transporting these taxed his ingenuity. Shipped up from Lake Ontario by sled and oxen, they were monstrous thirty-two pounders weighing two tons each. Daniel strengthened an old Durham salt boat, loaded the cannon with a makeshift crane, and kept the boat, water almost over its gunwales, very close to shore as his men rowed furiously for thirty hours straight.

At midnight the first day a storm rose suddenly and the heavy rolling of the seas carried away their rudder and mast. The weight of the cannon so warped the boat's bottom planks that water rushed in. The men were screaming in the rain that the boat would sink, yet Daniel wound a coil of rope about the boat, and turning it like a tourniquet with a gunner's handspike—all the men bailing and rowing at once—he managed to keep the craft afloat.

The villagers of Presque Isle likewise helped. Resenting the arrogance of British cruisers, many villagers camped at the American shipyard, laborers by day, watchmen by night. Women stitched heavy canvas, and the community donated its largest building—the courthouse—to serve as a sail loft.

Toward the end of May the two large ships were nearly finished and four smaller gunboats were begun. Perry was called down to Lake Ontario to help command a ship in the siege of Fort George. Daniel sailed with him as far as Buffaloe Creek. The two had developed a mutual respect, and while Daniel would say of the young officer, "He ain't the sort you'd share a mug of ale with," he admired Perry's ability to command men, how sharply his orders were given, and how quickly criticism, blame, and punishment were doled out.

When Perry left to fight on Lake Ontario, Daniel greatly

cherished the few days with his family. Both he and Carrie knew this might be the last time they'd see each other, but neither mentioned it. They lay in each other's arms, talking in low voices, caressing as they hadn't done since courtship. As Daniel prepared to return to Presque Isle, news reached town of an American victory. Fort George had fallen the night before, and now the British withdrew their forces from Fort Erie, down to Ontario. As he passed through Buffaloe Creek, Perry would not talk about the battle, but certain of his men regaled the patrons of Cook's Tavern with accounts of his bravery, how he had walked untouched through the rain of bullets and shells.

With the British gone from Fort Erie, Perry ordered Daniel to run the five ships out of Black Rock at night. Only the *Caledonia* could sail under her own power. Daniel's men fixed oars to the others, and hitching a team of oxen to pull each against the Niagara's current into Lake Erie, one by one the ships cleared the sandbar. At daybreak, linked with cables, the five ships hugged the coastline, wary of British cruisers, and they proceeded toward Pennsylvania.

They arrived in two days and crossed the sandbar into the harbor to join the *Lawrence,* Perry's flagship, and her sister ship, the *Niagara*. By late July four additional smaller boats had been built, armed with carronades and cannon to guard the launching of the bigger ships.

From time to time British patrols appeared on the horizon, sailing just out of range of the guns in the fort. Each time the Brits appeared, a palpable fear ran through the Navy yard, yet Daniel with a pleasantry here and a shout there maintained discipline and kept the men working. At the end of July the squadron was ready to sail. Perry planned to float the smaller boats of shallow draft over the bar unequipped, and he did so in two days. He anchored them just beyond the reef, and his men hurriedly ferried out their guns and fixtures. Soon the seven smaller ships, bristling with guns, stood as sentinels to guard the emerging flagship and her sister.

The big ships drew eight feet of water even before loaded with guns, equipment, and provisions. Daniel devised an ingenious way to lift them over the bar where the water ran five feet deep. He sank long scows and attached them to either side of the *Lawrence*. Pumping and bailing furiously, the extra buoyancy as the scows were emptied lifted the big ship up the needed three feet so it could scrape over the sandbar.

The villagers shouted and applauded at the proceeding. But just as Daniel was ordering his men to bring the *Niagara* into place to repeat the lifting operation, a shout went up. On the northern horizon a sail had appeared, then another behind it.

Perry gave his prearranged signal, and all the sentinel boats massed below the guns of the fort. The British ship sailed closer. "If they attack us now, we're finished," Daniel muttered. He hammered upon an iron bar to get the men's attention. "Leave it for the gunners to watch the Brits, lads. Come on, we've got work to do."

Again they positioned the hull near the sandbar, sank the scows, attached them, plugged the holes, pumped and bailed until the *Niagara* rose up and scraped into the lake. Watching through telescopes, the British waited until the operation was completed, then sailed away. Perry feared the entire British squadron would return in the morning. There was no time to rest. If caught unaware, the American ships could be quickly sunk before they ever sallied forth into battle. All night by the light of pitch torches, Perry and Hedges and the men ferried the cannon, equipment, and barrels of water, as well as salt pork and biscuit, coils of rigging, and great bundles of sail canvas. Makeshift cranes lifted the goods and swung them aboard and down into the holds, then raised the masts and quickly secured them with stays. Crews unfolded the sails and strung ladders and rigging.

The men worked for two full days without sleep. When they were done, Perry ordered them to sling their hammocks and get twelve hours' sleep. But for the men in the crow's nest, all that could be heard for those twelve hours was snoring.

Yet Perry allowed himself only four hours' sleep. After the herculean effort at building his fleet in five months, only one component was lacking—men. Constantly he had petitioned his superiors for shipbuilders and sailors. Groups of fifty, sixty, and ninety men had been sent to him from time to time. Perry now had enough men to sail the ships, but he needed more to fight. He dispatched a messenger to his superior asking for a hundred and fifty men.

Later that afternoon the *Silver Pearl* visited the fleet. Lester rowed to the *Lawrence* and excitedly imparted news: "We was tacking past Isle du Plat when we saw something red. Turned out to be three Yanks escaped from the prison camp far to the north. Horrors they told would make a man prefer death, I tell you. They are nearly starving there, and they told, too, the British provisions are running low because the prisoners and the thousands of Indians and their squaws and families must be fed. There's no route from Detroit overland to Hamilton or York, so the Brits will need to make a run down the lake soon for provisions."

Though he didn't show it, this news greatly pleased Perry. A desperate enemy made mistakes. He put a few questions to Lester, then dismissed him. In the *Silver Pearl*, with the neutral cartel flag flying, Perry and Daniel sailed to Sandusky to seek troops from General Harrison. Realizing the importance of a naval victory to support his land forces, Harrison offered Daniel seventy Kentucky riflemen.

When Daniel conveyed the offer, Perry grew impatient. "We want sailors, not riflemen! Doesn't he have any from lake towns?"

Daniel, though, had a suggestion. "These sharpshooters, sir, can hit a silver dollar at a hundred paces. If we put them high in the rigging, why, they could pick off men at two hundred yards. The Brits like to vaunt their rank, so we could instruct the riflemen to snipe only at the cocks with the plumage, the officers. Without officers..." Daniel shrugged.

Perry accepted Harrison's offer and set a date to take them aboard. He didn't want to feed them until he could use them. In addition, a hundred sailors had been sent up from Lake Ontario, and with the Kentuckians, Perry's manpower would swell to five hundred. Spirits ran high, and Perry staged wrestling matches on shore to spur their combative spirit.

On August twelfth the fleet weighed anchor and moved out smartly. Colored ensigns had been distributed along with coded signal keys. The flagship *Lawrence* led the fleet, and the green or white or red flag that Perry hoisted signaled the ships following to tack, to close in, to form the order of battle, to sail within calling distance.

At first Daniel had been given command of the *Ohio,* the smallest ship of the line. But Perry decided to leave the smallest two ships behind because he didn't have enough sailors to man them properly. He invited Daniel to join him on the bridge of the *Lawrence* and give advice on the lake's winds and currents.

The enemy was nowhere on the lake, so Perry used the buoyant August days to drill his commanders and their crews. Back and forth they tacked, forming a battle line, running before the wind, drawing up into attack formation, falling away to regroup. Aboard the ships the commanders ceaselessly drilled the sailors and gunners. By repetition and trial and error, the men soon came to know their tasks and to perform them flawlessly.

Daniel was fascinated by Perry's tactics in commanding men. He saw how Perry simplified procedures so that individual judgment was minimized, and how through repetition the men came to act without thinking. Daniel saw that his own friendly, paternal attitude aboard the *Silver Pearl* would never work on such a large operation. One moment's hesitation could ruin the entire enterprise.

The men grew impatient for battle. Daniel marveled how calm and benevolent the lake seemed. Often he daydreamed of his smuggling days and the evenings so long ago when he courted Carrie. And he thought occasionally of Eleanora and imagined her regally insulated from the threat of war.

They sailed at last to Sandusky to meet with General Harrison and to take on the riflemen. Harrison brought twenty Indian chiefs down to the lake to view the "big canoes," and they panicked when Perry ordered his men to fire a salute. "Tell your brothers," Harrison spoke to the chiefs, "that these canoes will make war upon them if they give aid to the men in red coats."

Harrison sent the Kentucky "marines" to Perry, and the commander drilled them for two entire days on clambering up the rope ladders with their rifles and powderhorns.

Twice Perry sailed his squadron to the mouth of the river to lure the British fleet out from Detroit, yet the British would not accept his challenge. Anchored at Put-in-Bay, the American fleet drilled, rested, checked and rechecked that all was in order for battle. Then early on the sunny morning of September tenth, the cry of "Sail ho!" snapped the fleet awake.

"Where away?"

"North'ard," cried the lad, "from the Detroit River." Bosuns' whistles sounded and men sprang to their battle stations. All eyes looked to the masts of the flagships for the signal flags. A blue flag followed by a white flag was run up the mizzenmast to summon all commanding officers for a hasty council of war. Nervous anticipation filled the cabin, yet Perry seemed remarkably cool and calm.

"We will form in a line with the *Lawrence* leading." Daniel handed out copies of the secret code describing the colors of the flags and what they signified. "We will join with the enemy when this"—Perry unrolled a blue banner with white letters—"is run up the mainmast." The flag read: DON'T GIVE UP THE SHIP.

Perry instructed the captains to feed their men at eleven, just before battle would be joined. "Men fight better on full stomachs, and the grog will settle their nerves." When there were no questions, Perry gave them encouragement: "Do your utmost today, and victory will be ours." With a handshake to each, he dismissed them.

Back at their ships the commanders weighed anchor, and with sails unfurling and fluttering in the late summer breeze, they followed the *Lawrence* on a tack around Rattlesnake Island. By eleven o'clock the full British squadron was in view eight miles north. The hulls were freshly painted, and their white sails were dazzling in the sun. The Union Jack and red ensign flags fluttered aloft.

"What is your impression?" Perry asked Daniel.

"The wind will die within an hour."

"No. I meant the Brits."

"Formidable, sir. Formidable."

Perry ordered the noon meal distributed with a shot of rum. He himself took no food. True to Daniel's prediction, the wind fell to three knots, and slowly the two fleets drifted nearer. When he could see the enemy standing in its rigging, moving along the rails, Perry produced his signal flag. "What say you, men?" he cried from the bridge. "Shall I hoist it?"

"Aye, sir!" shouted the sailors, gunners, and sharpshooters, all anxious for battle.

Perry handed it to his bosun, who clipped it to a line and ran it up the mainmast. It unfurled and the white letters blazed: DON'T GIVE UP THE SHIP.

Now Perry went on a final inspection, looking at the guns, chatting amiably with the men. He instructed that sand be spread on the deck to give traction when blood started to flow. He had left the bridge to Daniel, who peered through the telescope at the British squadron. His nerves tingled and his blood raced. Only the midnight raid with Elliott compared to this sensation. A bugle rang out in the British fleet, then a full brass band played "Rule, Brittannia!" Perry climbed back up on the bridge.

"Ready, Mr. Hedges?"

"Aye, sir."

A signal flag was run up the foremast, and the American ships clustered near the *Lawrence*. Together they bore down upon the British line. The first shots from the British flagship fell short, sending up high streams of water. Yet with adjusted sights, the second volley slammed into the *Lawrence*, tearing sailcloth and rigging. Men upon the foredeck screamed in pain.

The guns of the *Lawrence* fired, and clouds of black smoke enveloped the deck. Another volley exploded from the British gun ports, and men amidships screamed and fell. One was helped, his arm mangled, to the hatchway door and Surgeon Parsons below.

"We have a light but favorable wind," Perry told Daniel, as if he couldn't hear the screams. Daniel scrutinized the commander's face, astonished how cool and calm he remained.

Now the two ships drew near one another, and three of the British gunboats reinforced their flagship, the *Queen Charlotte*. Explosion after explosion rocked the *Lawrence*. As Daniel attempted to read the wind and plot a course, he could not tell which ship was firing.

Relentlessly the cannonballs flew. Spars fell to the deck, the rigging tore from the masts, and sails hung in shreds. Gaping holes were opened in the planking, and the deck was pervaded with the stench of gun smoke and the screams of wounded men. Arms, legs, and heads had been carried away by enemy cannonballs. Blood flowed freely, staining the deck red, running into the scuppers.

"We're losing men quickly," Perry cried above the screams and explosions. "Go to the hatchway and order the surgeon to send up any man who can walk."

Daniel leapt down to the deck, and slipping on the blood, stepping over bodies in gruesome positions, he reached the hatch and threw it open. His gorge rose in a thick clot, and he turned aside and vomited his breakfast. Below, men with bones sticking through their flesh, with horrible head wounds, with legs missing and abdomens riddled by musket balls, screamed, moaned, writhed, and shook in horrible pain. The smell of open bowels was stronger than the stench of gunpowder on deck. Among them the surgeon and two men moved, amputating limbs, setting broken ones and applying splints, administering what opium they had to ease pain.

"Dr. Parsons!" he cried above the din. "Send up any man who can walk!" He wiped his mouth on his sleeve.

In a file a dozen bloody, bandaged sailors slowly climbed the ladder. Daniel pointed them to the guns where their mates had been carried off. High in the spars the Kentucky riflemen were firing, aiming at the officers' plumage, yet cannonballs carried away the rigging and the spars, and in twisted tangles of rope, timber, and canvas, the Kentuckians fell to the deck.

"Mr. Hedges!" Daniel looked up toward Perry. "Man the helm. Our helmsman's gone."

Daniel rushed to the wheel and grappled with it to bring the ship back on course. The helmsman had just been carried overboard by a cannonball. Relentlessly the firing continued. Daniel peered to his left, and to his surprise saw the rest of the American fleet standing idly and safely away from the battle. The *Lawrence* had taken severe punishment alone and was nearly disabled. The tangled rigging and sailcloth hardly caught a breeze, and the gaping holes in its sides flooded the hold with lake water, drawing the ship down.

Men stumbled about the deck, nearly fainting with fatigue, loading and firing the cannon by sheer instinct. Again the call went down to the surgeon to send up any man who could haul a line, and eight men, unable to walk, crawled out of the hatch and took the ropes handed to them.

Suddenly all grew very quiet on deck. All eyes turned to watch the colors descending the mast. "We're surrendering!" one man cried, yet others quieted him. As the stars and stripes reached the deck, Perry draped the flag around his body so it wouldn't be dragged through the blood, then he walked across the deck to the railing and climbed down the rope ladder into a waiting boat. The boat cast away its line, and two men rowed him toward the *Niagara,* Perry standing in the bow wrapped in the American flag. As soon as he boarded the other ship, the stars and stripes were run up its mainmast. A shout of exultation rang out through the American navy, and the *Niagara* moved up to join battle.

Perry boldly maneuvered the *Niagara* to shoot through the British line. Both port and starboard guns blazed as he flew through, cutting the squadron in half, the fire raking the decks, Kentucky riflemen picking off officers. The move was bold and calculated to send the British into confusion.

Meanwhile, try as he might, Daniel could not get the *Lawrence* to respond to its rudder. Heavy and listing, it fell away from the engagement, the blue banner still fluttering: DON'T GIVE UP THE SHIP. Soon the sounds of battle far away were muffled by the screams of dying men aboard. Daniel turned away from the fighting and scanned the deck where the wreckage and carnage of a mere two hours lay. He was disgusted. For ten months he had worked day in and day out to build these ships. From all quarters they had searched and hunted, bought and begged the materials to outfit the fleet, and had enlisted men to fight. In two hours all his work was undone. Men lay everywhere crying and screaming, and the stench was revolting.

An annoying pain announced itself in his shoulder, and Daniel was surprised to see blood flowing from an open wound. He'd been hit during the battle but hadn't noticed. Useless to steer the disabled wreck, he let her drift and went below for a bandage and to help the surgeon administer to the wounded.

From the deck of the *Lawrence* it was unclear how the battle went. Both fleets were hopelessly interlocked, and two British ships, entangled in each other's rigging, punished by American fire, held each other in a death embrace. After an hour of speculation among the able-bodied men, a feeble cheer went up: the British colors had been struck. The Brits had surrendered to Perry.

Daniel helped stitch the bodies of the dead into their hammocks along with cannonballs for weights. Twenty-two men had been killed, sixty-one wounded. They lined the hammocks of the men who had not been swept overboard along the deck. Officers would be buried ashore, a privilege of rank. Late that afternoon, Perry's rowboat pulled aside. He climbed up to the deck, read a short prayer over the corpses, then the bodies slid down a plank one by one, splashing to a watery grave.

"Return the *Lawrence* to Put-in-Bay," Perry ordered Daniel. "Make such repairs as necessary. We shall patrol the lake now that it is ours."

And that was all. Perry, curt and military in his bearing, flushed in victory, departed from his flagship. He sailed that very night to Presque Isle to arrange parole for the British commander and to see about his immediate promotion and transfer away from the frontier.

15

*D*aniel refused to discuss the battle. The townspeople dogged him for details, but all he would say was, "We won." This time they whispered that his heroism made him conceited. He heard this but didn't care. He felt cheapened by the battle. Perry sailed away unscathed after he had used everyone and everything. Perry got a promotion and a new assignment, but others suffered so much. The image of the *Lawrence* haunted him, the disabled ship, crippled, listing away from the guns, limbs and corpses and groaning men strewn in gore and splintered wood.

He would only discuss the battle with his wife, and only on the morning she told him that he'd tossed violently in bed, crying out and making retching sounds.

"Whatever were you dreaming about?" she asked.

"The battle," he said. "It was horrible, Carrie! Horrible!"

"I didn't want you to go, Danny. I was so worried. You were wounded, and you might have been killed. Then where would we be?"

"It was foolish," he admitted. "It seemed honorable, but to see how quickly Perry left us all behind . . . he used us, came here and used us, then moved on. He won the battle, that's true, and there probably isn't another who could have. But it was at such a price."

"Danny?" Carrie embraced him and whispered in his ear. "Do you remember back in August when you came to get the cannon and we were together? Oh, Danny, I think we're going to have a baby!"

Tears welled up in Daniel's eyes. "Oh, that's wonderful, Carrie. Out of such chaos, such destruction and death . . ." He held her. "I've been thinking quite a lot since the battle, girl, and I consider that there really ain't much a man can count on beyond his family."

Tears were flowing down her cheeks, too, as she pulled

away, and she smiled through them. "Oh, Danny, we'll be so happy."

"There won't be any other missions, any other causes. You and me, Carrie, and the children."

In the next few weeks Daniel came to see that a sense of challenge, of adventure, had been stimulated by his first journey to Albany. Instead of smuggling, he had looked toward Albany and serving the government as a worthy use of his time and talents. Now he saw things differently: He might have been killed, with no provision for his wife and babies. Daniel vowed to learn a lesson from the battle—that in a gamble, whether for money through smuggling, prestige in serving the canal commissioners, heroics in daring missions, or the love of beautiful Eleanora, it was extraordinarily easy to lose all he cherished. And even then his winnings would be paltry. He vowed that he would take no more unnecessary risks.

Winter swept over the lake, and by mid-November it was icebound. In past winters wolves came out of the Canadian forest to forage among the settlements, yet now a worse danger was ever present as British raiding parties threatened to descend on dogsleds and snowshoes to attack the Americans.

The Brits mounted a strong offensive early in December. Attacking Fort George below Niagara Falls, they drove the Americans back. As he retreated, General Samuel McClure burned the village of Newark and murdered Canadian women and children on the pretext of depriving the British army of lodging. This infuriated the British command. McClure's massacre became a rallying cry. The Brits crossed the river and marched on Black Rock, and as they came, panic seized the Americans. No leader could muster troops. Joseph Ellicott sent three hundred settlers from Batavia, and they formed a battle line outside Black Rock, but as the British came during a gray Christmas Day blizzard, the Americans broke and fled into the woods. The British streamed into Black Rock and burned the customs house, the wharves, warehouses, and ships in drydock. For three days they hunted settlers and turned them over to bloodthirsty Indians who tomahawked and scalped them.

The Batavia contingent fell back to Buffaloe Creek, attempting to regroup. A stormy meeting at the courthouse was held December twenty-eighth, and wild tales of the depredations of Black Rock only fanned the flames. No one thought clearly.

"Please!" Daniel cried, rising to face the clamor. "Hear me!" He waited, staring at the more vocal in the crowd until they fell silent. "The British will be here tomorrow or the next day. Their blood is hot, and they want revenge. We could stand and fight, but they'd soon overpower and kill us. I say we organize a retreat inland to Batavia, that we collect all our food and ammunition, our women and children, and then set out tonight together."

"Coward!" someone screamed.

"We must face facts!" Daniel protested. "They will burn our homes. There is no reason for us to be in them."

"We must face them!" cried a young man. "Victory will be ours if only we have courage."

"No," Daniel cried, "we'll be overrun!"

"They said you was a hero!"

"Sit down!"

"Coward!"

So Daniel left the meeting and walked home to pack. The Army had confiscated all the horses long ago, so Daniel made up packs of valuables, clothes, and food for himself, Carrie, and the two children. They could reach Batavia, thirty miles east, by midnight the next day. Joseph Ellicott would give them shelter and food, and Marian would comfort Carrie and the children while Daniel decided what to do next.

They set out at sunset. The children, sensing the danger, were silent. They had dressed in their warmest furs and leggings. Daniel made their packs as light as possible, only blankets and food. Yet after seven hours the biting wind had little Eli whimpering and Rachel faint.

"I think we should rest," Carrie said. She was nearly five months pregnant, and the trek had tired her.

Daniel did not want to stop, because they might be overtaken, but looking into her face, he saw how weary she was. "All right," he said. "But we must get away from the road."

For an excruciating half hour the refugees trudged on. By now little Eli was sobbing, his fingers and toes frostbitten. It was midnight when Daniel spied a thick clump of pine across a snowy field, a hundred yards from the road. They waded through four-foot drifts and made camp. Carrie began breaking off dead branches, but Daniel stopped her.

"No, Carrie, I'm sorry. We can't risk a fire." He had Eli's leggings off and was rubbing blood back into his frostbitten toes. "The British and Indians are everywhere."

She nodded grimly, spread a blanket on the snow, took Rachel to her and covered her with the bearskin robe. Daniel heard them sobbing.

"It'll be all right," he said. "We'll be with Joseph and Marian tonight." He wrapped a bear robe about himself and his son, lay down and drifted off to sleep.

Daniel awoke to muffled voices. He pulled back the robe and peered out. It was gray dawn, and a biting wind blew from the west. A scouting party of three English soldiers and eight Indians in fur tunics was on the road. Carrie heard them, too, and peered out.

"They've seen our tracks," Daniel said. "I should have covered them. Maybe they'll keep on."

One of the Indians grunted, pointed his war club directly at them, and they all started through the snow drifts.

"I'll go and meet them. I'll bribe them, and they'll go away. Don't make any noise." Daniel pulled back the robe. "It'll be all right, girl." His legs were asleep, and it took great effort for him to stand and walk. He clenched his fist as a sign he would prevail, and flashed her a smile. Carrie looked pale, weary, and frightened in the cold light.

As Daniel emerged from the thicket, the Indians cried out. The British regulars pointed their rifles at him and were about to fire when Daniel called: "Don't shoot! I'm a friend!" He held up his hands and waded through the deep snow toward them. The corporal in command ordered them to keep their rifles trained on him.

"Gentlemen." Daniel approached the group. "I'm a tradesman of Buffaloe and only my family is with me. We're traveling toward Batavia, and we are carrying nothing but food and blankets." He tried to seem casual, but it was difficult in the gaze of the soldiers and the ferociously painted Indians. "However, I have a thousand dollars in gold, and you may have it in return for our freedom."

This offer made the corporal grin. "Yes?"

"Yes." Daniel still held his hands high in the air. "If you'll allow me to get it . . . ?"

"Step closer." Daniel approached the group. Slowly they surrounded him, training their muskets on his head. "Let's see the money."

With his left hand Daniel reached cautiously into his coat, pulled out a pouch, and handed it to the corporal. The Englishman opened it, looked inside, and nodded with approval. "You say it is only your family? How many?"

"My wife, my son, and my daughter."

"Very well." The corporal smiled and nodded. "Very well, very well, very . . . well . . . very . . ." His words echoed again and again and his voice sounded far away, and suddenly a searing white pain filled Daniel's head and he felt disembodied, floating. Something was tremendously funny, wonderfully ironic and funny, and the cool darkness was pleasant, and he laughed as "Very well, very well, very well," echoed.

"Daniel?" A voice came from very far away. The cool darkness was so pleasant he did not want to awaken. Why were they trying to wake him up? Let him sleep, he was so very tired. It was cold and dark and pleasant. His fatigue made even the act of hearing painful. "Daniel?" It was a man's voice, a familiar voice. "Daniel!"

With great effort Daniel opened his eyes and looked up into the painful light of the sun. Joseph Ellicott stood above him in a fur cap. "Daniel!"

"Joseph!" he whispered hoarsely. A tremendous thirst made his tongue thick and sluggish.

"Lie still, Daniel."

"What are you doing here . . . ?"

"Lie still."

"Carrie? Where is Carrie?" He raised himself up on his elbow, but the pain nearly blacked him out. He lay back down, gasping. "Where're Carrie and the children?"

Ellicott said nothing. Slowly the world pieced itself back together, and Daniel looked suspiciously around. He was lying in the snow, and his blood had melted and stained it all around his head. "Where's Carrie?" he cried, bolting up. "Where are the children?" And then he knew, he knew surer than he had ever known anything. He could read it in Joseph's expression and in the look of the four others peering down in pity. He sat up and looked toward the road. The pain was excruciating. Then he looked toward the clump of fir trees.

"I must, I must go to her!"

"No, Daniel."

Daniel closed his eyes and his mouth worked with agony. "No!" he whispered. "No!" he said breathlessly. Then he cried, "No!! Nooooo!!" He looked up at the others, his mouth trying to form words. "They didn't! They couldn't! Oh, Carrie! She's going to have a baby this the spring! Joseph, we're going to have a baby! No! Noooo!"

"I'm sorry," Joseph said, and helped Daniel to his feet. By then other men of Batavia were dragging bundles wrapped in bearskin from the clump of trees.

Daniel rose to his feet and started toward them, screaming like a wounded animal. Joseph grabbed him and wrestled him by the shoulders. "Don't look, Danny! Don't look. You mustn't!"

"Noooo!"

"Come with me, Danny. We'll return to Batavia."

"No! Joseph, we're going to have a baby! A baby!"

Hugging Joseph, Daniel stumbled through the snow toward the roadway. He looked back at the clump of trees and only saw two men in red uniforms facedown in the snow.

At Joseph's house in Batavia Daniel lapsed into a delirium for two weeks. A fever shook him night and day, alternately burning and sweating, shivering and chattering, he rambled incoherently. When the fever broke, Daniel was still not convalescent for a month. Marian and the girls sat at his bedside, nursing him, talking pleasantly, avoiding the one topic he wanted most to discuss.

It wasn't until February that Joseph told him the details. Marching with two hundred men to aid Buffaloe Creek, they had happened on Daniel facedown in the snow. Turning him over, they saw he was still breathing but had suffered a violent blow to the head from a war club. Tracks led into the woods, and suddenly they heard Carrie scream. Rushing toward the clump of trees, they found the Englishmen and the Indians holding her captive. The children had been murdered—Ellicott didn't tell Daniel his eight-year-old daughter had been raped—and the men were raping Carrie. They used her as a shield, trying to buy their freedom from Joseph and his men, but one of the Indians lost his temper and clubbed her dead with one blow. Joseph and his men opened fire.

Daniel heard all this in grim silence. Three days later he left Joseph's house. The thirty-mile walk to Buffaloe Creek gave him time to think. How empty and still everything was, how overcast and dismal and dead. Entering the village, he saw the courthouse had been burned. He knew he couldn't live in the house without Carrie and the children, yet the choice had been made for him. Only a charred and roofless shell remained. Daniel walked about the deserted streets as if in a nightmare. Every home had been burned, as well as Clark's Hotel and Cook's Tavern. The few people he encountered did not seem to recognize him, everyone numb, forgetful, and suspicious. Daniel walked to the harbor and gazed for a half an hour upon the charred hulk of his beloved *Silver Pearl*. Then he looked past her, out over the lake. The western sky was the color of iron, and the stiff wind assaulted him. There was nothing but a blank and frigid expanse of snow.

"And other men have suffered like this!" he murmured. Tears flowed down his cheeks in the icy wind. "It is no use," he groaned, clenching his fists, his face twisted with agony, "My life is at an end."

16

Napoleon had abdicated, and with no French foe, England turned its full attention to the war in North America. DeWitt Clinton had lost his presidential bid 89 to 128 votes in the Electoral College, yet as the nation plunged into war, he was elected Lieutenant Governor of New York State, and he remained New York City Mayor. Fearing a British invasion of New York in the spring of 1814, he built fortifications in Harlem and along the East River, and reinforced the Battery at the tip of Manhattan. He set up signal stations on Governors and Staten Islands to warn of an approaching fleet with bonfires. He planned forts for either side of the Narrows with big guns to blow any advancing squadron into driftwood. For this, though, he needed money, and again he looked to Washington.

When Clinton's invitation came, Eleanora asked if Kate would accompany her. So despondent had Kate become with the news of Joel's capture, Eleanora believed the journey would cheer her. Together they sailed to New York in a river sloop, then went overland in Clinton's coach to Washington.

They arrived in mid-August as the small town sweltered in muggy Potomac heat. Clinton had brought Edward Carr, his secretary, and the party of four took a suite of rooms at the Washington Hotel, across from the federal treasury. Their timing was bad. Reports that the British fleet was patrolling up and down the Atlantic coast caused President Madison and his cabinet considerably more concern about Washington than far-off New York City. Day by weary day Clinton and Eleanora called upon senators and representatives in the twin buildings of the Capitol, yet such confusion reigned about who was doing what and what was likely to happen, they accomplished nothing.

Throughout the countryside volunteers were called up, yet the dandies reported more from a sense of chivalry than from any desire to fight. After a week of no success, Clinton and Eleanora dined at Mason Gardens.

"This is the third time," he said. "All our efforts in Washington seem doomed. I suppose we should remain up north and rely on our own resources. Let the Virginians have their way. But it galls me how they're so hell-bent on destroying the country. Jemmy Madison is riding out to inspect the troops himself tomorrow, as if some presidential derring-do will rectify all the death and injury and destruction of property. He can start a war well enough, but he doesn't know how to wage it."

"And the British get closer each day." Eleanora sipped her brandy. "The fever makes poor Kate tremble, and in her weakened state she fears she'll be taken prisoner as her husband was."

Clinton smiled. "They'll never get close, Eleanora. At the last moment soldiers will come rallying to defend their homes."

"It is rather tantalizing, waiting to see what happens."

"Yes, but after I complete my meetings tomorrow, we should start packing. Hopefully this will be the last time we return home empty-handed from this godforsaken city."

The next day Eleanora conducted the packing and made arrangements for their transportation. But they arose the following morning to a new panic. The British had crossed the Potomac at Bladensburg and were fighting the hastily-summoned American forces.

"It's useless for you to go north," Clinton said to Eleanora at breakfast. She had managed to hire a coach and four. "Better to take the ferry to Maryland and head directly for Baltimore."

"You sound as though you're not coming."

"I'm not. There are a few services I can render here in the capital if the British reach it."

Eleanora scowled. "Services?"

"Yes. Madison and his cabinet are rushing pell-mell around the countryside. No one shows a cool head. If I can speak with the British commander, perhaps I might negotiate terms. It is in times such as these, my dear"—he touched her patronizingly on the arm—"that reputations are made."

"Well, then, I am staying with you," she said firmly.

"No, you must leave. A woman such as yourself...there's no telling what barbarity—"

"I can care for myself well enough."

"I'll make arrangements."

As the morning wore on, dust and smoke filled the northern sky. Toward noon dust clouds on the road drew nearer. Many horsemen were riding hard. The anxious populace strained out of windows to see and hear news of the battle.

Just after noon a hatless rider dashed through the streets. "Flee! The British have broken through our lines! They're attacking! Flee!" His sweating, frothing horse spun in the middle of the street, rearing high. Clinton grasped the bridle, then hauled the man out of the saddle.

"What is it you say?" He shook the man.

The man was angry at this treatment. "The British have smashed our line! They'll be here by afternoon. Three times we fell back and three times we regrouped. And still they came on. There's no stopping them. No one opposes them now. Look!" He waved his arm up the road, where a hundred men were running toward the center of the city. The man broke Clinton's grip, vaulted onto his horse and galloped off, screaming, "Flee! Flee!"

"Eleanora," Clinton pleaded when he found her in the hotel garden. "You must leave the city at once. The British will be here by nightfall. The looting and destruction will be horrible. No one will be safe."

"I cannot," she said. "Though my jewels and gowns are packed, the coach you hired has been gone for two hours. Someone stole it to escape."

"Then we must get you another." Clinton called his secretary and told him to find any sort of vehicle. By now the streets were mobbed with fleeing soldiers and frightened bureaucrats. Many of the wealthier folk buried their silver, jewelry, and banknotes in the boardinghouse yards, and a line of refugees streamed from the city toward Alexandria. President Madison himself drove back to the Executive Mansion after viewing the battle through the clamoring streets, and citizens hurled insults and mud clods at his coach.

Carr returned in an hour with a hay wagon and two old horses. "Fine," Clinton said, "leave as soon as possible. Dress as farmers and take the road to the Navy yard."

Kate and Eleanora dressed in the most ordinary clothes Kate had packed. Carr had a hotel porter load the trunks of gowns and jewelry onto the wagon, then covered the cargo with hay. Eleanora and Carr climbed up into the seat as two men gently lifted Kate into the hay. She was very ill and nearly in tears.

"I leave under protest," Eleanora said, clasping Clinton's hand.

"The bridge by the Navy yard is still up, and you may make good time. The road is deserted."

"And if we encounter the enemy?"

"You won't. They're marching in from the north. Make haste over the bridge, though, for I understand that when the British enter the city, the Navy yard will be exploded and the bridge burned."

"Shall we wait for you in Baltimore?" Carr asked.

"No." Clinton handed him a packet of letters. "Leave a note that you're safe at the Eldridge Hotel. Stop there overnight if you're tired. But if the British are successful here, they'll move up the coast. Get back to New York as soon as you can and deliver these letters to the Common Council. I'll follow in a few days."

"Yes, sir."

Clinton motioned them onward. Carr snapped the whip and the old horses plodded east toward the Capitol and the river beyond. The road was filled with refugees fleeing westward, wailing infants and worried parents. Against this human current they made slow progress. Past the Capitol, the throngs disappeared and Carr urged the horses into a trot. They paid their toll and crossed the rickety bridge, then all breathed a sigh of relief at being in Maryland.

"I'll keep to the main road," Carr said, "and so avoid getting lost." The level turnpike offered speed and comfort. Eleanora had never ridden on a haywagon, and though rough and jostling, the novelty pleased her despite the circumstances. Kate lay quietly, prostrate with fever. They traveled all afternoon, and when the sun set, they discussed whether to camp for the night or continue.

"Are you all right to keep on, Kate?"

"I'll be just as sick anywhere we stop, mum."

"Then let us continue. We'll reach Baltimore by noon tomorrow."

As the night thickened, a red glare filled the western sky. "It looks like the entire city is burning," Eleanora said. "I hope DeWitt is all right."

"He'll be all right. He'll emerge as the only hero from all this," Carr said. "When the smoke clears, he'll stand head and shoulders above that coward Madison, who went fleeing like a dog back to his Virginia estate."

They drove for two more hours, and Carr finally persuaded Eleanora to climb up into the hay with Kate. The hay was soft and fragrant, and the night moonless and starry. Eleanora lay back, gazing into the heavens, enjoying the thrill of adventure. She looked from star to star and remembered Daniel Hedges. He could chart a course by reading these very stars. How often must he look up into the heavens and feel secure.

"Halt!" The command startled her awake. She felt she had been sleeping for a very long time. "Who goes there?"

"Why, say, what's that?" Carr spoke in a deliberately foolish accent. Eleanora raised her head and looked down to see the blue uniform of a British marine. Behind him stood four others, and they held rifles and bayonets.

"Step down from the wagon," the marine ordered.

"Well, sure, sure thing."

"What are you hauling?" The officer's voice was soft but menacing.

"Hay. I'm hauling hay. Goin' yonder to Nottingham with it."

"Who's with you?"

"Why, my wife and her sister, both asleep up there in the wagon. It'd be such a shame to wake them, as Kate's quite ill."

Two of the marines advanced and searched him, one pulling a pistol out from under his coat, the other drawing out a thick packet of letters.

"Bring a torch," the officer snapped. One of his men ran for the torch, and scanning the addresses on the dispatches, broke the seal and remarked: "Fortifying New York harbor." He turned to his men. "Spies. Search the wagon."

Three of the marines jumped up and roused Eleanora and Kate. They swept back the hay to uncover the trunks, then hauled them down, broke the locks with the butts of their rifles, and threw them open. The soldiers pawed through the gowns, lingerie, and jewels until their officer instructed them to close the trunks and carry them back toward Benedict as confiscated property.

Eleanora watched indignantly. Kate, weak and sick, leaned upon her, mumbling incoherently.

"So, you're spies."

"No, sir, we're private citizens trying to return to our home."

"Take them," the officer ordered, and they were seized, bound, and roughly heaved back up into the wagon. One marine sat facing them as a guard and the other drove. The journey seemed endless. Kate was mumbling deliriously when the eastern sky grew light. Tired and afraid, Eleanora was despondent. It was futile to say anything or even move, so she sat and watched like a cornered animal. She hoped only that Kate would be all right.

The marine drove them down to Pig Point, a small bay on the Patuxent River. Another sweltering day had dawned. A crowd of three hundred prisoners was collected on the muddy shoreline. A British officer at a table with a ledger and a quill took information from prisoners in a single file, and they were led off to eight mastless ships, hulls that fleeing Americans had left to block the river.

"Oh, mum," Kate groaned, "whatever are we to do?"

"We must bear up, my pet," Eleanora said, but the weariness in her voice belied her words.

Clinton believed the British would march into the capital in orderly rank and file, their officers in firm control of the troops, that they would occupy the Capitol and the Executive Mansion and garrison the city until receiving orders from higher up. He would be an envoy, since the president and the entire cabinet had fled, and he would negotiate on behalf of the nation with the occupying force. He would vindicate his loss at the polls by repairing Jemmy's botched war. Yet Clinton completely misjudged the situation. After a deathly quiet of four hours, the first British troops and marines poured into town, vanguard for the main force. Suspiciously, aggressively, they moved through the streets, weapons aimed, bayonets fixed, calling out for all citizens to stay indoors.

Clinton was sitting on the veranda of Samuel Blodgett's hotel as they approached. He had been discussing the war with some acquaintances, and seeing a British officer, he stepped into the street and tipped his hat.

"Permit me, sir. I am DeWitt Clinton, Mayor of New York City and Lieutenant Governor of New York State—"

The soldier pushed him back with his rifle. "We're searching for the president."

"The president and Mrs. Madison have fled. If you'd be so kind as to take me to your commanding officer..."

"Return to the hotel and you won't be shot." The officer began to move up the street. Rebuffed in front of his acquaintances, Clinton docilely returned to his chair.

"We must wait until they take formal occupation," he explained. "The commanders have not yet arrived." And yet the rebuff surprised him. He had an unsettling suspicion that the afternoon and evening might not turn out as he'd expected.

The tide of British regulars and marines swelled. When shots were fired upon two officers from Robert Sewall's house, the mansion was immediately searched, looted, and torched. It burned high and violently, an example of what resistance brought. Soldiers broke windows along the street, and yelling and cursing filled the city. The British officers tried with some success to restrain their men with threats that looters would be shot. They tried to limit the destruction to public property, and tried to make it methodical. As a thick, humid dusk descended, a chorus of voices in the street rang out. "The Capitol! The Capitol!" Clinton looked toward Capitol Hill. The wooden passageway connecting the House to the Senate was ablaze, flames licking out of the windows of each chamber, blackening the white limestone facades. People watched in disbelief. Soon flames burst through the roofs and the blaze spat and sparked, rolling high against swelling rain clouds, lighting the lower portion of the city like hell itself.

Behind the flaming Capitol the Navy yard was touched off by the American commander to prevent ships and supplies from falling into enemy hands. Soon that was a raging holocaust. Flames flew out along the spars, sails, and tarred rigging, barrels of tar exploding. As if it were the backlighting on a stage, it lit the sky behind the burning Capitol theatrically.

"The British commander is at the President's house," a man whispered to Clinton as they watched the fire from the porch.

"Will they make their headquarters there?"

"Don't know, sir."

"Very well," he said, and rose to walk to the Executive Mansion. The burning Capitol imposed an ominous silence in the streets.

As he approached the wrought-iron fence, two British sentries called: "Who goes there?"

"DeWitt Clinton, an American citizen, Lieutenant Governor of the State of New York."

One sentry went inside. Returning, he said, "The admiral requests the pleasure of your company at table." This greatly puzzled Clinton, but he acquiesced to a search, then went inside with the sentry.

Admiral Cockburn reclined in the president's chair at the head of a table set for forty, resting his muddy boots on the fresh linen. "Wonderful Madeira, wonderful bouquet." He held his glass to the light and smacked his lips, concentrating mightily on the wine and ignoring Clinton.

Clinton peered around at an incredible scene. In the presence of their commanding officer, British soldiers were stuffing their pockets with the president's silver plate and silverware. Paintings had been ripped from the walls; clocks, lamps, firedogs in the hearth taken; and the upholstery torn in a mad search for valuables and money. Down the stairs came a British officer, boasting as he buttoned one of President Madison's frilled shirts.

"Drink!" Cockburn yelled, and slapped a plump little man who sat near him, a small bookish fellow, very ill at ease. "Drink to Jemmy and Dolly! They set this fine table for us. Drink!" The admiral turned to Clinton. "Speak!"

"I've come to ask for your terms." Clinton used as haughty and commanding a voice as he could muster.

"Terms?" Cockburn quaffed a glass of the Madeira and threw the crystal goblet into the wall. He turned again, and smiled. "Private citizens and private property will not be touched if no resistance is met. Any house with guns or powder will be burned immediately, and anyone offering resistance will be shot."

"And public property, sir?"

The admiral sneered, picked up a china plate, and by way

of an answer, hurled it into the wall. He motioned the soliders to take Clinton out, and roughly they led him by the arms and desposited him on the east lawn. They left him alone, and he listened a moment to smashing plate and glassware. Enraged, he clenched and unclenched his hands and struggled to control his breath. Deliberately, the British were defacing and destroying the seat of government, obliterating the Americans' faith in their public institutions. Madison had allowed this to happen! If only Pennsylvania had voted sensibly! Twenty electoral votes would have won him the presidency, and this outrage never would have occurred. Clinton brushed his sleeves off, adjusted his collar and hat, and walked as calmly and as erectly as possible. Now all would be burned—the libraries, the patent office, and courtrooms, the newspaper. Certainly they would not touch the houses of worship! Yet here were barbarians—Clinton shook his head sadly—barbarians who claimed to serve a Christian king.

The Capitol smoldered like an expended pyre, and the Navy yard still blazed. Clinton watched the spectacle silently. It would be this way all up the coast. Baltimore would be next, then Philadelphia, then New York. New York. He had come to the capital to get funds for two redoubts at the Narrows, and yet Madison had rebuffed him. Madison was now in hiding. Clinton saw clearly where his duty lay. He could accomplish nothing here. He must find the funds and build the forts immediately. This must not happen to New York.

As he approached the Washington Hotel to pack, someone cried: "The President's house! Clinton turned to see flames erupting inside the windows as British marines, done plundering, touched off their black powder and rockets. Room by room the great white limestone mansion glowed like a giant lantern until the windows exploded, the roof blew upward with a hot rush of wind, and a brilliant volcano of flame exploded into the sky. Clinton pushed disgustedly through the fascinated crowd.

Kate was too ill to weep. In the dim light below the deck of the prison ship they had been thrust the first day, the cowering fear in the eyes of the other prisoners caused Eleanora to despair. Yet she must not give in to such feelings, she told herself; she must nurse and comfort Kate.

Kate's fever worsened. The British had not separated men

and women, and so the prisoners had hung blankets up at either end of the fetid hole for latrines. Kate vomited until nothing remained, then, exhausted, she alternately slept and retched. Eleanora escorted her to the latrine for most of the first day. Children cowered in their mother's arms, complaining and crying dejectedly. Toward midnight a gentleman who had been wounded by a British musket ball died, and his two little daughters wailed and slumped over his corpse until someone called a guard and they dragged the body up from the hold, its eyes and tongue lolling and the head banging upon each rung of the ladder.

Eleanora sat that night in mute terror, one whale-oil lamp illuminating the clusters of prisoners. She stroked Kate's forehead, trying her best to provide comfort. By morning she was incensed.

"Where are you going?" an older man asked as she climbed the ladder.

"I'm going to talk with our captors." Her boldness sparked a faint hope in the others. She rapped on the hatchway, and it opened. The guard was shocked to see a woman, and Eleanora climbed out.

"My maid is ill and needs a doctor."

Fearing one of his superiors might see he'd let her up, the guard stood at attention, looking directly ahead.

"I said, my maid is ill and requires the attention of a physician," Eleanora repeated. "I demand to be released to find a doctor."

The guard stared blankly ahead.

"I refuse to remain down there and watch my girl die," Eleanora cried, then turned away from the sentry and started for the railing of the hulk. Roughly he grabbed her. She resisted, her eyes afire with rage. "You can't let her die! All I ask is a doctor to look after her!"

The guard dragged her back. Now Eleanora's anger took over. She beat upon his chest with her fists. "You can't do this! You can't!"

Hardly looking at her, the guard led her to the hatch and threw her down. Her foot struggled to find a hold on a rung of the ladder, her hands lurched out at the lip of the opening, but she hit her arm, spun halfway in the air and landed in a heap at the bottom. The other prisoners gasped and cried out as the hatchway slammed shut and Eleanora lay dazed upon the floor.

*   *   *

Reaching Baltimore late the next day, Clinton looked in vain for a message at the Eldridge that they had passed through Maryland. He inquired at all of the hotels but could learn nothing. Frantically he retraced his steps, hoping that in his haste he had neglected to ask someone, to see or hear something.

For three days Clinton tried in vain to locate them. He considered returning to New York and searching for them there, but the British were now moving upon Baltimore, and if she were still in the area, she would be in peril. The dead ends maddened him. On the fourth day of his search Clinton learned that a cartel boat had reached Fort McHenry, and he rode south from Baltimore and asked the burly old captain whether he knew of any prison camps.

"Sartinly do, sir. 'Tis prison hulks at Pig Point where they keep 'em."

Clinton slipped him a five-dollar gold piece. "And how would I make inquiry of a lady who may have been captured?"

The fat old man licked his whiskered lip. "Why, I can pass through the line."

Clinton considered embarking with the fellow, then realized he would make better time overland. The British would consider him a prime prisoner if he were caught, yet he disregarded all caution, determined to take the chance. In a warm summer shower that afternoon he set out on a rented horse.

When she awoke on the fifth morning in the ship, Eleanora didn't want to stir. Kate had slept soundly through the night for the first time, and even now was slumbering. Eleanora looked on Kate's features. She felt responsible for the predicament, feeling that she should have insisted they stay with Clinton. She vowed she would lease a large farm to Kate and Joel on minimal terms when she returned to her estate. Good, kind Kate, her closest ally and confidante for years. Eleanora reached over to brush a strand of her hair aside, and was startled by Kate's white, waxen color, the chill of her skin. She pulled her hand back involuntarily. "No," she moaned. *"No!"* A sob welled up as she realized she was holding a corpse. "Oh, Kate," she cried, "what have I done?"

Some of the other prisoners rose and walked over. Eleanora fell weeping upon her maid's lifeless breast. "Oh, Kate! Oh, my girl Kate! What have I done to you?" She didn't know whom to turn to, as she remembered vividly how they had dragged the dead man out.

After talking his way through three sets of guards, Clinton finally summoned all his negotiating skill and successfully bribed an officer to secure Eleanora's release. He paid half again as much for her maid and his private secretary.

The sight of the prison hulks beached on the swampy shore depressed him. He had sent the three away to this, and he had stayed behind for false heroics. He presented his papers to the officer in command and a marine was dispatched. Clinton learned then that Edward Carr had been hanged as a spy. Shocked and upset, he did his best to control his rage in front of the British. Better to get Eleanora and Kate out safely.

The hatch opened upon a despondent throng of prisoners, each man, woman, and child staring blankly ahead. For an entire week they had dragged on a dire existence, eating thin soup and moldy bread. No sunshine pierced the gloom. When the sentry called her name, Eleanora stared blankly ahead. She hardly heard him.

"Pardon me, ma'am," a boy said, "but he's calling for ye."

She looked up and squinted into the dusty rays of sunshine. "Yes?"

"Come with me," the sentry said, escaping back up to fresh air.

Eleanora rose to her feet stiffly, her dress in rags, and felt her way among the stretched-out bodies on the floor. She climbed up, her joints cracking from disuse, and peered over the edge of the hatchway. DeWitt Clinton stood below, waving his hat.

"You came!" Her cracked lips formed the words, but her voice failed. "You came!" Tears flowed down her cheeks.

"Eleanora!" Clinton sighed as she was helped out into the fresh air then down to the muddy shore. He waded into the water, knee deep then waist deep, and as he lifted her up, she clasped him around the neck and buried her face in his breast.

"Isn't Kate coming?"

"Kate's dead," she said hollowly.

"Oh, Eleanora, Eleanora, I'm so sorry, so very, very sorry. My heroics—"

"No, DeWitt!" Eleanora pulled back. "If only...if only..."
She broke down then. "Oh, DeWitt," she sobbed convulsively,
"if only it had been me!"

"You mustn't say that, you must never say that!"

"But I mean it! I am so weary, so very weary of it all! Kate
had so much to live for, and I have nothing. If only she had
been spared, and it had been me! Oh, the world!" She fell
against his breast, weeping bitterly.

"Bear up, Eleanora."

"Oh, DeWitt," she sobbed, "take me away from here,
please. Take me away from this awful place."

"Bear up. They mustn't see this. Be strong." And Clinton
let her down upon the shore so she could walk on her own.

BOOK III

17

War clouds still hung over the western frontier, and the inept American military command offered no defense. Daniel Hedges had no stomach for fighting and couldn't bear to remain in Buffaloe Creek. With a bedroll, shot and powder, an axe and frying pan, a week's provisions and five pounds of salt, he took up his musket and set off toward the shaggy mountains of Cattaraugus and Allegany.

On the south face of a peak he set up camp. Two boulders had come to rest above a creek. In front of the boulders Daniel built an entrance, and behind, a hearth of stone and a chimney of mud and sticks. From the door and from the wide ledge where virgin pine protected him, Daniel watched the storm clouds gathering and sweeping up the mountain slopes, obscuring the peaks then passing eastward toward Philadelphia and New York. The panorama pleased him.

Daniel's theology was decidedly Iroquois. An old Seneca chief, quietly smoking his pipe in the winter lodge, had once told him, "To walk among the mountain peaks, a man needs long legs." Although he had abandoned his Iroquois identity, "Eye of the Bright Water," and had taken the name carved in a leather satchel he carried—perhaps his father's, perhaps the name of a tomahawked Yankee peddler—Daniel Hedges believed now, as his beard grew and fur replaced his leather and woolen clothing, that sorrow gave him the "long legs" the chief had described.

When the spring thaw broke up the ice, a family of otter built its barrow in a pool directly below the ledge of Daniel's home. He sat on the lip of rock as the spring gushing subsided, and watched them, sleek and quick, carrying branches and bushes, playing and plucking fish from the water in their long snouts. When their home was finished, the otters frolicked on a smooth rock slide that fell fifteen feet into their pool. They scrambled up the rock, then slid, squealing with delight, down into the pool. For entire mornings Daniel watched them, envying their joy.

A profound sadness filled him as he watched the otter family play. His life had been as simple and happy once. He regretted now the time he had spent away from home, smuggling and trading on the lake, surveying for the canal, building ships for the battle. The memory of Eleanora stung him with guilt. Only the memories of long winter afternoons, listening to his children play and his Carrie sing, only those nights in the cabin with the wind in the pine, seemed worth remembering.

Summer brought swarms of black flies which laid a siege upon his hut and shut him up in the smoky chapel for whole days. Then swarms of mosquitoes laid him low with fever which he treated with bark tea. Weak and shivering, he lay upon his bed of skins listening to water race and boil in the creek, listening to the birds chirp, to the thunderstorms shake the earth, to a wolf howling in the forest. At last he recovered, sallow-skinned and weak. He did not know how long he had been sick, yet the summer nights had lengthened and a scent of autumn was in the air. He noticed the otters had left, and it made him sad. Yet he saw, too, his sentimentality, and that there was no time for it. He dragged his wasted form about the mountain, trapping hares, chopping wood, preparing to meet the winter, trying not to listen to a voice that whispered its indifference as to whether he lived or died.

Eleanora returned to Claverack chastened by the war. Although family and friends tried to shake her from such despondency, she shut herself up in her mansion, wrapped her lands about her as a cloak, and swore she would bear her hardship alone.

She peered out of the window each day numbed and indifferent. Late summer bloomed, then mellowed into a rich harvest, yet she despised the fruitfulness of her lands. When she heard of a farmer's family welcoming a new son or daughter, she fought to control her malice and envy. The creeks ran and the millwheels turned. Her barns swelled with hay, fodder, and winter wheat. The sheep grew heavy with wool, and the beams of smokehouses and milk houses groaned with the weight of pork, beef, and cheeses. Her lands insulated her from the buffetings of war and politics, but Eleanora saw them only as her prison. The estate owned her, fixed her identity in the eyes of others, and didn't even have the grace to be as barren as its mistress. She refused all invitations to balls and parties, even to the customary Harvest Home celebrated by her tenants. She bit her pillow in the night and wept. An enormous aching emptiness engulfed her. All she saw was wretched and ugly.

Nor did news at Christmas time cheer her that America won the war and the fighting was over. The great matters of state, the causes and issues she had championed, seemed in retrospect so much wasted effort. What did it matter that America with its tiny army and fledgling navy had vanquished the most powerful empire on earth? What did it matter that universal celebrations of the treaty heralded a new era for the nation? She was alone, and she'd been roughly shown how cruel and indifferent the world was, and how vulnerable she could be. She locked herself in her room for days at a time, hardly eating meals from the tray Hilda brought.

Eleanora lapsed in and out of fevers and ailments. Dr. Edwinston could only prescribe rest and herbal tea, though out of earshot he confided to the student who accompanied him, "What she requires most only a man could administer, and the dose should be liberal." The young man, smitten by the beautiful aristocrat, replied: "It's always the apples highest on the tree that go untasted."

In the prison ship Eleanora had seen how cheap life was. She longed to challenge that revelation, yet she couldn't. Her lot was preordained. She blamed herself, her naiveté. She had never dreamed a man could prefer to love other men as her husband had. Jacob Van Rensselaer's revels in various hunting lodges up and down the Atlantic seaboard must indeed have startled the beasts of the forest. And the damnable agreement her father had made! Mistakes, all mistakes, and the dead hand of her family and Jacob's family would guide her every decision until she died.

Two months after the Treaty of Ghent, a ragged, bearded stranger presented himself at Eleanora's Claverack mansion, inquiring about Katherine Kipp. To replace Kate, Eleanora had selected Hilda Bruen, daughter of a German Palatine. Hilda now conveyed the stranger's query to her mistress.

"What is his name?" Eleanora asked.

Bashfully the girl stared at the floor. "I didn't ask, ma'am, but he can be nothing more than a wanderer. Shall I feed him some scraps and send him along?"

Eleanora glared at her. "Show him in." The flustered girl left, returning in a few moments with a bent, haggard man in rags.

"What is your business, sir, and how do you know of Katherine Kipp?"

The man looked up and his penetrating gray eyes fixed Eleanora with their sadness. "She is my wife, Lady Eleanora."

"Joel?" Eleanora was startled. "Joel Kipp?" He looked down and slowly nodded. "We had thought you died in the prison camp."

"And I nearly did, mum. Is Kate still working hereabouts?"

"I'm sorry, Joel," Eleanora said quietly. She looked up and tried to control her grief. "She died in my arms. We, too, were captured by the British, held in a prison hulk. The fever took her."

Joel lowered his head until his chin rested upon his breast, then he turned and started to leave.

"A minute, Joel." Eleanora was on her feet, and she took his arm. "You'll need a position now, and... and a *home*." This word sounded queer to her even as she said it. "New tenants have taken over the farm you and Kate shared after your wedding, but we shall find you a house and a station." Quickly, before he refused, Eleanora instructed the girl to take him to the kitchen for a meal then to Edward to be barbered and fitted with clothes. Hilda nodded and took Joel by the hand.

That evening Eleanora summoned him: "I have inquired about where we may locate you, Joel." She smiled kindly. A startling transformation had taken place. Shaven and dressed, rested and fed, he seemed nearly as vigorous as formerly. He certainly was as handsome, and the sadness in his eyes made him even more so. "I have decided, if you find it satisfactory, to employ you as a member of my household staff."

Joel was visibly surprised. "And what will I do? Serve your meals?"

Eleanora laughed softly. "No, not as a servant. I shall need someone to supervise the stables and to recommend what sort of improvements should be made to the house, barns, and fences. I am in need of someone to collect the rent, someone with tact and diplomacy. You are highly regarded among our people. And Joel, I should like someone to travel with me."

Already Eleanora had instructed that an apartment above the stables be readied for him. He shared a glass of claret with her, discussing his new position, then he stood. "Lady Eleanora," he said, "I deeply appreciate this kindness. I shall do my best to earn it."

She took both his hands. "Your courage speaks for itself, and it will be Kate's memory that binds us."

She watched as he left, then sat again and sipped her wine. His reappearance had changed everything for her. He had suffered far more than she. He had seen battle, mutilation, death, starvation. She had lost a servant, but he had lost a wife. His return shook her out her despond and self-pity. A passing fancy even occurred to her that she might take him as a lover, but this soon passed. He had always been an energetic, capable, and affable man. Now, sipping her wine, she knew why she had acted so quickly—Joel Kipp reminded her of the ship captain, Daniel Hedges. Joel was younger and not nearly so wise, not as capable, yet he had a quality of resilience. She wondered what Daniel was doing now. Perhaps he had grown rich on war contracts. Perry's fleet had been celebrated throughout the nation for its victory. Perhaps Daniel had left Buffaloe Creek for Washington. A thought stung her: perhaps he had fallen in action on the western frontier. She shrugged, and took a last sip. Loyal, obedient, and strong, Joel Kipp would bring a welcome change to Claverack, a change the estate needed. She called Hilda and prepared for bed.

That night her dreams were filled with Daniel Hedges. She dreamed of him aboard his *Silver Pearl,* as she had imagined years before. She dreamed of him as a babe, borne away in the arms of dark heathens into a land of wolves and wildcats. She dreamed of him as the lanky westerner she had first met at the General's Ball. But above all she dreamed of him as her lover, his strong arms, powerful hips, comforting laugh, and gentle kiss. She awoke at sunrise and felt refreshed. Languorously she stretched as the cocks crowed, and she hugged her pillows. Only Daniel could stir such passion, and the effect was immediate and strong.

"Hilda! Hilda! Prepare my bath. I feel like bathing today. And tell Samuel to saddle Hecate. I will ride also."

Hilda had yet to learn unquestioning obedience. "Why not bathe after you return from riding?"

"The bath, Hilda. When I wish to bathe, I wish to bathe."

The flustered girl left, and Eleanora peered into the mirror. She saw new hope in her face.

As the days passed, the change in the household was so dramatic even the servants began to wonder how it had come about. New furnishing replaced old. In a month wall hangings, carpets, chaise longues, and sofas had replaced those used for three decades. The exterior trim of the mansion was painted. In the spring a landscape gardener changed the approach to the house, laid out new flower gardens with two new fountains, and planted evergreens, Oriental trees and shrubs. Nothing had been done to the mansion since Jacob's death, and now within a year Claverack's dilapidated aspect gave way to a modern, handsome, and cultivated charm.

Nor was the change wholly physical. Eleanora hired a new chef from France, and the sauces and pastries were celebrated throughout the manor. No longer was her door only open to landed gentry. Now, heeding Joel's counsel, she invited certain of her more prosperous tenants to her table. The effect upon her people was remarkable. Flattered that they had been recognized, and seeing what changes were taking place at the mansion, they improved the appearance of their holdings too. The bickerings between farmers, between the miller, the smith, the tavern keeper and their customers, grew far less frequent and far less intense.

Late in the spring a spirited horse with an expert horseman trotted up the drive. The tall rider dismounted, stepped up the three stairs to the new veranda that looked favorably over the Berkshires, and took the view that before knocking.

In her counting room Eleanora was projecting when the new schoolhouse could be built.

"Gentleman by the name of DeWitt Clinton, ma'am."

"I'll receive him in the parlor presently, Hilda. Escort him in."

Eleanora darted up the back staircase to her room, quickly combed her hair, applied a touch of rouge, and slipped into an informal gown of Chinese silk. She had not seen Clinton for a year, and he had appeared unannounced.

"Eleanora, you look wonderful." He placed a kiss on her cheek and led her to the sofa. "A year has brought many changes, all for the better." He looked approvingly about the drawing room.

"We've been working hard to rebuild, DeWitt. Please, sit down."

"Ah, yes, the spirit is everywhere." Clinton began to pace. "People have put the war behind them and are seizing opportunity. Our unexpected victory over Britain gives us such ambition to build, and we must harness this energy. You heard they've ousted me as mayor again?" Eleanora nodded. "That damned Tammany crew. They play such games with the common weal, and yet my freedom from the mayor's duties gives me time for grander things."

"DeWitt, sit down."

He scowled at her directness, then sat upon a chaise lounge. "I have come to ask for your help."

"The canal again?"

"Of course."

"I wonder whether such projects aren't beyond me now. I have changed."

"Beyond you?" He knit his brow. "Never! You have always been up to it."

"But the war taught me much, DeWitt. I am no longer thinking in such grand terms. Instead I concentrate on the people close to me. Why, you yourself have even remarked upon the result. I truly don't see how I can help you now."

Clinton brightened up—she was not outright refusing. "I am now organizing a meeting of the first citizens of New York City for December thirtieth at the City Hotel. We'll form a committee to revive the canal both in the public mind and in the legislature. I have received many favorable responses so far. Speculators see much money to be made in selling land out West. Legislators see many votes to be won in promoting such a bold project. Landowners see the value of their lands rising. Everyone I speak with sees immense value to our state, and I must use this support before it dissipates. You can help vastly with your charm and your quick pen."

"I don't know . . ."

His voice changed key. "Won't you come this winter? I'm sure life up here must get tedious that time of year, and there are so many diversions in New York."

Eleanora laughed, and folded her hands at her lips, considering. Her eyes glanced back and forth, looking for an excuse. Finding none, she threw up her hands. "Your sneak attack has worked, DeWitt. You don't give me time to find a reason not to, so I guess I must."

"Wonderful!" He clapped his hand. "The enthusiasm we once knew has redoubled since the war. Certainly the war has taught us all many lessons about who we are and what we're about. Even those who preferred war to the canal three years ago acknowledge the convenience it would have provided in shipping men and munitions to the Canadian frontier. Now there will be no stopping until we finish. We are on the verge of a new era. For all its hell and horror, the war has drawn us together, and we see we need fear nothing now." He raised his index finger. "One task I'd like you to do to begin."

"Yes?"

"Have you been in touch with that surveyor fellow?"

Clinton certainly remembered his name, and his oblique reference irritated Eleanora. "Daniel Hedges?"

"Yes, yes, do you know where he is?"

"No, I don't. The last time I saw him was in Washington with you, three years ago."

"Could you contact him? We'll need him in New York."

"Is it appropriate? Wouldn't it be better if the commission notified him?"

Clinton shook his head. "No, Eleanora. I doubt he'd respond. But he'll respond if you ask. See if you can reach him. Ask him to join us in New York late in December. Tell him his expertise is essential and that he will be well rewarded."

"I'll try to reach him, but I can make no promise."

"Good." Clinton stood. "Keep me abreast on any development. If you haven't heard from him by October first, let me know and we'll try something else."

As she stood upon her porch, watching him ride westward toward the capital, she folded her arms and sighed. "So, DeWitt employs a siren's song to lure Odysseus." As she turned to go inside, she feared that Daniel would not respond to her letter, then she feared he would.

Daniel weathered the winter on his mountain peak. But after the ice broke he journeyed down among the lowlands. He had no money and only some dried venison strips for food. People noticed, and feared his wild appearance even in the remotest settlements. He offered labor here and there, and slept wherever he ended up at night.

Traveling from village to village that summer, it slowly

came to him that he must go west. Solitude and independence had spoiled him for living among men—he had to strike out into the virgin West and leave behind all his old memories and ghosts.

Daniel entered Buffaloe Creek in late August, 1815. He had been away sixteen months, and the village had fully recovered, had even grown. New buildings stood on old foundations and new names hung on the signs of stores and taverns. New ships rode at anchor in the harbor. At the site of his home, squatters had built a one-story structure above his foundation. Daniel saw children in the yard. He had no desire to identify himself and lay claim to the land. There was plenty of land to be had in the West. He ambled down the path to the waterfront and booked passage on a shining new sloop for Sandusky.

Because the sloop left in three days, Daniel took a room in the new Hicks Inn in return for chopping wood. Evenings he sat alone by the taproom hearth and listened to the men's talk. They discussed commerce and the price of real estate. There was some talk about the canal, but it was very speculative, and the project depended to a great deal on what the legislature did next term. One vocal critic of politicians stated that the canal had been merely a prewar fantasy, now abandoned. Daniel said nothing.

On his last night in Buffaloe Creek he sat an extra hour at the hearth. Just as he was rising to go upstairs to bed, the door burst open and in stumbled a drunken threesome shouting for whiskey punch.

"Keep 'em coming, lassie," one man said. Daniel recognized the voice of Lester Frye.

He walked over and extended his hand. "Lester!"

The man had nearly doubled in size, and his face was a florid red. He scowled. "I know the voice, man, but not the cuts of ye. Who is it?"

"Daniel! Daniel Hedges!"

Lester looked him over from the crown of his shaggy head of hair and his long knotted beard down to his moccasins.

"No, you ain't!"

"Yes, Lester, it's me—Danny!"

Lester scowled and tipped a lamp into his face. "The eyes are similar, but . . . ? What happened to you, Danny?"

This was the first time Daniel took any notice of his own appearance. He hung his head. "Tough times."

"By the cuts of ye, Danny, looks as though you come back from the dead. Why, I wouldn't recognize you in a month of gazing. Have a drink?"

"Sure."

Lester hammered his palm on the table. "Lassie! Another tankard of punch, and step smart." He turned to Daniel. "Where have you been?"

Daniel's answer was hesitant and evasive, so Lester turned to his two friends as the girl brought the tankards and set them down. "Do you know this man? It's Danny Hedges, best ship's captain on Lake Erie. 'Course, you'd have to cut back the brush to see him. Was Danny and me what captured Black Jack Layland the pirate, and 'twas Danny and me what captured the *Caledonia* during the war. Danny here built the fleet for Perry and served in the battle. A real honest-to-God hero, though he's too modest and won't do no bragging."

The serving girl looked keenly at Daniel, and the other men turned to scrutinize him. Daniel drank his punch.

"You look prosperous," he said to Lester, to draw the attention away from himself.

"Aye, Danny, I'm a rich man now. The money we made together"—he winked—"helped me purchase land when it was cheaper than week-old fish." Lester described some of the real estate he had bought after the British invasion, when people needed cash, and how valuable those holdings were now. "Danny, come join me. I've got an opening for a man with your skills and smarts. You always were one who could drive a deal."

"No, thank you, Lester."

"It'd be like old times."

"No, Lester. I have other plans."

"Aw, Danny!" Lester then regaled the others with smuggling stories.

Daniel quickly drained off his punch. "Was nice seeing you again, Lester." He shook the fat man's hand. "I hope our paths cross again." Lester responded with four or five questions about where he was going and what he was going to do, but Daniel evaded them and left to go upstairs. The tavern girl stopped him in the kitchen.

"You don't remember me?"

He looked closely at her. "No."

"Edna Kay, Captain Hedges. You rescued me long ago from a British ship and kept me out of the prison camp."

Daniel squinted, then saw it was the young girl who had

been cabined with the British commander. She had grown up in three years. He bit his lip. "Yes?"

She dropped her eyes. "I came to the American side as soon as the treaty was signed, and I asked about you. I heard your wife and children were murdered by the British, and I searched far and wide for you. No one knew where you'd gone. I wanted ... I wanted to thank you."

Daniel nodded noncommittally.

"I wonder, Captain Hedges..." A faraway look came into her eyes.

Daniel gently placed his hand on her arm. "I'm sorry, but I thank you." He turned away and started toward the stairs.

"Captain Hedges!" She followed him. "Even if ... even if you don't wish to ... I thought you should know that Oliver Forward stopped by last week. He has a letter for you, but no one had seen you in well over a year. I just ... I just thought you might want to know."

"Thank you, Edna." Daniel turned away. It had been many months since he'd slept with a woman, and he shied away from the complications it would bring.

The next day he breathed more freely, knowing he was to set sail. It was a crisp, clear September morning, the lake gleaming, gulls squawking, and the breeze full in the pines. On his way to the sloop, Daniel stopped by the post office.

An old woman sat behind the counter, and she riffled through a packet of envelopes for his letter. He let out a small gasp when he recognized the handwriting and the return address: E. L. Van Rensselaer, Claverack.

"Is something the matter, sir?"

"No, ma'am. That's correct. Thanking you."

He walked down to the waterfront and sat for half an hour, wondering if he should open it. The return address and the handwriting brought many memories crowding in. He watched the sloop being loaded, and he dangled his legs over the water. No harm would come of just reading it, he decided, and tore open the envelope.

Claverack
August 12, 1815

Mr. Daniel Hedges
Buffaloe Creek

Dear Mr. Hedges:
    Mr. Clinton requested specifically that I write to ask

if you would do him the valuable service of attending a meeting at the City Hotel, Broadway, New York City, on December 30 this year. He has secured the support of many influential men, and believes that after the lapse due to war, the canal project can again be undertaken. Your expertise in these matters is valued and needed.

I will be attending as well. I trust you weathered the war, as I understand from the supervisor of my estate who fought in Niagara that it was particularly severe on the frontier. I look forward to renewing our acquaintance and have much to discuss with you.

Please make every effort to join us then. Hoping that you will respond at your earliest convenience, I remain,

Your humble svt.,
E. L. Van Rensselaer

Now, here was a predicament. Daniel sought solitude and independence, and she was offering him employment. Why should he return to be manipulated by them? He held the letter gingerly above the water. If only he could let it slip away, forgotten.

But then her image was before him, her aristocratic bearing, her blue eyes and pale lips, her fair hair, long and fragrant. The ship was nearly loaded. He was all packed and ready. But he was no longer married, and he might court her openly now. He reread the letter. "I look forward to renewing our acquaintance and have much to discuss with you. . . ." He glanced back at the ship. Before him, over the water, lay a vast wilderness. Yet from the civilized East a grand lady had summoned him.

Daniel read the letter a third time, and with each word his certainty grew, until he wondered how he could have any doubt. He walked to the sloop and accepted half of his fare as a refund. Then, whistling and light of step, he returned to the village to find a barber and a bathtub.

18

Martin Van Buren knocked at the door of the address given him by O'Hanlon, but it seemed unlikely "the Master," as O'Hanlon referred to him, would inhabit such a place. It was a low one-story shack, long and narrow, the rest of the lot filled with discarded iron and wooden crates. A beautiful black-haired girl opened the door. "Sir?"

"Is the colonel at home?"

"Yes, sir, and may I tell him who's calling?"

He flashed his grin. Though he currently held a judgeship and a seat in the State Senate, he said simply, "Martin Van Buren, Miss."

She closed the door. Van Buren looked with dismay around him. How could a man even enter such a place? At last the girl opened the door and with a courteous smile said, "Please follow me." Van Buren obeyed. In such a narrow hallway he feared for his linen. She opened the door to a small chamber where a small, handsome man with graying hair sat at a table loaded with law books. A fire burned in the grate, making the narrow room hot. The man looked up.

"Judge! Judge! So good of you to come!"

Van Buren was taken aback by his friendliness. "Sir?"

"Ah." The Master rose and stepped around the desk, extending his hand. "It's a pleasure to meet you at long last!" A frank smile played upon his lips. "Sit down, son, sit down!" The man motioned him to the only chair in the room. Van Buren complied.

"Perceive life"—Aaron Burr theatrically waved his arm at the squalor—"when things go awry."

Awry. Van Buren nodded as Burr scrutinized his features closely. This remarkable man whose mind ran in terms of conspiracies, empires, dark plots, armies of Spaniards and Indians, beautiful women—many of them, gifts of flowers and perfume, treason, dueling, exile, and whose only child perished at sea, used the word awry. All the suffering had not dimmed his sense of irony. Van Buren was immediately enchanted.

"O'Hanlon said I should call upon you."

"O'Hanlon's a whore," Burr said candidly. "Do you owe him anything?"

Van Buren preferred to approach things more delicately. "No, sir, I don't believe so."

"Good. Good. You know enough to keep people in your debt. That is as it should be." Suddenly his expression changed to woe. "Poor, poor Theodosia! She wrote me of you and of your accomplishments. Since returning, I've inquired into your background. Your lack of formal schooling and of family connections may be overcome. You have demonstrated great ability. If we work together, you shall pluck the golden apple, Matty." He pulled an imaginary apple out of the air. "The presidency."

"I only had the pleasure of meeting her once."

"And your generosity to me in my time of need will never be forgotten."

"She told you?"

"There were never secrets between parent and child," Burr said, and the way he raised his left eyebrow made Van Buren feel uncomfortable. Burr seemed exceptionally bright, unpredictable, unhinged. "Twenty-five dollars, and you with a young wife and babies. Well, it provided many a warm fire that November, and some vintage claret, and a good many bouquets for the wenches." Burr fixed him with a penetrating gaze. "And now I mean to help you."

"Sir?"

"Behold this old man! Behold how I must live. You would not think but the golden apple was once within my grasp"—he reached up again—"yet it slipped from me. I knew so little then. But now"—his eyes grew narrow and sly—"you shall have it in my stead. You shall be president, Matty, and vindicate, for this poor old man, his years of disgrace and exile."

"You flatter me, sir."

"Nonsense. Your abilities precede you. I want only to keep you from repeating my mistakes."

"Well, then, how stands the game?"

"Ah-ha," Burr cackled. "Yes." He rubbed his hands together. "The game! Yes. Of course you recognize the three ways to gain power—inherit it, build it, or steal it?" Van Buren nodded. "Well, Clinton inherited power and is expanding, building upon it even since he's been ousted from the mayor's office. His followers are legion. Without connections or fortune you have no choice. You must seize power, and who better to steal it from than Clinton? Therefore, Matty, Clinton must fall. We must bury him in that ditch he wants to dig. O'Hanlon and the Tammany boys plan a demonstration for the night he tries to sell this canal project. I believe we must keep them involved, and what better way than having them show their strength in the street? But our plan shall be more discreet, behind the scenes. The imperious, aristocratic Clinton! That bombastic, platitude-spouting prince could very well pluck the golden apple in his own right if we don't intervene."

"So, how shall we proceed?"

Burr tapped his temple. "Wisely." He then asked a series of questions, elicited responses, interpreted the information, and translated it into directions, suggestions, strategies to be followed. At one point he noted, "We can also attack him through his advisors. Whom does he trust?"

Van Buren placed his fingertips together. "Almost no one. Clinton keeps his own counsel. There is one person, though, a woman." Burr's eyebrows raised at this news. "No, nothing like that. She is rather adept in politics. She is intelligent and extraordinarily beautiful, and she lends a certain perspective to his projects. She is unrivaled in communicating with the common folk, for she loves and helps her tenants considerably on her estate in my home county. I don't believe she herself understands how vital she is in his undertakings."

"So much the better," Burr said. "Yet I caution you, never underestimate women! When they are wise, they are far wiser than men. My poor Theodosia."

"I shan't. But if I could cut her away from him, I should effectively cut away what gives the man's politics flesh and blood."

"What is her name?"

"Eleanora Livingston Van Rensselaer."

A smile spread across Colonel Burr's face, and he nodded. "About twenty-seven or twenty-eight? A handsome woman? Fair hair?"

Van Buren nodded. "Yes."

"And she married Jacob Van Rensselaer, nephew of the general?"

"Yes. You do astonish me, sir."

"And the young man had peculiar tastes, liked Latin and Greek and other scholars who shared his interests, male scholars?"

"The same."

"The Livingstons are a blackhearted clan, my boy. They rival the Clintons for lying and double-dealing. Mark my words, this woman, if she is as close to Clinton as you say, can be his Achilles heel. Aim an arrow there. Not only is that spot unguarded, it begs for a wound. What of her—her"—his right hand circled in the air—"her appetite?"

"She is chaste, I believe."

Colonel Burr laughed and shook his head. "No one, Matty, is chaste. Chastity is not a natural condition. People are just good liars. Simply find out what stallion rides that mare and you will undo her."

"For having an affair?" Van Buren asked doubtfully.

"No, for breaching a convenant she made with the Van Rensselaers." He nodded at the perplexed Van Buren. "Yes. When I was yet in power, I was privy to an agreement, a covenant she made, the families made with her and her husband. It was much discussed in the profession then. The happy couple was conveyed the vast estate named Claverack, Van Rensselaer land of six thousand acres to which the Livingstons joined four or five thousand, the girl's dowry, with one simple and unalterable condition." He raised his finger instructively. "If the Livingstons are shrewd, the Van Rensselaers are shrewder. Old Van Rensselaer required them to agree that if his son died, the girl could possess the entire estate only so long as she remained a widow. If she remarried, she would be dispossessed of all the lands, including her dowry, and the estate would revert to the Van Rensselaers."

This small bit of news magnified very quickly in its usefulness as Van Buren considered it. "But I know of no impending wedding," Van Buren said.

Now Colonel Burr grinned diabolically. "Hmm! Would be interesting, though, to see what a judge might hold in the event of unwidowlike conduct."

"And I might even judge the case!" Van Buren nodded at the simple beauty of the plan.

"Precisely."

"And then who would take possession?"

"Ah," Burr said with a gleam in his eye, "that is what you must find out. Find out who is the remainderman and have him do the more unsavory work. He will dog her and spy upon her and then bring the case to you. Whisper in his ear that this woman has a lover, for she must, my boy, she must. Tell him that they plan to wed secretly, to have children in violation of the covenant, make up the details or investigate a bit yourself. He will not sit long upon his rights. It is a most handsome estate, as I remember. And when he begins to hound her, the girl will have nothing else in her mind but how to keep hold of her property. She will care nothing for the lover, nothing for Clinton, and nothing for the canal. That, my boy, if what you tell me is true, could very well be the breach in Clinton's wall. Make the passage but a little wider and his whole lofty edifice will tumble."

"Brilliant!"

"And all the better since neither she nor Clinton will suspect you are behind it."

With that settled, they energetically discussed legislative measures in the forthcoming session. Burr had found a most willing protégé.

19

After a long, tooth-rattling stagecoach journey, Daniel Hedges reached the metropolis Christmas Day. A light snow had fallen, and Daniel walked the streets, their quiet broken only by sleigh bells and church bells. Daniel enjoyed walking New York's streets alone that day in the snow, because he felt anonymous and the air was crisp and cold and the snow softened the harsher edges and eased the memories of past Christmases.

Although Eleanora had already checked into the lavish City Hotel, she was spending Christmas at Clinton's Flushing mansion. Daniel's room, reserved by Eleanora, was directly next to hers and connected by a common door. He heard noises in her room when he awoke next morning. He quickly shaved, dressed, and knocked upon the hallway door. He did not presume the connecting door would be opened to him just yet. A young man answered. "Yes?"

"Has Lady Eleanora arisen yet?"

"And who be you?"

"Daniel Hedges, chief surveyor for the canal commission." Joel Kipp closed the door. Daniel leaned back and waited. The door opened again. "She'll see you," he said curtly, and Daniel brushed past him through the anteroom and into the parlor. The parlor was bright and airy, sunlight reflecting off the new snow through her high windows.

"Ah! Daniel! So wonderful to see you again!" Eleanora rose and extended both her hands. "Too long, too long, it's been far too long." She kissed him on the cheek. Daniel held her at an arm's length. She wore a pink peignoir and slippers of silver brocade. She looked casual, fresh, well-rested. "You must tell me everything," she said excitedly, and she sat and folded her hands in her lap. Daniel glanced toward Joel. She nodded. "Joel, please go help Clinton's men in the ballroom. And Hilda, take your sewing into the bedroom."

Both servants left and closed the doors. Daniel and Eleanora stared intensely at each other for a very long moment.

"I have thought of you often," he said. "The war was very long and trying along the Niagara frontier."

"And on us. I lost my serving girl during the burning of Washington," Eleanora explained. "We were captured and held in a prison ship. It was terrible. We were very close, she and I."

Daniel nodded, and after a long pause: "I lost my family."

Eleanora leaned closer to read his expression, the tone of his voice. "Your babies?"

"Yes, my wife and little ones." He tried to seem casual. "They were murdered by the British as we fled the burning of Buffaloe two years back. Christmas is not my favorite holiday."

"Oh, Daniel, I'm so sorry!"

"Yes, the war rearranged much." He shrugged and watched for a reaction other than sympathy, but in vain.

"Everyone lost. Joel too." She indicated the door where Joel had left. "He was captured by the British and held in a camp, and he nearly starved. His wife was my girl who died. I took him in because of her. He's ever so capable protecting me."

"Protecting you . . . from what?"

Eleanora smiled. Her fear, brought on by the capture, seemed excessive now in peacetime. "Often from myself."

Daniel considered he might have presumed too much. "I was glad to receive your letter, quite by accident too. It gave me a direction I lacked. Now it's time to bring some things together, to build for the future after the war."

"And the canal project proves even more exciting now than before. . . ."

He winced. She had deflected the talk immediately into

the canal, listing recent developments, then said, "Let's get down to business."

For three days Eleanora and Daniel pored over newspapers, pamphlets, speeches, maps, geologic readings, commerce predictions, altitude measurements—digesting all that had been written about the canal. Each evening they met with Clinton, who had spent the day calling upon people, gathering questions, and persuading them to support the project. He posed questions he had heard that day, asking Eleanora questions about public sentiment and Daniel questions about the survey and engineering. By the day of the mass meeting they had viewed the issue from every possible side, and Clinton felt confident discussing it in depth in public.

The noisy, smoky ballroom filled with applause as DeWitt Clinton, Eleanora Van Rensselaer and Daniel Hedges entered with the canal commissioners. Clinton raised his hands to quell the clapping and cheers, yet it only grew louder as they sat and Clinton ascended to the rostrum.

"Ladies and gentlemen of the great state of New York," he cried, his hands spread wide, and the hall exploded with enthusiastic applause. "The war is behind us. A new age has dawned. Tonight we begin again that great work that will open the gates of our bountiful West and will make New York the greatest state in this great nation!"

More applause, and Clinton motioned for silence. He proceeded to deliver the speech Eleanora had written based upon their research and the questions many people had asked. Again and again applause erupted, again and again Clinton motioned for quiet.

"And in the weeks and months to come," he concluded, "I encourage you to contact your legislators. Each vote will be critical to secure the necessary funds. We have not a moment to lose. If the funds are forthcoming, digging will begin this summer. With East linked to West, West to East, the great city of New York will be the fairest port in the world!"

The crowd was on its feet. Landowners, manufacturers, shippers, merchants, and gentlemen clapped, whistled, and cheered, anticipating vast gains. But as Clinton was stepping down, a stone shattered the window behind the dais with a loud crash. Silence fell and men and women watched. Despite the freezing temperatures, Clinton ordered three men to open a pair of French windows to a balcony. "A mob!" one man said. Fifteen hundred men carried torches in the snowy street below. Clinton turned to climb out on the balcony. "Don't go out," Eleanora whispered. "They'll ridicule you." He was already at the window.

"I must. No mob will undo what we've done tonight." He stepped back to the rostrum. "Ladies and gentlemen, every cause has its opponents, and the leaders of this mob are ours. Why? Not because they object to the canal! No. We encourage divergent opinions. Divergent opinions help us see any flaws in our reasoning. No. They are our enemies because they want to reduce the canal to a partisan issue. Yet the canal will benefit all New Yorkers, even them. We must keep it above party politics. I shall reason with them and send them home." He motioned to Eleanora and whispered, "That's the constable yonder. Tell him to collect some men in the lobby and stay there until I call for him."

Then Clinton stepped through the window and was met by boos and catcalls. The steam of his breath encircled his head as he raised his arms.

"People of New York!" A loud jeer met his words. "Listen to me! Compare what I say with what your leaders tell you! I am calling on you as I call upon those inside to join with me in a great effort that will put money in each and every pocket."

"It's a conspiracy!" a heckler called.

"Immigrants want our jobs!"

"Gentlemen! Gentlemen!" Clinton called. "I ask the Sons of Tammany who have long led this great city in making reforms to help me. I ask you not to forget your frustrations or criticisms, but to vent them in a proper forum. This destruction of property and hazard to life and limb"—he waved to the broken window—"serves no one, and only defeats your purpose."

"Only the rich will benefit!"

"No tax for a goddamned ditch!"

"I ask you as a fellow New Yorker not to go home and forget, but to meet among yourselves. Return to Martling's Tavern. Organize. Appoint five delegates to meet with us tomorrow. We shall discuss our project thus far and listen to your concerns. This canal is not proposed to benefit any one segment of our state, but to benefit all."

"Liar! We know different!"

Another brick sailed out of the crowd. Clinton ducked and

it flew through the window. Clinton was furious. "I will not respond to heckling or to force. If there's a man among you, prevail upon your friends. I have made my offer and I will receive five of you tomorrow for as long as you wish to talk. Tomorrow, peaceably, reasonably, we shall smooth our differences, not tonight in the street."

Clinton climbed back through the window to the resounding applause of those at the banquet, and he held up his hands to quiet them. "We welcome different opinions, but we will not countenance mobocracy!" Again wild applause, during which Clinton leaned over to Eleanora and Daniel. "Get ready to flee if they pelt the building."

"You don't mean they'd dare?" she asked.

Clinton rolled his eyes. "You can never tell."

But the mob did not pelt the building. Confronted by Clinton himself when they expected him to huddle in fear, invited to discuss their differences, the crowd lost its spirit. Many went back to Martling's Tavern with words of admiration for Clinton's courage.

The orchestra had begun in the ballroom, and men at nearby tables expressed admiration for Clinton in endless toasts. But Clinton was impatient, and as soon as he could, he summoned Eleanora and Daniel to his suite on the fourth floor.

"This is precisely what we must not have," he said when the door was closed. He paced the floor. "Controversy! Controversy! No damned controversy! A torchlight mob in the street!"

"You handled it marvelously, DeWitt." Eleanora's excitement had not abated. "You advanced our cause by five years tonight! You stood up to them!"

"But I despise their tactics. I see someone's hand in this and it troubles me. O'Hanlon is surely involved, but he's just a stooge. Possibly Van Buren. I hear he secretly opposes us." Then Clinton's expression grew very grave. "But possibly someone else too."

"Who?"

Clinton paused and looked from Daniel to Eleanora then back. "Aaron Burr."

"Burr?" Eleanora seemed puzzled. "Why would be be involved? His political career is long over."

"That is precisely why. He cannot keep out of it, and not

being able to involve himself directly, he works through others. I hear he has taken Van Buren as his protégé."

"But why?"

"Burr misses power. He wants it back, and Van Buren thinks as he does. Burr can live vicariously. A mob in the streets! I haven't seen that tactic used in years. Burr will oppose us with all the guile of Satan himself. He wants revenge for the disgrace he has suffered. He and the Clinton family were always enemies." Clinton nodded. "We must get to him, hurt him, make him bleed. But how can you hurt a man who has nothing to lose?" Then Clinton cleared his throat and looked up at the two of them. "But Burr and Van Buren are my problems and need not concern you."

Then they discussed a "Memorial," an essay they could publish in newspapers throughout the state. For Eleanora Clinton sketched the broad political outlines, the arguments he wished explored. He discussed with Daniel what engineering details were necessary. "Take all the technical mystery out of it. Make it so simple that a father could build one for his child, or better yet, the child could build it for the father. See if you can have a draft for me by morning."

"By morning?" Eleanora was surprised. Clinton simply turned and looked at her, and she was silent. As he reiterated a few points, a knock sounded at the door.

"Four farmers from Brooklyn, sir," a young man said. "They have a contribution, and they would· appreciate a word."

"Very well." Clinton dismissed Eleanora and Daniel. "I'll see you at breakfast. Nine o'clock."

They left the room and passed the four farmers waiting to speak with the great man. They went downstairs to Eleanora's suite, and Eleanora told Hilda and Joel she'd need them no longer that night. She and Daniel began at ten o'clock, while in the ballroom a riotous canal party celebrated Clinton's triumph over the Tammany mob.

Four hours later they had twelve pages of persuasive text which Eleanora delivered to a scrivener for copying. "Are you tired, Daniel, or shall I send down for champagne?"

"I'm all right. The excitement stirred me up."

Eleanora sent for the champagne, and it came in a silver bucket filled with snow. Daniel opened it and poured.

Eleanora held up her glass. "To the canal on the night of its rebirth."

"To us," Daniel replied.

She smiled. "You, myself, and DeWitt."

Daniel nodded.

They discussed the arguments they'd refined that evening. Then Eleanora said, "DeWitt admires your capacities, Daniel. I watch him watch you."

"I admire his," Daniel said evasively.

"He has all sorts of engineers feeding him all sorts of technical details, all sorts of inventions men wish to promote. Yet when you speak, he listens."

"Well..." Daniel tossed off the wine and stood. "That is what we're both doing here, isn't it? Helping him?"

She looked down at her finger circling the rim of her glass. When she looked up, the soft expression of her lips and the intensity of her eyes surprised him. "Partially." She waited for him to say or ask something, yet he did not.

He set his glass down and looked into her eyes again. "I should get some sleep."

"So should I," she agreed, "but not yet. Sit by me, Daniel." She placed her glass on the cluttered table. Daniel crossed the room and sat next to her. Her voice grew husky. "I have often thought of the night we spent together."

"So have I." He touched her ear and looked into her eyes. The vast intelligence of those eyes, the depth of their sorrow... but tonight he saw something else. Excitement, yes, but also joy. He leaned over and kissed her lips, and her lips and tongue were delicious with the wine.

"I lived as a hermit for a year, alone on a mountain, gazing into my fire and out at the stars. I thought of you then."

Eleanora kissed him passionately, and she drank in the sweetness of the wine on his tongue. "Daniel?" He pulled away. She swallowed and struggled for control. "I know that without a wife now you have no need for... for *discretion*. You have no reason to keep silent about our... our association."

Daniel cringed. "Association?"

She looked sad suddenly. "See how guarded I must be!"

"I love you," he said softly. "I have no difficulty in telling you or in telling the world."

"And I love you, Daniel." She sighed; the admission relieved her somewhat. "But I must ask a favor, an enormous favor that you could very well refuse me. Yet I must ask you to promise you will never ever discuss our time together, our love—never discuss it with anyone." She looked down, ashamed. "I'm sorry, but I must ask that."

Daniel saw in her eye sorrow and fear. He wanted to ask why, yet he didn't. "I guess if you could tell me the reason, you would."

She nodded and tears welled in her eyes. "You don't know, and you never will, what it is like. Please!" She reached for him, pulled him toward her and kissed him on the lips with new hunger. "I love you, oh, Daniel, I love you so! Forgive me! Promise me! Ours shall be a secret love! Only we shall share it! No one will know, and it shall be even more sacred because we do not profane it to others."

He nodded. "And this reason, this reason for our silence, it can never be removed?"

"Never!" she cried. "Never! And that's what makes it so horrible." She fell upon his breast and wept. Daniel felt her warm tears on his neck, and he lifted her chin and kissed them away. Slowly he stood, lifted her from the love seat and carried her through the door into the darkened chamber. He lay her on the bed and lay down beside her. "The secret," he said, then corrected himself, "*our* secret will be kept."

"Oh, Daniel!" she moaned, and tangled her fingers in his hair, encircled him with her arms and legs, and kissed him passionately.

Comforted by the sound of his breathing, Eleanora drifted into sleep contentedly, her dreams happy and bright. She slept that night in the deepest slumber she'd enjoyed since before her capture. Yet when she heard a door close outside the room, she bolted upright. Daniel was still beside her. Sunlight streamed in the tall windows and sleighs passed below in the street.

"Daniel," she whispered, "you must go."

She watched him awaken, register where he was, then look at her.

"Good morning," he said easily, drifting back to sleep.

"Good morning," she answered. His ease calmed her a bit. The situation was comic enough. "Daniel, you've got to find a way out of here unseen."

He opened his eyes a second time. Far off a church bell rang nine times, muffled by the snow.

"I must be dreaming."

"We're late! We're supposed to meet DeWitt at nine. This . . . this will never do."

"Yes it will, Eleanora, my love. Does very nicely, if you ask me." He leaned his head back, opened his eyes, and gently stroked her hair.

They went down to breakfast separately. Clinton had read their draft and he praised much of it, criticized some, and suggested changes. As he finished discussing it, he reached out and took Daniel's hand in his left, Eleanora's in his right.

"I know in the hurly-burly we lose sight of our overall objective." He smiled warmly to each. "A man could never ask for two wiser, more loyal, more capable allies that you. Last night we built a firm foundation for our efforts to reach the public, and we learned much, even about how the project will be misperceived by our enemies. When this Memorial is finished, and three or four more drafts should suffice, I'd like both of you to travel together across the state promoting our cause in villages and townships. We need to put pressure on all our legislators, and the best way to reach them is through the people." Clinton squeezed their hands firmly. "This will be our triumvirate, then. Let us go forward together, and together we shall accomplish what small minds now consider impossible."

Gracefully Clinton placed their hands back on the linen. "Now I must meet with O'Hanlon and the Tammany Bucktails." He left.

Still glowing from their night of intimacy, Daniel and Eleanora gazed into each other's eyes. During the next few months they would be together constantly.

"We have much to celebrate at the New Year's Ball tonight." Eleanora said.

A hundred couples had been invited, but so great was the positive reaction to the canal project, seventy additional couples came uninvited. Clinton stood at the door, greeting each couple, wishing them a happy New Year. The orchestra played lively new waltzes, and the wives of these men of wealth and power had dressed in the sheerest Parisian gowns. The dancers swirled gracefully, bathed in the candlelight. Displays were set out around the ballroom, a birch-bark canoe, a stuffed wildcat, a wooden Indian in buckskin, a Durham salt boat, one of Oliver Perry's cannon. When all the guests and party crashers had arrived, Clinton gave a short address, then left

Eleanora and Daniel and hastened to a private room adjoining the first-floor bar.

Two men stood outside. "Is he alone?" They nodded. Clinton pushed into the room and latched the door.

Martin Van Buren had been waiting impatiently for half an hour. "I was about to leave," the small man announced from the table where he sat. Light from the hearth fire glowed in his reddish-blond hair. "I thought you'd forgotten me."

Clinton ignored this. "I asked for a meeting to reconcile our views about the canal. Thank you for coming."

Van Buren inclined his head slightly, a smile playing at his lips.

"I spoke with O'Hanlon and four Tammany sachems this morning," Clinton said. "They oppose the project and will fight it in the legislature. They are shortsighted and cannot see the potential it will have for the port of New York. They see all sorts of conspiracies and menaces that simply do not exist. Where do you stand on the issue, Judge?"

"I remain curious." Van Buren inclined his head thoughtfully. "I need to know more before making up my mind."

"My people will give you any and all information they possess."

"I am endeavoring to collect information, sir, slightly less biased."

This annoyed Clinton. He glared at Van Buren for a full minute. The little man stared directly back, again a sly smile on his lip.

"What exactly are your reservations?"

"I want to determine the canal's popularity."

"Popularity?" Clinton demanded. "It will be popular if we make it popular. This is what I'm endeavoring to do. The canal will be the single most important issue in New York for the next decade!"

Van Buren smiled and looked down at the table. "Perhaps there are men who look beyond your promises, Mr. Clinton. You assume state government should engage itself in building a waterway. I don't know if a majority of the people would agree with you, at least a majority of those who vote. Many believe private companies are better suited since they must turn a profit at what they undertake."

"No such company has come forth."

The Manhattan Water and Canal Company may be interested."

"Burr's people? Never. He's far too slippery. Even Ellicott and the Holland Land people have washed their hands of Burr."

Van Buren shrugged. "Well, then, some other company."

"We don't need a private firm!" Clinton grew impatient. "All benefits will accrue to this state, to the public at large, so it is only right that the cost should be borne by the public. No private firm has sufficient capital."

Van Buren shook his head. "Yet this obligation could very well bankrupt the state. Without a more positive showing, sir, I am afraid I cannot support it this session."

"And so you and Tammany Hall will obstruct a funding bill to begin digging?"

"Unless you can satisfy me the project is sound and the people want it. My associates and I will need more than letters in the newspapers, and speeches, and"—he nodded toward the door—"New Year's Eve parties. While a certain visionary capacity is to be admired in leaders, particularly religious leaders, prudence and caution are far more important in public men."

"So you hang back as the voice of prudence and caution on this issue?"

Van Buren smiled and nodded.

"And so we must convince you and yours that it is prudent to proceed?"

Van Buren spread his arms in candor. "That is all we ask."

"Very well," Clinton said abruptly, extending his hand for Van Buren to shake. "I just hope you don't regret someday not joining us sooner." And he turned from the small man, unlocked the door, and left.

Van Buren waited with a bemused smile. Seeing Clinton lose his composure was pleasurable. And yet the night could bring more pleasant news. Within five minutes a knock sounded at the door and a thickly built Loyal Son of Tammany entered.

"Yes?"

"Your suspicion was right. A surveyor feller. Name's Hedges. Their rooms are connected by a door. Uh, Mr. Van Buren, sir, I uh . . . I had to bribe a chambermaid. . . ."

"Sure, my good man," Van Buren said, and counted out five silver dollars.

*   *   *

"The arrogant little upstart!" Clinton thundered. "How can the bastard son of an innkeeper hold our grand canal in his waistcoat pocket? I loathe these politics. Madison was bad enough. Van Buren is intolerable! I see Burr's treachery behind this, Burr the schemer, like a spider spinning his evil web. Before he is done, there will be many ruined lives. Now Van Buren postures himself as the protector of the public purse. He's only waiting to see if the canal can help his career, and when it will, he will fall in step with us. He and Burr are one in their thinking—such voracious appetites for gaining political offices, and none of the integrity required to hold them."

"His colleagues always vote in a bloc," Eleanora observed. "He has the votes needed to push or obstruct any legislation. Of course, bribery and blackmail are always at his disposal too."

"Yes." Clinton set his lip. "He does have his political cronies in Albany who vote with Tammany Hall. Yet we shall have the people on our side." Clinton thought a moment. "We must appeal directly to them, energetically and soon." He warmed to a new idea. "Yes, we shall hunt the little fox. As I said this morning, you and Daniel make arrangements to travel through every crossroads hamlet in this state and stir up enthusiasm to send a clear message to Albany. Speak to farmers' markets, churches, taverns, wherever four or five voters congregate. Carry our message to the hustings. The good work you've done here will serve you well. We shall work up such a canal fever that Van Buren should sooner seek to halt the advancing tide."

There was a knock at the door. A waiter entered with a tray of glasses and a bottle of champagne. Daniel passed the glasses as the waiter removed the cork with a pop and poured the wine.

"I propose a toast for the New Year," Clinton said. "To our association, the three of us. May success be ours together."

"Together." Daniel smiled to Eleanora.

"Together." She lifted her glass and clinked it with DeWitt's and then with Daniel's.

20

Returning to Hudson, Martin Van Buren told his clerk to see if the deed to Claverack had been recorded. The clerk produced the copy with its red seal, and Van Buren perused it. Set forth were the metes and bounds of the estate, part Livingson and part Van Rensselaer land conveyed in fee tail to Jacob and Eleanora Van Rensselaer. Van Buren scratched his head. Jacob had died without offspring. The land should have reverted to the Van Rensselaers, with Eleanora maintaining only a one-third dower interest for her life. Yet she still held the entire estate.

"Henry, you've been clerk for twenty years. Do you recall anything unusual about the Claverack conveyance? Something is missing here."

Henry scowled as he read it over. "No, your honor."

"Tell me, then, why would a widow keep the entire estate at her husband's death instead of only a dower share? And why mention the wife at all in the deed? Her family was trying to protect something, but they'd never get back title to the acres of her dowry."

"Ah!" Henry's eyes lit up. "I do remember something strange, a scheme by the Van Rensselaers. Yes, yes. They made a separate covenant before the wedding to agree on certain unusual terms. I remember Chancellor Livingston involved himself in its drafting, and the families wished to keep the terms of the covenant private."

"Do you know the terms?"

Henry winked. "A few of them. It seems both families wanted to assure the estate remained intact and passed to their descendants. They wanted only the offspring of this union to inherit. Yet they foresaw—wisely as it turned out—that one of the couple might die before children were born. Jacob, the husband, of course, would have seisin of all the land. If he survived Eleanora he might remarry and pass the estate down to Van Rensselaers. But what if Eleanora survived, as indeed happened? The Van Rensselaers didn't want her claiming an interest in other property Jacob held. That's why they put her on the deed."

"Yes," Van Buren said, "the statute of 1787 would prevent that so long as she held Claverack."

"The Van Rensselaers also worried that she might remarry, and if she did, the heirs of her body not named Van Rensselaer might inherit Claverack. Chancellor Livingston advised an agreement whereby the bride gave up her widow's right to dower for the right to keep the entire estate for life, on the sole condition that she not remarry. If she remarried, she lost everything."

"Excellent, Henry! Do you know where the covenant is?"

"I believe each family kept a copy. They were duly signed and sealed."

"Is there any way, my fine Henry, that you can get me the specific language?"

"I know the Livingston accountant quite well. I'll see what I can do, your honor."

Three days later Henry produced a verbatim copy of the covenant. Van Buren read it with pleasure. "Under the terms, she holds the land 'so long as she shall honor her nuptial vows, and if she remarries'"—Van Buren looked up, smiling—"*forfeiture*."

"Quite."

"One last matter, Henry. If she forfeits, who takes?"

Henry put his finger to his lips. "Let's see! Let's see! Primogeniture controls, I believe. Where the conveyance fails, it would be the next oldest brother. There were three sons— Master Jacob, Master Edward, and Master Randolph. Master Edward died in the war. Master Randolph, it seems."

"Where might I find him?"

"Oh, he's a young man of low habits. He's always at the Burgomaster—a tavern at the docks—with a pretty hard crew." Henry accepted a five-dollar gold piece. "Thank you, your honor. It's noon now, he shouldn't be too drunk yet."

Van Buren left immediately for the docks where whaling vessels were anchored. New England warehouses, saltbox shops, and houses lined the shore, built by captains transplanted from Nantucket. The inland port of Hudson seemed more like a Nantucket harbor than a bay on the Hudson River. Van Buren stepped brightly along. The irony of his plan pleased him. Landed aristocrats used such deeds, wills, and covenants to keep their wealth and power consolidated. Van Buren had long resented such wealth and privilege. Now he was using the very instrument of conveyance to divide and conquer. He'd separate Lady Eleanora from her property and security, and perhaps split her from Clinton.

He located the Burgomaster Tavern and asked for Randolph Van Rensselaer.

"Randy? Why, he's over there." The bartender nodded with disgust.

Van Buren crossed the low dingy room to where a thin young man sat at the hearth, a shock of red hair dangling in his eyes. "Mr. Van Rensselaer?"

The man's startled expression soured into anger. "Whatever you're peddling, I don't need none."

"On the contrary, sir, you will be very interested in what I have to offer." He introduced himself, then sat down. 'I'll come directly to the point. You stand to inherit your brother's estate of Claverack if you can demonstrate certain conduct and the intentions of its current occupant."

Randolph scowled. "I'll be dead before I see that. Father gave Jacob and his bride the home and lands. Then Jake died, leaving that barren bitch in the house." He swigged from his pewter tankard, licked his lips and asked. "So what's it to you?"

"Are you aware of an agreement that if she remarries, she must leave Claverack, and it becomes yours?"

Years of drink and smoky taprooms gave Randolph's skin a sallow cast, and it wrinkled as he scowled again. "No."

Van Buren's eyes twinkled. "Yes." He nodded. "Yes."

"Ah, but she won't marry. Who'd have her if she was dispossessed? Besides, she knows what she'd lose, and she's a sly bitch, she is."

Van Buren raised his finger instructively. "I hear she is secretly seeing a man, and has plans to marry."

"Fine!" Randolph grew surly. "When she does, I'll eject her."

"But they plan to be secretly wed. Your father and brothers are all dead. You didn't even know of the covenant, man. So she need only wait until you are gone, your claim will be moot, then she will perfect title in herself."

"Leave off the legal doubletalk, Judge." He narrowed his eyes unpleasantly. "Do I have a claim or not?"

Van Buren backed up. "As a member of the bench I cannot practice law, but I'd suggest you look into the matter. The covenant provides she may hold the lands only so long as she honors her nuptial vows. The threat of a charge of adultery or fornication, and the publicity of a court battle, might just convince her to leave."

Randolph's eyes brightened, and he took another swig of punch. "What do you gain by all this?"

"Your perpetual friendship, and the pleasure of seeing the estate returned to its rightful owner."

"Who is the man she's seeing?"

"That will be for you to determine, but I suspect it is the surveyor on this wild canal project. Daniel Hedges is his name." Van Buren stood. "You must look into it further. I cannot become involved, you understand. And I trust you will keep this conversation confidential."

Randolph nodded. "Want a drink?"

"No, no thank you. I wish you luck in this endeavor. Perhaps I may help when it ripens into an action."

Randolph smiled. The judge tipped his hat and left. "Ah," Van Buren said to himself as he pushed into the fresh sunlight, "Informed self-interest. As dependable as gravity."

The change in Randolph was quick and dramatic. Slovenly, lazy, drunken before, he now hired a valet, bought new clothes, trimmed his shaggy hair, and with a walking stick and a three-cornered hat, affected the air of a landed gentleman. In his father's strongbox he found the Van Rensselaer copy of the marriage covenant and he showed it to Berthold Van Jagg, a Hudson attorney.

Eleanora returned from New York City, then left on a journey across the state. She traveled with Joel Kipp, Hilda, and Daniel Hedges. Armed with copies of the finished Memorial, they went westward in three large sleighs to Schenectady, Rome, Utica, Oswego, Salina, the little cluster of buildings called Rochesterville, then along the Ridge Road to Black Rock and Buffaloe Creek. Joel secured them lodging in each place, and they met local officials and major property owners to discuss face-to-face what the canal would accomplish.

Usually the evening they arrived, Joel tacked up broadsides in the taverns and post office that a public meeting would be held the following night at an inn or a church. By nightfall the next day a curious throng had assembled. Daniel and Eleanora allowed local officials to share the dais, and usually after some introductory remarks, the mayor or town justice introduced Eleanora.

The men and women who came were surprised that a woman took the rostrum, yet because it was a woman, they listened more attentively. Eleanora described how funds would be raised and spent, what it would cost, how long the canal would take to build, then what benefits would accompany its completion—larger cities, greater wealth, schools for the children, local industries, and the access to manufactured goods from the East and Europe.

"In the words of Mr. Clinton," she concluded, holding up the pamphlet she and Daniel had written, "'It remains for a free state to create a new era in history, and to erect a work more magnificent and more beneficial than has ever been achieved by the human race.'" She sat to their resounding applause.

Daniel followed. He identified himself as a former merchant from Buffaloe Creek. With a map he showed how trade generated in the Ohio Valley, the Great Lakes territories and beyond, would naturally flow either down the Mississippi to New Orleans or down the St. Lawrence to Montreal.

He lowered his voice. "Like many of you, I fought in the war to defend my home. My house was burned, my wife and babies massacred. Why? Because the government in Washington could not defend us. A cannon costing four hundred dollars to cast, cost two thousand to ship to Niagara! An eight-dollar barrel of pork for the men cost a hundred dollars to ship to them! This canal will channel commerce through our state, but more importantly, it will help prevent another invasion from Canada."

He then described the canal's dimensions, how a lock lifted boats, how aqueducts would carry the canal over rivers and creeks, how the towpath would accommodate teams going in both directions. His final point piqued local curiosity.

"Now, as to the men needed to dig—we'll be using local contractors mostly. You have the plows and the shovels. You know where granite and limestone may be quarried, where white oak for the lock gates and scaffolding can be cut. When the funds are approved by the legislature, a state agent will contact you to see who is willing to work. His strongbox will be filled with silver and gold. If some of you want to subcontract, you may dig two or three miles of the canal. The money you earn may build you a new home, buy new livestock or tools, purchase new fields and pastures. From the day the legislature acts, you all will benefit."

Daniel sat to polite applause, then Eleanora urged the people to contact the representatives they had put into office and demand a favorable vote. She asked them to sign a petition. During this western sweep, five ledgers were filled with over ten thousand signatures.

Daniel and Eleanora enjoyed the time together immensely. They were a team now. She brought vision and political savvy, he brought backwoods common sense and engineering skill. They saw each other's strengths and weaknesses, and their admiration for each other grew.

The visit to Black Rock and Buffaloe Creek unlocked emotions in Daniel that he was at last able to share. A rivalry had arisen between the two communities as to where the western end of the canal would be. Without making commitments to Joseph Ellicott, whose vast holdings in Black Rock caused him to want it there, or to Daniel's old neighbors who favored Buffaloe, Daniel and Eleanora channeled the furious enthusiasm into letters and petition signatures. To celebrate their most promising meeting, they decided to remain a day longer at Buffaloe. It was the first of May, a glorious sunny day, and tender green buds stood out against the deep green of the pine forest.

"Show me where you once lived," Eleanora said brightly at breakfast. Her eyes held a girlish enthusiasm. "I want to see everything you have told me about."

"Everything's changed."

"Good morning, Mr. Hedges," Daniel heard at his back, and he turned to see a pretty young woman. "I attended your lecture last night, and I thought you and the lady were wonderful!"

Daniel bristled when he recognized her. "This is Edna Kay, Eleanora," he said. "Edna, Eleanora Van Rensselaer." Edna curtsied.

"So nice to meet you. If there's anything I can do to make your stay more comfortable, please let me know. I have been promoted to head chambermaid."

Daniel congratulated her, and she left. Before he could explain how he saved her during the war, how she located Eleanora's letter that sent him East instead of West, Eleanora smiled roguishly: "I see some things haven't changed."

They walked out together in the clean spring sun. Eleanora wore a long frilled gown of yellow saffron and carried a small parasol. Daniel described how the village looked before its burning, what sort of goods had lined the docks, where he moored his *Silver Pearl*, how they'd ignored the embargo. And Eleanora's questions demonstrated her excitement at the adventure and romance of his former life.

They paused at a small shack whose chimney belched wood smoke in the morning air. "What is this?"

"This is where my home stood." He looked upon the site with dismay. "It was a large house, a fine house for raising children. The British burned it."

"Who owns the land now?"

"Why, I do. These people are squatters."

"Then you must evict them! This is valuable property, and its value will increase tenfold when the canal is dug." She stared disgustedly at the shack. "Property, Daniel, property is something you must seize and hold, else it will slip through your fingers."

"They have children." He pointed to a clothesline. "I can't do that."

"But they will perfect title if they squat here long enough."

Daniel shrugged. "It doesn't mean that much to me now." He led her into the woods a distance until the overgrown path disappeared among the briars. "I own this land as well. It's so overgrown. About twenty acres. We, uh, I built a cabin on it, and our children were born here."

"I should so like to see it."

"But your dress!" Daniel didn't want to admit there were other reasons for keeping her away from the cabin. He and Carrie had been so happy. He looked into Eleanora's eyes and saw sympathy. "Very well. Come along." And he started into the briars, parting them for her.

The cabin still stood, rough-hewn logs and clay chinking, but its roof had partially caved in. The yard was completely overgrown. They walked around the cabin, then paused at the doorway. As reluctant to enter the cabin as he was to relive certain memories, Daniel took Eleanora's hand. She slowly put her arms around his neck, stepped up and kissed him on the lips.

"Oh, Daniel," she murmured close to his ear, "it is so beautiful here! A man and a woman could believe they were beginning the human race again, free from all its mistakes and shortcomings." She kissed him again, more passionately this time. Daniel responded, and when they parted, they were both breathing deeply, striving to control themselves. "Are we desecrating her memory?"

"No." He shook his head. "Carrie loved life so very much, and she showed others how to love it as well. She was never petty or jealous."

"And yet so many seek to control us from the grave."

"But they can't if we don't let them." Daniel believed she was speaking of her husband. He led her inside. The place looked very much the same as when he had stripped it of its furnishings the day they moved. The caved-in roof had deposited a heap of pine needles on the floor. After peering here and there, Eleanora turned to Daniel and kissed him eagerly.

"Oh, Daniel, I want you now."

He dropped the embrace and crossed the room. From a high shelf he took a small toy boat, a model of the *Silver Pearl*. "This was my son's." He put it back. "It's cold in here, Eleanora. Come outside. I know a place." He led her through the chirping forest to a mossy glade by a stream. The ground was elevated, and from the bed of moss they could see down to the village and the harbor where ships rode in the breeze. Daniel covered the moss with his coat, and they lay upon it looking toward the lake.

"It is so serene!" She sighed. As he kissed her, she wrapped her arms about him and curled her hips into his. "Oh, Daniel!" She sighed again, and her eyes grew misty. "I could be so happy here with you!"

"If only—" he began to say, but stopped himself. He was about to mention the strange promise she'd extracted from him.

"If only!" she sighed.

He kissed her deeply with his tongue, then stroked her back, hips, and thighs. She rolled on top of him and playfully unbuttoned his shirt. "This Eden is no place for clothes!" She pulled off her own. With joy and abandon she explored his body. This was no hidden encounter at her town house, or in the City Hotel, or in five of the many inns where they'd had the courage to meet in the dead of night. Hers was a new innocence today. Happily they romped on the soft moss, urging each other to new heights of pleasure. At last they lay together, calmed.

"It feels so wonderful to be out of doors."

"It could be like this always."

"If only it could!" Her tone ended that subject. Daniel watched the high, fleecy clouds, thinking, then he bolted up: "Let's go sailing!"

"Oh, yes, let's do!"

"I'll show you how I used to make my living."

Quickly they arose, dressed, and returned to town. Daniel rented a small skiff while Eleanora brought her cloak from the inn, and soon they were out on the lake, tacking in the brisk breeze. The little boat responded immediately to his hand, and they reached ten knots.

Eleanora lay back, watching the wind in his hair, the sun and shade upon his face as they tacked; listening to his calm, mellow voice describe what he was doing and how it affected the boat.

"I love it here!" she cried.

Daniel smiled, watching the wind whip her fair hair, watching as she held her face proudly into the wind. The sun sparkled gloriously on the water, and silhouetted against it, Eleanora seemed far more beautiful than he had ever seen her. This, he told himself, was their happiest day together. He regretted the sun's passing across the sky, and the moment arrived when he said, "We should start back."

As he came about, the setting sun lit Eleanora with a deep rose color. Paying out the lines, Daniel ran before the wind, and with no skippering to be done, he thought a moment, then said, "This journey with you has made many things clear."

Eleanora nodded. While sailing out, she had remarked to herself, "He is the finest man I've ever met." Yet she didn't want to speak now.

"I've got to ask you something, Eleanora."

"All right." She was suddenly tense.

"Why can't we stop all the hiding and whispering and sneaking around? Why don't we tell the world to be damned and live our lives as we see fit?"

She breathed with relief. She had thought he was going to propose. She stared thoughtfully into the setting sun. "There are many things about me, Daniel, that you don't know."

"I know enough to want to know more."

"And yet I have very good reasons for asking this favor of you, reasons I cannot tell you."

"Maybe not tonight or tomorrow, but why not next week or next month?"

She sighed and looked out over the water. "I love you, Daniel, and it grieves me that we can't be together openly. It grieves me even more that I can't tell you why."

"Share it with me, Eleanora. I may be able to help you."

"No," she said firmly.

"Why?"

"Because if I shared it with you, you should think terribly of me and you wouldn't love me anymore."

"Nonsense."

"It is my own secret, Daniel, one I must live with alone. I do not wish to burden you with it, and you only add to my sorrow when you pressure me."

He regretted he had mentioned it. "I don't mean to do that."

"I know, so let's not talk of it further, please. I cannot read the future, Daniel. Perhaps there'll come a day when I can explain, but I don't want to promise what may never be. Please trust me."

He squinted into the sparkling waves. "I do. I do and I will."

21

While Daniel and Eleanora promoted the canal through the western territories, DeWitt Clinton politicked in the river counties: Albany, Rensselaer, Columbia, Greene, Ulster, Dutchess, Putnam, Rockland, Westchester, and his native Orange. Yet Van Buren and Tammany Hall were campaigning, too, preying on fear that western produce shipped by canal would flood the market and lower prices, and that tenant farmers would depart for more fertile bottom land they could own outright. The legislative session would be the battleground.

"But how do you know you can trust him?" Hannah Van Buren lay across the bed, watching her husband adjust his silk cravat in the mirror.

"He has nothing to gain or lose."

"But why is he offering you this help?"

Van Buren turned and flashed her a boyish smile. "It's the nature of the game, my love. Once accustomed to manipulating men and controlling events, he can't stay idle. No one retires from politics, they are forced out."

"But why did he pick you to help?"

"We think alike. He has tremendous experience, and he admires my methods. I do believe I'm brighter than he is, surely less extreme in my methods. He gets too involved in plots and conspiracies and revenge, in punishing enemies. I am steered by ambition alone. Yet he sees me as his protégé, his understudy. It is convenient for me to have someone with whom I may discuss affairs." Van Buren turned back to the mirror. "I genuinely like him too."

"But if it should become public you're involved with a convicted traitor..."

"He's discreet, Hannah. While there are excesses, and sometimes he seems a bit unhinged, for the most part his advice is sound." He faced her. "Don't worry. Although he might see me as his avenging angel, I keep my own counsel. I'll ride with him only so far as he drives in my direction." He crossed the room and kissed Hannah's forehead. "Only so long as he benefits me and my family."

Albany blazed with excitement for the canal. Debate about the canal funding dominated the last two weeks of the 1816 session. The night before the vote, Clinton staged a torchlight parade through Albany's streets to show public support. With trumpets blaring, a bass drum pounding, and thousands shouting and cheering, the parade passed through the street by the Mansion House.

"Nice effect." Aaron Burr dropped the heavy velvet curtain of his window and turned to Martin Van Buren. "The mob. *Coriolanus* and the mob. Voracious beast, never satisfied."

"Clinton has much support." Van Buren didn't like admitting he didn't recognize literary allusions. He was nervous, too, about the vote.

"Never rely on the mob, Matty. No one can control it. Rely only on men who hold office, and their families. Once you give a dog his dish, you can easily slip the leash about his neck."

"Clinton seems to have the mob on his side."

"Only temperarily, Matty. Yes, you'll have a good floor fight tomorrow. Are your votes firmly committed?"

"We'll see tomorrow."

"Just keep to the high ground, Matty. You may have to retreat once or twice as the battle heats up. Speak sparingly. Watch where your support threatens to erode. If you've prepared the troops sufficiently, you'll know what arguments to use in swaying the weaker ones to stand and not fall back."

"Clinton's people have been working."

"Yes, I hear from an ally in the Holland Land Company that the Van Rensselaer woman's oratory, wit, and beauty garnered much support in the western counties. Have you done anything to neutralize her?"

"Randolph Van Rensselaer has been gathering evidence, but his attorney doesn't believe they have enough yet to bring an action for ejectment."

"My friend told me she was cavorting rather openly with the surveyor there." Burr winked. "Tie those two together, and Clinton's little triumvirate will be blown apart."

"Van Rensselaer's agent is checking registry books at the inns to see if they ever signed as man and wife. And yet the woman is cautious. She keeps a strapping young man as a bodyguard and chaperone. We need to be patient."

"A few gold coins in the proper hands could get you the evidence you need. How about a town justice swearing he performed a wedding ceremony?"

Van Buren just smiled. "No need to suborn perjury yet, sir. We'll uncover something."

At Eleanora's town house DeWitt Clinton, Daniel Hedges, Eleanora, and four senators from the north, south, central, and western portions of the state were finishing dinner.

Clinton turned to Daniel. "We shall waste no time. Immediately after the appropriation, you should travel to Rome and begin hiring contractors. If all goes well, thirty or forty miles of the canal may be dug by the first frost."

These senators had assured Clinton they had the necessary votes for victory. Now each basked in the radiance of being a member of his inner circle.

"It's essential we proceed quickly." Clinton led the way to the drawing room for brandy and cigars. "With the public on our side, the clamoring of Tammany Hall will seem mere whining."

As he and Eleanora had arranged, Daniel left the dinner party first. At his rooming house he changed clothes, waited half an hour, then returned to the town house. Satisfied everyone had departed, he walked up the alley to the gate of Eleanora's small flower garden. He paused. Sensing someone watching him, he noticed a man slouching against the stable. Boldly Daniel crossed the alley to confront him, but seeing he was noticed, the man threw his cloak over his head and bolted up the alley. Daniel looked warily about but saw no one else.

Unlatching the gate, he saw the candle in the window—their signal. He let himself in and forgot about the loiterer.

Next morning the steps to the Capitol were crowded with politicians holding last-minute conferences. The Senate convened at ten. In the high hall with green velvet curtains and oaks desks, debate raged between Henry Yates, Clinton's senator from central New York, and Henry Seymour, a Van Buren follower from Utica. For three hours the other thirty senators sat, weighing, evaluating, considering the arguments. Van Buren watched the proceeding warily. He did not wish to cast himself and his followers as obstructionists.

DeWitt Clinton, as lieutenant governor, presided over the Senate. He was pleased to recognize one of his allies on the floor who called for a motion to demand the previous question. Two thirds, twenty-two votes, were needed to close debate and bring the issue immediately to a vote, yet only twenty-one "Ayes" were tallied. The motion failed, and discussion continued, splintering Clinton's solid support.

"Mr. Chairman, may I have the floor?"

"The chair recognizes Senator Martin Van Buren, Columbia County."

Van Buren stood before the body and began to speak. His voice was reedy and thin, and at first he seemed nervous. Yet soon his logic overcame the lack in his oratory.

"...even conceding the project should be undertaken, must we proceed blindly? Should we levy a tax of five dollars upon every man, woman, and child of this state to conduct an experiment? The Canal Commission has explored many possibilities as to how and where it should be built, yes. And yes, the people have expressed a desire for the canal. Yes, surveys have been made and engineering studies done. But is there one conclusive fact before us that such a project can be built? I say no. It is too speculative at present to warrant funding.

"Consider, gentlemen. The Canal Commission has sought

to retain noted engineers from England and France at seven thousand dollars a year, a princely sum. Has anyone accepted? No. They say the project is impossible. Do we have an engineer? Perhaps. The name of a surveyor, Daniel Hedges, has been mentioned. What are his qualifications?" Van Buren spread his arms at the rhetorical question.

Sitting together in the gallery, Eleanora clasped Daniel's arm.

"Has he ever built anything like this before? Not to my knowledge. And who will dig the ditch? Where will the men, the horses, the oxen come from? Mr. Yates says the work will be contracted out to local inhabitants, but he must know there are vast tracts of unsettled wilderness. Will the canal simply end at a cliff or a forest? As for the canal route, where will it be? There haven't even been any stakes driven to show farmers where their fields will be crossed. How long will the digging take? No one knows. Nothing like this has ever been attempted. Five years? Ten years? Twenty? And each year will they come back for more money to save their foundering project? And will we pour more money after what has been wasted. I say, no, gentlemen. No."

Van Buren shook his head. "We have given this canal project a great deal of attention. I move we call the previous question and vote immediately upon this construction appropriation."

The chamber gasped at Van Buren's audacity. He had held out so he could have the last word. Now, his vote joining the other twenty-one would provide enough to put it to the test while his arguments were fresh in the legislators' minds. And on the appropriation, only a majority was needed. While twenty-two senators wanted the matter resolved so they might get on with other business, it would be difficult for Clinton to secure a majority, particularly after Van Buren's persuasive speech.

"Clerk." Clinton hammered down his gavel. "Call the roll."

Exactly twenty-two votes supported Van Buren. The floor of the Senate buzzed with excitement as it seemed Van Buren had swayed a few to his side. The matter would be voted on without rebuttal now.

"Motion: Whether to appropriate funds for canal construction, amount to be set if majority approves."

"Mr. Van Buren's motion is on the floor. Clerk." Clinton hammered the gavel again. "Call the roll once more."

Eleanora tightly clapsed Daniel's arm. He looked with disdain upon the politicians. "If we get sixteen," she whispered, "DeWitt will break the tie." One by one the votes were counted, and the chamber gasped at each.

"Fifteen ayes," the clerk called.

The place exploded. Seasoned senators leapt up sputtering, pointing fingers at those who did not vote yes. Furiously Clinton hammered his gavel, crying "Order! Order!" And while shouts and recriminations filled the chamber, Clinton glared at Van Buren, and Van Buren inclined his head ever so slightly and smiled.

That evening Clinton stormed into Eleanora's parlor, took a chair, and glanced from her to Daniel. He deliberately folded his hands and sat stock still, striving for control.

"What was the telling blow?" she asked.

"Not driving stakes into the ground to mark the route." He rolled his eyes. "No wonder they call him the Little Magician. He defeated our motion to call a vote, got his arguments before the chamber, then succeeded in passing his own motion to call a vote after convincing one of the fence-sitters to be cautious and side with him. He knows how to play the game. We knew he had twelve, but he picked up five additional votes. I'd like to learn what he promised in return."

"It's madness how he opposes us," Daniel said.

"Mad and shrewd. He builds his power by tearing our support apart." Clinton raised an eyebrow. "He's an anarchist, profiting from confusion and dissension, and he's an accomplished demagogue. Today he has emerged as the leader of the canal opposition. He has positioned himself as the single vote we must win over and keep if we're to function." Clinton shook his head in disgust.

"Now what?" Eleanora asked.

"I have spent the day regrouping. Adversity must only make us stronger, more determined. We have a year to prepare for the next battle, and the fair-haired boy from Kinderhook will learn how to swallow defeat. I have dispatched young Canvass White to England to study and make drawings of canals and locks, and also to hire diggers. Napoleon's defeat his left many English soldiers idle."

"White is a very able man," Daniel agreed. "He helped me survey the central section of the canal. Have you plans for me?"

Clinton nodded. "I want you to begin at Buffaloe and survey for the last time, hopefully, every inch of ground to the Irondequoit. We'll have others do the central and eastern sections. We'll need altitudes, soil composition, the ownership of the land, the depth of gullies and streams to be crossed, as well as plans for aqueducts and culverts." Clinton gently pounded his fist on the arm of the chair. "By next year we shall have the most exhaustive survey of any strip of land ever conducted. Let Van Buren oppose us then."

"And I?" Eleanora asked.

"A special effort, my dear. In this state hundreds now languish in prison for debt and other petty offenses. Why not turn their idleness into productive labor? We could allow them to work on the canal until their sentence has run, and pay them the same wage as other men. I have attorneys looking into the constitutional issues of clemency. You should visit the prisons in the guise of a reformer and look into conditions there. See Thayer for details. He'll escort you."

She nodded.

"Well," Clinton said, lightly slapping the arms of the chair and standing. "The canal lost a year today, but gained much direction. Let us put this setback behind quickly and prepare for the next skirmish." He shook Daniel's hand heartily and kissed Eleanora's, then bowed and walked from the room.

They sat and stared intensely into each other's eye for a long, long moment.

"And so we must part again?"

Daniel nodded, and set his jaw.

"Oh, Daniel, will it always be this way?"

"Only so long as the canal is all we share." He stood.

"You're not leaving?"

"Yes, I am. I'm tired, and I have a lot of thinking to do."

"Oh, Daniel, we can't part this way! We can't! I won't see you for six months." Her eyes darted back and forth, and she spoke more quickly. "I have a plan, Daniel, a plan that occurred to me this morning when Van Buren was speaking. We'll appoint you chief engineer for the actual digging. You can manage the work, I know." She was clasping his arm, staring with anxious hope into his eyes. "That's what we'll do. DeWitt will do it, I know he will, for me, for you, for us."

Daniel looked down at her. "Let's take things one step at a time. We trip over ourselves when we think too far in advance." He turned to go.

"You'll not part from me this way?"

"No. I'll call tomorrow before I leave."

He kissed her gently, and she backed away from him. After the door closed, she threw herself on the love seat, sobbing. "Oh, this wretched, wretched business."

Across the city Van Buren and supporters celebrated Clinton's defeat and their own rise to power as a force to work with Tammany Hall.

"We demonstrated today," Van Buren said, raising his glass high into the candlelight, "what may be accomplished when we vote together. Today marks the beginning of a new era in state politics. Yes, gentlemen, we in this room"—he looked slowly about at the twenty-three assembled—"will shortly control all offices of this state. And our Regency shall win the emulation and respect it deserves."

"Here, here!" the others cried in unison.

As Van Buren went about the room talking with each man individually, a waiter approached him and whispered in his ear. "Yes," Van Buren said, "I'll be up presently." Excusing himself then, he proceeded upstairs to a private room. Aaron Burr was seated on an ottoman, a fire blazing in the hearth despite the warm summer weather.

"Come in, my boy. I hear the most glowing accounts of your speech in the Senate this morning. I quite regret I could not attend."

"You do me great honor, sir."

"You play the game extraordinarily well, turning the tables so quickly on your opposition. You have raised yourself up as the leader of a powerful faction Clinton will have to reckon with soon. You alone shall control the offices dispensed in every county of this state!" Burr chuckled, then narrowed his eye. "You have learned much from watching others. Now learn from one old man. You have an able enemy in Clinton, and the further you push him and all of his people down, the higher you will rise. But Clinton has a great following, as did Hamilton. Use Clinton as you will"—he raised an instructive finger—"but take care how you dispose of him."

"Dueling is no longer fashionable." Van Buren seemed fairly cocky since that morning. "I shall employ other means."

Burr grew very serious. "Yes, Matty, but remember that in politics you can never kill a man too dead, never, for his reputation and his followers will rise and stalk you all your days."

"I learn much from your example, sir, and am flattered by your attention."

Burr nodded at the homage. "You offer me the chance to rectify certain mistakes, Matty. It is a good alliance when both parties benefit." Burr grew more cheerful. "Now, be off with you to enjoy the praise you have earned. There will be many setbacks to offset your victory tonight, so savor it deeply. Leave an old man alone to reminisce about his past victories."

22

*B*ack across the state Daniel Hedges rode to measure and catalogue every pertinent fact for the legislature. He finished by winter, and decided to remain in Buffaloe Creek. He repaired the roof of his cabin, and hunted for meat on his land between the Seneca reservation and the village. The solitude pleased him, and he often gazed into the fire upon the winter night, remembering the sweet times he had shared with Carrie in the cabin, remembering the joy of his children.

Occasionally Daniel strolled past his lot in town and gazed at the squatter's cottage and the children in the yard. One afternoon early in March Daniel saw a woman leave the hut, her shawl wrapped tightly about her. She barely glanced at him, but he recognized her. "Edna?"

She turned. "Captain Hedges?"

"Do you live here?"

"Why, yes."

"And these are your children?"

"Yes."

"I didn't know you were married."

"A woman hardly needs a husband for that."

"Quite so." Her saucy expression made her quite pretty. "May I walk you to the tavern?"

She nodded, and her eyes bored into his. "If you do not mind being seen with me." She kept talk to neutral topics, about what had brought him back to Buffaloe Creek and how long he would be staying. As they parted at the inn, Edna extended her hand, "I hope we shall speak again, Mr. Hedges."

"I'd like that."

He had seen for the first time how pretty she was. Each other time he had been distracted by something else—the raging battle, Lester Frye, Eleanora. Now here was a dilemma. He pondered it long and hard for a week. Three hundred miles separated him from the woman he loved, who would not publicly acknowledge him, and here at hand was a most attractive woman he'd rescued years before, who had children he might help raise and care for, who even lived on his property! It would indeed be practical to court Edna. Yet, Daniel reflected, cursing the perversity of human nature, men always want what they cannot have, and the more unattainable, the greater their desire.

Even as he avoided Edna and watched for her children each time he passed the lot, his letters to Eleanora, both to Claverack and to the Albany town house, went unanswered.

Yet there was good reason why she didn't write back. After touring the state prisons, Eleanora returned to her estate, and the solitude she enjoyed at Claverack was shattered in mid July. She was playing a wistful Mozart sonata alone in the candlelight of her drawing room when Hilda burst in breathlessly. "Ma'am, Joel's here and he's mighty agitated."

"Show him in."

Joel's eyes smoldered, and his frame trembled with rage.

"Beggin' your pardon to call at such an unreasonable hour, ma'am, but I just come from the Chatham Inn, and a scoundrel named Gleason taunted me terrible." She looked up and frowned. "No, I didn't brawl with the red-nosed Irish bast—Beggin' your pardon, ma'am, but on your account I should have busted his nose!"

"What about? I don't know the man." She arose moved the candlelabra to a side table, and motioned Joel to a chair.

"He railed on and on about the estate and about you, ma'am. He called you names I ain't heard since the prison camp. It was more than I could stomach, so I told him to be still. Well, an Irishman can't keep still even when he's stone cold sober, and that certainly warn't the case here. He turns on me and says that he and his master will be running you and me off Claverack before long because of your, er, your *friendship* with Mr. Hedges."

Eleanora's heart missed a beat. "Hilda, bring two glasses of brandy." She fought for control, attempted to appear cool and indifferent. The brandy provided a welcome interruption, and she sipped it slowly.

"Did he mention who his master might be?"

"Yes, ma'am. Randolph Van Rensselaer, that rum-soaked drunk out of Hudson."

"Jacob's brother!"

"Yes. Gleason said he's been surveilling you upon your 'jaunts,' as he called them, and he's kept a watch outside the house in Albany, and that they have enough to run you clean off the land." Joel poured his brandy off in one gulp. "Evil business."

Eleanora was silent.

"Would there be any truth to what he said about running us out of Claverack?"

Eleanora tried to smile. "Of course not! Randolph has been famous for his delusions of grandeur."

"Aye, and still is. Encountered him Saturday at market. He's strutting the streets of Hudson with all new clothing, dressed like a peacock. There's a suspiciously smug look to him these days."

"Pay no attention to it," she said offhandedly, but her voice wavered, and she saw that Joel noticed.

They discussed back rents and Claverack's mills and carding house, then Joel left. For half an hour Eleanora gazed into the candlelight, hardly breathing. Before her she saw only sordid name-calling, endless court battles, vicious, greedy grasping for the land. Once she had stood above it all, a lady, a woman of property, deserving of respect. Now she would be dragged down in the eyes of her peers, her tenants, her family for allowing herself the simple, all too human pleasure of loving a man. She cursed her stupidity.

Eleanora could not sleep that night. She paced the room like a caged beast. Whom could she tell? No one. To admit her conduct with Daniel Hedges would be to dispossess herself. She paused at the window. The fields and barns were bathed in moonlight. She might lose this land she loved and nurtured merely because she loved Daniel, yet she did not love him any less. What could she do? Eleanora closed her eyes, slumped to the floor, and stretched full length on the cool oak. It soothed her cheek and forehead, and she pressed her breasts, hips, arms, and thighs against its polished smoothness. These lands, this house, this estate was hers, as much a part of her as was her name. Yet tonight she felt a kinship with the wretched prisoners she had seen. She must fight for these lands, and she must avoid Daniel at all costs. She regretted that she couldn't tell him why, yet she must not. No one must know. "The dead hand," she murmured in the darkness, her brow pressed to the floorboards, "the dead hand steers my life."

Soon Clinton summoned her to Albany. "You look pale and thin," he said as he kissed her cheek. "But never mind. I am running for governor, and our work will put the rose back in your cheek." He described the tremendous support he'd received for the canal project and for a gubernatorial campaign. "It seems as though we've been working on this forever, dear Eleanora. Daniel's study will be presented next week, and we will call Van Buren's bluff. What possible objection can he raise now?"

"I see none." The mention of Daniel affected her noticeably.

"Canvass White, our young genius, has returned from England with drawings of canals, towpaths, locks, bridges, and canal boats. He brought a man back with him, an Irishman, J. J. McShane, a hardy, unlettered fellow who shows precisely the muscle we'll need for the digging. How did you fare at the state prisons?"

"Oh, DeWitt, what a pitiful lot! Nowhere but in Dante have I encountered such horrors, such despair. The cells are only four feet wide and ten long, and the men are stacked to the ceiling on wooden slabs like bookcases, two or three to a cell. They sleep on moldy hay in the most unbelievable stench, and the places crawl with insects and rats."

Clinton nodded gravely. "And many simply can't pay their debts."

"They didn't look human. Their heads were shaved to prevent lice. With downcast eyes they shuffled in chains."

"I can't imagine any of them opting to stay in prison when they can be in the open air, digging." Clinton considered. "I was impressed with that Irishman McShane. The great proportion of the prisoners are Irish. He seems just the man to keep them in line. We'll use the work gangs to dig where private contractors do not respond to the letting of bids."

"I assume this young man White will oversee the contractors and the work gangs?"

"No." Clinton shook his head. "He will certainly be invaluable as an engineer, but I want to hire Hedges to oversee construction. I heard of the work he did for Commander Perry during the war. I'll put both White and McShane under him."

Hearing Daniel's name again, she involuntarily looked away. "I see."

Clinton scrutinized her. "Have you an objection?"

"No." She felt faint.

"Have you any objection?" Clinton asked again.

"No," she said, failing her attempt to be nonchalant.

"I thought you enjoyed the man's company."

"I, I do. And yet... and yet..." She was losing her composure in front of a man who'd risen to power reading the truth in the faces of men and women.

"You don't think him competent?"

"Of course he's competent."

"What is the difficulty, then?"

"None."

His voice dropped. "Eleanora?"

"Something personal."

"Something personal!" Clinton exclaimed in exasperation. "I knew it. I told you at the outset that personal feelings must not interfere with our great work, and you agreed, and now..." His voice trailed off.

Eleanora was silent, but her face flushed red. She felt she had betrayed him.

"What am I to do?" he demanded of her. "I must rely on both of you. I *need* both of you."

She stared back silently. Her own sorrow and loss far surpassed any damage to Clinton, yet she couldn't tell him. Him and his damned canal!

"I am running for governor of this state." Clinton held his hand out as if striving to grasp something intangible. "The state, the state, Eleanora, is the repository of all our hopes and dreams, it embodies our ambitions and our desires, and gives us an identity as a people. The state and the state alone provides whatever justice and protection from fear we enjoy. Men put their trust into the state, and from the state they take direction in leading their lives—what they can and cannot do. To rule, Eleanora, to rule the state nothing, *nothing* can stand in the way of guarding men's interests in liberty and property. I wish to be worthy of such a sacred trust. I cannot afford to have such, such personal difficulties in my way, particularly when they can be avoided with a little self-control."

Eleanora flinched at his lecture. She considered an angry outburst, but knew it would accomplish nothing except make her look foolish and defensive. Clinton saw her expression, and his voice softened. "You have been by my side, Eleanora, in so many undertakings. How many times have we been to Washington? Above all our other efforts, Eleanora, this canal will change the thinking of men. The completion of this canal will be the greatest hour, not only for New York, but for our nation. It will show the world the best that our system of government can accomplish. You have been most helpful, my most helpful ally, from its inception. Daniel Hedges has been invaluable since we began looking past political issues toward the actual digging."

Now his voice became conciliatory. "We cannot afford to splinter apart. That is exactly what Van Buren wants. There is too much pressure from outside to allow any division in our ranks." He reached down, and she placed her hand in his. Slowly she looked up into his eyes. "I ask you, Eleanora, to put aside any feeling you may have for the man. Work with him as another man might. Only together will we succeed. Apart we all shall fail, and fail miserably."

"Of course, DeWitt." She bowed her head in homage. "Of course I shall do so."

"Very well. Then contact him and set up a meeting. Use a subordinate if you must. We should meet soon after election day to orchestrate our drive for funds in the legislature."

"I will do so directly."

Clinton showed himself out. Eleanora sat for the better part of an hour, her mind in a hot confusion. Of course she must never tell Daniel any of this, yet if he tried to reestablish intimacy, she must fend him off and return their association to one of strictly business. She'd deal with Daniel through Joel Kipp. Let Randolph Van Rensselaer and Gleason make innuendos—they would never have proof.

23

April's special election swept DeWitt Clinton into the governor's chair, 43,310 votes to 1,479, a staggering mandate to proceed with the canal. Clinton remarked to Eleanora as they prepared for the inauguration, "Now let Van Buren obstruct us."

The *Albany Argus,* usually a Van Buren mouthpiece, editorialized that the canal's time had come, and urged a speedy passage of the funding bill. On inauguration day 1817 Daniel Hedges entered Albany on a rented horse. The ale houses, hotels, and streets were filled with drunken crowds cheering Clinton and the new age he'd usher in. Daniel proceeded to Mrs. Pratt's, but it was full, and he asked at five others until he found a room.

"'Tis a grand eve, sir," the serving girl remarked as she opened his room.

"Yes, but crowds have a habit of turning, and I wouldn't want this one against me."

"But there's no effigies burning tonight. Everyone's of one mind." The chambermaid was correct. Martin Van Buren had not even complained.

Earlier that morning Van Buren had met with Aaron Burr.

"Now, Matty, is the time to show your statesmanship," Burr said. "You must show you're bigger than their petty politics. You alone listen to the people and proceed cautiously. I read the *Argus.*"

"I proceed cautiously because today it's Clinton's mob."

"It is never wise to ignore the mob. Like a baby wailing, there's often more wisdom in what it says than in all of our philosophy."

"Yes, for a time I must support the canal."

"But cautiously, Matty, cautiously. In politics you should never close all the doors behind you. All too often you need an escape."

198

Busy that day throughout Albany in responding to what many considered a telling defeat, Van Buren returned at six to his new home on State Street for his usual change of linen.

"Everyone tells me that Clinton has bested you, dear." Hannah selected him a shirt.

"Ah, love." Van Buren removed his other. "Issues in politics are like these shirts. You wear them until they're soiled, then you change. Last year we were merely asking for more information. They complied. Now we can support the project."

Hannah shook her head. "Politics is second only to law in confounding me."

Meeting with the members of his Regency, Van Buren found them less likely to change their shirts. At the evening caucus he pleaded with them to give in.

"But we'll seem inconsistent, weak."

"Clinton will carry the day with or without us," Van Buren predicted.

"But our position will erode."

"Our position is untenable," Van Buren said quietly, his pale eyes quickly darting about. "As for consistency, the only consistency I care for is to be on the right side of this issue."

Still the men protested, vented their frustration that Tammany Hall would object to changing their votes; that Clinton now was governor, and so many relatives and friends would lose jobs; that if they didn't continue their opposition, the canal would be dug and their former votes would seem shortsighted. Van Buren watched them, listened, and smiled to himself, for he knew that by persistence and persuasion he'd eventually have his way.

Daniel passed through the streets as if he'd awakened in Bedlam. Drunken men capered on roofs howling and screaming; they leapt off wagons, danced roundels with plump women; and tavern doors flew open, spewing ragged songs and streams of revelers from their smoky taprooms.

He was glad to see lights in the windows of Eleanora's town house. He stepped up the stairs, rang the bell, and noticed a curtain sway in an upper window. The door was a long time in being answered.

"Yes?" It was Joel Kipp, and he wasn't friendly.

"Joel!" Daniel said with familiarity.

"What do you want?"

"Why, to see Eleanora, of course."

"She's receiving no one," he said flatly.

"Is she ill?"

"Yes," Joel glared, patently lying, "she's ill."

Daniel paused, looked down, then back up. Joel's expression was inscrutable. "Well, then, tell her I called and that I hope she is feeling better."

"Yes, Mr. Hedges, I'll do that." Abruptly he closed the door. Daniel paused on the porch, and noticed the window curtain above sway again. Everything seemed topsy-turvy tonight, a night they should be celebrating. He stepped to the street, shoved his hands deeply into his pockets, and ambled back to his room.

For the next two days Albany buzzed with anticipation over the canal bill vote. If approved, funds would at last be set aside for digging. Tammany Hall was unalterably opposed, yet Van Buren had mollified his voting bloc into keeping an open mind.

The vote came on the last day of session. In the gallery Governor Clinton and Eleanora hoped for passage, but steadied themselves for defeat.

"There's Daniel." Clinton pointed. Eleanora seemed startled as Daniel turned and waved. She looked away, blushing.

Four times that morning the bill was shuffled from the Senate to the Assembly for modifications. The tall clock read eleven-twenty; only forty minutes remained until adjournment. "Damn them," Clinton muttered. "They'll defeat us with their delay and their procedure." Eleanora placed her hand over his, and stole a look at Daniel. He sat in a relaxed posture, indifferent to the goings-on. A sob welled up within her. The excitement, the disappointment, the nearness of Daniel, yet the distance she must maintain—she felt she would burst into tears. Then Van Buren asked for the floor, and the Senate chamber grew very quiet.

"Now we're undone," she whispered, and threw up her hands. Clinton looked dejectedly at the floor. Van Buren would filibuster until the clock ran out, and another year would have to pass before they could begin digging.

"Gentlemen of the Senate," the little man said, "we were asked to consider such funding last year, and before us this bill returns."

"He'll draw out his *coup de grace*," Clinton muttered. "He's despicable!"

"I have studied what our able surveyor has compiled for

us, gentlemen, and I am staggered by the enormity of the project and the size of the financial commitment we are being asked to underwrite. Nowhere has a state built public work of this order."

"Why won't he thrust in his sword and have done with it?" Clinton said through clenched teeth. He rapped his walking stick impatiently on the floor.

"Last year we asked for this additional information to be able to make an informed decision. This year we can make that informed decision."

The clock read 11:51. In despair, Eleanora looked at Daniel, and he still viewed the goings-on dispassionately.

"The minor adjustments we have made over the last three weeks allow me, gentlemen, to stand before you this morning and say I believe the time for the canal has come."

Pandemonium erupted. Four justices in the gallery, canal opponents and intimates of Van Buren, nearly tumbled over the railing. Clinton's mouth dropped. Again, again, again the new lieutenant governor rapped his gavel. "Order! Order!"

Van Buren raised his hands for quiet.

"I have heard much about our fox from Kinderhook," Clinton whispered. "He is the ablest politician I have seen." He nodded to the clock. "He has become the savior of the canal, the champion of this year's session."

"Yes," Van Buren called. "We have ample findings here to commit state money for one year of digging."

Instantly Clinton was on his feet and down the stairs. He passed the sergeant-at-arms and joined Van Buren on the Senate floor. Many cheered seeing the two together, and Clinton shook Van Buren's hand warmly to signal to his followers that they should follow Van Buren's lead.

"You have shown yourself a statesman this morning." Clinton was flushed and enthusiastic.

"It will be a pleasure to unite for the good of all," Van Buren said.

Waving to his enthusiastic supporters, Clinton left the floor for the final vote. The bill passed by one vote—Van Buren's—and the chamber erupted with applause as the clock rang twelve times and the lieutenant governor adjourned. Eleanora looked at Daniel Hedges, and he was staring at her.

"Decisive vote! Decisive vote!" The canal supporters flocked to Van Buren and escorted him from the hall.

Yet when he reached the sunlight outside and the crowd

thinned, Van Buren replied to a friend's question: "Yes, we've given Clinton the money to dig his ditch. Now let's bury him in it."

Daniel vowed to see Eleanora that night. The streets were loud and joyous, and the happiness was contagious. Again the lights were on in her town house. He rang the bell and waited. The door was opened again by Joel Kipp. "Yes?"

"Please announce me to Lady Eleanora."

"I'm sorry, sir, she's receiving no visitors."

"Please announce me." Daniel glared at the young man. "Allow her to make her own decision."

Joel paused, closed the door, was gone just a moment, then returned. "I'm sorry, sir, Mrs. Van Rensselaer is receiving no one."

Daniel grew angry. "I don't believe you."

"She told me she would talk with you tomorrow at the canal board meeting."

"I don't believe she said that at all!" Daniel was furious. "I want to ask her myself."

"Sir, you should probably go."

"I tell you, I saw Lady Eleanora this morning, and I want to discuss an important matter with her."

Joel looked over Daniel's shoulder. Daniel turned and saw a man slouching against a house across the street. He thought this was a diversionary tactic. "Announce me at once!"

Joel stammered something behind the door, then the door opened fully, revealing Eleanora. Daniel had no words.

"Why don't you believe my servant?" she asked quietly.

"I didn't believe he told you what I said."

"My servants obey me. I have implicit trust in Joel, and you should as well."

Angry, humiliated, bewildered, Daniel bowed and muttered, "I am sorry to have upset your household."

"Good night, Mr. Hedges," she said with icy formality.

Daniel quickly turned and stepped to the street. As he started on his way, the man across the street called: "Care for a pint of ale?" He came to life suddenly and fell in step with Daniel. "Name's Gleason."

"Hedges." Daniel shook his hand. "Daniel Hedges."

When Daniel left, Eleanora dashed up the stairs. Joel watched, barely understanding what had happened. Eleanora ripped open the bedroom door, slammed it behind her, and threw herself on the bed. She had turned away the only man she had ever loved, and he was not likely to return. Oh, how she missed Kate! If Kate were here, she could rail and cry and pour out her heart.

Desperately Eleanora tried not to remember, but it all came back, the first night with Daniel, in this very room, the tenderness of his lips, his touch, the joy in his eyes. Now, four walls and an empty bed. No, she told herself with clenched teeth, she must not descend into self-pity, but even as she vowed not to, the sobs and the hot tears came. Oh, how she loved him! And she could never tell him the reason! She was not some silly girl who threw all she had to the wind. She felt old and sad and weary.

Meanwhile, Daniel accompanied Gleason to a warehouse on the riverbank. Inside, planks on sawhorses made a bar, and in the center of the floor a boxing ring had been roped off. Everyone spoke in Irish brogues. The crowd pressed up to the ring, cheering the boxers. In the ring two mountains of humanity battled, hairy and brawny.

"She's a game lassie, though?" Gleason leered.

Daniel ignored him, ordered two tankards of ale.

"Could you imagine returning home to that each evening?" Gleason smacked his lips and winked. Daniel paid for the ale. A roar of the crowd signaled one of the boxers was knocked unconscious. The bookmakers chalked odds on their blackboards.

Gleason licked foam from his lips. "So, how do you know her?"

"We work together on the canal project."

"Aye." Gleason saw Daniel's irritation and fell quiet.

"And now," the referee cried, "from County Cork by way of Liverpool, that battlin' brawlin' son of old Erin, J. J. McShane!" Boos and catcalls filled the air.

Into the ring stepped a wide, barrel-chested man of forty. He raised his clenched fists defiantly and strutted about the ring.

"And opposin' McShane, gentlemen, five times champion at Hannigan's Saloon, Irish Sean Malloy!" The place went berserk over the local Albany favorite. A slimmer, younger man danced into the ring, punching and feinting. Bookies chalked their odds and betting began. Some the odds were four-to-one against McShane.

"Let's get on with it, Paddy," McShane called impatiently.

The referee discussed rules, the bell rang to start the fight, and they came from their corners. Still the bookies scribbled. Malloy staggered McShane with a punch, and McShane seemed redfaced, out of breath.

"Are ye a bettin' man?" Gleason asked Daniel.

"Not usually, but I feel like gambling tonight." He thought of Eleanora. "Five dollars on the older fellow."

"He won't last three rounds!"

"But Malloy has no odds. It ain't worth risking the money."

Gleason shrugged, took the five-dollar gold piece from Hedges, and placed two bets. J. J. McShane groped around the ring like a lumbering bear. The younger man danced and jabbed and ducked and circled. Tempers rose and men screamed. When the odds reached eight-to-one a bookmaker called: "Bets are closed, gentlemen."

Now a change came over McShane. His chest expanded, his legs grew limber, and a keen defiant look flashed in his eye. He danced, feinted, and jabbed at Malloy. Each of his punches was well placed and shook Malloy to his frame.

Men pressed closer to the ring, crying desperately for Malloy to guard, to hit back, to duck. McShane's withering blows rained upon the younger man despite his fancy footwork.

"Your boy's in the winnin'," Gleason cried. Daniel nodded.

Malloy's face was a bloody mess, blood smeared down his arms and chest when one of McShane's shattering punches sent him to the sawdust. He lay there, trying to rise, sawdust clinging to the blood. The referee asked if he would return to the fight. He shook his head. As McShane crossed the ring, bent over and helped Malloy up, a small group of men who'd been standing together cashed their bets.

"Looks like you won."

"Yeah, tonight's my night for winning," Daniel said with irony.

"Shall I collect your winnings?"

"By all means," Daniel said, motioning him toward the bookmakers. Gleason returned with forty dollars in gold. Daniel watched McShane accept congratulations from the small group of men who had won by betting on him.

"We thought you were done this time," one said.

"You waited long enough."

"Only till they closed the books," McShane said, toweling himself off. "We got enough for a round of whiskeys and some rooms? I'm tired of sleeping on the floor."

"Aye, J.J. Enough for two weeks of both."

"Then let's drink!" The Irishmen moved to the bar. Four whiskey bottles appeared, and without glasses they swigged and passed them man to man.

"Good boys," Gleason observed. "Just off the boat. Probably left wives and gals back home whilst they seek their fortune." He squinted at Daniel. "You married?"

"No," Daniel said flatly.

"Do you fancy the lady?"

Daniel looked Gleason squarely in the eye. "She's a beautiful woman, 'tis true, but what would she ever see in me?" The question hung unanswered for a full minute.

"You're right."

"Well, Gleason, time I get some sleep." He clinked down ten dollars. "Buy those Irish boys a drink."

"See you again?"

Daniel nodded, pulled on his hat and left. The air off the river was cool and damp, and the river ran smooth, still, and dark. Why had Gleason been outside Eleanora's house? Daniel wondered. Then he thought of McShane. How he had played the crowd and milked their bets pleased him. Daniel thought of the deck of the *Lawrence*, red with blood after the battle. He remembered how he felt that day when Perry left, and how he felt tonight as Eleanora turned him away. Tonight it made him feel good to watch one man beat another man senseless.

He slept well and awoke refreshed. Lying in bed, he thought about what he would do now. Perhaps the canal commissioners needed something else done; if not, he should return to Buffaloe Creek. Edna was there and perhaps still single. She was more like he was anyway, more common, easygoing. Daniel realized he had misplaced his trust by putting it in Eleanora. The future was refreshingly open to him now. He would enjoy turning in his surveyor's notebooks and collecting his salary. Then he would owe no one anything, and he might leave Albany forever if he chose. Ellicott was in town. They could ride home together. Ellicott, he reflected, had been right so long ago.

Dressed in buckskin, Daniel attended the commissioners' meeting the next morning. He was uncomfortable as he, Simeon DeWitt, and five canal commissioners waited for the governor. In the dusty office they discussed geology and topography until a clerk announced Clinton's coach. Daniel watched through the window as Clinton helped Eleanora down and escorted her up the steps to the Capitol. Daniel noted that they made a fine couple.

"Thank you for coming," Clinton said. Eleanora sat regally, her eyes fixed with admiration for her governor. Today Clinton spoke with new authority. Like a military commander, he ordered them as his troops. Daniel watched Eleanora, but she did not turn his way.

"And for the digging, I have carefully considered this appointment." Daniel watched Eleanora—how inscrutable she seemed! "You'll all be pleased, as will the public when I give this to the press—Daniel Hedges will superintend the digging of the first phase of the canal."

Daniel started to clap, then Ellicott nudged him. All eyes were on him. He heard the words echo, then he looked at Clinton. The great man was clapping his hands and nodding. Taken by surprise, Daniel didn't want to embarrass himself or anyone else by refusing. Eleanora smiled and clapped her gloved hands. Ellicott was beaming congratulations.

"I shall be honored," Daniel answered their applause. Clinton motioned to one of the lads, and the young man opened the door. Bruised and smiling, J. J. McShane stepped in, folded his arms and gazed around.

"At Canvass White's behest, Mr. McShane has emigrated here from Liverpool with valuable experience in digging canals," Clinton explained. McShane nodded. "He and his Irishmen will accompany Mr. Hedges to Rome, and he will help get the digging under way." McShane waved, then left the room.

As a last item, Clinton set the official opening ceremony for July fourth. As they adjourned, Daniel watched Eleanora. She brushed past him and murmured, "Excuse me, Mr. Hedges."

Daniel met McShane in the hall. "I saw your fight last night," he told the big man. McShane had a shock of red hair and heavily freckled skin.

"Didn't lose no money, did ye?" He winked. Daniel shook his head. "Good. Always bet on J.J., Mr. Hedges. Me and the boys were a wee bit short of capital, being in America and all, and that's the handiest way to raise it."

Together he and Daniel walked outside. Daniel listened to his account of the voyage, trying desperately not to watch the slender form in a yellow gown and parasol helped into Clinton's carriage.

"Ah," McShane said, filling his lungs with fresh spring air, "ye've got the sweetest air on earth, Mr. Hedges. America!"

"Call me Daniel, J.J."

"Aye, Dan-o then it is."

"We've got a lot of work ahead of us." Daniel watched the carriage pull away as the woman sat back in its shade and closed her parasol.

Again McShane breathed deeply. "Aye, it's a new era being born, Dan-o, a new era indeed."

"So it is." Daniel nodded. "So it is."

24

As the sun rose that Fourth of July, a small cluster of men stood in a meadow outside the ruins of Fort Stanwix. Along the flat plain to the east and west, a line of stakes had been driven in the rich black soil. The men talked in low voices.

Dressed in woollen trousers, shirt-sleeves, and a beaver hat, Governor Clinton smoked a cigar. "Gentlemen, today we realize the fruit of many years' labor. We have triumphed over the disbelievers, the indifferent, and the overly cautious. Forty-one years ago today a courageous group of men put their signatures to the Declaration of Independence and gave birth to our nation. We must remember that the Declaration only signaled the beginning of a bloody seven years' war. Now we must level hills, bridge streams, scale heights, and cut through mountains to join Lake Erie with the Atlantic."

Nearby, a mule hitched to an upright plow flicked its tail. A bluejay screamed across the sky. Daniel scanned the serious faces of the other men—Eleanora had not attended the ceremony. He looked to the east, where the stakes disappeared over the horizon, then to the west. This small informal ceremony pleased him.

Clinton continued: "At last we have the funds to dig, and we shall dig as much as possible this year. Yet we must not forget our project has its enemies, able enemies. Funds may very well dry up before we dig much farther. So let us work vigorously to show the world what a free people with fore-sight and vision can accomplish on their own."

Clapping was light in the open air.

"Let us then proceed." Clinton threw down his cigar and took the handles of the plow. "Giddyap!" The mule awoke and pulled upon the reins, and the plow sank into the rich black soil and turned up the first furrow of the canal.

Daniel shook McShane's hand. "We've got much to do, J.J."

"Aye, Dan-o. So let's get on with it."

BOOK IV

25

By September contractors were digging forty miles of canal. Anxious to earn extra cash, farmers contracted and subcontracted themselves, their teams of horses and oxen, their hired hands, and their sons. Where the route had been staked out, they stripped trees and brush and dragged out stumps and root systems. They grubbed the land with plows, hauling loose earth to the sides to form embankments. Forty feet wide at its lip, sloping to a width of twenty-eight feet at bottom, the ditch was four feet deep. The sloping sides formed a prism, with a berm on the south side, a towpath on the north, and horses and oxen plodding back and forth packed the banks firmly.

Only three locks were needed along the level ground between Rome and Salina. Canvass White carefully designed the locks from sketches drawn in England. J. J. McShane scouted for suitable granite to quarry, and White experimented until he found limestone with the proper chemical composition to make hydraulic cement—cement that hardened further the longer it was exposed to water. An outcropping between Salina and Onondaga Lake provided the desired limestone.

Daniel traveled back and forth along the canal bed that summer, supervising the dig, making sure the prism was uniform, paying the contractors from a strongbox in his buckboard. He enjoyed supervising. He understood the pioneer contractors, honest, direct, and simple men who welcomed the chance to link their hamlets and farms with the markets and factories of the East. Daniel credited Oliver Perry with showing him how to command men, and yet his style was far less exacting, arrogant, and military. He paused with each contractor as if visiting, asked about difficulties, made suggestions, then offered them a swig of corn liquor from a jug beneath his buckboard seat.

Soon McShane had his forty-five Irish mates cutting and dressing granite for locks. They hauled the great granite blocks along the towpath on rollers, and measuring and checking levels, they build the first twin lock chambers, one for eastbound, one for westbound traffic. J.J. demonstrated how to caulk the lock gates of white oak with tarred hemp rope, and they hung the gates and fixed levers to open and close them. By mid-October the first lock and fifteen miles of canal were ready. The testing of the ditch and lock drew a thousand people. At a signal from a cannon the dams of feeder canals were opened and water poured into the canal ditch. A resounding cheer rose from men and women, squeals of delight from children.

Just south of Salina, J.J.'s natural showman's flair came out as he tested the Milan lock. With a flourish of his arm he commanded the downwater gates be closed, the upwater gates opened. Water poured into the lock chamber and lifted a boat on which he had placed three children. The children's fear turned to delight as the boat rose, and the crowd applauded wildly until the boat was eight feet above its former level, a gate opened, and a team of mules towed it eastward.

Praise for this small stretch of canal was universal. Daniel found the digging immensely rewarding compared to trying to garner public support and legislative votes. He took satisfaction that out of the turmoil of politics, the canal was becoming a reality under his guiding hand. Yet in his tent late at night Daniel thought fondly and sadly of Eleanora. He remembered, as he balanced his books, how happy they had been, and as he blew out the oil lamp and lay down on his cot, he felt an emptiness no amount of work or success could erase.

Eleanora's problems deepened. One muggy August afternoon Joel announced the Columbia County sheriff. "And he's got some paper, some order with him too."

As she swept into the foyer to meet him, the sheriff doffed

his hat. "Sorry, ma'am, but I must serve these papers from the court."

"What are they?"

"A summons and declaration for ejectment."

"Ejectment?" Joel demanded, advancing on the man, "I'll show you ejectment."

"Joel!" Eleanora said, then extended her hand for the papers. "Very well, Sheriff." She took them.

"Sorry, ma'am." He fumbled with his hat, glared at Joel, then left.

"But why?" Joel asked in disbelief.

"This is a matter for lawyers and courts, Joel. Don't concern yourself. I will attend to it." After dismissing him, she wished she felt the confidence she'd feigned. Upstairs she took an iron box from a secret compartment in her bedstead. The box held her mother's jewelry, twenty-three thousand dollars in gold, the deed to the Claverack estate, and the Livingston-Van Rensselaer covenant. Eleanora removed the deed and the covenant from the other papers, replaced the box, threw on her riding cloak and went to the stables.

"Saddle Arabel," she told the stable boy. He led the chestnut mare out, and as he was pulling the cinch tight, Joel Kipp appeared.

"Let me accompany you."

"No," Eleanora said firmly. "I will ride alone."

The mere taste of owning land had replaced his fondness for drink, and Randolph Van Rensselaer aggressively applied himself to advancing his claim. Though Gleason had seen Daniel Hedges enter the back door of Eleanora's town house only once, and though Gleason had been unable to draw Daniel out during the night of drinking and betting, Gleason had returned from the West with affidavits that they had shared a room nine times. "Cousin" Randolph didn't bother to ask whether the witnesses could be produced, or indeed if the evidence were truthful, and neither did the judge in issuing his order.

"Calm yourself, Lady Van Rensselaer." Alan Van Zandt escorted her to a chair. "You may challenge this, certainly. This is only a preliminary move to put you on the defensive." A florid man of fifty with great shocks of white hair, Van Zandt motioned for the documents and spent half an hour poring over the deed and the covenant, murmuring, "Hmm!" and "I see." He looked up. "Very interesting case, most interesting indeed."

Eleanora nervously adjusted herself in the chair.

"Have you read this covenant lately?"

"I'm afraid none of it makes much sense to me."

"Well, Lady Van Rensselaer, the deed is good and legal and proper. But the covenant modifies your rights to occupancy significantly." Eleanora suddenly felt faint. "Are you all right?"

"It's just the heat."

Van Zandt poured a glass of water and she sipped it.

"There's one very troublesome phrase." He scanned the parchment again. "You are granted possession of all of Claverack so long"—he read—"'as she honors her nuptial vows to foreclose the possibility of issue, and unless and until she remarries.'" Van Zandt looked up. "There's no telling how a court will construe that. It is very poorly drafted; the intent of the parties is hopelessly vague."

"Issue?" Eleanora frowned.

"Children. That clause prevents any child you may conceive and bear either in a subsequent marriage or out of wedlock from claiming the property. Chancellor Livingston included you on the deed"—he pointed to the other paper—"and so any issue you might bear would have a colorable claim to the land."

"That's preposterous!"

Van Zandt raised his eyebrows. "Don't underestimate the Van Rensselaers. They do not lose or give away property. They foresaw the possibility of Jacob predeceasing you. For their part this clause clearly intends that your becoming pregnant would dispossess you and the child, but the question is, does it forbid an affair of the heart?"

Eleanora's cheeks flushed a brilliant red.

"Certainly in your wedding vows you promised to be faithful, but that promise extends only till death may you part. Upon your spouse's death that condition is fulfilled, and, I would submit, you are released. Interesting, most interesting case."

Eleanora sat with folded hands as he read the documents again. "Mr. Van Zandt, will you represent me?"

"Not your cousins? Why, the Livingstons have the finest legal minds in the state."

"They say the chancellor helped draft that covenant," she

pointed out, "and you see how bothersome it is. In any case, I consider the whole affair too delicate for my family to become involved."

Van Zandt scrutinized her. "Does Randolph have any case at all?"

"Meaning what?"

"Meaning have the usual standards of widowhood been breached?"

"Of course not!" Eleanora lied with indignance.

Van Zandt nodded. "Then the case will hinge on the strength of their proof. I had a case of this sort regarding the custody of a child. They found the poor mother, only a girl herself, had taken a lover, and they subpoenaed him, gave him the oath. Unfortunately she wasn't frank with me. His testimony undid her. She lost the child to her in-laws. Terribly messy affair." Van Zandt peered deeply into her eye, and she felt he could read her heart. "Though nothing like your case, eh?"

"Nothing at all." She stared back at him. "So you will file the appropriate papers to challenge this ejectment, and I can ignore it?"

"Yes. You have not remarried, you are not pregnant, and you have no lover. I will suggest the delicacy of the situation to the judge and try to see what evidence Randolph has collected. Unless he has something substantial, and we both know he cannot have what is not there, that will be the end of it unless he demands a trial."

"Very good."

"You might consider a journey if he seeks a trial. Your absence from the state would delay the day of reckoning after I challenge the writ. We needn't rush into a trial."

"I'll consider it," she said.

As her horse ambled homeward, Eleanora imagined the disgrace of a public trial, the humiliation of being stripped of her lands, her dignity, her station in life; of being pauperized and turned out. She imagined Daniel in the witness box testifying. How could he or she describe their love to twelve yeoman jurors? Why should they? It was private. How could she ever face Daniel again? And what of him? Despite the consequences, Eleanora knew she would do it again, and her weakness shamed her. Daniel wasn't suffering. He had no inkling of this horrible affair. She envied his easy acceptance of life. She wanted to weep, and yet as the gables of Claverack rose into view around a stand of pine, she was filled with resolve, and spurred the horse into a trot. She must take a journey out of the state. Europe would be a suitable place to hide for a few months, perhaps a year. She would write immediately to Washington Irving in London.

26

The canal commissioners met in the governor's executive chamber to discuss the first construction season.

"Quite an elegant change, General," Simeon DeWitt said, observing the new velvet drapes and Persian carpet.

"Yes," Van Rensselaer replied. "Reflects the majesty Mr. Clinton brings to office. Quite."

Clinton emerged from his private office with Eleanora Van Rensselaer. Involuntarily Daniel turned away, then caught himself and turned back. As accustomed as he was to the labor camp and his bachelor's tent, her grace and beauty quite overwhelmed him. A diamond necklace gleamed above her pale yellow gown, and her quick blue eyes looked from man to man until they rested on Daniel. She inclined her head inquisitively and a smile quivered on her lip before she turned to Ellicott.

"Thank you all for coming." Governor Clinton sat. "We have much to discuss this morning, so let us begin."

With maps and charts Daniel reported to the commissioners that fifty-two miles of canal had been begun since July and fifteen miles and two locks were completed. He described McShane's work crew and offered his book of disbursements.

"Thank you, Mr. Hedges." Clinton folded his hands and slowly looked around the table. "I think we're all of one mind, gentlemen, that progress is far too slow." The others nodded seriously. "Our powerful adversaries in the legislature will fasten on these paltry fifteen miles to suggest it will take twenty years to complete the project. Should construction lag next year as badly, our defeat is certain."

Daniel had expected praise, and he was annoyed. Others

responded with suggestions for speeding the dig. Clinton turned to Daniel. "What do you say, Mr. Engineer?"

Daniel peered at Eleanora, and she smiled radiantly. He turned to Clinton. "We started late this year, July fourth, yet we soon had fifty miles under contract. While private contractors can supplement the digging, I believe we need a large, reliable, *permanent* work force."

Eleanora encouraged him. "You need an army, Mr. Hedges, an army of men who will dig."

"Yes. Send me a thousand, two thousand men, and our progress will surprise even the most optimistic." Other commissioners murmured that his idea was farfetched—an army of men digging. Then Clinton recognized Eleanora.

"I have visited the prisons, gentlemen, and there are seven or eight hundred able-bodied men languishing in cells for the pettiest crimes, most of them for debt. We could use them in the digging until their sentences expire."

"We have considered that," Clinton nodded, "but to use my clemency power, I need assurance they won't escape."

"Hire guards," General Van Rensselaer suggested.

"Too cumbersome. We need someone who will control and work them."

"We have such a man in J. J. McShane," Daniel offered.

"The Irishman?"

"Yes. He is tough, stern, and demanding. He can do it."

Clinton considered. Discussion followed, and the others, seeing Clinton warming to the idea, warmed to it themselves. They began to support it, even push it.

"Then let's proceed with the convicts," Clinton concluded. "And with the Irish pouring in through New York harbor. Let's get a recruiter down there and sign them up as soon as they step off the boat."

They discussed some logistics, then Clinton left for an appointment. As the meeting broke up, Daniel noticed Eleanora staring at him, and to his surprise, suddenly she smiled, walked around the conference table, and stood behind his chair.

"Hello, Mr. Hedges and Mr. Ellicott. It has been a long time indeed." Both men returned the greeting, and Ellicott excused himself.

"You look well," Daniel said. Eleanora's eyes sparkled and a mischievous smile played at her lips. "I am. I am journeying. I leave next week for Boston, then for London."

"How nice." Daniel considered, then looked up boldly.

"Would it be possible to see you before then?"

Startled, Eleanora glanced left then right and gave an embarrassed laugh. "Would that be wise?"

Daniel smiled broadly and nodded. "Certainly. London, eh?"

"Yes. Kind Mr. Irving has invited me to enjoy his literary circles there, and I find life tiresome here, now that the digging is actually under way."

"Tiresome? There are enough challenges at the dig."

"I'm sure you're equal to them."

"You should visit us sometime."

"I'd like that. After London." She whispered then: "I'll send word tomorrow night."

Returning from the dinner the legislators held that evening, Joseph and Daniel talked of Eleanora. Only men had been invited to the dinner, but her name came up repeatedly. Joseph was feeling his champagne.

"I thought that after Carrie's death you would make a bid for Eleanora's hand. You're the sort of man who needs a wife."

"She's remarkable, but unpredictable. Seems so warm and full of life sometimes, and other times so cold and distant."

"My boy, she's simply an aristocrat. You and I can never understand that. She will have things her way always and everywhere. To her, people are objects moved about like chess pieces on a board."

"But she is so far superior to other women!"

"So much so, she's unattainable." Again Ellicott patted him on the back. "Forget about her, Danny. Find yourself a woman of your station in life and get married again."

Daniel thought of Edna Kay. "But I measure every woman by Eleanora and they all come up wanting."

"A woman is a woman," Joseph said. "Forget her. Get on with your life."

Daniel did not answer.

The next day Daniel was so evasive about his evening plans, Joseph went out alone. Daniel waited for word as the church bells rang eight o'clock, then eight-thirty, then nine o'clock, then nine-thirty. When the bells rang ten, he put aside the drawings and geological text he was studying, stood, stretched, and started for the bedroom. At that moment he heard a faint tap on his door, and opening it, he saw Joel Kipp.

"Come quickly."

Grabbing his coat, Daniel followed Joel down the back stairs to a waiting coach. They rattled through the icy streets in the moonlight, neither speaking, then north along the riverbank, past the general's gracious manor house. A mile farther they halted at a small cottage by the river.

"I'll return in three hours," Joel said. The moon was nearly full as Daniel crossed the frozen yard and knocked on the double Dutch door. Eleanora opened it. She was dressed in homespun, a linen apron and bonnet.

"Why, *Vrouw* Van Rensselaer!" Daniel folded his arms and admired the effect. The simple warmth and comfort of the cottage pleased him.

"It belongs to my maid's sister," she explained. "Come in."

"And the clothing?"

"A disguise for me to get here unnoticed."

"A disguise," he repeated sarcastically.

Eleanora took a small pot from the hearth and poured hot chocolate into two delft cups on the table. "I'm afraid I'm not very good at this."

Daniel took one. "Neither am I at hiding and skulking around. Why must we go through this charade? We're adults, not youngsters."

"Please, Daniel, let us just be together tonight. I'm leaving for Europe. Let's not quarrel."

Yet Daniel meant to be heard. "I want to know, Eleanora, why you turned me away last spring. All summer I slogged through the rain and mud, haggling with woodsmen and contractors, watching over the birth of the canal—the canal that you and I and Clinton have dreamed of for so long and worked so hard to realize—and I resented being there. I despised the slowness of its progress, the sweat and the strain of cutting through forests, the plodding oxen and mules.

"Now you're leaving the country. You must know that our grand vision can easily be lost in the reality of rain and mud and fleas and mosquitoes. It was pointless, absurd to be digging a ditch when money may dry up, especially after you stopped loving me."

"Oh, Daniel, don't ever think that!"

"Your words and actions are not consistent. Why can't we be seen together? Why must we hide from the world?"

Her eyes narrowed. "Daniel, you must trust me. There are reasons, good reasons, why we must not just now. I cannot explain beyond that."

"Very well." Daniel stood to go.

"Can't you trust me? Won't you?" She stood and walked to him. "What do you think it does to me? Night after night I must lie alone, thinking of you, dreaming of those precious few times we've been together. Then I awaken to the four walls of my chamber. Life mocks me, Daniel. I, the mistress of all I see, envy my tenants their children, my mares their foals."

"But why don't you do something? Why?"

She sobbed and embraced him. "Oh, Daniel, I love you, I love you so very, very much. I cannot tell you. You must trust me. You must!" Eleanora pulled away from him, her eyes wet with tears. "Let us lie together, tonight, now!"

She led him to the recessed bed closet near the hearth. Daniel reached down and swept her up, and she parted the curtain as he lay her on the quilt. Instantly he was beside her.

She outlined his face with her finger. "Oh, Daniel!" she signed. "I want nothing but to be with you always, yet I must deny us both. I've been so foolish, and I'll not be back for months. I want to remember us together as we are tonight."

Tenderly he brushed a strand of her hair aside and touched her lips gently with a kiss.

"Oh, Daniel," she sobbed.

Slowly he kissed her, and she responded, then they gently made love.

"Oh," she sighed sleepily. "If it could only be like this always."

Daniel did not say what he thought. They lay in each other's arms for a time, then made love again.

"Daniel? It is time for you to go."

Awakening, he heard the horses jingling in their traces.

"Yes."

"Oh, Daniel, I envy you so. You live among the stars and the rocks, the forests and the water, the forces of earth and air. And I have only my four walls. I sit alone at night and dream of your digging, your commanding the men."

"You must visit us on your return. Wear the clothes you wore tonight."

She smiled and kissed him. The horse whinnied outside,

and Daniel sat up. She reached out and embraced him. They heard boots on the snow. Daniel swung his legs out of the bed closet by the hearth as a knock sounded on the door.

"I must go."

"I love you, Daniel, and I shall miss you."

"Until your return." He kissed her again, adjusted his garments, and pulled on his coat. Outside it was snowing furiously and the horses hung their heads, waiting to pull the coach along a road fit only for sleighs. Daniel paused on the threshold and peered fondly back into the simple cottage. Then he pulled on his hat, raised his collar, and walked with Joel through the snow.

"You'll be home soon enough, sir," Joel said with encouragement.

"Home." He settled into the bearskin robe and stared out at the snowstorm, the frosted trees, and the river flowing silently and dark.

Eleanora awoke with a start. Gray light seeped in through the bed curtains, and she sat bolt upright, momentarily forgetting where she was. The memories of the night returned then, and she sobbed and hugged her pillow. At last she arose, crossed to the washstand, and looked into the glass. She saw new lines along the corners of her mouth and wrinkles in her forehead that made her look older. She scrutinized her eyes. They seemed cold and sinister this morning.

Her imminent departure for London had made her adventurous with Daniel, yet in the cold light she heard his plea for their togetherness. "Oh, you fool!" she said to her reflection. "What if you are pregnant? You perfect fool."

27

*D*aniel sat in his tent reviewing maps of the work. The fifty-two miles under contract were an alternating strip of finished stretches, land scarred by a few passes of the plow, land barely cleared of brush and stumps. He heard J.J.

call out and he stepped outside to see the first group of convicts arrive.

"So, ye've been sprung by the guv'ner to dig his ditch, and your heads are all filled with dreams of whiskey and women." As J.J. circled the group, the men huddled closer together. "Ye didn't know there's a lot of backbreakin', soul-splittin' work to be done, nor did you counter on not having a place to sleep tonight. But first things must always come first, so send out the toughest man among ye, and I'll meet him presently."

J.J. walked over to Daniel. "Hard cases, eh?" Their heads were shaved, their canvas prison clothing filthy and ill-fitting. Some were barefoot on the cold mud. Daniel nodded. "Yet most are good Irish lads, Dan-o. You'll be surprised at the spirit I'll get out of them. First, though, I must slip the bit between their teeth. Pity it's always got to be this way." J.J. walked back to the group shaking his head.

From the group a great hulk of a man stepped out. His fists were the size of hams, and his forehead low, his jaw immense, and his shoulders massive knots of muscle.

J.J. put his hands on his hips. "You're the toughest of the lot?"

The man sneered. "Shamus Fitzgibbon's a name you won't be forgettin', I'm sure."

"Well, well, well, Shamus Fitzgibbon, welcome to the canal. Here we work from sunup till sundown. You'll have four meals a day soon's we get the cookhouse built. You'll get a quart of whiskey spaced out in shots during the day and forty cents wages. Now, there ain't no walls, for this ain't prison. This is the frontier. Ain't nothin' in them woods but wildcats and wolves and maybe some crazy Injuns. Do you see that man?" J.J. pointed at Daniel Hedges. The group nodded. "His word is law. He is sheriff, judge, and jury. He's the one what can land you back in prison to start serving your sentences from day one. And me, I'm the one what enforces his law." So saying, J.J. sucker-punched the big man with an uppercut and sent him reeling backward.

Shamus was shocked, then pained, then furious. He snorted, wiped blood from his nose, then crouched and ran at McShane. J.J. grabbed Shamus by the collar, rolled onto his back and pulled the big man down, set his feet in Shamus's groin, then flipped him over in the air. Dazed, Shamus stumbled to his feet, growled, and advanced again. He dealt J.J. a withering blow to the stomach, and J.J. countered with a punch to the man's jaw that nearly broke his fist. The man squeezed J.J.'s neck, and it looked like he would simply pluck J.J.'s head off his shoulders, until J.J. buried his heel in the man's instep then sank his knee in the man's groin. Shamus expelled a loud rush of air, his eyes rolled back into his head, and J.J. reached up, striving on the bald head to find hair to pull. Instead he grabbed Shamus's ears and brought his face down upon his upraised knee four times.

As Shamus struggled to stand, J.J. hauled back and with all his might landed a blow upon his nose. Shamus fell back sprawling in the mud and melting snow, and after a meager attempt to rise, just sighed and lay still.

"Now that we understand each other," J.J. said, catching his breath, "we'll begin by building you boys a camp so you won't be sleeping under the stars." He reached down and helped Shamus Fitzgibbons up. "But first, I know you've been languishing in state's prison, so let's have a drink."

A cheer went up. J.J. rolled a whiskey keg from his tent, and the men clustered about it, reaching for the few tin cups he handed around or cupping their hands and straining toward the tin dipper. Daniel returned to his maps and drawing.

Soon the woods behind his tent were ringing with whoops and the blows of axes felling trees. For an hour they worked, sang, and shouted. Suddenly the men were screaming wildly and a pistol shot rang out.

"'Tis only a snake, lads," J.J. called. "When St. Paddy drove them from the holy ground, why, like you, they come slitherin' to the New World. Sure and if the land hereabouts ain't crawling with snakes. But take heart—only the poison ones can hurt ye."

How will we ever survive the Irish? Daniel mused.

Daniel's fears were allayed when he saw them dig. Energetic, fond of laughter and song, the Irish sprang to the digging each morning; they joked and dug and drank their sixteen rations of whiskey, and ate their four meals with abandon. Many had been bogtrotters and peat cutters in the old country, others had raised horses, and so showed great prowess as teamsters.

More arrived constantly. Clinton granted hundreds clemency, for he saw the canal's future depended on the 1818 digging season. Agents along the New York City docks signed

Irish immigrants as soon as they stepped down the ramp to "come and earn a steady wage."

They arrived on the frontier in waves, trudging in gangs over the turnpike and towpath. J.J. devised an organizational structure as new camps sprang up along the staked-out course of the canal. He searched for physical toughness, for lieutenants who commanded respect. According to his merit system, if another man "whupped" his boss in a fair fight over an issue considered fair in J.J.'s judicial opinion, he would be promoted to gang boss, and the unfortunate loser was demoted or moved to another crew.

"New blood, Dan-o, we always need new blood. If they believe they'll advance, they'll work and fight like dogs. That's the secret, Dan-o. Every Irishman is a king in his heart. So long as an Irishman believes he's his own master, there's nothing he won't do to further his interest. But cage him up, press him down, cut off the hope that tomorrow will be better, and he becomes a vile, nasty customer."

J.J. imposed the routine, and steadily the canal crept westward. He kept a sharp eye on the lines of the berm, the prism, and the towpath to assure they were true. Rarely did he bother Daniel with questions. For days at a time Daniel and Canvass White left the dig to ride west and prepare the route for autumn and the following spring. Five locks would be needed to drop the canal into the dreaded Montezuma Swamp, then nine or ten more to lift it to high ground farther west. They took borings at each lock site to find bedrock, and they scouted likely quarries for granite and limestone, and stands of white oak for lock gates.

By late summer three thousand Irish immigrants and convicts were working on a hundred miles of canal. They lived in ramshackle bunkhouses, shanty towns of bark huts where each night they collapsed and snored so soundly on slabs, they rarely noticed the clouds of bloodthirsty mosquitoes.

As he moved his tent and belongings westward to keep on the forefront of the digging, Daniel became friendly with many of the workers. When the leaves blazed and frost gripped the earth, Daniel moved his tent to Montezuma to survey a course through the swamp. On a warm Sunday morning during Indian summer, he and J.J. walked down to the edge of the Cayuga Marsh.

"Aye, but 'tis a foreboding place, Dan-o. I shan't be too keen on working through this next spring."

Behind them on the hill the trees were gold and crimson. Before them lay a morass of tangled roots and dead limbs, as if the very life of the trees had been sucked down into the black water and green scum.

"There's many a fever lurking in there, J.J."

"Aye. We'll lose many boys."

"Canvass is trying to design a way to dig in that muck. We'll need to race through as quickly as possible."

"Aye, but it'll take a season at least."

Then they scaled the hill and left the swamp behind. "I say, Dan-o, but autumn makes the heart sad, don't it?'

"I suppose." Daniel had asked J.J. many questions about England and London, and he used these descriptions as backdrops for imagining Eleanora's travels. From the camp across the meadow came a melodic lilt of the Irish elbow pipes. The resplendent sky, the brilliant leaves, and the sweet sad sound of the Celtic melody caused Daniel to ask: "What is that tune, J.J.?"

"Ye have a fine ear, Dan-o. 'Carrickfergus,' an ancient air that come down from heaven, to be sure. Did you ever take a wife?"

Daniel was shocked at first, but then he saw J.J. was remembering his own lost love. "Yes, yes, I did. A wife and two babies. They were killed by the British during the war."

"I'm sorry, Dan-o. And since then, lad, has there been anyone?"

"Just one, but she couldn't decide whether to wed, so it came to nothing. You?"

"Aye." J.J. nodded. "I made the great mistake. Turned a sweet-tempered milkmaid into a mean-spirited shrew. Astonishing how they change! Bore me two sons and a daughter, she did, before she left. I was in Liverpool. She returned to her Da in County Mayo. Took me wee ones too. Ah, I was hard at the liquor for a while over that, but me mates brought me about. Wasn't too long afterward old Canvass came snoopin' about with his spectacles and sketch book, and I'd heard stories about American women." He spread his arms in the sunshine. "So I'm here. But where are they?"

"What did you hear about American women?"

"That they're independent and saucy."

Daniel smiled, applying the epithets to Eleanora.

"'Course, it wouldn't do just now to involve meself with a woman. Got to stay mean. There's many of the men itching to knock down the straw boss and take me job. But when the diggin's done..."

They drew near the shantytown named Kilkenny by the men, and a tin whistle and fiddle and the Irish pipes sent sweet notes quivering high into the bright sunshine among the gold and crimson leaves.

"Whatever is that tune now? It's so sweet and haunting!"

"'Tis an old air about a sailor who fears he'll never see his true love more."

Daniel listened carefully to the Irish air. He was a sailor in his heart, lured inland by Eleanora, trying with sweat and strain to link Lake Erie with the sea. The song conjured up emotions only a sailor could know. Daniel murmured to himself, "If I might only open my landlocked heart!"

J.J. threw his arm over Daniel's shoulder. "I suppose you and me are two of a dying breed, because we won't sit still. But let's not get glum and moody, Dan-o. We'll have Mick strike up a rouser, and I'll demonstrate a few jigs."

They entered the camp. The melody that had tinged the afternoon with a lovely sadness wafted off into silence, and the men called out for more. J.J. filled two tin cups at the whiskey cask. Daniel felt uncomfortable among the wild and motley group. He listened to a few songs, shared the whiskey, then returned to his tent.

At sunset Daniel lay upon his cot. He thought of Eleanora, and remembered how she had looked as a simple Dutch vrouw. Her elegance, her grace, her passion made such a simple presence grand. It was impossible for him to favor another woman, he knew, and the ineffable sadness of the Irish pipes gave this sad feeling a voice. Especially that one lovely Irish air, quivering high in the autumn sun. But the air had ended, the men clapped and drank whiskey and cried for more lively tunes, and his precious moment of insight was trampled beneath jigging, roughshod boots.

When Daniel closed his eyes, he dreamt not of bright autumn leaves, the bright skies of Indian summer, or sweet Irish airs, but of the foul, murky swamp that lay before them.

28

*L*ady Eleanora booked passage aboard the *Ariel* and left Boston harbor early in April. She stood at the railing watching the land recede behind the massive gray swells. Exhilarated by the clean sea air, she remembered fondly the afternoon upon Lake Erie with Daniel.

A month later the Isle of Wight rose into view, and the *Ariel* soon passed on to Southhampton. As the ship was moored, Eleanora saw Irving among the crowd, and she gaily waved her lavender scarf. Down the gangplank she hurried, and he met her at the bottom with a kiss. He seemed far older than the last time she'd seen him. Gray streaked his hair, his skin was sallow from too little sun, and he seemed tired and drawn.

"You look ravishing, Eleanora!" He held her at arm's length. "You don't know how ecstatic I was when you wrote. How long can you stay?"

"As long as I'm welcome." She kissed him on the cheek.

"Then you shall never leave!" He skipped gaily about. He led her arm in arm along the quay to an inn where he'd secured lodging for the night.

Over dinner that evening—"English food is very bland," he told her, "they steam and boil the flavor out so you need to spice it up with ale"—Eleanora relayed news of Clinton and Van Buren, the politics and the canal. "Forgive me for thinking this way," Irving said, "but I cannot see how anyone could take all that seriously."

"But the canal will bring wonderful prosperity to our state!"

"I'm quite sure it will. But all the strategies, the feints and jabs—I would find it tiresome. And dear Eleanora, what is won when the shouting and the smoke clear? Headaches and responsibilities that you never bargained for, and the awful midnight fear that someone else will take away your power. No." He shook his head and held up his tankard for a refill. "Political office is not worth the price it exacts."

"And yet I remember a certain author who befriended Dolly Madison and sought an appointment."

Irving shook his head sadly. "That was shortly after poor Matilda died, and I sought an ambassador's post in vain. Matilda, then Theodosia. Ah!" he sighed, and seemed about to weep. He swigged his ale. "This world is too cruel to allow such beauty to survive. Why, we should be absolutely frantic, dear Eleanora, if anything happened to you."

"We? You and who else?"

"Why, me and my characters. I have been ever so prolific these days!" He grew excited. "Last autumn I visited the great man himself, Sir Walter Scott, at Abbotsford. He had read a few of my sketches, and how encouraging he was! He said that in my work America had produced a new voice, a new sort of literature, and he told me I must keep writing."

"Well of course you must. Sir Walter Scott! How wonderful."

"To write accurately about America, I'm convinced, you must live as an expatriate." He finished his ale and ordered another. "I've got some sketches for you to read, sketches about the Hudson Valley, I've developed the most charming characters from folk tales you and I were weaned on. I hope to publish them next year. But you must be kind in your criticism. They're not quite finished."

"Of course, of course."

They talked awhile longer, then Eleanora went upstairs, leaving him glassy-eyed, gazing into the hearth, ordering yet another mug of ale. In her room Eleanora was saddened by her first encounter with Irving. He seemed defeated, resigned, his "sketches" as much an escape as the ale.

They hired a coach next day to carry them up to London. As excited as a schoolboy, Irving pointed out everything he could along the way. A gray sky hung over the green land, and when Eleanora remarked about this, Irving said: "It is always so. You must go to Italy and Spain for sun."

"It seems rather melancholy."

"No, my dear, *thoughtful*—thoughtful is a better word." They stopped for dinner in Winchester, and Irving led her through the sanctified cloisters of the cathedral, where the moody gray light softly infused the stained glass. A choir practiced an intricate hymn, young boys' voices rising like the singing of angels into the dim Gothic vaults.

"Imagine the legions of nameless, faceless laborers who worked upon scaffolding generation upon generation to raise up this house of worship," Irving whispered. "Some of them carved their own faces and faces of their wives and children high in those vaults. Sort of like my characters."

"What faith and dedication! It is inspiring, Washington. How different from our stern Protestantism."

"Our modern era offers nothing to compare."

Eleanora didn't agree as they strolled through the dim, echoing chapels. She saw a parallel, yet she didn't relate it to Irving because he would scoff. She saw the grand canal as a later day effort, motivated not by religious faith, to be sure, but by the desire for commerce and trade. Yet it was on the scale of this cathedral—a grand, communal work, an embodiment of a people—and Daniel was its architect and builder. Clinton's efforts were meant to crown himself king by undertaking the great project, she thought; Irving's works mere embellishments, gargoyles.

London enchanted Eleanora: the crowded, jostling streets; the taverns and teeming waterfront; the lavish town houses and public buildings. Since Waterloo an energetic spirit filled the city. The empire was expanding, and the prosperity and pride infused people's conduct with hope and joy. So, too, would New York State be, Eleanora reflected, when the canal was completed.

Because Irving was a celebrity, invitations were frequent. "I try to keep amused," Irving answered when she asked him if the social whirl ever stopped. And he did. He danced, he applauded from his theatre box, he traded *bons mots* with witty young playwrights, he flirted with duchesses and dowagers, and constantly he drank. He drank ale for breakfast, Madeira at dinner, whiskey at tea, claret or Chablis at supper, champagne at parties. Eleanora was alarmed. When she mentioned it, he only shrugged. She tried to ignore it after that, but she saw his talent being dissipated. It saddened and disgusted her.

True, he masked his true feelings with happy, sentimental prose, with doggerel and gay laughter. True, his expatriatism gave him an objective view of his homeland. True, he was well-regarded. Yet as the weeks wore into a month, Eleanora sensed his profound sadness beneath it all. Whether caused by the death of his beloved or his absence from his brothers, the sadness had conquered him, and he made no effort to rid himself of it, but merely drank it into dullness.

Although invited everywhere, Irving was only on the periphery of the city's, the nation's, the empire's life, she saw.

The royalty, the nobility made the policy that expanded the empire. They ordered the troops to the field, the navy to the seas. Irving was merely an artist. Eleanora longed to involve herself in a far greater enterprise than the pursuit of fun. She missed the bold courage of Daniel Hedges. As primitive as it was, it stood for something. At the end of two months she knew she must return to America.

Their farewell was painful. For three days after Eleanora announced she wished to return to America, Irving remained blind drunk, weeping in private. She told him he talked "sweet nonsense" when he said that of all the women he had ever met, she alone had the will, the integrity, and maturity he admired. She booked her passage. Still he was determined. He hired a private dining room at Gray's Inn and instructed the cook to prepare a savory roast mutton. He had champagne brought up, and under the guise of a farewell dinner, he toasted Eleanora.

"My dear," he said during the soup course, "a plan has been forming itself in my head of late."

Eleanora peered up roguishly. "Another plot, new characters?"

"Yes." He sipped the wine and warmed to the idea. "Absolutely! You and I, Eleanora, we're not what they call young—"

Suddenly she knew what was coming. "I'm terribly flattered," she tried to head him off, "but I cannot remain. Oh, Washington. I never knew you felt so."

"Stay, Eleanora! Stay here! London is the place for you, not the wilderness of Albany and the West. Your spirit needs gaiety, the finer things, civilization. Our mutual regard over the last twenty years has matured. If you prefer, we might live together as brother and sister. Just allow me the smallest chance that we might marry—no, no, no, you needn't decide tonight! I'd rather you took time for mature reflection. I merely want to open up the possibility for you."

"I'm very touched, my dear, dear friend." Eleanora saw his sadness laid bare, and it greatly upset her. "You have been so very kind these last two months, but I'm afraid I shall live and die an old maid."

He quaffed his wine and poured another. "Was . . . was your life with Jacob so very rich you can't bear another?"

"Partly," she lied.

"Please, Eleanora, I beg you, don't dismiss the idea out of hand. Think upon it. I shall write. Answer my letters. Perhaps in a year or so."

"I am rather set in my ways."

"Oh, I can accommodate that! I will accommodate anything for you! But," he said then, with false nonchalance, "let's discuss the matter no further tonight. I only wanted to acquaint you with a thought I'd had," and he shrugged off her refusal by plunging into the next course and the next bottle of wine.

A week later Eleanora watched the Isle of Wight recede behind the gray-green seas. Gulls screamed and sharply banked, and the bright August wind snapped the colorful flags.

"I forgot others had heavier burdens," she murmured, and made up her mind, as the sunset burnished the North Atlantic, that she'd put her life in order, resolve the property dispute, see the canal finished, and come to some sort of understanding with Daniel.

Upon reaching New York that September, she learned DeWitt Clinton was at his Flushing estate. She also learned that Maria, his wife of twenty years, had died. Immediately she hired a coach, ferried to Brooklyn, and proceeded to his mansion.

Black crepe still hung from the windows and doors of the great house. Old William showed her to an anteroom. "I'll tell the governor you have come. Things, as you may understand, are not as they once were."

In a few minutes a door opened and Clinton limped in, hunched over a cane. "It's good of you to come." He looked pale and weak.

"Oh, DeWitt! I just heard about Maria! I'm so very sorry." She rushed to him and embraced and kissed him.

"Come in, come in," he said, ushering her into a large rear parlor whose chilly gloom was not relieved by the small fire in the grate. Eleanora asked many questions. Maria had died of consumption in late summer. "Three of the boys were with me at her bedside, and Sadie, of course." He sighed, and it shook his large frame. "Not long after the funeral I fell off Zephyr while riding to the hounds. I have been as you perceive me, a cripple in body, heart, and soul."

"Oh, DeWitt!"

"It wouldn't be so bad for me now that she's gone, Eleanora, if I hadn't neglected her so these last fifteen years." He peered up at her, and his overwhelming grief shocked her. "Everything came before Maria. Politics, scientific research, the canal, the war, the smallest, most tedious affairs of state— and she, kind heart, stood back in the shadows and bore it all happily, patiently. She'd not see me for months at a time, and when I returned, worn down from an expedition or throttled by a debate or a series of newspaper editorials, she'd sit in my lap like Sadie does now, and she'd hold me. 'At least we have this time together,' she'd say. 'You make me so very proud and happy.'" He cradled his forehead in his right hand. "I have never fallen off a horse in my life. Trying to forget my grief, I agreed to go fox hunting, and I fell off Zephyr, the mildest in my stables!"

There was a long silence as the man sat and gazed into the fire.

"DeWitt, may I remain with you here awhile?"

He looked up, surprised. He squinted as though he had just noticed her. "Of course, as long as you wish. I don't need to be in Albany until session begins after New Year. Stay with me until then."

"I'd like that." She went to him and entwined his strong fingers in her own. "I'd like that very much."

Clinton sighed and touched her hand. "Good, kind Eleanora. We must build up the fire, warm up the place for you. I'll call William." Stiffly he started to rise.

"Now, just sit there, DeWitt. I'll see that everything is done."

29

The 1818 digging season was an unqualified success. Sixty-two miles of canal were open, greatly reducing shipping costs from central New York to the Mohawk Valley. Yet only five of sixty locks had been built, and the canal threaded through relatively flat lands. They still faced enormous engineering problems—rivers to be bridged, cliffs to be scaled, and three hundred miles to be dug. The greatest immediate threat was the Montezuma Swamp.

"Aye, Dan-o, I worked peat bogs as a lad. Tough duty, believe me, but nothing like what's waitin' for us next summer."

Daniel and J.J. were riding through the snow with their yearly report for the Canal Commission. Daniel was absorbed in other thoughts. Ellicott had told him that Eleanora had returned and was staying in New York City. Three days ago a whiskey merchant told him the governor's wife had passed away. Daniel drew the conclusion that Eleanora was living with Clinton.

"We'll need more men and teams," said. "A pity we can't work the lads all winter. They'll be like an army itching for combat by spring."

"Yes," Daniel agreed. "Waiting is always the hardest to do."

After delivering his report to Clinton and the commission, Daniel paused on the Capitol steps while Clinton limped down the icy stairs on a cane. A coach and four drove up State Street and stopped. When the door opened, Daniel saw Eleanora inside.

Nearby, one of the canal commissioners said: "She's been living with him since last summer. Shameful. His wife wasn't cold in the ground yet, and he took up with that Van Rensselaer widow."

"Oh," said another in a superior tone. "They've been carrying on secretly for years. Everyone knows that."

Daniel turned, enraged.

"She's a spirited one, they say. Uses her widowhood to conceal her affairs. Be interesting to see if she can get Clinton to the altar now."

Daniel was stupefied with rage. Just then he saw J.J. coming to meet him. Daniel hailed him.

"How did it go, Dan-o?"

"Well enough, well enough."

"You don't look like it did."

Daniel glared at him. "I can't get away from here fast enough."

"Well, friend, there's a lot of good whiskey to be drunk, and if there's any left in Albany when the sun rises tomorry, why, it won't be my fault!" He led Daniel to a tavern.

They spent the afternoon in waterfront bars. For sport J.J. battled a hefty stevedore and won a fifty-dollar prize. They drank poteen, ale, and corn liquor, and J.J. sang and danced Irish jigs with men playing fiddles and squeezeboxes. Daniel awoke in a room that reeked of perfume and saw a tousled head in the bed next to him. He moved to rise, and the girl turned, clacked her tongue and opened her eyes. She was an Irish beauty with dark hair and deep violet eyes. "Leavin', me love?"

"Yes." Daniel was mortified that he couldn't remember what had happened.

"Well, do come again." She laughed lasciviously. He saw some greenbacks on the bureau, and he dug into his pocket and left two more for her. "Now ain't you the sweetest?" Downstairs Daniel discovered they were in a fancy bordello. J.J. sat on a sofa talking with disheveled girls as if he were the owner. "Top o' the marnin', Dan-o. Sleep well?" Daniel muttered something in reply. "Katie here's from County Kerry, Jane from Cork, and the twins"—he smacked his fingers—"the twins, they're from Dublin City."

"Let's go."

"Sure, Dan-o, sure." Promising to return, J.J. bid farewell. In the morning light Daniel remembered what he had heard yesterday and had been trying to forget all night. "We'll pack and start back this afternoon."

"Ah, Dan-o! 'Tis a long, long year on the dig. Another day, a coupla more women..."

J.J. fell quiet at Daniel's sharp glance.

In the governor's suite farther up the hill, Eleanora had arrived from her town house for breakfast. Clinton was in an unusual mood.

"You seem awfully cheerful today," she remarked.

"I am." He showed her to the table and they began a breakfast of herring, eggs, and toast. "I have made a great decision, a wonderful earth-shaking decision."

"Does that make today different from others?"

"Quite." He glowed with joy and pride. "I'm going to remarry." Eleanora nearly choked on the herring. "You must be happy for me."

"I am, I am. Who...who will be the lucky Mrs. Clinton?"

He saw her dismay, and reached across the table. "You are to be the first to know, Eleanora, because I need to share my joy with my dearest, closest friend. I must pledge you to secrecy until the formal announcement. Catherine Jones."

"I know Kitty. I'm very happy for both of you."

"We must wait until the legislative session is far along, so the wedding will not distract my enemies or the public from the issues."

"I understand, of course." Her appetite flagged. "Isn't this rather sudden?"

"Oh, we've been seeing each other since Maria passed away."

Eleanora scowled. She had believed she knew Clinton before. Now she knew him better. She had been at his side for two months and never suspected his romance. Thus, she silently concluded, he had been seeing Kitty before Maria's death. Catherine's father was a banker and would be most useful in financing another presidential bid. She could see them together, hugging, kissing, while in the next room Maria lay dying. She regarded Clinton, who now ate with a healthy appetite.

"I wanted her to join us for breakfast today, but she preferred I tell you alone."

"Oh, so she's in Albany." This depressed Eleanora, because she realized that she had been Clinton's decoy for two months—allowing people to see them together, mourning his Maria while he'd been carrying on a secret love affair.

"I have often wondered, Eleanora, why you did not remarry." She glared at his impertinence. "I simply cannot get along without someone sharing my life," he added. "Life is far too short to forego such intimacy and companionship."

"I would rather you spared me the sermon!" She was indignant, angry, bitter. Tears pressed at her eyes. She abruptly threw down her napkin, rose from the table, and realizing she could not very well flee, she went to the window, breathing deeply to calm herself.

"I'm sorry." Clinton was at her back, his hands on her shoulders, "Please forgive me. I am too often insensitive to the feelings of others." She turned to face him. He looked sympathetic. "Your feelings have not been altogether platonic?"

"Yes, DeWitt, yes, they have. I have enjoyed our companionship these last few months, and I regret it will end."

"Why do you not find someone?" he asked again. "Why not remarry?"

She narrowed her eye. "I can't."

"Why, of course you can!"

"No, DeWitt. I cannot."

"But why?"

She turned away from him and leaned her hands on the windowsill. "When I was betrothed there were negotiations between my family and the Van Rensselaers regarding Claverack. We agreed on the eve of the wedding that I might keep all of the estate in the event of Jacob's death only if I did not remarry. A future marriage would mean I'd forfeit everything. My two sisters are spinsters without property. I have seen how they live."

"But that's absurd. Even if you give up Claverack, you still have the right to one-third of its income for your life."

"No, we bargained that away."

"*You* did?"

"Well, my father did. He and the chancellor wrote out the covenant. You know what a woman's desires and legal rights are worth. Without her father or her husband agreeing, a woman has no rights at all. They hold all her property, and they can dispose of it at their whim."

"But not without her releasing her rights. Did you sign the covenant?"

"Why, I must have." Then she thought. "No, I don't believe I did. No, I didn't."

"Then you are entitled to dower, the right to income for your life in one-third of all Jacob owned."

"That's what I should have, but I have no longer. The contract. They told me about the contract. In any case, what use is mere money if I lose my beautiful Claverack?"

"But the contract doesn't bind you because you didn't sign it. Perhaps the chancellor wanted to hoodwink the Van Rensselaers. Perhaps your father thought he was securing you far greater rights than you would otherwise get. They knew the value of Claverack, and either didn't consider the right to remarry that important or believed a second husband could support you as well."

"But I'm afraid you're wrong." Eleanora turned and stared at him for a long moment. "The next in line to Claverack, Randolph Van Rensselaer, has brought an ejectment action to dispossess me, and I have consulted a lawyer."

"A lawyer? Eleanora! I'm the governor!" Clinton held her by the shoulders. "The Van Rensselaers knew Jacob preferred the company of men. No doubt they wanted to discourage you from other love affairs to keep his reputation unsullied."

"But the chancellor?"

"He must have known your antenuptial contract wasn't worth the wax that sealed it. No doubt he was appeasing the Van Rensselaers. Perhaps he got something else from them. And after all, you have been allowed to enjoy all of Claverack since Jacob's death. The chancellor knew you couldn't be cheated of your dower. No doubt that's why he had your father sign. It was a big hoax, Eleanora, each family trying to outsmart the other."

"And so I have suffered under this delusion for years? Just because they played tricks with the law?"

"What have you lost? Nothing."

"Nothing," Eleanora whispered. "Nearly a decade. All that time, DeWitt, time that cannot be recovered. They manipulated the law to cause me untold embarrassment and shame! I have lived as a widow because of their law."

Clinton shrugged. "I can't speak for your families, but don't blame the law. It will be that very law that will save you, and obtain at least your dower's interest. Why didn't you consult me about this before?"

"I wanted to keep it secret, DeWitt. They are hanging their case on my . . . my, indiscretions." She dropped her eyes. "And there have been a few, all too few."

He shook his head. "When you want a favorable decision, don't go to a lawyer, go to the judge."

She looked up sharply. "You aren't that cynical."

"Cynical? That's precisely what to do. You must get to the judge before he renders an opinion, so there will be no chance the opinion will be adverse."

"DeWitt, you're not suggesting we tamper with the courts?"

"Not tampering, just assuring justice is done. You must win, Eleanora. You cannot believe how many wrong decisions are rendered. Your rights are guaranteed by the laws of this state, and you must get what you're entitled to." He scrutinized her very closely. "Are you sure you did not sign the agreement?"

"Yes."

"Absolutely?"

"Yes. I have it at Claverack. It is easy enough to prove."

"Then let me talk to the judge—Judge Edmonds isn't it?"

She nodded, then dropped her eyes. "I wish you wouldn't get involved in this, DeWitt. I thank you for your interest, but if the law is as clear as you say, I won't need your help."

"Never mind, never mind, just let me take care of everything." It was Clinton's way to make amends. He embraced her. "It's a grand day for us all, isn't it?"

"Yes." And Eleanora surrendered to the safety of his arms.

Daniel returned to the work with a hollow sense of duty. The Montezuma Swamp lay before them, stagnant and foul, its muck offering small promise for a channel, a firm berm, or a towpath.

Daniel ordered the convicts and Irish out of their winter quarters early to fell whole stands of oak, and he constructed a sawmill to cut the logs into piles and planks. Only by driving piles and building a wall could they keep the muck they shoveled out from oozing back. Nor were his spirits lifted by the news from Senator Hartwick of Oneida that Clinton was remarrying. This shocked and hurt him. She has loved Clinton all along, he thought, and he felt foolish and used. Work was his only comfort now, the canal his only mistress. He worked feverishly.

Ice was on the fetid water when they began digging that year. Frost reached three feet into the ground, and the congealed muck made easy digging, yet the sloppy last foot of black slime showed them what they would be encountering all summer.

One by one Daniel built five camps through the swamp on what high ground he could find. The men nailed up their shanties, bunks, and cookhouses, but the swamp prohibited a connecting roadway.

"Only way out of here is to dig," J.J. told the work gangs he led in. "So let's get on with it." The men responded, and the ditch progressed.

"Dan-o, Dan-o," J.J. said one afternoon as Daniel poled a barge out of the swamp to the lumber dock for another load. "Ye've got to slow down, lad. Your second trip today. Leave the third for the men. Won't do to get yourself sick."

"We must make progress before the mosquitoes rise. You've never seen the malaria."

"Aye, but take precautions so you ain't one what gets it. Leave the barge. My man Feeney'll pole it back to them inside. Come dine with me tonight. I have a fine bottle of the Irish."

Daniel accepted. In the six weeks of digging, he'd taken great comfort in J.J.'s expansive good nature. At an old campsite overlooking the swamp, J.J. built a fire. They fried salmon, trout, and bass with potatoes and onions, and they drank the Irish whiskey.

"Ye've seemed sad recently, Dan-o."

"It'll pass, J.J. It'll pass."

"Progress is good so far, and I heard tell Ben Wright is opening twelve miles next week." J.J. waved his arm toward the setting sun. "Now ain't that a sight, Dan-o?" The sky was a fiery lake as storm clouds massed in the west. The sun reflected a red gold in the water of the canal, smooth and straight and due west.

"Behold, J.J." Daniel waved the neck of the bottle at the canal. "Behold what one man did for the love of a woman."

"Aye, Dan-o, he built her a highway of gold, a highway to the sun."

"No." Daniel shook his head, and swigged the liquor. "Straight into a swamp."

Governor DeWitt Clinton presided over the Council of Appointment, the body that appointed all officers in the state, including judges. Power had seesawed on the council between Clinton's faction and the Tammany Hall Bucktails. Tammany needed one of Clinton's men to secure an appointment, and they had succeeded in turning one in 1816 to get Martin Van Buren appointed attorney general. When Van Buren resigned his judgeship and left Hudson to reside in Albany, the council appointed Nathaniel Edmonds to succeed Van Buren as surrogate and soon Edmonds advanced to the state Supreme Court. Edmonds knew what hand fed him. When Clinton summoned him to Albany, a sense of gloom descended. Tammany had put him in office, but he mustn't irritate Clinton. He hated politics, but he enjoyed wearing the judicial robes.

Clinton, though, was affable and relaxed, not at all angry when he entered the executive suite. "So kind of you to come, Judge," he said, and asked about the judge's family before the two talked about the weather.

Then, obliquely, Clinton asked: "Are you aware of an action for ejectment pending against the widow of Jacob Van Rensselaer?"

"Why, yes, yes, I am, Governor. There have been several stays requested and it's finally come to me for trial."

"Yes. What do you see as the merits of the case?"

"It is highly unethical to—"

"Of course, of course. But you understand the petitioner has a heavy burden to bear in proving his case."

"Quite."

"My interest, Judge, is purely curiosity. I assume the losing party will appeal to the chancellor for equitable relief, but the plaintiff's claim appears to have so little merit, while its potential damage to a woman's property interests and reputation would be grave. Do you agree?"

"Quite right, sir. I agree fully."

"Good."

Clinton abruptly stood, signaling the meeting was over. "Let me stress again, Judge, my interest is only that of curiosity, yet any leeway you may extend will be noticed, rest assured."

"The matter will receive my most careful scrutiny." Edmonds shook his hand and left the Capitol relieved. A simple ejectment! The triviality of it made him laugh, and he strolled down the broad thoroughfare of State Street in high cheer. Then his eye caught a lawyer's shingle: MARTIN VAN BUREN, ESQ. He tapped his cane and decided to visit his old friend.

Van Buren's clerk answered the door, and the senator happened to be home. Van Buren bustled out from the back room, his eyes sparkling, and he pumped Edmonds's hand with vigor. "What brings you to the capital?"

"Why, the funniest thing." Edmonds scratched his head. "I was summoned by Governor Clinton over a simple ejectment proceeding."

"You don't say." Van Buren directed him to his office. "Come in, do come in."

After Van Buren told certain gossip mongers that DeWitt Clinton was tampering with the courts in Columbia County, the whispering campaign began. A week later a letter to the editor ran in the *Albany Argus*:

SIR:

A matter of burning importance concerns me today.

QUERY: What state official recently met with a Supreme Court Justice, threatening to rescind his appointment if a case was not decided in a particular way?

ANSWER: An official wishing to help a widowed lady keep lands she occupies wrongfully. This high official, influential with the Council of Appointment, believes he is above the law.

Such blatant court-fixing offends every citizen of this state and cries out for an investigation. At the very least we should closely watch the calendar of the Columbia County Supreme Court.

CATALINE

"This is abhorrent!" Clinton raged, hurling the paper into the love seat in Eleanora's parlor. "I made it exceedingly clear to that oaf Edmonds that I took only a passing interest in your case!"

"But you spoke robed with the power of your office, DeWitt, and the judge interpreted it so." It quite upset Eleanora to see her case in the press. A profound weariness came over her. She'd planned to leave for Claverack to consult with Van Zandt, but Clinton had just arrived unannounced and beside himself with anger. "I urged you not to become involved, DeWitt! I knew this could happen."

He glared at her, first angry she could think her judgment superior to his, then outraged that her case had generated such a malicious rumor.

"It's Van Buren," the governor said hoarsely. "That snake. I can read it in his methods." Clinton held up a clenched fist. "And how do you cripple a snake? You must cut off his head. I will strip that snake of every office he enjoys. He won't be attorney general past tomorrow."

"Why does he do this?" Eleanora asked with exasperation. "I've seen politics played many ways, but never like this before."

"He's an anarchist. he'll set a building afire, scream 'Fire! Fire!' and then take credit for saving lives by sounding the first alarm."

"But why?"

"It's his only tactic to gain power. Burr used the same one. People admire men who seem to predict events, never suspecting them of causing those events. Van Buren needs to keep us on the defensive so we'll be so busy tending to our affairs that we cannot undo him. He may strengthen his Regency in perfect security."

"So, what can we do now?"

"Delay," Clinton said. "We must rely on the shortness of people's memories. We must postpone your suit at least until my reelection next year. If the matter should come to bar, we will lose either way. Either you're dispossessed and I am criticized for meddling, or you win and the public howls for my blood."

"But what of the progress of the canal? That will surely offset people's acrimony."

"Hedges and his Irish are the brightest lights that shine today. But it's a sad truth in politics—just put one public farthing in your pocket and it discredits everything else you've done. Alas, Eleanora, people only recall the mistakes of their public men."

30

*B*lack flies rose suddenly in clouds one June day. Till then the men dug methodically, cranes and massive stones on ropes driving piles into the soft ground, then the men connecting the piles with planks. Diggers scooped up the muck and threw it beyond the wall on each side of the channel. Black flies ended that. They flew into the men's ears, noses, and throats, and coated their brawny arms, shoulders, and necks. Worst of all, they swarmed into their eyes.

"Aye, lads," J.J. McShane called. "Clothe the naked parts now. Rig up a hood when you got cloth to spare." Yet before they could blink, or between blinks, three, five, eight flies attacked.

Night was worse. Into the rude shanties the flies swarmed, and the exhausted men, usually sprawled snoring upon planks of pine, now cursed, spun, and swatted them. For two weeks the men arose from sleepless beds and fled into the open air, only to be assaulted by the orange sun and new legions of flies. Suddenly the flies were gone.

"Like Moses' plague upon Egypt, Dan-o. Gone."

"Other plagues will follow."

"What be there?"

"Besides the leeches and black flies and water snakes? Only the worst—mosquitoes. Swamp fever. Malaria."

"Ah, 'tis a hellish place they send us."

Daniel looked up to the barren limbs of the dead trees which writhed toward low gray clouds. "It's flat, sure, and the best course for the canal, but those that will use it later aren't the ones that dig it, and that, J.J., is a mighty difference."

When the black flies disappeared on the clean westerly wind, the men's temperament improved. Knee-, thigh-, and waist-deep in the muck, hurling the black slime over the wooden wall, they joked, laughed, and sang. Yet this good humor was soon to end.

Eleanora returned to Claverack confused and depressed. Clinton had succeeded only in drawing universal public attention to her case. He despised her now because disgrace had followed. He was getting married, and didn't need her. She despised him too. He had acted high-handed with her sisterly affections, using her as a decoy to draw attention away from his secret love affair with Kitty. Worst of all, a year must pass before she could be certain as to her fate.

Van Zandt notified Eleanora, and she met him in his office so her farmers and servants would learn nothing of the matter. He informed her the case was on the court calendar for September.

"Is it possible to delay?"

"Perhaps. How long a time?"

"A year."

Van Zandt frowned. "Considering its notoriety, Edmonds might not be willing to do that."

"Well, don't you have tricks to stall?"

"Perhaps."

"I need the case delayed at least a year."

"You'll be hanging in the balance for that long?" She did not respond. "You may be accountable for the rents you collect during that time if we lose."

"A year," she repeated. "I need a year."

Outside his office her face burned with indignation. A year; she was reduced to begging time from an attorney! She rode along in the sunshine. The bright cheery day thrust her spirits even lower. Like a sentence for those poor convicts she had visited, she could do nothing but wait for her freedom.

A thought she'd had before occurred to her now, but this time she didn't repress it. Why not throw the whole thing off? Why not give up Claverack? Go west, live with Daniel? The happiest days of her life were those times they'd politicked together across the state. She spurred Arabel into a trot. Giving up Claverack was far different from having it taken away.

She considered the impact on Clinton. He wanted her to place a year of her life as a sacrifice on the altar of his political ambition. For what? The canal was being dug—Daniel was seeing to that. She had brought Daniel to the project. Why all the secrecy? What did Clinton want her to be? A confidential secretary. What had Washington Irving wanted? A mother. And what had Jacob wanted? She clenched her teeth, for it infuriated her. He wanted a woman to live in his house, to be beautiful and accomplished, to keep up appearances while he went off with his young friends. She had served them all. She had gone to each of those men, and after helping them, had nothing for herself.

How different Daniel was! He wanted her only to be a woman, nothing more . . . and nothing less. He cherished her womanhood. He wasn't frightened or envious or domineering. He loved her. Right now he was literally moving mountains for her, and she had been too blind and foolish to see.

A year. The cavalier way Clinton asked for that time angered her. He expected it, took it for granted. Why, she might conceive and bear a child in less time. Her thirtieth year had passed. She couldn't wait another year. Certainly the suit could be delayed that long, but she needn't live in its shadow. And she would live! Let the property look after itself. If it was hers after the suit, so be it. If not, what had she lost?

With the decision made, it was as if she'd gained that year. Eleanora spurred Arabel into a gallop, and she drank in the wind. The strong muscles of the horse's neck, the rich red mane, the clouds above and the streaming sun: she was suddenly glad, for she knew then she must go to Daniel, her wonderful joy not lessened by the possibility that he might turn her away. She was sure of his love. It was the only thing in all this time that she could trust.

She rode hard until the gables of Claverack came into view. She left Arabel with the groom to be cooled down, and walked to the house flicking the riding crop upon her thigh.

Late June brought mosquitoes. They attacked the men in relentless swarms and with diabolical accuracy found holes in shirts and trousers, stinging tender flesh, siphoning blood, injecting the deadly malaria. Order broke down and the digging slowed.

The disease announced itself with a shiver of cold sweat. Disregarding it, the men continued to dig. Many hung smoke pots about their net, and in earthenware cups on rawhide they burned green sticks. But smoke was a poor substitute for oxygen in their lungs, and the mosquitoes clung to their backs. Fever raced through the work gangs, and chills and shakes laid the men low, until the shanties were groaning hells as the stricken men lay shaking and moaning.

J.J. McShane walked a blessed path. He had found a rag of cheesecloth and draped it over his broad-brimmed hat to keep the insects out. In his leather coat and blacksmith's gloves, he lumbered through the dwindling crews like a faceless gladiator, encouraging the men to dig, watching closely for deserters. And they deserted in droves. The convicts knew that the cool breezes of Lake Ontario only twenty-five miles north offered safety from the disease, and that they might escape to Canada and freedom. J.J. alerted gang bosses so workers might not use the canal bed as an escape route. Still, many fled into the wilderness and perished among the swarms of mosquitoes. Some reached Canada. But most of the three thousand men remained at the dig, mingling groans and delirious rantings with the croaking of bullfrogs.

A doctor rode between work camps, but he could do little else than give the men feverwort, green pigweed, snakeroot, and kerosene. Nothing abated the plague. In a matter of days able-bodied diggers fell where they dug, groaned and twitched in the bunkhouses, then were carried to a common grave. As the weeks wore on, men died by the hundreds and the work came to a standstill.

"We've only got a hundred men and four teams on this stretch, and the pile drivers hang limp," Daniel complained to J.J. one August morning. "How many behind and how many up front?"

"Thirteen hundred still working, Dan-o, but they're weak and slow. Four hundred up in front, eight behind, and one here. The lads have lost their spunk."

"It's a sorry time for us all, J.J."

Daniel protected himself with tight clothes, gloves, and a cheesecloth veil hung from his hat brim. He attended the mass burials out of duty, never considering he'd succumb.

He ignored the first shiver. He rode fast and hard along the towpath, hoping that a sweat would carry the poison from his body. But the second shiver lasted a long and alarming minute, and he knew he was ill.

"J.J.," he said, "I'll be in my tent." He threw himself on his horse, and clinging to its neck, rode the five miles back to his tent. By the time he arrived, he was shaking and sweating. Then he lay on his cot, certain he would die.

* * *

Water snakes whipped through the green scum, hungry mosquitoes sucked at his blood, leeches clung to his thighs and genitals, and the swollen red sun grew larger and larger, until it filled up the sky and the whole vast jumble of rock, swamp, and forest was falling into a fiery lake. He cried out for water, but his parched throat cracked and no sound came out.

Suddenly it was quiet and cold. His sweat made him shiver. He was so very cold and wet, he huddled in the blankets upon a bed of ice. In barren trees the white wolves sat, yellow eyes peering at him, and silver mist filtered in the dark. The warmth drained from his body into the cold empty night. His teeth were chattering.

He heard voices during the fevers and chilling, but they were of a different dimension, disembodied voices, and in a circle his parents, his wife, his children seemed to float just beyond his sight, his hearing. He sensed while his throat burned again for a countless time that a benevolent hand touched his face and forehead. Cool waves passed through his flesh, and his burning thirst was slaked. He wept. His mind was playing tricks. He ground his teeth together and pressed his eyes tightly shut, then with an extreme effort, threw them open.

Light nearly blinded him. Far above him he saw her face. Her blond hair was tied back and her blue eyes looked kindly down upon him.

"Daniel?"

He grit his teeth even tighter and wept, despising the trick his delirium played.

"Daniel?"

The voice was sweeter than a melody. He opened his eyes and saw her again.

"Daniel!" She smiled. "Your fever has broken." He blinked, licked his parched, cracked lips. He tried to speak, but his voice caught in his throat. He reached out and touched her hand.

"Eleanora!"

"Yes. I am here." She pressed his hand between hers, and they were cool. "I won't leave you."

He turned upon the bed, pressed his face into the damp sheets—*sheets!*—and wept. "Oh, at last!"

* * *

As a convalescent, Daniel was impatient. He longed to get back to the digging and push forward, but Eleanora stood firm. He must rest in order to be of use to anyone. She told him days later of the harrowing week she had spent trying to locate him, how she and Joel Kipp had ridden west on the turnpikes and along the towpath, only to find a plague on the workers. Albany knew nothing of it; it was all kept secret to forestall political opposition.

"At the first work camp all we could hear was groaning. The men's teeth chattered, and they shivered in their bunks with chills. Joel approached a man sitting alone with flies buzzing around him. He was dead. Everywhere dead men lay as we pressed farther into the swamp, their stomachs bloated from the heat and decomposition. The stench! When we asked why they weren't buried, we were told no one could lift a shovel."

She told him how they had discovered him shivering in his tent, and had rescued him in a buckboard, hired a spacious stone farmhouse, and treated him. "As soon as I saw the fever"—she held up a bottle—"I sent a rider to New York City, and he returned in a week with this. They call it Jesuit bark and it seems to work. Bark from a South American tree. That's what brought you around."

"If only we had more."

"Most are beyond help." Then she mentioned Van Buren and frustrations with the digging.

"No talk of politicians! Tell me of J.J."

"Joel says he is impervious to the illness. Nothing bothers him." She described how he tried to maintain order, get men buried, keep those who could work on the dig. "It must be all the whiskey he drinks."

"I have to return!"

"I'll tell you when that day arrives."

And yet despite his impatience, Daniel enjoyed how she doted on him. For hours at a time she sat at his bedside reading, talking, and singing. She dressed as a woman of the land—homespun skirt, loose woollen blouse, a wide black belt, and simple boots. She let her hair fall free. Daniel lay in his bed and luxuriated in the aroma of baking bread. The farm fields had been planted by the owner, and soon workers were harvesting.

"What about your obligations?" he asked one morning in late September.

"What obligations?"

"Your estate and the matters before the legislature, and...and Clinton." He spun his hand in the air as if the list were endless.

She smiled, "I have only one obligation now and you keep me busy enough."

The leaves were turning when Daniel could walk outside. He walked with her in the pastures and meadows. Together they picnicked during the warm, sunny Indian summer. For two weeks their lives were bliss. Then one evening Daniel announced they would dig all through the winter.

"It was a mistake going into that swamp in summer. Cold congeals the earth and makes it far easier to dig. We'll work all winter and be through the swamp by the first thaw."

Eleanora said nothing.

"What is the matter?"

She paused in their stroll, took his arm, and looked up sadly. "What about me?"

He scratched his head. "I was accustomed to your making your own decisions."

"Very well, then, I shall!" She lay her head on his shoulder. "I'll stay here, where I belong."

Daniel reached down and kissed her. The delicious scent of harvest was in the air, and a bird screamed across the bright autumn sky.

"You make me so very happy." He kissed her again.

"I love you, Daniel, so very, very much."

31

Clinton's marriage pleased New York society. The handsome, energetic governor could not have chosen a more beautiful or accomplished wife than Catherine Jones. It was assumed that her father's banking connections would someday finance DeWitt Clinton's successful presidential bid, and then all of New York society would benefit.

Immediately after the letter in the newspaper, Clinton convened the Council of Appointment and ousted Van Buren from the attorney-general post. Now Van Buren only held his State Senate seat, yet his Albany Regency was a powerful political machine, passing or obstructing laws and budget bills. And soon afterward, when a New York seat fell vacant in the United States Senate, Van Buren had himself appointed and left for Washington.

"He has a remarkable appetite for political office," Clinton observed to his wife. "The result, I suppose, of his low birth."

"We should pity the less fortunate, dear."

"He has single-handedly cost our state years of work and progress on the canal to advance his selfish political ends. He must be punished."

But Van Buren thought otherwise. By championing the cause of those who hated Clinton, he had built a solid reliable power base both in New York City and in Albany.

"Ah, Matty," Burr used to say, "power is like fire, it consumes what feeds it and requires more and more to burn brighter, higher, and hotter." Van Buren soon discovered new fuel in the malaria epidemic and in the Financial Panic of 1819. If he only could associate all the negative aspects with the governor, Clinton's political funeral pyre would blaze into the sky.

Van Buren asked his Regency to get a death count from the Canal Commission, and the commission duly sent Daniel Hedges a letter requesting the information.

"Have you counted the dead, J.J.?"

"For them politicians? They sit comfortable in Albany with their tarts and their votin' games, so why don't they let us get on with the work?"

"How many died, J.J.?"

"All of 'em, Dan-o. Tell 'em that. All of 'em."

Daniel modified this response: "Too many. I was one of the few who recovered. Many fled into the forests and perished there. An accurate count is impossible." Not wanting to open the issue, the Canal Commission forwarded Van Buren a letter saying it hadn't kept count. Van Buren then focused upon the Panic of 1819 to impede the canal's progress. He couldn't blame Clinton for the recession, but he could prevent money from being spent on the canal, arguing the state couldn't afford the expense.

The winter passed quietly along the course of the canal, and Daniel and Eleanora were happily together day and night.

Though in Albany it would have been thought highly disgraceful to live together openly without a church wedding, fronterismen paid little attention to the happy couple. Eleanora said nothing of her pending lawsuit, but harbored a defiance toward matrimony that Daniel found puzzling.

"Why should the state be able to invade our lives and tell us we cannot live such as this?" she asked as they lay together in bed. Dying embers took the edge off the October chill and tinged her skin a deep rose. "Why can't we live as Adam and Eve, man and woman, why must it be man and *wife*, the woman as the man's possession and ward?"

"Ah, my love, who cares? I never think of such things. I'm happier now than I can remember."

"But it's infuriating! Even now I suppose there are rumors rampant in Albany."

"Let them squawk. We can't hear them. It won't get the ditch dug any quicker."

Eleanora considered their lack of a marriage contract, and also the one she had executed long ago. "But we should at least think about Albany, for we have been summoned there." Daniel groaned. "DeWitt has some problems with funds for next year."

Daniel's fists clenched. "Goddamn them!" He sat up and punched his right fist into his left hand. She was surprised. "Goddamn them."

"You don't understand."

"No, Eleanora." He pointed his finger at her. "I do understand. I understand all too well. We have been dying out here, hundreds of men, perhaps a thousand, laying in unmarked graves. These petty politicans are now threatening to cut off the money to pay us? No! Our diggers have not died in vain! We must finish it, if only for them."

"But the legislature makes the decisions."

"You understand all that far better than I ever want to. I am going to work these men through the winter. Why? To keep them warm, to keep them busy, to keep the canal progressing. What will the politicians be doing? Drinking and wenching. I'd put the young boys who run whiskey on my mudline against them politicians anytime."

"Daniel, be reasonable."

"Reasonable? What else have I been? How far can a man bend for the politicians? I have done their bidding. I understand their troubles. I don't even care if they understand mine, but if Clinton calls us, you go, I won't. And you tell him how I feel."

Angrily he rose. Eleanora pulled the quilt up about her neck. "Daniel, please." He spun about in the firelight and pointed his thumb eastward.

"Right now they're worried about what they're going to have for breakfast, if their wives will catch them fornicating, how many votes they can steal. They have no courage, no honesty. Give me J. J. McShane anytime because J.J. *is* his word."

"Daniel!"

"No," he cried, "don't pretend with me that they are more important to this work than we are. I would have died if it hadn't been for you. I owe you my life, but I owe them nothing. All debts have been paid in full. Let Clinton find some way or another to keep the money coming so I can pay my men. He's never shy about taking all the credit for the work." Daniel threw on his clothes and left to exhale his frustrations in the frosty moonlight.

Clinton did do something. He planned a celebration in late October to open the finished portion of the canal from Utica to Rome. The ceremony, replete with speeches, a brass band aboard a canal boat, politicians praising each other, and gun salutes, greatly impressed the locals. Yet the *Albany Argus* complained that at such a rate the canal would require twenty years for completion and would surely bankrupt the state. The newspaper continued its charge of judge-fixing. Clinton was fighting for his political survival as the recession plunged merchants into bankruptcy, forced freeholders off the land as banks foreclosed, then ran those very banks into oblivion.

Yet with a stroke of genius Clinton turned the panic into an advantage. He appeared personally before the legislature and urged passage of a funding bill to allow the state to pay farmer-contractors a higher wage. This wage, in turn, would allow them to pay their mortgages and thus pull the economy of the central and western part of the state up by its bootstraps. The bill passed in both houses.

Despite this ingenious plan, ugly rumors persisted about Clinton's reclusive ways, his drinking habits, his new wife's control over policy. Even though ninety miles of canal connected Rome with the Seneca River by July fourth, Clinton squeaked through the election with less than a one-percent margin.

"I grow weary of it all," Clinton confessed to Kitty. She peered up from her novel. "I wonder sometimes why I have worked so hard."

"So do I," Kitty agreed. "DeWitt, let us leave Albany. This is a horrid little place, so dull and cramped. I don't care in the least whether some woodsman can ship his lumber or furs, or a farmer ship his wheat more cheaply. You've done more for these people than they deserve. Let's return to New York. You have holdings, and Papa will help us get started. You'd make a perfect bankers' attorney."

"We shall see, my dear." While her plea had not fallen upon deaf ears, Clinton watched as she returned to her novel, and involuntarily measured her against Eleanora.

32

*J*oel Kipp brought the news. Eleanora read on his face that she had lost the suit. Daniel wasn't there to comfort her. With the funds for the canal at last approved, the crews had dug all through the winter of 1820-21, and as the canal proceeded out of the swamp, she remained as he went west for three days to scout the Irondequoit Valley and the turbulent Genesee.

"I went to the courtroom, ma'am, and I listened to them," Joel said, and shook his head. "Van Zandt made all manner of excuses for you not appearing, but you could tell it angered Judge Edmonds. The judge said there were some irregularities alleged in your ... in your, ah ... *conduct*, that Van Zandt did not dispute. The judge kept saying 'acquiescence' ... that you 'acquiesced' and so forfeited Claverack."

"I simply could not appear." She dropped her eyes to the simple dress she wore, and looked about the kitchen and into the fieldstone hearth. "It would have been humiliating, and would not have helped the case."

"Van Zandt agreed." Joel handed her a letter. She focused upon this passage:

The court held that the covenant between your father and Jacob VR Sr. was a valid agreement between two landowners conditioning the conveyance, and that they might impose any conditions they desired. I argued that 'Till death do us part' was a condition subsequent and Jacob's death released you. Thus, you might comport yourself as you saw fit so long as you did not remarry. Yet the judge looked at the parties' intent. Plaintiff's proof as to midnight liaisons and your current living arrangement was damning. Your nonappearance was considered acquiescence on your part and fatal to your claim. The motion for ejectment was granted. Still, I suggest we appeal to Chancery for reinstatement of your dower right.

Inasmuch as his claim was granted, plaintiff Randolph VR requests you remove all personal property from both the Claverack house and the Albany town house by September 1, 1821. Any personalty left after that date will be sold at public auction.

Eleanora sighed and lay the letter on the table. "And now we must find you a position, Joel."

"Why, after I look to your effects and all this is settled, I'll work here, on the dig."

She nodded. "Yes. Daniel is due home this evening. Put up at the inn in Pittsford. I want to tell him in my own way."

"I'll stop tomorrow before I return to Albany."

Daniel arrived at sunset, excited by what he had accomplished. "We took soundings in the streambed of the Genesee, and the bedrock is only five feet under gravel and silt. We shall begin the footings in August when the water is low. J.J. and I have devised a way to bridge the Irondequoit too."

As she prepared a supper of trout, new potatoes, fresh bread, and ale, Daniel discussed the contest between Black Rock and Buffaloe Creek for the terminus of the canal. Joseph Ellicott, with a long-standing feud against Buffaloe and with property in Black Rock, championed the Black Rock faction. Lester Frye led those of Buffaloe. "Of course, I favor Buffaloe," Daniel admitted. "I own land there, true, but it is also the better entry into the lake." He squinted. "Eleanora, is something wrong?"

"Why, yes." She turned and fought back a sob. "Something terrible, something awful has happened to me." Tears flowed down her cheeks.

"What?" He clasped her hands and held her to him. "What is it?"

"Oh, Daniel, I cannot hope that you will marry me now!"

"But you have always railed against the notion of marriage." He scowled. "What is it?" She wept bitterly on his shoulder.

"I so much, so very much want to be your wife, and now..."

He held her, repeating over and over, "It's all right, it's all right."

When she had calmed, he helped her to a seat. "Now, what makes you think I'd let you get away this time?"

She looked up into his broad smile and his sparkling eyes, and smiled faintly. "I have nothing. I have lost my estate, the home in Albany attached to it, my station in life. Everything. I'm destitute."

"How?"

"There was a condition in my marriage agreement with Jacob that I did not fulfill."

Daniel nodded. His eyes grew wide and he whispered with sudden revelation: "They prevented you from remarrying! That's it! That's what it has always been!"

"Yes, yes, oh, yes." She dropped her eyes, ashamed. "And now you believe that my lands were so important to me that I put them above my love for you." She turned away, sobbing. "But that wasn't it. My beautiful Claverack, my home, the land and the people that I loved... I couldn't abandon it until I saw that fighting for it meant hurting you. Until I came west, that agreement prevented my remarriage. Now... now my poverty does. You're all I have, Daniel, and I don't even know if you'll have me."

"Eleanora," he whispered, sitting on the hearth beside her chair, "you saved my life! I knew there was some other reason, but I thought it was another love, or that it was me—who I was, where I came from."

She turned. Tears streaked her face. "Oh, no, my love. Oh, no. From the first I loved you, hopelessly. I couldn't show it. I fought it. I tried to deny and forget it, but I couldn't, Daniel! Oh, and I felt so foolish, so torn. I believed the dead hand of my father controlled me, yet in you I saw such life, so much love. Before I met you I lived alone, chasing after things I cared little for—poetry, politics—believing, hoping they would acquire value for me. Then when we were together, I knew I could love, I must love, but I wouldn't accept it, not until this evil business began. I came west because I couldn't drag us—drag you—through the public rebuke, the newspapers, the gossip mongers, the screaming of DeWitt's enemies. It would have been such a scandal! They would have ignored all the fine work you've done. Yet I had to be with you. I *have* to be with you!"

"Then I bless the day this evil business began! I am grateful to Clinton's enemies!"

"And yet, I bring nothing to the union, Daniel. I am a pauper."

He laughed and reached for her. "We don't need a dowry. We don't need anything at all. You saved my life!"

She nodded, and smiled through her tears. "And my own as well, though I've lost all else."

"Let it go!" he cried. "You're well rid of all that. Let them have Claverack. We'll build a new life, a happier life, together." He pulled her to her feet, lifted her off the floor and spun her around. "Oh, my Eleanora, this is the happiest day of my life! What children we shall have!"

"Children?"

"Of course. Oh, Eleanora, I've dreamed about this day for years. What a mother you will make!"

"I'm . . . I'm quite . . ."

He kissed her passionately and spun her about.

"What about supper?" she asked.

"It'll wait." And he carried her up to the bedroom.

BOOK V

33

*A*fter the court decision Eleanora Van Rensselaer felt and acted like a different woman. The worst had happened, and she awoke from her long-standing fear to accept her new life. Freed from worrying what people thought, she adopted a western pioneer attitude, setting out to work and earn what happiness she might.

She sewed trousers and a jacket for herself, and announced to Daniel: "I'd like to command a group of diggers." Unfortunately this request ignored J. J. McShane's manner of discovering and promoting gang leaders—those who beat the boss in a fair fight won control of the gang. Yet Eleanora was not to be rebuffed. As J.J. began the mile-long earthworks necessary to carry the canal eighty feet above the Irondequoit Valley, she asked Daniel if she could assist in setting up the three new workers' camps. He agreed, and detailed some older workers to her.

Before, not much thought had gone into building the work camps, and most of the thought about provisions concerned only whiskey. The men's fare was usually Irish stew, boiled salt pork or beef or game with whatever carrots, potatoes, turnips, and onions could be bought from neighboring farmers, and the stew and biscuit washed down with coffee and whiskey. The lanes of the work camp were ankle deep in mud and smelled of excrement. Rude bunkhouses held only wooden shelves where the men collapsed after sixteen or eighteen hours of digging.

"With a little planning we can greatly improve this," she remarked to one of the thirty old and injured men she commanded. At three sites near bright springs she laid out a compound two hundred feet square and marked out bunk-house sites at each corner. Instead of rude, overflowing ditches for latrines, Eleanora had four-holed privies built farther downslope. She left nothing to the judgment of carpenters, but designed on paper a new spacious bunkhouse floor plan that centered around a hearth and sitting area, bunks set off from the central area by panels.

She journeyed to Rochesterville and arranged with a merchant for a shipment of blankets and towels, barrels of flour and yeast. Budgeting funds, she bought cattle, swine, and sheep. She hired a boy for each work camp to graze the cattle on the central green, and had pens built for the pigs. She arranged for a special meal each Sunday of roast beef, pork, or mutton. She showed the mess hands how to bake bread in Dutch ovens, and the fresh bread each night alone won her universal acclaim among the men. She added cake and pastry when sugar or molasses could be obtained. The men responded. Each Sunday they held prize fights, "sings," cockfights and rat races on the greens.

"She's a rare angel," J.J. told Daniel. "The men love her. I believe if anyone was to lay a hand on her, why, he'd find a Dublin blade in his back. Dan-o, I'm getting half again as much work out of the boys, and miracle to end miracles, the whiskey rations have gone down!"

"Yet she grows impatient since that work's done, J.J. She needs a new challenge. I've been thinking of giving her command of a gang."

J.J. shook his head. "Again, Dan-o, the men would resent taking orders from a female, no matter she don't wear skirts. Would upset the dig. Why not give her five or six men and have them spur along them private contractors who're slacking off?"

This appealed to Daniel, and soon he dispatched Eleanora with three men to report on progress and contract for any stretches not being dug.

With Canvass White Daniel worked and reworked the aqueduct plans for spanning the Genesee River while J.J. and the crews quarried granite and sunk massive footings in the riverbed for eleven fifty-foot arches. At Rochesterville the Genesee was turbulent and rapid. Spring thaws brought two-ton ice floes that the pilings must withstand. As the pilings rose that summer, so did the spirit of the men.

However, harmony and enterprise were not universal. A vicious battle waged between Black Rock and Buffaloe Creek. To sound more attractive to the Albany legislators, the citizens of Buffaloe Creek dropped the *Creek* and the *e* from the name of their community, and *Buffalo* now competed with Ellicott's Black Rock to be the western terminus. Ellicott argued Black Rock's advantages: a shorter distance to dig, a wider harbor; yet Clinton opposed him. In disgust and frustration, Ellicott resigned from the Canal Commission.

Seeing this rift, Van Buren conferred with Aaron Burr, then approached Ellicott directly.

"Perhaps you might share your dissatisfaction with the western counties?" Van Buren suggested over dinner in an Albany tavern.

"Clinton's flaw is that he won't compromise once you fall afoul of him." Ellicott shook his head. "You can never again get near him no matter how close you were before. He's intractable."

"And we both know," Van Buren said with a smile and a flourish of his hand, "that public men must be flexible." The senator then discussed ways to turn Holland Land Company farmers against the governor.

Using every means, Van Buren eroded Clinton's popularity and support. His long years of plotting and building an organization based on patronage would bear fruit if the powerful Clinton were gone.

As the construction season of 1821 ended, Daniel and Eleanora set up housekeeping near Rochester. Only a cluster of homes with a mill until a year before, the village had quickly become a boomtown, and so it dropped the *ville* from its name. Land doubled and trebled in value. Foundations were laid for homes and warehouses. The canal would soon link Rochester with the Hudson River and New York City.

Eleanora's help and enthusiasm this season had been extraordinary. The invigorating outdoor life tanned her skin, bleached her hair, and put a new sparkle in her eye.

"We do make quite a pair," Daniel said one day after regaling her about a man's astonishment at seeing a woman in trousers.

"Yes, and beyond the bit of gossip from churchgoing

women, it's surprising how few people notice our living arrangement."

"Does this mean you don't want a wedding?"

She glared at him. "Not at all. In fact, we should probably plan it soon."

"I thought you wanted to wait until the canal is dug."

"I thought so, too, but what if we were to be blessed with a baby?"

"You're not...?" Daniel's eyes suddenly lit up, at first with panic, then with surprise and hope.

She laughed. "No...no, I'm not. But it might happen, especially during the winter, when we're so idle."

"Next week, then."

"No, I think we should let DeWitt know. He'll certainly want to attend."

"Clinton, eh?"

"Oh, yes! If it weren't for him—"

"All right. You make the arrangements."

Eleanora wrote DeWitt, and he wrote back that he'd visit on a campaign swing while he was securing his party's nomination. Yet that winter he did not come, since his support was eroding in the lower Hudson counties. In February they set the day for late March, just before the party would select its candidate.

In mid-March Daniel journeyed to the western escarpment to take some further measurements of the canal's last great obstacle. This cliff, home of eagles and rattlesnakes, would require a flight of five twin locks—a grand staircase of water, each lock spilling into the one below, one side to lift boats, the other to let them down.

Meanwhile J.J. and the men quarried stone for the Rochester aqueduct. After blasting or cracking stone with water poured into bored holes that froze and split the rock, the men dressed the blocks and dragged them to the riverbank on oxen-drawn sleds. All lay ready the day Daniel returned, March eighteenth. The men had vigorously celebrated the feast of their patron, St. Patrick, and lay hungover in the work camps. Daniel and J.J. discussed his impending wedding ceremony and how work would begin the day after, when Daniel and Eleanora left for their honeymoon.

Returning home that night, he was surprised no lights were on. Inside he found only a note:

March 16, 1822

Dearest Daniel:

A very important matter compels me to go to Albany.
I hope you understand. I will write at my earliest
convenience.

Love,
Eleanora

At his first reading, Daniel shrugged, deciding he could
get along alone for the month. Then, with a start, he remembered their wedding was set for the twenty-fourth. Next day
he told J.J. the wedding would be delayed and that work
should start immediately.

"What is it, Dan-o?"

"Pressing business drew her away."

"Aye. Pressing business, eh?" J.J. asked nothing further, yet
Daniel sensed J.J. didn't approve of Eleanora's conduct. He
didn't approve himself. To forget, he threw himself into the
work of damming and diverting the course of the Genesee so
they could begin to build.

Yet Eleanora's journey was hardly for pleasure. A week
before, she had met Assemblyman Atwater in the street, and
he had triumphantly announced that Clinton was not seeking
reelection. Eleanora believed he was joking until she consulted a
state senator later that evening. "No," Senator Clayburn said,
"he is not running this year. The party wouldn't give him the
nomination. Van Buren's faction is too strong."

Daniel wouldn't return for two days. Eleanora felt as if
some devastating blow had stunned her, the canal project, and
her impending marriage. Immediately she packed, left her
terse note, and boarded the stagecoach to Lauraville. Already
the canal was in service eastward, and she traveled from
there in a passenger boat day and night until she reached
Rome. The boat was close at night and filled with men's
snoring, but it was far smoother and quicker than a stagecoach. At Rome she boarded a stagecoach and set off along
the gravel turnpike. By the morning of the third day she
was in Albany. Calling at the governor's suite, she found to
her dismay Clinton had left for New York City the day
before.

With her town house gone, Eleanora stayed at Gray's
Hotel that night, then caught the steamboat *North River* in

the morning. Within a week of her departure she was at Clinton's house in Flushing.

When the butler announced Eleanora, Catherine swept down the hall. "Oh, Eleanora, it's so good to see you!" Yet the alarm in the socialite's voice was foreboding. "DeWitt is not himself. Perhaps you should spend the night elsewhere and speak with him in the morning."

"I heard he is not running for office this year, and it seemed so incredible, I just had to speak with him."

A loud cry in the back of the house and a crashing of glass interrupted them. Catherine looked in horror toward the sound.

"Please." Catherine pressed Eleanora's hand between hers. "I think you had better go. There's an inn. George, our footman, will—"

Another groan and a crashing sound.

"No, Kitty, I must see him."

"He is in no condition to entertain. I must insist." Eleanora glared at her until Catherine spun about and went to the back of the house. She returned and said, "He would like to see you, but please, please don't press him. He's been through a terrible ordeal."

Eleanora followed her. The rear parlor was dark except for two candles. Six empty wine bottles stood on the table. Another one lay in pieces on the floor, and the wall and carpet were stained red.

Clinton stood in the middle of the room, an impotent giant, snorting in rage. He worked to focus his eyes. "It is you. You have come."

"She'll be stopping at the inn tonight," Kitty said primly.

"Leave us, Catherine!" Clinton commanded, pointing to the door. Both women were surprised. As Catherine left, Clinton looked at Eleanora with a sidelong glance. "So, you have come."

"I heard you weren't running, and I had to talk with you."

"Glass of wine?" He poured himself another tumbler. "My only solace these days." He drank it and poured another.

"Yes. I'll have one with you." She accepted it. "You look terrible, DeWitt. You need sleep."

"Sleep? Sleep is the one thing I've forgotten how to do." He struggled to compose himself. "It is true ... what you heard—that I'm not running—but it's not my decision. The party ... the party refuses to back me."

"But why? The canal progresses ever so well."

"Why?" he whispered hoarsely. "Martin Van Buren, that's why. That little snake has made my reelection impossible. While I've been devoting my time to serving the people, he's been consolidating his power within the party."

"But surely you overestimate... *they* overestimate him."

"No!" Clinton howled. "No! That was our mistake all along. We underestimated him. While we've been building the eighth wonder of the world, he's been building a party structure. That bastard son of an innkeeper. God! Is there no justice?"

Eleanora had never seen him quite this worked up, though she had comforted him before. The sight of this massive man howling like a wounded beast terrified her.

"He's everywhere. He called a convention and rewrote our state constitution to abolish my powers on the Council of Appointment. So now the men I've put in office, the men I've fed for a decade, turn on me and turn to him. My own men eating out of his hand!"

"But it's not that hopeless," she pleaded. "His trickery, his deceit will undo him. The people of this state—"

"The people?" Clinton cried. "What do they know? They cannot see into men's hearts as we can and read their motives. Their sight is clouded, their memory short. They believe the damned newspapers, and the editors believe Van Buren. I am undone!" Clinton's eyes grew wide and his voice was insidious, a theatrical whisper. "Soft you, a word or two before you go—Shakespeare's moor. I have done the state some service, and they know it. No more of that. I pray you, in your letters, when you shall these unlucky deeds relate, speak of me as I am. Nothing extenuate, nor set down aught in malice." Now his voice dripped with sarcasm. "Then, then must you speak of one that ruled not wisely, but too well!"

"DeWitt!" she scolded.

"You have never suffered political exile, woman. You do not know how it is to be stripped of the robes of office, turned out to limp along. Tiresias the beggar, limping, limping, laughed at, vilified by men who once genuflected." He thromped his chest. "I do! I was twice turned out as mayor. Now as governor."

She sipped her wine, then spoke softly. "And you forget. I have been dispossessed of my estate, turned out with nothing but the clothes on my back."

He looked up. "Ah." He quaffed his wine and poured another glass. "Fortune plays the whore with us both."

"Yes, but tomorrow is another day. I shall talk to you when your senses have returned. Know this, DeWitt, that I have never been happier since I lost my lands. And you—you must get control of yourself. Kitty must find me a room in this drafty house of yours. Be kind to her, she is not the cause." Eleanora turned and walked from the room, leaving Clinton looking down at his wineglass as if he just noticed it in his hand.

"How long has he been this way?" Eleanora asked Catherine, who had been eavesdropping in the hall.

"Two days. It terrifies me."

"He'll be better in the morning," she said, and clasped his wife's arm.

The governor joined them in the airy conservatory for breakfast, a trifle haggard but in far better spirits. "Eleanora, I have never seen you look so well! You glow like a country wench. You're positively robust!" He kissed her. "Good morning, Kitty." He kissed his wife and signaled for the servant to bring cider and cocoa. "It must be Daniel's influence. And he, a lucky man to be marrying you. One can always tell when a woman's in love."

"Yes, it's him, mostly. But I've been working on the canal also. If our lazy class would only do something physical, we'd see the impact of our commands on the lower orders. Lower orders! Hah! I myself have been reduced, haven't I?"

"And so you must appeal to Chancery. Equity would never allow a woman to be cheated of her dower."

"We shall see."

"We shall do more than that. I'll have the attorney general look into it personally and confer with your lawyer. I may as well use the office I hold for as long as I may hold it. Now tell me about building the great pyramid, my political tomb."

She regaled him with stories of the contractors, the hard-drinking, brawling Irish, the constant migration of people to western lands to farm and to trade. She described the elephantine pilings that would carry the canal over the Genesee, and the mammoth excavations needed farther west.

After breakfast Clinton asked her to join him in his library. "I'm sorry about my behavior." She was astonished, having never heard him apologize. "I cannot believe what is happening to me, Eleanora. It's reprehensible."

"The tide will turn," she said brightly.

"I am so weary of the cadres and cabals and conspiracies of men! Like hounds dragging down the stag, they set upon me from every side."

"You must forget them. If you will not be running this year, so be it, DeWitt. But do not resign yourself to anonymity. You must see the awe our canal produces in all who behold it. It is more than a highway for transporting people and goods, DeWitt. It is enterprise, ingenuity, raw perseverance. That's what captures their imagination."

He nodded. "Your enthusiasm is welcome."

"Oh, DeWitt, you must come out and view the great work. Accept the tribute and accolades of a thankful people who line its banks. Forget Van Buren and his pack of dogs. The canal is a work of surpassing beauty. The West is a land where no possibility is limited—ambition and enterprise count for all. I have never felt freer, happier, more useful. Visit us this summer. You'll draw surprising strength from it."

"Perhaps, perhaps."

"Daniel will show you the marvels he and McShane have worked in earth and stone."

Clinton gave a laugh. "Rumors abound about your scandalous life-style."

"Oh, yes." She blushed suddenly. "Nowhere is the difference between East and West more apparent than in that attitude toward a man and a woman. In the West men and women join together often without a ceremony, because they face a struggle for survival. They build a cabin, clear the fields, plant the crops, and raise their children. Cruel nature is our enemy, not sin."

"When will your wedding be?"

"You've delayed it twice. We were going ahead without you, and scheduled it for today."

"Today? What are you doing here?"

"I heard you weren't running, and I had to come. I know you far too well, DeWitt. I knew how you would react, and I was correct. Daniel will understand. Another few weeks won't hurt anything." An idea occurred to her. "Why don't we postpone our wedding until your visit?"

"So I could attend?"

"No." She smiled broadly. "So you can perform it. Who

has more authority to join man and wife in this state than the governor?"

"I'd be flattered. I have always admired Daniel. His efforts have kept the construction on course, even during the slowest dog days. If I had five men like him, I'd be president by now."

"Wonderful!" She clapped her hands. "Then it's settled. I shall write him directly. Oh, this is an unexpected joy. Daniel will be immensely pleased!"

Yet Daniel was far from pleased. In flagrant disregard for his feelings, she had left with only a terse note. He'd thought she'd changed. In the days ahead he realized how much he loved her, how disoriented and alone he felt, and also how no marriage vow would keep her from doing this again.

He tried to occupy his evenings at the tavern with J. J. McShane, but he always returned to the empty house and stared at her empty chair by the cold hearth. He was finally relieved when a letter arrived:

Flushing
March 24, 1822

My Dearest Daniel:

I am staying with DeWitt and Kitty another two days, and then I shall return. I shall explain everything upon my arrival. Please know that my action has helped our project immeasurably—soon we will have DeWitt's personal attention to rely on. He has agreed to view the work in June, and he will perform our wedding ceremony!

I go to sleep each night with thoughts of you, my beloved, and I miss you so very much. Thank you for your understanding, and know that I love you.

Your own
Eleanora.

"Clinton," he muttered, "again, Clinton." Impatiently he slapped the letter in his hand.

34

On a mild June afternoon, work ceased early on the Rochester aqueduct. Blocks hung idle from cranes above the massive stone arches that marched across the foaming river with Roman determination. In this frontier hamlet of woodsmen, trappers, riverboatmen, traders, farmers, and housewives, the townspeople paused frequently to contemplate the aqueduct, for it symbolized the great age of commerce and civilization to come. Yet on this day everyone had paused together, even the workers.

On the western side a larger crowd had gathered, a hundred fifty workers, eighty-five townspeople, and a rustic band that played the Irish elbow pipes, the tin whistle, a squeezebox, a fiddle, and a drum. They played jigs and reels, and the men sipped freely from a whiskey keg. A tall man in a dark suit stood near the unfinished bed of the bridge which soon would be filled with water. Governor Clinton was waiting for the ceremony to begin.

A whoop went up among the men as the door to the foreman's cabin opened and a young girl in a yellow gown stepped out, green ribbons fluttering in her hair. She was followed by Eleanora Van Rensselaer in a long flowing white gown. Many of the men had only seen her in woollen trousers and jacket, and an awed hush fell upon them. As she moved into the sunlight, a halo of blond hair was accentuated by the pure white of the veil. Judge Rochester, father of the maid of honor, stepped to Eleanora and took her arm.

Near the governor Daniel Hedges stood in a dark suit, and at his side, tugging at the high, uncomfortable collar, stood J. J. McShane. The crowd fell back as peasants recede before a queen, and Eleanora gracefully bowed, scanned the great stone breastwork, then looked at Daniel. They exchanged nervous smiles.

As the squeezebox, pipes, and fiddle played a wedding march, the judge solemnly escorted her to Daniel, and he bowed. Daniel returned the bow, looking into Eleanora's eyes, and his nervousness disappeared. The slightest smile curled at her lip, and her eyes were misty.

"Who gives this woman in matrimony?" Governor Clinton asked.

"I do, sir." Then Judge Rochester stood aside. Eleanora glided to Daniel and stood at his side, facing the governor.

Clinton bowed to them, then took out a small book. Informally he welcomed them: "It is fitting you have chosen with your wedding vows to sanctify this grand work that joins East to West. You both have worked so very long with me, with these men, and with the people of our state. Eleanora, Daniel" —Clinton's voice quavered—"you have helped give birth to what was once a dream but is quickly becoming a new age for us all. Generations of New Yorkers will be in your debt. I am grateful, and yes, humbled, by the honor you do me to say these few words that will join you together as man and wife."

Men cleared their throats and women sniffed and sobbed in the crowd. "Daniel, do you take this woman Eleanora as your lawfully wedded wife, to love, honor, and cherish from this day forward, in sickness and in health, till death do you part?"

Daniel looked into her eyes, filled with emotion. "I do."

"And do you, Eleanora, take this man, Daniel, as your lawfully wedded husband, to love, honor, and obey from this day forward, in sickness and in health, till death do you part?"

Eleanora looked up at him. She paused, then said, "I do."

"If you would place the ring upon her finger, Daniel." Daniel looked to J.J., and the Irishman was so taken up with the formality, he went blank. "The rings, J.J." The Irishman patted his waistcoat, produced a small jeweler's box, and handed it to Daniel. Daniel opened it, removed the smaller gold ring, and took up Eleanora's trembling hand. He placed the ring upon her finger and repeated the pledge Clinton recited. Then Eleanora took the larger ring, placed it on Daniel's finger, and gazing into his eyes, made her pledge.

Clinton spoke in a deep, official voice. "With the authority vested in me as Governor of the State of New York, I now pronounce you man and wife."

They kissed. The words were no sooner uttered and the kiss exchanged when a deafening holler erupted from the men, the band struck up, and the Irishmen, whiskey in their veins, linked arms and jigged.

"Congratulations." Clinton clasped both their arms. "I am

so very happy for you, and I wish you all the best." He waved his arm at the great aqueduct. "May you be the happiest couple in the land today and in the years ahead."

"Thank you, Governor." Daniel warmly shook his hand.

"You have made us very happy," Eleanora told him as she kissed him on the cheek. "Today I know at last what happiness is, and you shall, DeWitt, with our help, know it the day the canal is open. Thank you."

The crowd flooded in. Judge and Mrs. Rochester congratulated them warmly. J. J. McShane embraced Daniel and gave a shy kiss to the back of Eleanora's hand. The gang leaders were next. Each one advanced to deliver his good wishes. Then workmen pressed forward, and they all started in a procession, the young Rochester girl strewing flowers on the road.

Yet the governor did not participate in the festivities. He walked back and forth the width of the aqueduct, then the length, admiring from every angle its straight, clean lines. He leaned over the side then and watched the water swiftly flowing. "That was perhaps the last good thing I'll do in office," he said, speaking to the foaming water. And remembering a tale of an Indian chief swept into the river's current and carried over the falls, a tale Daniel told him when they viewed the Niagara cataract, Clinton muttered, "And the stoic pagan chief surrendered to oblivion." He flung a stone into the swirling river, and returned alone to his lodgings.

The wedding reception brought out the gaiety and festiveness of the Irish.

"Aye, Dan-o, nothin' to an Irishman's liking as a good wake or wedding."

"I'm happy we chose the latter."

The men's joy demonstrated to Daniel how tightly knit a team J.J. had forged. The band played all afternoon, and the men danced strenuous jigs and reels. A ring was set up in the tavern yard, and boxing matches brought the clamoring, gambling men to wager on two giants who mauled and gouged each other till they couldn't stand. Whiskey, porter, and lager beer flowed freely, and barroom choruses shook the rafters.

The wedding couple departed in a carriage early in the evening. Already men were snoring in the corners of the tavern. Daniel had secured a cottage downriver, near Carthage, for four days. In a tall stand of pine just back from the river, the cottage was built of logs, and the sound of the river and the wind in the pines lent a peaceful, cleansing, timeless air.

Eleanora sighed contentedly as they sat together in the candlelight where the moths circled. "Tonight," she whipered, "we could be the only man and woman in the world."

After lighting the fire and drinking a glass of champagne, they made slow, languorous love in the great feather bed.

"Oh, Daniel," she sighed after catching her breath, and cradled his face above her in her hands. "I am so very happy to be your wife."

He smiled down upon her. "And I'm the luckiest man alive."

They slept in each other's arms, content and perfectly at peace.

Upon waking, Eleanora stretched, yawned, and looked outside. Daniel stood knee-deep in the river with a fishing pole. She called to him. Outlined by the sun sparkling on the water, he turned and waved. "I've caught breakfast. Put the skillet on the coals."

They ate outside, trout, bacon, fried potatoes, and eggs. The larder Mrs. Rochester had provided included a round loaf of Irish soda bread, and Daniel cut and buttered slices of it. With appetites whetted by their night of passion and the anticipation of a long afternoon of the same, they ate heartily, and lingered over coffee.

"We are so very lucky, Daniel. Three years ago I would have said this was impossible." She looked about her. Birds called in the forest, and the sunlight slanted down through the canopy of pine. "I thought losing my estate would be the very end of my life." She laughed. "But it was really only the beginning. . . . All my life, Daniel, I have sought something I couldn't define and couldn't find. Anywhere. I looked for it in poetry, then in politics. I always needed more than the social whirl of balls and parties. And I believed my love for a man must be more than a furious and fleeting passion that burns bright and hot, then dies when the passion is spent." She smiled and held his hand.

"I always believed my love would be joined to some noble work, a work my lover shared. Together we would grow and learn and mature. And I knew, Daniel, from the first time you came to my house, that if I could get you involved in this grand work, then perhaps, just maybe, my dream would come true. And it has, my love, it has . . . better and richer than I ever considered possible."

"So that was it." He shook his head in mock dismay. "You

hid your motive well. You don't know how many nights I lay awake on my cot wondering what on earth I was doing digging a ditch toward the lake where I used to sail wild and free. Yes, I'd remember sailing in my *Silver Pearl*, and think of leaving this work, of building another brig and returning to the lake trade. Certainly it wasn't the salary. My old first mate now owns half the lakefront in Buffalo. I thought many times, too, that you were just using me to help Clinton, that your true affection lay with him."

"With DeWitt?" Eleanora feigned shock.

"Yes. You were always together. He saw more of you than he did his wife. His needs always came first, always before you considered mine. Even this March."

"Daniel!" she scolded.

"But all the signs were there."

"One thing about DeWitt you have seen, no doubt, is that he needs attention, acclaim, admiration. That was difficult for me at first, as if he had no self-confidence. I don't admire weakness. I sometimes thought he had the appetite for attention of a gigantic prideful child. That offended me. But soon I saw another side to his genius, a tender side. He spends so much time reading and pondering, politicking and planning, that when he reawakens from those long spells, he desperately needs to be with people he can trust, to feel that he is as mortal and ordinary as everyone else. He is only asking people to thank him for his effort."

"You love him very much."

"I do. He is a remarkable man, but he is also a distant man, cold and often bitterly cynical. He lapses into depressions gloomier than the Cayuga swamp, and when the rage erupts that he strives to control, it seems only I can reason with him. He trusts no one. Both his wives have been simple, beautiful girls who bore his children, kept his house, and allowed him his way."

Daniel nodded. "I thought you'd marry him when his wife died."

She gave a short laugh. "Many people did, evidently. How far appearance always is from reality! I could never live with DeWitt. He is far too demanding. But after that story you told me about losing your parents in a massacre, I saw you as quiet, stoic, accepting."

"And yet all that time I only wanted an interest in Claverack."

Eleanora threw back her head and emitted a peal of

laughter that joined with the sound of the rushing water, the sparkling sun, and the deep, fragrant wood.

"This is nice." He nodded at the woodland around them.

"Yes." She thought. "That wedding reception was a far cry from my first. Aristocrats in powdered wigs, dowagers in brocade gowns, the orchestra that filled Clermont with waltzes, and Jacob..." her voice trailed off.

"Mine too." Daniel thought back.

"Let's go inside," she whispered.

"Inside? On a beautiful morning like this? How can you think of it?" He cast a glance into the forest. "I bet we can find a fine bed of moss if we were to walk along the river."

"Oh, yes." She grew excited and clasped his arm. "Let's."

They stood and kissed, and he led her into the forest, where the morning sun slanted majestically and the birds, chipmunks, and squirrels soon came out of hiding for the breakfast scraps.

35

*A*ll too soon the honeymoon ended, but a new enthusiasm had filled the work crews. As flooring was laid for the channel and towpath on the great Genesee aqueduct, Daniel let contracts for the next big push, along the ridge. He put Canvass White and J.J. in charge of the cut through the great cliff seventeen miles east of Niagara Falls. He and Eleanora rode eastward to tour what had been completed and to give a final inspection to the portion soon to open.

In August Eleanora took charge of the Holland Land Company farmers who contracted to work while Daniel and J.J. rode to Buffalo. From the back of his horse Daniel pointed out the wide harbor. He described his capture of the British vessels during the war and how he built Perry's fleet.

"Aye, Dan-o, the Brits are nasty sods, truth to tell. Once the Yanks beat hell out of them, why, says half the Irish population, America, that's the land for me."

"What will you do when we finish digging?"

"Ah, find me another canal to work on, sure enough.

What else can a great big bellowin' buck like me do? 'Tis certain I'm getting too old for prize-fighting."

"Look over Buffalo, J.J. It could be to your liking."

"Ah," he said disgustedly, "I ain't the kind to be settling down, Dan-o. Ain't in my blood." He clucked at the horse, pulled on the rein, and they ambled on.

Lodging at the renamed Eagle Tavern, Daniel invited Lester Frye to dine with them.

"Only luck, Danny, only luck pulled me through those times," he boasted. "I come in after the war and bought up frontage for a song. So convinced was everyone the British would capture the shoreline, they sold and fled." He grinned at J.J. "Me and Danny was in business together, see? Anyways, them pair of villains, Ellicott and Porter, why they're trying to steal the port of our grand canal for their little township of Black Rock, and that's what's got me concerned."

J.J. nodded.

"They're boasting how they run Dee-Witt Clinton, Dee-Witt Clinton himself, out of office over that there tug o' war. Oh, Danny and me seen some high old times, we did. We made this area what it is today. Them johnny-come-latelies trying to cash in, why, Mr. McShane, it's downright disgusting."

Lester buried his disgusted face in his tankard of ale, and emerged with foam on his lips. "Didn't tell you, Danny, that I got something of yours. Sold the *Pearl*."

Daniel glared at him. "The *Pearl*?"

"Yep. I sold her to some salvagers. You weren't nowhere around and weren't much left of her but the hull and some fixtures. They inquired of me, so I up and sold her."

This angered Daniel. "And what did you do with the price?"

"Invested it, Danny-boy. Been keeping it for you. All safe and secure. In fact," he leaned across the table, "I got a wharf what's yours, and I been keeping it. You build a warehouse toward the end of it and you're in business again. The future, Danny—got to protect your investments for the future."

The waitress brought another round of tankards. She bent down and whispered in J.J.'s ear, then left.

"You own a wharf here in Buffalo—prime dockage—and if the canal winds up terminating here, why, we'll both be rich."

"How much did you get for the *Pearl*?"

"Three hundred. She took a lot of punishment."

"And the dock? How much did it cost?"

"It's worth about—"

"Not what it's worth. What did you pay?"

"Two fifty." Lester reached into his vest. "Here." He slapped fifty dollars in gold on the table. "That's the balance, and you've got good title to the wharf."

"Dan-o," J.J. said, "all this talk of finances makes me a wee thirsty. I'll be in the taproom awhile, and if I'm gone when you get there, why, I'll see you tomorry."

Daniel turned and saw Edna Kay removing her apron and glancing their way.

"See you in the morning, J.J."

"So," Lester resumed, "don't mourn the *Pearl*, Danny. We'll build a whole fleet of vessels. This place is exploding with opportunity. When they hear the canal is definitely coming to Buffalo—and you can deliver the news to me whenever you know—the building spree will be crazy." Lester leaned closer. "But you can tell your old mate, can't you, Danny?"

"You haven't changed, Lester. I'll do what I can."

"Your word is like the jingle of coins in my pocket, Danny." He pushed the gold pieces nearer Daniel, and Daniel picked them up and put them in his vest.

"Which wharf?"

"End of Washington Street."

"Thanks, Lester." Abruptly Daniel rose from the table, leaving Lester with the bill.

He walked through the streets of Buffalo and remembered back to a former time when the village looked far different. He remembered Carrie, Rachel, and Eli, and he remembered his peace of mind when he walked down to the harbor to board the *Silver Pearl* and sail out upon the lake. He smelled the wind, and the clean lake air beckoned him to be sailing again. He walked out on the pier at the foot of Washington Street. Lester was trying to bribe him for a favorable decision, but he was inept even at that. Daniel decided he'd accept the wharf. He reached the end of the pier, and the lake lay black and silent, gently rising and falling on the pilings. Instinctively he reached into his pocket and clutched the ten gold pieces. He used to moor his *Silver Pearl* out there; her trim lines, her speed upon the lake had made him proud. "I'll build another," he said. "I'm not meant to be on land." He took the fifty dollars from his pocket and considered hurling it into the water as a proper farewell, then slipped the coins back into his pocket. They'd make an initial payment on materials for the new brig.

*   *   *

Next day Daniel walked his property with J.J. "I'll build a house upon this rise." He scanned the shore of the lake.

J.J. pointed. "There's a good stand of oak that'd supply you."

"No," Daniel said. "Stone, it must be built of stone. I had a wooden house before, and I had a wooden ship. I will have a house of stone."

"The lass told me something about you rescuing her. . . ."

"The war was difficult out here, J.J. She was in a compromising situation, and I helped her out."

"Aye," J.J. said, "she's a game lassie, though." Together they scanned the lake. Daniel saw it with new eyes today, planning for his wife and a new family, returning home. J.J. prattled on. "I'll tell you, though, Dan-o, it's been a while since I've been with a woman, but she was sweet, sweeter than the liquor that drips into the jug. She weren't no female with a whine in every word, but she ain't no breezy day neither." He spat, then turned to Daniel. "I'm getting old, mate. She showed a rare ability last night. I've been thinking of settling down."

"Ah-ha!" Daniel slapped J.J. on the back. "As soon as the canal is completed, we'll be partners."

"Nay, Dan-o. I meant the settlin' to be a state of mind, not a location. I must keep moving because the familiarity causes me to sit and ponder and mull over things I wasn't meant to plumb. But she is a game lassie." J.J. looked upon the clouds over the lake. "As life gets shorter, Dan-o, I wax philosophic. But 'tis a grand canal we've dug, and few men can boast such a friend as you."

"I own the site where Edna lives," Daniel said, to change the subject. "I'll deed it to you if you're of a mind to remain."

"Can't do it, Dan-o. There's a canal madness over the land, now they are seeing what we've done, and I believe I'm heading down Philadelphia way." He laughed. "The lake's mighty sweet, but my impatient Irish heart needs to be nearer the sea."

"Have you asked Edna if she'll accompany you?"

"No!" J.J. was shocked. "Never give a woman such a say!"

"There you're wrong, J.J. Women are wiser than we can ever hope to be. Talk to her. If you decide you want to stay, the site of the house is yours."

J.J. turned to him and reached out his hand. "You're a

good man, Dan-o. I did promise her I'd stop by this evening, so can we tarry here till tomorry?"

"Absolutely, my friend. Absolutely."

DeWitt Clinton spent the summer of 1823 on the canal. Freed of the governor's hectic duties, he took an obsessive personal interest in the great work. He dressed in the casual clothes of a gentleman farmer and moved among the men with encouraging words and handshakes. In general he seemed more relaxed, yet a trifle sad.

"Ah, Daniel, it's much like myself being ripped up," he said one June day as they looked down upon the massive blasting and earthworks at Lockport. Cranes hung above the cut, swinging baskets of rubble up and out. "Looks like a gaping wound just now, with the explosions and showers of rock. But once filled with water, it'll be placid and serene."

"You give the men much encouragement with your interest in their work," Daniel remarked.

"That's Eleanora's doing. She wouldn't allow me to sit in New York brooding. She loves this work, and the change in her is astonishing. She looks a decade younger and livelier in the year since your wedding."

"She certainly prefers this to politics."

"Ah, Hedges, but it's hell to be out of power."

"Surely you'll rise again!"

"Surely? There's nothing sure in politics. That reptile Van Buren is consolidating power day and night, purging my name from people's memories."

"Yes, he is." Daniel looked at Clinton questioningly. "What drives a man like that?"

"Raw ambition. He's ruthless and expert at seizing power. He'll take the glory for the canal. I'll be a private citizen when it opens. Ah, the people, a fickle mob. Deep appetite and shallow memory."

"I have more confidence in the people, Mr. Clinton. Yours is simply a temporary setback."

Clinton ignored his optimism. "You, Daniel"—he waved his arm over the furious activity spread below them—"you have done the best of the three of us that started this. Eleanora has been run off her lands, and I've been run out of office. But you . . . you're still engineer, and you have lovely Eleanora." Daniel saw a gleam of admiration in the great man's eye.

"But you're still on the Canal Commission!"

"For how long? My terms ends next year."

"They never would take that from you."

"Never say 'never' in politics. The impossible can and usually does happen. In any event, I have some news for Eleanora about her Chancery suit, promising news."

"Let's find her."

"You're a lucky man, Daniel."

"We both are," Daniel answered.

Eleanora was laying out a luncheon of cold ham, chicken, Canadian cheddar, fresh bread, pie, and coffee. "Welcome, DeWitt, so good to see you."

They sat in the shade of an ancient oak. Over lunch Clinton talked about the new sense of energy and enterprise along the canal, and about the festivities planned for the fall. "I've come to ask you if you both would accompany me and reap some of the praise."

"You didn't tell him?" Eleanora asked. Daniel shook his head. She turned to Clinton. "We'd love to, DeWitt, but I'm five months pregnant, and that will be my time for lying in."

"Congratulations!" Clinton circled the table and embraced her. "I'm so very happy for both of you. What an unexpected joy!"

"Yes, and if it's a boy, his name will be Daniel Clinton Hedges."

Clinton's eyes filled, and he tried to hide his emotion. "You do me such honor." He cleared his throat. "I bring you good news, Eleanora. Your suit has been heard in Chancery. While the court upheld Randolph Van Rensselaer's claim to Claverack because you acquiesced, it also awarded you dower. As I expected, your father's signature was not a release of your right, and so you shall get a life income equal to one-third the rents and tenements Jacob held while you were married. This works in your favor. As long as you remained at Claverack, the 1787 statute limited your right to income from that estate. Now you may collect one-third of the income from everything Jacob held, and his holdings in Manhattan were vast. Your attorney Van Zandt is now seeking an accounting, and you'll get arrearages back to the date you were first ejected. Since Claverack was roughly one quarter of Jacob's property, you'll realize slightly more than all you were earning when you held the estate."

"That all seems so long ago and far away," Eleanora said. "It is good news, DeWitt. Thank you for looking into it."

"Yes, it will be welcome with a baby, particularly when your husband works for such a meager wage," Clinton joked.

"I'll correct that presently, just as soon as I retire from state service," Daniel said. "Opportunity knows no bounds in Buffalo today."

"Yes? I shall consider that. I'll be retiring soon."

"Retiring?" both cried.

"Yes."

"Nonsense. Just you wait until this is completed, DeWitt. You alone will be the hero of a grateful people."

"The people," he scoffed. "We shall see."

Construction was hectic as work gangs blasted a mile and a half through solid rock. Yet Daniel had delegated most of the work so he could stay home with Eleanora. They lay together talking for long hours each afternoon, remember the past and dreaming about the future.

She went into labor in mid-October. Daniel brought old Doc Barnes. The labor was long and difficult, and Daniel sat at her bedside applying cold compresses to her forehead for thirty hours. He wept when she was not looking, regretting he had reduced such a grand lady to a thrashing animal, screaming in pain, expelling blood, urine, and excrement.

Yet when the baby was born and Doc Barnes exclaimed, "It's a boy," Daniel's joy knew no bounds. He walked with the babe out into the sun of a late summer morning and held it to the sun. He murmured an Iroquois prayer, lowered the babe to his cheek, and as little Daniel Clinton began to wail, he embraced him. "Oh, my son!" He rocked him a moment, looking into the forest, then far out over the lake, before returning him to his mother's breast for his first suckle.

36

"*A* grave mistake, Matty," the elder statesman said as Van Buren revealed the plan he had just put into motion. "If you have any power to stop it, do so."

"You think it too extreme?"

"Yes, and not subtle, not oblique enough. For years you have successfully eroded Clinton's support here and there, and have succeeded in undoing him. This confrontation meets him face to face on his own battleground. The best you can hope for is a draw. And you'll probably lose."

"The Regency supported it to a man."

"The Regency is not infallible. Driving Clinton from the Canal Commission will prove to the people that he has been a victim of political intrigue all along. Yes, we have harried him about his damned canal. I never thought it would get dug myself. Still, he has it nearly finished, and it's immensely popular. This plan—you say Judge Skinner proposed it? It will backfire. Too harsh. You must distance yourself from Regency's vote."

"But I am their leader."

Burr winked. "Only when it serves you to be. Say you were busy with federal issues, that you support Clinton's reappointment. Better yet, get out of town."

"But they've got the votes to oust him—downstate, the mid-Hudson counties, Ellicott's western counties."

"Legislative votes mean nothing in the face of an angry mob, Matty. And that's what you will have." He held up his index finger. "There is a maxim: 'You may kill a man in politics, but you can never kill him too dead.' I learned that inescapable truth the hard way. Was my duel with Hamilton merely the settling of a private grudge? I thought so. But nothing is private with public men. I brought the wrath of the American people down upon my head and won a place in infamy. They hounded me, tried me, exiled me. And in those hovels in London and Paris, I saw Hamilton nightly, bleeding and groaning, stalking like Banquo's ghost through my dreams. Let us leave town together. Sometimes retreat is the only alternative."

"There is no honor to be had in this?"

"None, Matty. Believe a man who has seen too much."

"Very well, I shall call on you at six in the morning."

"I hope Mr. Fulton's engines are repaired. If we hadn't had to stop at Kingston on the way up, I should have been here to avert this debacle."

In addition to the transport of goods, the canal speeded the transmission of news. Daniel Hedges first heard of this latest political outrage two days after the April twelfth vote. He was inspecting the blasting operation at Lockport, and Clinton was due at the site that morning. "Guess I'll have to break the news, J.J."

"They'll be here about noon."

Just after the dinner bell had rung, horses and mules threaded down the path toward waiting canal boats. Clinton planned to journey east to Schenectady on an inspection tour. Daniel approached him, and they found privacy in the foreman's cabin. "I have some very bad news, Governor."

"I am used to it, Hedges. Tell me."

"The legislature voted two days ago to remove you from the Canal Commission."

"What?" Clinton knit his brow.

"They voted to take away your last public office, sir, to remove you from the commission."

Clinton shook his head. "They can't do that."

"On the contrary, sir, they have done it. Your appointment expired and they filled it with someone else."

"No," Clinton said impatiently. "They have the power to do it, of course, but they can't do it politically."

"Well, sir, they have done it." For the first time in their long association, Daniel considered Clinton obtuse. Then when Clinton rose, shook his hand and laughed out loud, Daniel believed he'd come unhinged.

"This is the happiest day of my life!" Clinton cried. "The fools!" And he laughed and laughed.

"I'm afraid I don't understand, sir."

"Did your man tell you what happened immediately on the heels of the vote?"

"Why, there was a torchlight parade protesting it, sir. But a mob can't reinstate you."

"Ah, so. But it will, Hedges, it will. And you and Eleanora have been telling me to trust the people. You should have counseled me instead to trust Van Buren's stupidity." He clenched his hands at his temples, "Oh, this is hardly to be believed. I didn't have the power to call a coach, to get my boots blacked. The fools! The pack of fools! By stripping me of my last office, they have in essence given me back all they took away. I was going east today. Let us instead ride west to Eleanora. I'll stay with you until the resentment builds to a crescendo, then I shall progress triumphantly across the state and allow the people to summon me back as their leader."

"We won't reach Buffalo until near dawn."

"Immaterial, Daniel. Let us set out now. Eleanora deserves to share in this, and I need a quiet place to stay for a day or two. Have they champagne in Buffalo?"

"If they do, I'll find it."

"Before we start..." Clinton reached for Daniel's hand. "I don't tell you this often enough. You have been a source of strength for me during all this. Now things have come full circle. Let me tell you before the riotous clamor begins. I could negotiate and fight down in Albany, certain that your work was steady and sure. Often your achievements were all that went as planned."

"I am honored," Daniel said. "Eleanora will be happy to see you thus, sir. I'll have my man find mounts and tell your party to go on without you."

Clinton clapped his hands and laughed, relishing the irony of it all.

Soon they were riding toward Buffalo as the spring sun set. "Tell me, Hedges, how fast could you finish the deep cut and these twenty-odd miles?"

"Two years."

"Could the work be speeded up?"

"With more men and more money."

"I am planning now to run for governor this year, and I'd like to see the work completed by 'twenty-five."

"So would I. I'm anxious to get back into the lake trade. When the canal is completed, there will be tremendous opportunities for making money, and frankly"—he nudged Clinton—"I have a family to support."

"But you could do it?"

"If you say it must be done, it will. Direction from Albany under this governor has been less than inspiring."

"Well, then, my good man, we shall finish in 'twenty-five, and we shall show the world what my enterprising leadership can do. Ah-ha! Onward!"

They rode through the sunset and the darkness and reached Daniel's large stone house at sunrise. Already up with the baby, Eleanora heard their horses and appeared on the porch. She waved and smiled, the baby in her arms. "Now there's a sight!" Daniel said, spurring his horse into a gallop.

"I didn't expect you till Friday." She handed Daniel the baby. "And DeWitt! Heavens! What a lovely surprise. You two must be famished. I'll have Hilda fix breakfast."

They sat in the clean, spacious kitchen while Hilda bustled about frying bacon, sausage, eggs, and fish.

"Have you heard what has happened in Albany?" Daniel asked. Eleanora shook her head. "The politicians removed DeWitt from his post on the Canal Commission."

"Impossible!"

Clinton nodded and smiled.

"Where will it end?" she asked.

"Right here and right now," Clinton said, accepting the baby from Daniel. "Already there are riots in Albany against Van Buren and his cynical politicians." Clinton bounced his little namesake on his knee. Soon Hilda had the breakfast ready. Eleanora set out cups and poured black coffee.

"Ah, little man," Clinton said to the baby, "it's a grand life you're beginning. Like your papa you'll stand up to it, and like your mama you'll love it and make it rich for yourself and those around you. Your papa and mama and I have struggled through so much together. No one will ever know it all." He looked with satisfaction around the kitchen.

"If I have one regret, it is that I chose a public life over a private one," Clinton said. "I paid so little attention to my wife and family. There are few rewards in public life beyond the revenge I'm now enjoying, and so many sacrifices. Perhaps it is my nature, yet beyond his family and a few close friends, a man has little else to cherish or trust."

He cradled the infant, hugged him, then handed him back to his mother. Eleanora sat across from the two men, happy with them together in her kitchen. She loosened her bodice as they ate and talked, and placed the babe who bore both their names at her breast.

*　　*　　*

The reaction was even more dramatic than Clinton predicted. Immediately after the vote that ousted him, an angry mob rushed through Albany to the hotels and rooming houses of Regency members and clamored for an explanation. Aboard the steamboat *North River*, Burr and Van Buren enjoyed a gentleman's game of whist and admired the majestic Catskills.

By nightfall the news had reached Troy, Schenectady, and Kingston. Throngs turned out in the street, ten thousand in Albany's City Hall Park, angry faces burning in the ruddy glow of torches, and they marched in protest to what the legislature had done. Word reached New York City, already reaping benefits from the canal, and swept through Utica, Rome, the fledgling village of Syracuse near Salina, Rochester, Black Rock, and Buffalo.

Editorials deplored the petty political move and praised Clinton for withstanding a decade of hostile attacks. When the people of Buffalo learned Clinton was at Daniel Hedges's home, they assembled in a joyous crowd, marched there and called him out.

"And now the backlash begins," Clinton remarked as he prepared to go out on the porch. "It will be some trip across our state!"

"You deserve it," Eleanora said.

"Best of luck." Daniel slapped him on the back. Clinton opened the door and stepped out with raised arms to the rousing applause.

Clinton's triumphal journey across the state sent Van Buren's faction into hiding. A grateful people demonstrated its regard in banquets, parades, receptions, and interminable speeches. That spring Clinton was the unanimous choice of the Democratic-Republicans, and was elected governor by a gratifying plurality. His clear mandate from the people was to finish the canal.

J. J. McShane finally completed the mile-and-a-half blast through the deep cut during the summer of 1825. "Sixteen miles separate me from Buffalo and the arms of my gal," he shouted. "You lazy Irish luggards, let's get digging!" J.J. devised an ingenious way to encourage the Irish to dig. At intervals he placed casks of whiskey, and as the crew reached each cask, it was allowed fifteen minutes' rest to drink. Furiously his Irishmen dug, nor did the prism and the berm and the towpath suffer for their imbibing.

The Revolutionary War hero Marquis de Lafayette visited the canal on his tour to see how the American experiment in democracy was faring four decades after the Revolution. In flowery speeches he heralded the canal as proof of what men could accomplish untrammeled by monarchies, motivated by self-interest and free enterprise.

Daniel still visited the dig, but his engineering skills were needed no longer. During the summer he rented a berth in the shipyard, and with a hand-picked crew he built a brig according to an old plan, naming this ship the *Silver Pearl*. He constructed a warehouse at the wharf, hired Joel Kipp to manage the land side, and began reestablishing himself in the shipping trade on the lake.

Clinton scheduled the canal's opening ceremony for October 26, 1825, just before winter would seal it with ice. Along its length towns were booming with business and buildings rising day by day. The celebration committee had planned events and spectacles from Buffalo to New York, ending in a splendid fireworks display among the tall-masted ships in New York harbor. When Daniel and Eleanora received their invitation to accompany the party, they discussed whether to journey to the metropolis.

"Clinton will expect us to share the moment with him," Daniel said. "We cannot outright refuse him."

"But the work is all done," Eleanora protested. "I see no use in going. What would we do with Danny?"

"Truthfully, I don't want to go either. The nay-sayers will be out slapping each other on the back, everyone taking credit for what they didn't do."

"Well, then, let's tell DeWitt we'd be honored if he'd stay with us here before he starts but that we won't be accompanying him."

Eleanora used her most persuasive arguments, and finally warmed Clinton up to the idea that he and Kitty should lodge with them before setting out on the opening tour. Clinton "didn't want to be a bother," and had booked rooms at the Eagle already. Yet Eleanora prevailed, and he and Catherine arrived as the brilliant leaves were falling from the trees, and they spent an agreeable three days with the Hedges family.

Daniel had laid in special cuts of meat and imported wines. Although at first Catherine seemed apprehensive of frontier life, Daniel's comforting manner soon charmed her.

At dinner on the eve of the opening, Clinton proposed a

toast: "Let us drink to Daniel and Eleanora, the man and woman who transformed my dream into a highway of the future for all New York. May this household be blessed, and may they prosper with many more children."

They drank, and then Daniel stood.

"The canal will be open tomorrow, Governor, so I'll have my say. When I first heard about your canal, I was interested because it seemed such a challenge. And in the last ten years, I've done what we both set out to do, make water run uphill."

"Here, here!" Clinton cried.

"There's nothing else to say. We have completed the great work. I have married the fairest lady of the land, and the future lies before us with nothing but promise. I shall raise my glass, then, and simply say to you and to my lovely Eleanora, we did it."

"Yes!"

"Yes, we did!"

In the candlelight the three clinked their glasses together.

At the Eagle Tavern a United States senator was causing local people to stare. Martin Van Buren, the man who approved the first resolution to fund the canal, was enjoying the glow of popularity with his entourage of four. Already he had made arrangements for a canal boat to carry him in the triumphal party the five hundred miles to New York harbor. He had pondered on what to name his boat, and decided to keep it keep it simple: *The Senator.*

"Those people don't look normal," a waitress said to Edna Kay.

"They shouldn't," Edna replied, "they're from Washington."

"Let me get the table," the waitress said, "you've got a big day tomorrow, and then a big night." She winked. Edna and J.J. were to be married after the opening celebration the next day, and this was Edna's last night of work.

"No," Edna said, "I'll get it. I'd better get used to their sort, as J.J. wants to move to Philadelphia next month."

She found Van Buren affable and gentlemanly, and he left her a very large tip. As she crawled into bed with J. J. McShane for a night of prenuptial bliss, she told him she'd waited on Van Buren.

"Van Buren?" J.J. bolted upright. "Are you sure?"

"Why, yes, he's in room twelve."

"*Martin* Van Buren? A senator?"

"The very man."

"But what could he be doing in Buff'lo?"

"He said he funded the canal."

"Oh," J.J. said, folding his arms behind his head. "I see . . . I see . . ."

"J.J.? What's the matter? Don't think about him! Lie down! Lie down! Oh, I wish I hadn't mentioned it! Tomorrow we'll be man and wife. J.J.?"

"I'm considering, woman, I'm considering."

The next morning at seven, as Martin Van Buren breakfasted with his companions, a pretty waitress whispered that DeWitt Clinton wished to speak with him privately to discuss moving his boat up in the official flotilla.

"Very well." Van Buren folded his napkin meticulously. "I shall be back presently."

The senator adjusted his coat and stepped outside. Clinton had sent a coach for him, and he smiled as he stepped inside. This was a sign they might at last make amends. "Drive on!"

"Very well, sir." The whip cracked, and the horses awoke, and the traces jingled and groaned as the coach moved. Van Buren considered it sweet to be summoned to the great man. He wanted something, Clinton always wanted something. The senator had heard he was lodging out of town with the Van Rensselaer woman and her husband, the engineer. The senator enjoyed the rustic scenery. They drove for half an hour when he rapped on the trapdoor with his cane.

"Where are we going?"

"Few more minutes, sir."

Van Buren closed his watch and settled into his seat. A canal across the state—surely an extraordinary feat. He would make amends with Clinton, but he'd extract full price for his presence in the flotilla. Another half hour passed and he rapped on the door.

"My good man, you must have taken a wrong turn."

"Oh, no, sir. A mile and a half ahead."

The canal boats would be boarding at nine, and it was after eight now.

"Take me to the canal at once!" Van Buren commanded.

"Yes, sir, right away." Yet he did not change course. The sun was out the right window, and so they were going north. Impatiently Van Buren pounded his walking stick into the floor.

"Man!" he called. No answer. "Sirrah!" He pounded his

cane on the trapdoor. No answer. "I demand as a United States senator to know where I'm being taken!"

No answer.

Van Buren looked out at the passing forest and panicked. "I *demand*, I *demand*, sir, that you stop this coach."

Miraculously, the driver reined the horses. The driver expertly turned and backed up the coach, opened the hatch, and looked down at Van Buren. "Yes, sir?"

"Where are we?"

"We've reached our destination, sir." The driver leaned back, then produced two pistols. "Get out."

Van Buren's eyes opened wide with shock and indignation. "What?"

"Get out."

"But you don't know who I am!"

A deafening explosion sounded, and four inches from Van Buren's ear, a hole gaped in the upholstery. The senator laughed uneasily, "That is a fine game, driver, now take me to the ceremony."

The Irish lad lowered the other pistol, sighting it on Van Buren's nose. "Get out!"

Van Buren looked this way and that, then opened the door and stepped to the roadway. "Do you know who I am?" He pulled out his purse to offer a bribe. "I am a United States senator. How much to take me back?"

The lad flicked his whip, and the horses sprang ahead in the traces.

"Wait!" Van Buren cried. "Wait!"

The coach wheels picked up speed.

"Do you know who I am?" Van Buren cried with outstretched arms. "Don't you know who I am? I'm a United States senator! I demand you return!" But the Irish lad never looked back. And then the United States senator collected himself, looked about him, and saw he was deep in a forest where no one at all knew or cared who he was. He gave an uncharacteristic curse, brushed off his sleeves, his hat, and began the long trek back.

Daniel, Eleanora, and Daniel Clinton Hedges escorted DeWitt and Kitty Clinton through the clamoring village of Buffalo to their boat, the *Seneca Chief*. It was barely nine o'clock when they boarded, yet both sides of the canal were lined out of sight with well-wishers. All cheered as Clinton and Kitty boarded. The governor raised his hand for silence.

"As we go east we'll be swamped with odes and speeches and classical bombast, so I'll not engage in any of that now."

The crowd cheered.

"I congratulate the citizens of Buffalo today. I assure them their community will grow and prosper and will soon become a foremost city in this state. Let me also recognize your own son, Daniel Hedges, who built much of this great work...and I'll doff my hat to your new lady, Eleanora Livingston Van Rensselaer Hedges." He tipped his hat to Eleanora. The crowd cheered wildly. "Well, we mustn't keep the rest of this great state of New York waiting. Thank you for the support you have given us, people of Buffalo. May you thrive and prosper, and may God bless you and your descendants, who will inherit this new land."

Clinton gave a signal, and a cannon blast startled the assembled. The people cheered wildly, the small bell in the church tower rang, and the brass band struck up a tune. Clinton winked at Daniel and blew a kiss to Eleanora and the baby. The barefoot boy on the towpath flicked his switch at the white horses' flanks, and the horses started walking. The rope's slack lessened until it jerked the *Seneca Chief* ahead in the water. Far off another cannon exploded, then in the distance another.

"J.J.'s wedding is at two." Daniel took Eleanora's hand.

"We have time," she said.

"Time?"

"Yes." Eleanora bent down and kissed little Daniel Clinton. "Time for our own celebration."

"Good."

"Danny." Eleanora set the boy down. "You're going to play with Miss Hilda while Dada and I go to a wedding."

"Miss Hilda?" the two-year-old asked. He nodded and ran to the maid.

"Well, my love," Eleanora said. "Daniel Clinton mustn't be an only child."

"No," Daniel agreed, "we had better do something about that."

"I love you, Daniel."

"Ah, Eleanora, my wife." He slipped his arm around her waist and drew her to him, and together they watched the canal boats receding northward toward Black Rock. "It sure is a fine new day."

People were jigging all about them, the brass band was playing, and gun salvos exploded. Eleanora stepped up, kissed him, then whispered in his ear, "Let's go home."

"Gladly."

They held hands as young lovers do, and walked along the waterfront watching the canal boats proceed to their feasts, speeches, and fireworks. In the distance, like far-off thunder, another cannon boomed. In a relay the cannon blasts would progress eastward to Troy, then south along the Hudson to New York, where the guns of the Battery would respond, then the relay would return the five hundred miles to Buffalo.

"I'll bet we can be lying asleep in each other's arms by the time that cannon shot returns," Daniel said.

"Oh, yes." She smiled and kissed him again. "Oh, let's be."

To them the world had never looked quite so pure, so new, as they turned again to view the great waterway.

Meanwhile the cannon shot was quickly relayed from emplacement to emplacement. Many of Oliver Perry's cannon had been used in the West. The cannon of French, British, and American wars were called into service upon battlements in old forts farther east. Down the flight at Lockport the shot sounded, over the great aqueduct at Rochester, through the foul stagnant air of the Montezuma Swamp, echoing down the Mohawk Valley.

At Troy the cannon relay turned southward. By a prearranged signal the shot in Albany set all the church bells ringing. "It's open!" joyous crowds on the Capitol steps cheered. "It's open!" Down the meandering Hudson, the shots echoed through the Catskills and the sleepy Dutch villages where descendants of Washington Irving's characters paused to listen. Down through Tappan Zee and the Jersey Palisades it rolled until crowds on Manhattan docks cocked their ears and cheered wildly. "It's coming! It's coming!"

Cannon aboard warships in New York harbor answered with deep voices, then the fusillade from the Battery signaled that the Atlantic coast had been reached. The relay had taken an hour and a half. Now it turned back, and its answer raced up the Hudson and out along the route of the canal. Clinton's flotilla was approaching the flight at Lockport when the cannon shot returned. Standing in the bow of his boat, DeWitt Clinton raised his hat and joined the floating celebration in a loud cheer. And farther west, when the last reports of Perrry's cannon echoed over Lake Erie, in the master bedroom of their great stone house Daniel and Eleanora slept in each other's arms.

EPILOGUE

At every township along the canal the *Seneca Chief* paused to greet grateful New Yorkers now joined by the ribbon of water to the sea. The locals lavished Clinton's flotilla with feasts, toasts, speeches, songs, dances, odes, ballads, gun salutes, cannon salvos, and fireworks displays. No superlative lay idle. Eastward to greater and greater celebrations horses towed the boats; boats that carried barrels of Erie lake water, deer, bear cubs, raccoons, birds, Indian boys, logs of red cedar and bird's-eye maple to be fashioned into commemorative boxes; boats that carried canal comissioners, legislators, engineers, and foremen.

The flotilla reached Albany on Wednesday, November second. There the greatest celebration so far began, with a twenty-four-gun salute and the ringing of church bells, and in a rapture of balls and banquets, speeches and editorials, the capital city welcomed its hero. Three portraits were hung in the Assembly chamber that day: America's first president, George Washington, New York's first governor, George Clinton, and New York's first son, DeWitt Clinton. Martin Van Buren, who'd insisted on passing the celebration party in a closed boat, had reached Albany two days before Clinton. Despite McShane's practical joke, one that Van Buren ever after ascribed to Clinton, the senator took the dais at a formal state dinner honoring the governor.

Steamboats towed the canal boats down the Hudson next

day, and the flotilla reached New York harbor Friday, November fourth, dwarfed there by tall-masted ships from Europe and the Orient. New York City's ecstatic celebration outstripped all others together. Fireworks, balls, banquets, illuminations, parades, receptions and speeches kept the city awake the entire weekend and all but obscured the simple ceremony Clinton performed—the "Wedding of the Waters." To join the waters of Lake Erie with the Atlantic, Clinton had the *Seneca Chief* towed by steamboat to Sandy Hook where he poured a barrel of lake water into the sea. This simple wedding, as had another he performed, marked the beginning of a new era.

Immediately New York State reaped untold wealth from commerce flowing along the thin artery between the Great Lake territories and the sea. Tolls soon paid back the seven million dollars in construction costs, and revenues filled state coffers. Cities sprang up from the villages and boomtowns along its course: Troy, Schenectady, Utica, Rome, Syracuse, Rochester, Buffalo. So effectively did the canal tap into the vast land-locked territories of the Midwest—drawing commerce from Cleveland and Detroit, produce from Ohio, Pennsylvania, Indiana, Wisconsin and Michigan—that New York was soon named "The Empire State." New York City, the maritime port, arose as the nation's first harbor and financial capital.

DeWitt Clinton, who foresaw such immeasurable prosperity and employed his keen political skill and unyielding will for a decade and a half to achieve it, realized few personal benefits. Returned to the governor's office in 1826 by grateful New Yorkers, he died suddenly in 1828, before winning any national laurels. A legal judgment against his estate forced the sale of his home, his belongings, and holdings, and pauperized Catherine and their four young children. Over fierce objections from Van Buren's Regency, the state legislature finally settled a grant of ten thousand dollars on his widow.

Senator Martin Van Buren delivered a touching eulogy at Clinton's funeral, and with Tammany's support and Burr in the background, succeeded Clinton as governor. Yet he served only three months, preferring to return to Washington society. President Andrew Jackson appointed Van Buren Secretary of State, and Van Buren quickly became the most influential member of Jackson's cabinet and was elected vice president in 1832. With Jackson's support, Van Buren finally plucked "the golden apple" when he was elected eighth President of the United States in 1836, the year Aaron Burr passed from this world to advise, perhaps, the greatest schemer of all. Yet Van Buren's political skills surpassed his statesmanship. Tensions between North and South, and the Financial Panic of 1837, plagued his administration, and he lost in a bid for a second term to General William Henry Harrison, the Indian fighter who once supplied Kentucky riflemen to Oliver Hazard Perry. Van Buren retired to his Columbia County estate, Lindenwald, and despite a few unsuccessful attempts to reemerged, never again held public office.

J. J. McShane declined Daniel's offer of the property on Washington Street, and he and Edna followed the canal craze into Pennsylvania. Accustomed to the exclusive company of men, J.J. was blessed with five daughters, and returned each night from his labors to a happy hearth. Joel Kipp proved a loyal and capable agent for the Daniel Hedges Shipping Co. He married a Yankee girl and raised his family in the burgeoning city of Buffalo.

Lester Frye grew both in wealth and size. He ran two unsuccessful races to be Mayor of Buffalo, a city that soon became the second largest in the state. Lester always credited Daniel Hedges with giving him his start, and the "two hunnerd dollars" on the whiskey run as his first investment. Though he urged Daniel to involve himself in municipal concerns, Daniel preferred a very guarded private life.

Daniel and Eleanora lived happily and quietly together. Little Daniel Clinton Hedges had two brothers and a sister. He followed his father into the lake trade, became a skipper of considerable skill, then entered public life and was elected to Congress from Erie County for three terms. His brother Edward spent a restless youth in Nevada mining camps before joining the Army. He fell during the Battle of Gettysburg, fighting for the Union. John Jacob Hedges, the youngest and most beloved by his father, named after the burly Irishman J. J. McShane, attended Rensselaer Institute, a school set up by General Van Rensselaer during the last years of canal construction to teach the practical sciences, and he turned his talents to surveying and building the transcontinental railroad.

It was upon their daughter Lorraine that Eleanora showered her affection and placed her hopes for women of the next generation. She settled the dower income from her first marriage upon Lorraine to afford her freedom, and sent her to Emma Willard's Troy Female Seminary—the school Eleanora and Clinton had nurtured with public funds just after the War of 1812—to develop her passion for learning and accomplishment. For a time Lorraine joined with Elizabeth Cady Stanton and Susan B. Anthony in working to secure the right to vote and the right to own property for women.

When a wealthy brewer, Matthew Vassar, endowed an institution for higher learning for women, Lorraine accepted a teaching post at Vassar College in the Hudson Valley town of Poughkeepsie. In her thirty-third year she married a worthy sea captain who had made a fortune in the China trade. They lived on his estate in Dutchess County, and Lorraine involved herself extensively in the education of Vassar women.

Watching the nation grow from childhood to adolescence, Daniel and Eleanora lived on in their big stone house overlooking the canal and the port of Buffalo. From their hearth they could scan the lake when the moon was on the water, when dark squalls rose, when the sky brightened in autumn's glory, when the blizzards howled, and their love deepened and mellowed with the changing seasons. They raised their children, prospered in business and grew in the esteem of their community even as they jealously guarded their privacy. For they needed no acclaim. Together they had ushered in a new age. The canal, more crowded each year, and the rapidly expanding city, were constant reminders of what their private love and their dedication to a public cause had helped to build.

If, as the ancients say, life is a river born of earth and sky in the mountains, flowing ever downward to the sea, then the powerful and sometimes turbulent confluence of Daniel's and Eleanora's lives inspired and enriched their time, and the lives of those who knew them, who worked with them. Theirs was a unique mingling of virtue, passion, humor and sense, and only they knew how deep and how pure those waters ran. A reflection, finally, is all that others may see upon the surface of their lives, like the reflection of them walking hand in hand of a Sunday afternoon along the grand waterway. And with cannon silenced forever in that land, the words Eleanora once spoke to Clinton seem to echo still. What they had created was indeed a thing of surpassing beauty.

ABOUT THE AUTHOR

Jack Casey studied literature at Yale University and University of Edinburgh. After some restless years of traveling, he returned to his native New York State, and currently makes his home in Troy, New York with his wife June and their children Molly and John.